The Trinity Planets

The Helyan Series – Part Three

S.M.Tidball

DEDICATION

For everyone enjoying the Helyan Series so far, and for
Erin, my super-fan.

1

I'd taken to running the cliff path daily, using the alone time during the cooler early evenings to think through the thousand unanswered questions hijacking my mind. The outcome was always the same – frustration and sadness – but I did it anyway, hoping one day I'd have some eureka moment that would explain the events of the last month. It hadn't happened so far, but it had given me something to do since Primus Noah had put me under house-arrest. Okay, so maybe it wasn't that bad, but being banned from going on any off-world missions sure felt like it.

I'd run further than usual, preoccupied by a new theory for why it felt like I was being punished for something I didn't know I'd done. By the time I turned and headed back towards the monastery, the frustration had been replaced by an unease I couldn't explain. I tried to run through the anxiety rising in my chest, but I gave up, eventually stopping to catch my breath where the path was closest to the cliff edge.

My limbs felt heavy, my skin almost tingling, and the air was silent and still, just the persistent crashing of the waves on the rocks far below. I stretched my arms, staring out to sea. The pale pink sunset disappeared behind a veil of tissue-like clouds settling on the horizon, and I turned a slow circle, scanning the sky. Something wasn't right.

"There you are."

"Damn it, Ash! You scared the crap out of me," I replied, putting my hand on my chest to check my heart hadn't exploded.

"Dramatic much?"

"Funny. You know you shouldn't sneak up on people like that. You're lucky I wasn't armed."

"What? You think you could take me?" he taunted, his arms stretched out wide in invitation.

"Yeah, yeah, whatever. What's up?" I asked, adding concern to the long list of feelings fluttering under my ribcage.

"I was about to ask you the same thing. You're normally back by now, I was worried."

"Lost track of time, that's all. I was just…" A breeze broke the still air, passing over my skin like a billion mini-electric shocks, and the air practically crackled around me.

"Just what?"

"Did you feel that?" I replied, distracted. Rubbing the goosebumps my arms, I searched the horizon again. Nothing had changed.

Ash followed my gaze then turned towards me, frowning. "Shae, like I said, I'm worried—"

"There's a storm coming, Ash," I interrupted.

He sighed, and for the briefest moment I got a hit of sadness through the Link between us. "I know," he said simply. He sounded resigned, which confused me until he added, "I don't understand what's happening either. Things haven't been the same since we got home. I know you're frustrated and angry, and questioning everything you thought you knew, but I know you, Shae. Please don't do anything stupid; anything you'll regret. Don't go off all half-cocked and make things more difficult for yourself. I'll speak to Noah again, he's a reasonable man…" I pursed my lips and gave him my best, 'what the hell are you talking about,' frown before pointing out to the flat, gentle sea. "Huh? Oh, you mean an actual storm. I knew that. Just forget I said all that other stuff," he added, his trademark lopsided grin spreading across his strong face. He looked at the sky. "You sure? Looks okay to me. The bulletin this morning mentioned a couple of storms, but they're not due to come anywhere near us."

"I saw the bulletin too, Ash, but what can I tell you? You know I'm sensitive to all this atmospheric electric energy… stuff." I paused, thinking. "Things are going to get bad."

"Are we still referring to the storm?"

"I'm not sure. It's been a month since we were urgently called home after completing Operation Fallen Star. We haven't been allowed to go off-world since then, and…" I trailed off.

"And?"

"And I haven't spoken to Jared or Jake since we left Decerra."

"Noah told us they're both on some top-secret R.E.F. mission. It's not surprising we haven't had any coms from them." His voice sounded confident, but I knew him too well. I let down my mental roadblock and felt an undercurrent of uncertainty thrum through the Link from him.

"And how would Noah even know that?" I challenged. "It's not like the REF sends the Brotherhood mission bulletins."

"I don't know, Shae. Maybe for Guardian reasons?"

"Possible," I conceded. "But don't you think it's weird they got called off on another mission – together – only a day after we got the Third Seal safely back to Decerra? Especially as their previous orders were to take the *Defender* and the *Veritas* to Carmare for urgent repairs? Doesn't seem right if you ask me. And I know Noah said they were going off the grid for a bit, but I just thought…"

"You thought Jared would've told you himself? That he'd have said goodbye? Or still found some way to let you know they're okay?"

"All of the above, I guess. Or am I being selfish? Thinking Jared would risk a mission just to contact me? Don't answer that. I already know." I sighed deeply. "Seems like I don't know anything anymore. Everything just seems… wrong."

"I know, but I'm here. I'm with you, always," Ash replied, and that's all he needed to say for me to believe him, but I let down my roadblock anyway and felt his love warm my chest for a moment. "Anyway," he continued, "we can't do anything about all that right now, so let's concentrate on one thing at a time. Just saying you're right about the storm, how bad are we talking?"

I took a deep breath, puffing it out slowly, then closed my eyes and felt the breeze on my skin. "Bad, bad."

"Like the summer of my fifteenth birthday, bad?"

"Worse. Like worse than I've ever felt before, bad."

"That's not good. How long till it hits?"

"No clue. I can feel my chest vibrating already, and you hear that?"

"What?"

"Exactly. I don't hear anything, not even the gulls. We've got to get back, warn the others. You should go ahead, you're faster than me."

"No way, we do this together. I'm not leaving you out here alone. And don't bother trying to argue," he added as I opened my mouth. "My decision's final."

"Fine," I conceded.

We returned to the monastery as fast as I could run, Ash keeping pace with me, and by the time we got there, the sky had taken on an ominous crimson hue. Thunderheads gathered on the horizon and a volatile sea now crashed against the sharp rocks below the main complex. We hit the landing pads first, the *Nakomo* still looking incredible after the make-over the *Defender's* engineers had given her.

"Hey, what's the rush?" Brother Michael shouted as we pelted towards the stone steps leading down to the main complex. Ash skidded to a halt, and I almost ran straight into him. I'd run so hard for so long, I could barely get enough oxygen in my lungs, and I had to work hard to swallow the waves of nausea churning my stomach. I bent over, hands on knees, trying to get my breath back.

"A storm's coming," Ash replied. "Shae say's it going to be big, and it's going to be bad."

"Really?" Michael replied, looking to the sky.

"Really. When have you known Shae to be wrong about these things?" I looked up long enough to see the look of recognition on Michael's face before Ash continued. "I suggest you put Level Four storm protocols in place immediately."

Michael nodded his understanding, and the change in his demeaner told me he understood the severity. "We've only got three ships on the ground, plus the *Nakomo*. I'll have them locked down and the area cleared within an hour. We upgraded the power supply for the localised force shield last summer, so it should keep them safe from anything nature can throw at us."

"Excellent," Ash replied. "We'll leave you to get on with it."

He headed to the steps, and I followed, glad to be going at a slower pace. In the main foyer, the blue drapes adorned with the golden sun and rune symbol of the brotherhood, swayed in the growing breeze. Ash glanced around the room, assessing who was there.

"Brother Artimus," he called. One of the monks turned our way, his light-blue robes catching the wind, and he smoothed them down with both hands, colour creeping into his cheeks.

"What can I do for you this gloriously exquisite evening?" he replied, just a hint of his normal longwinded language.

"Find Francis and tell him to meet me in the Ops Room immediately."

Artimus's cheeks pinked further as he bristled. "I'm not your—"

"This is important, Artimus," Ash interrupted. "And serious."

"I… I…" Artimus stuttered, but then he looked between Ash and me, and stopped. He brushed down his robes again, composing himself. "Of course, Brother Asher. I'll find him right away."

"Thank you," Ash replied with genuine graciousness. Then, wasting no time, he turned to the other group of monks who'd been watching with interest. "Benjamin, Andre, with us."

They followed without hesitation as we took off again, through the doors into the main building. We passed meditation areas and classrooms, the smell of baking bread floating on the air from the kitchen. We drew further interest as we ran through the central courtyard, boots making muffled thuds on the flagstones as we headed quickly towards the Primus's office. Brother David sat at his pristinely organised desk, as always.

"Is he in?" Ash asked.

"Yes, but—"

Ash didn't wait to hear the rest of the sentence, he knocked on the door and walked straight in. "Forgive me Primus Noah, I…" We both stopped in our tracks.

Investigator Manus stood, tucking a long piece of thinning black hair behind his ear. "Do your people always barge into your office unannounced?" he said to Noah, but I noticed he was still watching me with intense, unblinking eyes.

"No, Investigator, they don't." Noah's tone was

cautionary, and clearly aimed at us.

David peered around me. "I did try to stop them, Primus. I didn't get the chance to explain you were in a meeting."

"It's okay, David. I know how..." he seemed to search for the right word, "determined Brother Asher can be when he has something on his mind. Perhaps you'd like to explain what that is, Ash."

"Of course. My apologies, Primus," Ash replied. David had been replaced by Benjamin and Andres, and I thought Manus's eyebrows were going to disappear forever into his hairline. "I wouldn't normally have disregarded protocols so blatantly, but there's a bad storm coming, and we think it's imminent. Shae thinks—"

"Oh, Shae thinks?" Investigator Manus interrupted, exaggerating my name. "So this hasn't come from the Ops Room? Because I haven't heard—"

"We need to instigate Level Four protocols across the whole complex," Ash continued, taking no notice of him. Noah stepped out from behind his large wooden desk.

"You feel it?" he asked. I nodded. "How bad?" he continued before Manus had a chance to say anything.

"I've never felt anything like this. It's like every cell in my body is vibrating. Honestly, I can't say with certainty what's going to happen, but what I will say is that I agree with Ash. We need to get ready. Because I have a feeling when this thing hits, it's hitting hard."

"You're seriously going to act on one person's feelings?" said Manus, not even bothering to hide the distain in his voice.

"When that one person is Shae, your gods damn right I am," Noah replied so firmly Manus took a step back. Lightning lit up the room briefly, and a few moments later, thunder rolled in the distance. "What's Ops got to say, Benjamin? The bulletin this morning said the storms were going to miss us by miles."

"I'm just as surprised about this as you, Primus. There was some indication that a third front might be building, but there was nothing to show we should be concerned."

"We're heading that way now to get an update," replied Ash, "but I wanted to get your agreement on the protocols first. We need to get the word out as soon as possible."

"I'll come with you to Ops," Noah said. "As much as I trust Shae's instincts…" he turned towards me and offered an apologetic smile. "No offence."

"None taken," I replied.

"I'd like to see some evidence of this threat for myself before I hit the panic button."

When we stepped back into the courtyard, I was surprised at how much the weather had changed in the few minutes we'd been with Noah. I pulled the band from my wrist, struggling to yank the flying stands of hair into a scruffy ponytail. The wind had already blown over chairs, and it whipped around the circular courtyard like a vortex. The sky had darkened dramatically, and the automatic chem-lights were flickering into life.

"Well, if this isn't evidence, I don't know what is," I yelled as we hurried across the yard.

The Ops Room was eventful when we got there. Plexi-screens displayed weather reports and telemetry, and a holo-screen in the centre of the room seemed to be running through a hypothetical scenario.

"Primus, I was just coming to find you," said one of the monks, sidestepping Francis to join us.

"Brother Oliver," Noah replied, "I hear we have a bit of a storm brewing."

"Yes, yes, that's exactly what I was coming to talk to you about. Following this morning's bulletin about two storms, we've picked up another nasty little bugger. A third weather front's forming a hundred or so miles north. Looks like things are going to get a little blustery for us, but nothing too serious. I was going to recommend Level Two storm protocols." Lightning flashed, followed by an ominous rumble.

"Level Two?" Ash challenged. "Noah, we need to start full Level Four immediately."

"Brother Asher," Oliver interjected. "I appreciate caution as much as the next monk, but Level Four is really unnecessary." He smiled politely, but his eyes narrowed showing irritation. "Come. Look at the screens and see for yourselves." We huddled around a large plexi. "There are the two completely separate and localised weather systems I advised about this morning, and there's the new one here between them." He touched the screen and telemetry for the third storm appeared down the side. His finger hesitated over some of the figures, and I noticed it began to shake slightly. "No, no. This can't be right."

"What?" Francis asked.

"It's... it's not behaving how it should. It's like..."

"Like what?" Ash pushed.

"Give me a minute." Oliver skimmed through data and reports, backwards and forwards until he sat back in his chair, his hand over his mouth. When he turned around, the first glow of sweat glimmered on his forehead. "Primus, I think you better issue that Level Four warning immediately."

Noah didn't hesitate. He accessed the nearest coms panel and opened a monastery wide channel. "This is Primus Noah. I'm initiating Level Four Storm Protocols. This is not a drill. I repeat, all areas initiate Level Four Storm Protocols immediately." From outside we heard instant yells of orders and activity.

"What's changed your mind, Oliver?" Andre asked.

"Hmm?" Oliver had turned back to his monitors.

"What's happened?" he prompted.

"I've never seen or heard anything like it. The three storms were completely independent, none of them close enough or strong enough to impact the others. But now...

I must've missed it."

"Missed what?" I pushed, getting irritated.

"There's a new low-pressure system pulling warm air into the third front, effectively super-charging it, and it's now heading our way. It'll soon be powerful enough to draw in the other two fronts, and when they merge... let's just say, I hope Level Four will be enough."

"There's no time to waste, then," said Ash. "Francis, I want you to coordinate everything from here. Andre, you're responsible for the main complex. Benjamin, I need you to take all the peripheral buildings to the East. I'll take the ones to the West and the dock."

"What about the shuttles?" Benjamin asked.

"Michael's already on it," Ash replied.

"What do you want me to do?" I asked.

"Help Andre with the main complex. We need everything and everyone inside by the time this thing really hits. Let's get this done, people. I want all our shields up in... Oliver, how long till it reaches us?"

"It's hard to tell. It's going to get bad over the next thirty to forty minutes, after that, it's going to get really bad, and then really, really bad."

"Okay, so that's shields-up in thirty. Be safe."

One of the key things Brother Benjamin taught me during tactical training, was never rely on technology – it can fail you at the time you need it the most. I reminded myself that with every hefty shutter I slammed tight over a window or door. Sure, we had the force shields, but I couldn't even remember the last time they were used. Technology was great... until it wasn't.

The wind buffeted me as I continued to work, and I narrowly avoided being decapitated by a thin sheet of flying wood I guessed came from the carpentry workshop. When I'd completed my allocated section, I hunkered down in an alcove, looking up at the swirling, black thunderheads. "Francis," I shouted over the noise of the wind. "I've completed section eight. What do you want me to do now?"

"Get your arse inside," he replied. Lightning flashed, bright and blinding, and the almost instantaneous boom vibrated into every bone. I felt the first hint of damp in the air and knew it wouldn't be long until the rain hit.

"Are all other areas secure?" I asked.

"The East and West buildings and the landing pads are as protected as they're going to be, and the main complex is almost complete."

"Almost?" I shouted. "Where's Ash?"

There was a moment's silence. "Ash is finishing off down at the docks, then he's heading back here to Ops. Get back inside. We're nearly ready to raise the shields."

"Copy that," I croaked, hoarse from yelling. I wiped a big, fat raindrop from my cheek and then another, and another. Before long, the sky opened and pounding rain soaked me to the skin within seconds.

The wind was fierce, and I could barely see through the driving rain. I edged my way around the building to get to the only unsecured entrance in my section. I pulled at the door, opening it slightly, but the wind was too strong. I tugged harder, but every time I thought I had it, it was like the wind blew harder still.

Pain shot through my ribs as a crate hit me side-on, ripping the door handle from my grasp and knocking me clear from the building. Away from its protection, the weather was even more violent. Lightning struck one of the buildings, stone and sparks flying, and I covered my head with my arms. I couldn't fight against the wind as it tumbled me over grass and stone, eventually slamming me into a low boundary wall. My cry of pain got swallowed by another thunderous rumble, and I covered my ears. Silver-blue shimmering light glowed as I picked stones out of my skin before edging along the wall, back towards my only way into the main building.

"Shae, what's going on? Your com signal's still showing you as outside. Are you okay?" Francis's voice was urgent in my ear.

"Slight delay," I yelled, cupping my hand over my ear so I could just hear him. "I'm trying, but it seems this storm has other ideas."

"We need to raise shields," he pushed. Lightning struck the building again, as if proof was needed. I pulled myself along the ground, staying as low as possible, but for every meter I gained, the wind blew me back two. Lightning struck repeatedly, the noise ear-piercing, and there was only one thing I could think of doing.

"Raise the shields, Francis," I shouted. "I'm in."

"Great. About time. Nothing like cutting it… hold fire… you're not in, are you?"

"Well, not exactly. But I'll be okay."

"Like hell you will." A familiar voice carried on the wind. I looked up, grabbing the hand being offered to me, and shadows in the open doorway pulled on the lifeline. We tumbled into the building, exhausted and slightly deaf from the storm. "We're in. Raise the shields," Ash ordered.

"You sure this time?" Francis replied sarcastically.

"Just do it," Ash grunted.

The roar of the wind was instantly replaced by the low hum of the force shield, except for the occasional crackling as lightning struck it. I pinched my nose and blew to clear my ears.

"How are we looking?" Ash asked Francis when we got to the Ops Room.

"You want the good news, or the bad news?

"Dealer's choice."

"Okay, the good news is all shields are fully operational and holding steady. The bad news is some of the outer, less substantial buildings took a bit of a hammering before we could get the shield up. The main complex also took some serious lightning strikes that overwhelmed the rods and caused localised outages with some blown power crystals."

"That's not too bad... considering," Ash replied, but he caught the expression on Francis's face. "There's more bad news, isn't there?"

"I'd like to say no, but I'd be lying. The storm is currently at about fifty percent of the destructive energy Oliver thinks it will get to. We don't have the power to maintain all the shields at full efficiency over a maintained period, so we better hope this weather doesn't stick around for long."

"Anything we can do to prolong the shields if needed?" I asked.

"I've diverted all power from non-essentials to boost them as much as we can, and we have some back-up powerpacks, which I've distributed around the monastery. We don't have many, so you better pray to the Gods that the main ones don't fail all at the same time. We also have one portable shield." He pointed to the red plastic box sat to the left of the door.

"That's it?" Ash asked.

"Yup. Just the one. But we can take it to any location should a main one fail altogether. After that, we're going to take a beating."

"So, what now?" Noah asked. "What's left to do?"

"Nothing really," Francis replied. "I've already stationed people around the complex to switch out the powerpacks if needed, and we're monitoring everything else from here. Nothing to do but weather the storm." Most of the people in the room groaned. "What? Too soon?" He grinned playfully and Ash gave him a half-hearted frown at best.

"Well, if there's nothing I can do here, I'm going to take a shower and get out of these running clothes," I said.

"Change, yes. Shower, no. That's part of the non-essential power diverts," Francis advised.

"Great."

"You'll just have to stay stinky."

"I'd punch you if my arms didn't ache so much from hanging on to things out there in the storm. You remember that? Remember I've been busy battening down the building? Oh, you might have missed that while you were chilling out here in warm, dry comfort."

"You want a piece of me?" Francis said, catching me off-guard as he jumped out of his seat, wrapping his arms around me in a bearhug.

"Hey! Let go, you big jerk." My words were muffled as he smooshed my face into his broad chest.

"That's enough," Ash said, and Francis released his vice-like grip. I punched him playfully on the arm and he reacted like I'd just walloped him with a fighting staff.

"You're such a baby," I teased. "And on that note, I'm going to wash and change... I assume the taps are still working?" I added sarcastically as I trotted out of the Ops room.

2

A couple of hours had passed, and so far, the shields were holding steady. Apart from the stoic few who'd been posted around the buildings on shield-watch, most of those who were left had congregated in the refectory. The continual soft hum of the shield generators, and the now more-frequent crackle from the lightning strikes, were masked by the rising merriment from the group. It was easy to forget the storm wreaking havoc only meters away.

Eventually, the excitement waned, and most of the Brothers cleared out, each heading to bed, or to prayer. Ash yawned heavily and stretched his arms above his head, one of his shoulder's cracking loudly.

"You're getting old," I teased.

"Getting old, my arse," he replied, his lopsided grin clearing away the frown. "But why don't you save my old bones and do the next coffee run, huh?"

"Anything to help an old man." I slid off the table where I'd been perched and side-stepped the swipe from Ash. Picking up the newly filled coffee pot, I headed out of the refectory towards the first person on watch. "Hey, Andre. What's up? Anything exciting happening?"

"Nope, not here. Shield looks fine and energy levels are holding steady. Thankfully," he replied. "If you're doing the rounds with that thing, though," he pointed to the coffee pot, "only Simon, Michael and I still have spare powerpacks. All the others have had to use theirs, so Francis relieved them. Without packs, there wasn't much for them to do."

"What if one of them fails again?"

Andre shrugged. "Whoever's still got a spare one will have to sprint it over, I guess, and hope they get it swapped out before the shield fails completely. But if more than three go while it's still blowing a tantrum out there, gods know what we're going to do."

The anxious look on his face reminded me just how serious the situation still was. The calm within the monastery had lulled me into a false sense of security, and over the hours I'd got used to the tingle under my skin to the point I'd forgotten about that too. I poured Andre a fresh cup of coffee, which slopped messily as I was practically bowled over by Francis as he skidded to a stop next to us.

"Easy," I said, righting myself, but he wasn't listening. He grabbed the power pack from the chair next to Andre and had already taken off before I could comprehend what was happening.

"With me, Shae," he yelled over his shoulder, already skidding around the next corner.

In my haste to follow, I practically threw the coffee pot on the nearest windowsill. It teetered on the edge, but I didn't stop, the crash and shatter of glass in my wake.

"Where are we heading?" I called after him.

"Library," he replied succinctly, but then he slowed and held the next door for me, adding, "The shield's weakening and Noah wants this one ready to swap out. No one thought the storm would go on this long, it should've blown itself out by now, and this is the last of the back-up powerpacks."

"What about the one's with Simon and Michael?"

"Both used. Like I said, this is the only powerpack left and the books must be kept safe, no matter what. Some of them are priceless, and that doesn't even include the irreplaceable artefacts in the vault."

Ash waited for us at the entrance. "What kept you?" he grunted above the rattling from the door. "We don't have much time. The shield's already weakening and has failed in some parts."

"Best not hang around then," Francis replied sarcastically.

The two men pushed the doors to the library open and I felt the sudden rush of cool, damp air. A large tree branch stuck through one of the spacious windows in the east wall, rain soaking the flapping pages of the books that had already fallen from the nearest stack.

"Francis, sort the power out. Shae, help me move these," Ash shouted above the whistling wind.

I grabbed an armful of wet scrolls, carrying them to the dry side of the room. "You need a hand?" I shouted, seeing Francis struggling to open the cover in the floor which housed the shield generator. He indicated he was okay, so I grabbed another set of sopping scrolls, peeling the parchment from my bare arms before I could put them down on top of the others.

"The power's almost depleted," Francis yelled. "I'm swapping in the new pack now." He pulled cables from the floor, working quickly to attach them to the power supply. "There may be a small interruption while the packs switch," he added after a moment. "Ready?"

"Do it," Ash shouted back, the wind now howling through the broken window. We both stopped in our tracks and watched as Francis typed in the override code before confirming the order to switch powerpacks. For a fraction of a second, the power ceased, and the storm sounded like the crack of a whip until the new battery kicked in. A fine spray of water settled on my arms and then everything was quiet and still again, except for the soft hum of the new power supply.

"Good work," Ash said, shaking raindrops from his hair.

"What's the damage?" Francis asked, getting up of the floor after replacing the shield cover.

"Doesn't look too bad… thank the Gods," Ash replied. "Could've been a lot worse. Fortunately, the shield loss was localised to the east corner and spared the more sensitive documents." He taped his compad and opened a link. "Oliver, this is Ash. We've successfully swapped out the power pack in the library, with some minimal damage. That's the last one though. What's happening with the storm?" He listened a bit before giving us the thumbs up.

"Good news?" Francis asked.

"Oliver says the storm's finally blowing itself out. Reckons the worst should be over in about thirty to forty minutes, give or take."

"That's great news," he replied. "We'll tidy up—"

The explosion stopped him mid-sentence, blowing the shield casing clear across the room, narrowly missing him before embedding itself in a bookcase on the far wall. I ducked and covered my ears, the shield instantly failing. Lightning cracked above, splintering the ceiling, and the resulting boom shattered the remaining windows. Over the roar of wind and the torrential downpour of rain, I heard Ash calling to Francis to make sure he was okay. Books and manuscripts fell from shaking stacks into wet heaps, and scrolls blew around the room as the wind rushed in. I caught one as it passed by, tucking it into one of the slightly more sheltered areas under a heavy reading table.

I heard Ash over my earpiece ordering the one portable shield we had to the library. While we waited, I grabbed as many books and documents as I could, my soaking hair whipping my face.

I registered the falling book stack at the same time I was bowled out of the way by Ash. I wiped the rain out of my eyes and looked at the heavy wood shelving lying just passed my left boot. "Thanks," I shouted, but my voice was drowned out by the wind. Ash nodded his understanding before grabbing a pile of books.

The doors to the library opened, and I saw the space on the other side was dry, protected by a separate shield generator. The brothers pushed their way through the wind and started grabbing everything they could carry, passing it back down the chain and out into the dry corridor.

The stacks shook and shuddered, and more books fell into sodden heaps. I picked up some of the scrolls I originally thought I'd saved, but they disintegrated into mulch at my touch. "Save what you can," Ash yelled as he dashed passed me. "Concentrate on the oldest," he added, nodding his head briefly towards the west wall.

The sturdy bookshelf was fixed securely to the west wall, but that didn't prevent it from vibrating under the storm's sheer power. I grabbed an armful of documents and headed back to the entrance, keeping low against the wind and trying to shield them from the rain as best I could.

I'd gone back for a second load when a flash of lightning hit the wall, opening up a black ominous crack and splintering the bookshelf from top to bottom. I instinctively dived out of the way, but a piece of flying wood embedded in my arm, and even though it hurt like hell, the pragmatist in me was glad it hadn't hit anywhere else. I clenched my teeth and grimaced in pain as I pulled it out, the immediate silver-blue glow lighting the area around me.

A glint of something, metal maybe, drew my gaze to the jagged edge of the fractured bookshelf, and for a moment I forgot the pain as I realised there was something else there. Something behind the stack.

One part of the shelf had opened marginally to reveal a hidden compartment behind. I unsuccessfully tried to wipe the rain from my eyes, surprised to find ancient parchments, old tomes, and mysterious artifacts. For a moment I was shocked, but I wasn't sure if it was because there was a hidden compartment containing secret items, or because, after all this time at the Monastery, I wasn't aware of its existence.

The wall crumbled further in a deafening crack, and I quickly decided to save what I could, and make sense of it later. I managed to grab about a third of what was there and then fought the wind and rain back the entrance, passing them off to a waiting monk.

Heading back, I passed several people trying to set up the new shield generator from the red plastic box. There was nothing I could do to help, so I carried on my task, but as I collected my second armful from the hidden compartment, the wall shifted further, and a rectangular wooden box fell from the top shelf. I tried to grab for it, but it slipped through my wet fingers, hitting the floor and springing open.

A piece of rolled-up parchment fell out, unravelling slightly, and I grabbed it before it could blow away. I was relieved the sheet had been preserved in a thin layer of plastic coating, the raindrops sliding off and causing no damage. Then I looked at it more closely. The bottom part of the document was jagged, like part of it had been torn off, and for a second my heart stopped.

In my room, safe and sound, was the torn part of parchment I'd been given by Finnian when I was much younger. The gift was from my mother and was the fulfilment of a promise he had made her to make sure I was given it. On the bloodied torn piece, in handwriting, were the words: Family, Honour, Courage. Nothing else. I know the shape and style of the paper like I know the back of my hand, which is why I recognised its counterpart in front of me.

As the storm raged on above, a separate, yet just as powerful maelstrom swirled in my head, and I could barely breath as I unfurled the scroll with shaking hands. The parchment, which looked like it had been torn from a large, ancient book, was covered in soft swirling patterns and bloody smudges.

Up until a few months ago, the only place I'd seen anything like it, was on the pendant I wore – another legacy left to me by my mother before she died. But everything changed on our last mission. In all my years with the Brotherhood of the Virtuous Sun, they'd consistently denied any knowledge of the symbols on my pendant, and had, in fact, gone further and denied being able to find any reference to the symbols anywhere else throughout the Four Sectors. Yet here, in this very monastery, was proof they had.

I was destroyed.

I don't know how long I stood there, looking at the very thing the Brotherhood had outright lied to me about for twenty-nine years, but a boom of thunder brought me crashing back to my surroundings. I quickly glanced around me to see if anyone was aware of my find, but everyone else was too busy shuttling books out of the library.

Without really thinking about it, I rolled up the page and shoved it inside my trousers. The wooden box I left open where it lay as I carried on my task as if nothing had happened.

"You okay?" Ash asked as we both deposited some books into the corridor at the same time. I wondered what feelings he was picking up from me through the Link, and for the first time ever, I was suspicious of his question. I let my mental roadblocks down to see if he knew any of what had happened, but all I felt was confusion and his usual concern.

"I'm okay," I lied, fixing the blocks back in place.

I didn't know what was worse – that the Brotherhood had kept the scroll from me, that they'd lied about it all this time, or that I now questioned the bonds I'd had with these people all my life.

I felt betrayed.

I wanted to leave and to go back to my room. I wanted to bury my head under my pillow and pretend this evening had never happened, but I couldn't. I couldn't because Shae gets stuck in and helps and does what needs to be done. Because Shae believes in the Brotherhood unreservedly. If I didn't stay to help protect the books, they would know something was wrong. So, I dug deep, and headed back into the library, fighting wind and rain, saving what I could.

There was a collective sigh and a few whoops as the replacement shield kicked in a few minutes later. The wind ceased instantly, the last raindrops fell, and a calm silence descended. It felt like an age since the first gennie had exploded, almost taking out Francis, but I don't think it had really been that long. Long enough to soak me to my skin.

I joined the monks in genuine celebration that the worst was over, but the hard work was just beginning.

"Oliver?" Ash said over coms. "What's the situation with the storm?" He waited a moment, listening to the response. "You sure? We don't want to be caught out again." He looked at me, raising both eyebrows in frustration as he listened. "Okay. Thanks." He tapped the earpiece to disconnect the call and then turned to address the room. "According to Oliver, the storm has passed us and we're just getting the tail end of it now. All shield generators are in the green and will last long enough to weather the last of it. No pun intended. There's minor damage to some other buildings, mainly the outer ones, but…" he gestured around him, "here is where we were worst hit."

"This is just terrible," said Artimus, and I wasn't sure if the glisten in his eyes was from the rain, or tears. "Such a waste."

"Yes, it is terrible," said Noah, entering the library, his gaze taking in the destruction. "But it could've been a lot worse. Let's thanks the Gods it wasn't."

"What now?" asked Andre, carefully picking up a book and smoothing down some pages.

"Now, we rebuild. We repair the walls, and the roof, and the shelves, and we save the books and parchments we can. Brother Adam keeps an index of everything that was in here, so we can identify what we've lost. But look at what you've saved," Noah continued, walking around the room, surveying the carnage.

He stopped near the cracked bookcase, flicking a barely perceptible look at the hidden compartment before clocking the wooden box on the floor. I wondered if anyone else noticed the brief look of panic on his face.

"We can restore most of these," he continued, bending down to pick up a few sodden books, but I noticed he also tipped over the open wooden box to see if the contents were still there. "It will just take time," he concluded, a slight waver to his voice. "Let's get some thermo-vecs in here tonight, and then tomorrow we can see what can be done once everything is dry. Brothers, Shae, I can't thank you enough for your hard work tonight. But for now, rest. We have a lot of work to do tomorrow."

"Man, I'm wired," admitted Francis as we filtered out of the library. "No way I can sleep just yet. What about you two? I don't care how wet I am, fancy a nightcap?"

"Sure, why not," replied Ash. "It has been one hell of a night. And it could've been a lot worse if you hadn't have warned us, Shae."

"I agree," said Noah, unexpectedly joining us from behind. "Once again, your gift has been heaven sent."

"I'm not sure about that," I said, trying not to be distracted by the manuscript page slipping down inside my trouser leg. "But, as Ash said, I'm glad it wasn't worse."

"True, true." He seemed distracted, and I could've sworn he was looking at me suspiciously, though that could just have been a guilty conscious.

"You know what? All that rain and dripping water has left me dying for a pee, so if you'll excuse me, I'll say goodnight."

"What, no drink? Come on," Francis said, reaching out to me, but I ducked him, afraid he might feel the scroll. "Have a pee then join us in the refectory."

"Once these come off," I picked at my trousers, "the only thing going on are my jammies. Goodnight guys, see you in the morning." I left before anyone could object further.

Back in the comfort and safety of my quarters, I peeled my trousers off with difficulty, removing the parchment page. The scroll was creased flat from being squashed against my leg, but the plastic had protected it and it hadn't cracked or degraded. For a long moment, I just looked at it; confused, angry, lost.

I needed to confirm. I had to be sure, but I didn't know if I had the strength to deal with what I already knew to be true.

I took a faltering breath and opened the deep bottom drawer of my desk, removing the carved wooden box Finnian had given me on my tenth birthday. We'd been on an off-world trip to the Trinity Planets, and I'd picked up keepsakes, or 'my treasures' as I'd called them back then, from each of the planets. Just little things – shells from Paradisum, pinecones from Arboribus, and fossils from Infernum. Finnian had given me the box to keep them safe.

Now, amongst other things, it held three of the most important items in the world to me: the data disc Finnian had left me after he died, the data recording I took in the catacombs on Tartarus, and the torn paper from my mother. I unfolded the blood-stained piece with shaking hands and placed it perfectly up against the larger part of the page. There was no denying that my part completed it, but it seemed odd that the piece from the hidden vault had no human writing on it, and the piece that I had, had no swirling symbols on it – just the handwritten words: Family, Honour, Courage. And I still had no clue what they meant.

I was confused and frozen to my core, but I wasn't sure if it was from the storm, or the betrayal of my brothers.

A hot shower later, and I felt marginally better; warm at least. I placed the two bits of paper in the wooden box and went to put it back in the drawer, but then pulled it back out. I'd never felt the need to protect anything at the monastery, but for the first time, I used the biometric sensor to lock the box. Sliding it into the drawer again, I wished Jared wasn't on his non-contactable, top-secret mission with Jake.

The next morning, I was tired after a fitful sleep, and my paranoia was in overdrive as I walked to the refectory. I was sure every person I passed knew I'd stolen the manuscript page and was silently judging me. The moment I saw Ash, I felt happy for the first time, like the churning sea in my belly had calmed.

"Hey, you," he said, standing to give me a hug and a brief kiss on the forehead. "We missed you last night."

"Yeah, sorry." We sat. "I just wasn't up to it."

He eyed me suspiciously for a moment and I felt my mental roadblocks thrumming as he tried to read me. After a moment, his eyes crinkled, and he smiled. "No worries, I think Francis drank all of the beer anyway. You okay?" A frown replaced the laughter lines.

Ash was the one person I had always trusted unconditionally. But now… I just didn't know anymore, and I hated myself for that. "I'm fine," I lied. "Just tired."

"Too tired to help with the library clean-up? We could do with all hands on deck."

"Sure. You know me, I'll be up for anything after a couple of mugs of coffee."

"Cool. I'm heading that way now, so just come over when you're ready." He stood and gave me another kiss on the forehead before striding off.

I hated that I didn't know if I could trust Ash. The possibility that he knew about the manuscript was the thing that hurt the most. If he did know, that would be the biggest betrayal of all, but if he didn't know, he was still the brother I loved and cared for. Why couldn't Finnian be here? If he were, he would guide me straight. He would...

He would what? Realisation slammed into me like a gut-punch. Finnian had known about the manuscript, he must've done. Was this the secret he was keeping from me my entire life? And if it was, there must be more to it than a piece of old paper. What other secrets where they hiding?

I didn't know if there was anyone on the entire planet I could trust anymore. Then, just as I was sinking into a panic I wasn't sure I was going to be able to pull myself out of, I remembered another part of Finnian's message: when I didn't know who to trust, trust Ash. That made me feel better, but I had to be sure. I downed the cold dregs of coffee and headed back to my room to listen to Finnian's message again.

Mildly bolstered by the thought there was still one person left who was on my side, I headed to the library to show willing, plastering on a happy face and doing what I needed to do to get through the day.

It was already a hive of industry when I got there, and it looked like Benjamin was allocating tasks. "Hey, Shae," he said cheerfully as I wandered over to him. "Good work on the early warning system for the storm. Damage would've been way worse if we hadn't been prepared."

"Thanks, but it was nothing," I replied humbly. "Where do you want me?"

"The thermo-vecs have dried the books on the tops of the piles, but the ones underneath are still damp. We need to separate them out. Dry books in reasonable condition are being stacked over there." He pointed towards the south wall. "The damp ones are going against this wall, and we'll put the thermo-vecs back on tonight. Any that you think are too damaged, put over there, and Adam is cataloguing them before we see if they're beyond repair." He sighed heavily, picking up a pile of mulch that only just resembled a book. "Unfortunately, some of these can never be replaced."

"I know," I said, rubbing his arms. "But there are many more that can be saved."

"That is true. You know what you're doing?" I nodded. "Then I'll leave you to it. Excuse me."

I started on the nearest pile, loading dry books in my arms until I was in danger of dropping them. Heading over to the stacking point, I noticed the heavy bookcase and gaping crack in the north wall had been cordoned off with bright orange tape and a danger sign depicting falling rocks. Thick black sheeting had been fixed across the whole shelving area, obscuring the hidden compartment, and when I walked closer to get a better look, David appeared out of nowhere, blocking my path.

"This part of the library's off limits, Shae," he said amiably. "It's still too unstable – don't want you getting hurt." He chuckled to himself. "Not that that would bother you."

"Just because I heal, doesn't mean I want to get hurt. But I see your point."

It was hard labour, and for the rest of the day, everyone was too busy working to engage in more than polite conversation now and again. It did, however, give me some time to think about what I was going to do next, and I realised the first thing I needed to do was get Ash alone, away from the monastery and everyone else in it. Without it looking suspicious.

Over dinner with Ash and Francis, I put my plan into action by casually mentioning that I'd be going on a run the following morning, knowing it wasn't Francis's thing. "You fancy it?" I asked him, just as he jammed in another huge piece of apple pie.

"Like hell," he spluttered, before raising his arms out to the sides, puffing out a broad chest. "This was built for combat, not for princy prancy running around aimlessly. If I want to get from A to B, I'll take a gods-damn rover." His chocolate eyes crinkled as he guffawed.

"Yeah, okay! A simple 'no' would've done it, Gigantor," I replied, but he just laughed harder.

"What about you?" I asked Ash casually.

"You sure you want the company? Normally you prefer to go alone. I want to clear my head," he mocked. To be fair, it was a good impression of me.

"What is it with you two this evening?" I quipped. "Look, the offer's there. I'd enjoy the company."

"You know what, count me in. It's about time I remind you just how much faster I am than you."

"Whatever," I replied, feigning indifference, even though Ash would've known the comment would rile my inner competitor. For a few minutes, everything seemed normal.

3

Early the next morning, I met Ash on the patio overlooking the bay and the Diamond Reef.

"Morning," he said, pulling some chairs back out of storage. "What's with the backpack?"

"Just some rations," I replied. "Water, energy bars, that kinda stuff."

"Don't be thinking you can use the extra weight as an excuse for me leaving you in the dust." His lopsided grin appeared as he stretched. "You want me to carry it?"

"No!" I replied too quickly, causing him to eye me carefully. "I wouldn't want you to use the extra weight as an excuse for me beating your arse." I think I recovered well, at least he thought it was funny.

"Come on then, let's go. We're still on library duty when we get back."

"Great," I called after him as he took off up the steps towards the landing pads.

Despite all his jokes about beating me, Ash kept pace without question or complaint. A couple of times we slowed for water, but I guess we'd been out about half an hour when he stopped dead and stared at me, hands on his hips.

"Okay, out with it," he said. It floored me for a moment. I thought I'd been so 'normal' about the whole thing, but then Ash was the one person who knew me better than I knew myself. I'm sure I looked guilty. "What's going on, Shae?"

"I…" I was momentarily frozen. I needed to know where Ash stood, but was I ready to find out if he'd been betraying me?

"Whatever it is, you can talk to me about it, Shae. You know that, right?" I didn't respond. "Is it about Jared, or Jake, or being on lockdown? Because I can talk to Noah again if you want me to. I'm not sure how much use that would—"

"It's not that," I blurted. "I need… wait a sec." I took my backpack off, rummaging inside it before passing a bottle of water to Ash. I took a second one and put it on the ground before sitting cross legged. Ash sat in front of me, looking even more confused as I took a small red box out of the bag, putting it on the ground between us. It beeped twice and then fell silent. He raised an eyebrow inquisitively. "I'll explain. One way or another, it'll make sense," I said. "I promise."

"Okay," he replied slowly. "Because you're not making too much so far."

"I know. Please, just bear with me. Ash, I'm going to ask you to do something, and you're going to think it's really strange. And then you're probably going to be offended. But I need you to do it for me, alright?"

"Okay," he repeated slowly again, deep furrows settling on his forehead.

"And I want to make sure no one else is listening. Hence the tech." I pointed to the little box.

"This is getting very weird, Shae, even for you." I nodded slowly, not taking my eyes off him. "It's a good job I trust you," he added, no idea of the irony. "What do you want me to do?"

"I want you to answer some questions."

"Is that all?" the frown lines smoothed over, and the smile reappeared.

"No, that's not all. Sorry. I need you to let your mental roadblocks down while you answer." The frown reappeared, but he remained silent. "I need to know whether you're telling me the truth."

"Okay, you were right. I'm officially offended. And I still don't know what the hell's going on."

"I'm so sorry, Ash. Like I said, it will make sense. Please?"

"You really need me to do this? For you?" I nodded. "Then okay. But you know this means you need to let your roadblocks down too?"

"Yes," I replied quietly. "And I apologise in advance for what you might get from me. Are you ready?"

He shook out his arms and cracked his neck. "Do it."

I tried to let my roadblocks down slowly, letting Ash in while trying not to dump my feelings on to him, but I failed. I was so emotional that all the fear and pain, confusion and anger bulldozed their way through the Link to Ash. He gasped, choking on his own breath, and I feared that something had gone wrong, that I'd damaged him in some way. I thumped his back and helped him to get his breath back, and when he had, tears rolled down his cheeks. I thought they were from him choking, but then I felt his own pain and anguish through the Link.

"This is how you feel?" he stammered. "This is how you feel right now?" He didn't wait for an answer, instead he scooped me into the tightest hug imaginable without breaking any bones. After a little while, he loosened his grip, but then pulled me back in for another bearhug.

"As much as I really like this, if you don't let go, we can't get started," I mumbled into his shoulder. He obliged, but when I saw his face again, he looked pale and drawn.

"I'll do whatever you need me to do," he said sadly. "And then, maybe, I'll understand why you feel so utterly betrayed."

"You will." I mentally checked the stability of the Link between us and took a deep breath. "When did we first meet?"

"Really?" he seemed surprised.

"Yes. I think it's best to start from the beginning."

"I guess…" He thought for a moment, then his eyes cleared slightly, and a smile tugged at his lips. "It was not long after I came to the monastery as an orphan. I was, what? Eight?" I nodded. "So you would've been six. That big kid with the big flappy ears was calling you names and then stole your cuddly rabbit. I punched him in the nose, gave you back your rabbit, and got called to the Primus' office for my trouble." All I got through the link was love and affection, as well as a hit of satisfaction.

"You were my protector even back then. But why did we become friends? How did I become your sister?"

"I don't understand."

"Out of all the kids, the boys you could've got close to, why me?"

"I'm not sure." He fell quiet, thinking. "I'm not sure it will make sense to you."

"Try me."

"I felt a… a connection to you. I felt like we were supposed to be family. That being close to you, protecting you, being there for you, was something I needed to do. Like I said, does that even make sense?"

"More than you know."

"What do you mean?"

"I mean, that's how I feel about you," I explained, but he laughed. "What?"

"You, my protector?" He laughed harder and I felt genuine amusement through the Link.

"Okay, wise arse, you know what I mean. I felt a

connection to you as well. Something I can't really describe. So nobody made you be my friend? Nobody told you to get close?" I paid close attention to the Link.

"Of course, no one told me to be friends with you. You can't make people have the feelings I have for you, Shae. I love you. You're my sister. I would do anything for you." The hit from the Link was so strong it was impossible to fake. "Hey, hey, I'm sorry. I'm not used to our mental roadblocks being down. I didn't mean to make you cry."

"It's alight. It's good."

"It is? You're still not making sense by the way," he added, but I could feel there was something left unsaid.

"There's more?"

"Finnian and I were on a training mission, but that was years later when I was maybe about fifteen. He asked about our relationship and said he was glad you had someone like me. He didn't tell me to do anything, but he said you were special, and whether you believed it or not, you would need someone like me to look after you." I checked the Link, and he was telling the truth. "I haven't thought about that day in forever, but now I come to think about it, it did seem a little weird.

"How so?"

"He asked if I would continue to be there for you. If I would commit to being your protector, like it was a job or something. Of course, I said I would – I mean, who else could put up with you?" I playfully swatted him on the knee. "Truthfully though, he got really serious. He said again that you were special, unique, and important, and there would be a time when you would be in true danger. I laughed and said when are you not in danger, you're like a danger magnet, but he didn't see the funny side. He said it was my 'purpose' to keep you safe, and he asked for my commitment, which of course I promised. But that wasn't the last time Finnian asked me to look out for you."

"What do you mean?"

"Well, you obviously know the off-world chaperone rule, but most recently, during our mission to stop ARRO, Finnian reminded me of my commitment to protect you. He said I needed to be extra vigilant, and not take your safety for granted. Then, when the Supremc Primus asked to speak to me before the naming ceremony, he said pretty much the same thing about me needing to protect you from danger. He was really serious, just like Finnian had been before. Made it sound like some kind of life-or-death situation, and I had no clue what it was all about. He said the Primus position was mine, if I wanted it, but asked if I would consider staying as an operator. Stay as a Guardian and continue to look out for you." I checked the Link again, and he was still telling the truth. He was just as in the dark about what was going on as I was. "That's why I got into so much trouble when I let you go off alone with Jake during Fallen Star. Doesn't change the fact that I would protect you with my life. Not because someone told me to, or asked me to do it, but because I would want do it. For you. Oh, stop it." He smiled. "I didn't say that so you'd get all weepy again."

"I'm sorry," I mumbled, wiping my cheek. "Let's change the subject before I run out of tears. Do you know who my parents were?"

"No idea. All records were lost in the transport explosion." True, according to the Link.

"Do you know why the *Nakomo* was in that part of the Sector?"

"Humanitarian mission, I believe." True.

"Do you know anything more than I do about my gift?"

"That's an abrupt change of topic, but no." True. "I'm just as confused by the developments as you are." True.

"Did you tell Noah about the newest evolutions?"

"No." He looked confused. "Though I'm not sure why. I guess I've just not had the right opportunity since we've been back."

"There wasn't the opportunity? Or it didn't feel right telling them for some reason?"

Ash thought for a moment. "Both, maybe? Shae, I don't like where this is heading."

I thought about Finnian's message, and the fact that his vows were so strong that he couldn't break them, even to protect me. Maybe that's why he'd been so keen on Ash taking up that role. Everything Ash had said so far had been true. Was it really fair for me to put him in the same position as Finnian?

"You know what, I've made a huge mistake. Let's stop here before we can't go back from this." I tried to stand, but Ash took my wrist and pulled me back to the ground.

"Whatever this is, we finish it now. Shae, I feel what you feel. It's already too late to go back."

"Are you sure?"

"Not in the least. But I have to know why you feel so deceived by the Brotherhood – and by me."

"Not you. Not anymore." Damn those wayward tears. Ash leant forward and brushed them away.

"Ask your next question."

"Last one, but it's a big one," I replied, checking the Link. Pulling out my pendant, and holding it towards him, I asked, "Have you seen these symbols anywhere other than on here?"

"These?" he asked, taking it in his hand and flipping it over. "No. I thought the scholars gave up searching for any reference to these years ago after they came up empty." He froze, looking overwhelmed. "I guess that was the right answer given the crushing sense of relief that just blasted through the Link."

"I'm sorry you had to go through that," I said after downing half a bottle of water. "But I had to know I could trust you."

"I still don't understand why you felt you couldn't."

"You need to see something... actually, you need to see

a few things, but we'll start with this." I stuck my hand into the backpack and removed a small pouch.

"Finnian's message?" he said, and I nodded. "Oh, Shae, you don't need to show me this. I'm sure it's personal."

"It is, but actually, Finnan himself told me to let you see it." I opened the drawstring and tipped out the small, silver data-disc before putting it into the portable holo-projector I'd also brought with me. "You ready for this?"

"Do it," he replied firmly.

"You may want to put your mental roadblocks back in place," I advised as I placed the holo-projector on the floor in front of Ash. As I felt the Link calm, I pressed play.

"My dearest Shae," Finnian began. "I suppose the traditional way to start one of these things is to say: if you're watching this, it's because I'm no longer with you. I hope mine was a truly honourable death, and that I didn't trip and fall over a cliff – or die in some other, equally embarrassing way. Oh, and I hope there was lots of singing and drinking at my funeral." Ash smiled sadly. "In all seriousness though, I'm truly sorry. Not because I've passed, but because I've left you... because I'll no longer be there to look out for you, to protect you. Although, after what I'm about to tell you, you may be glad I'm no longer around. And I wouldn't blame you."

I watched the confused frown pucker Ash's forehead.

"The Brotherhood has been my whole life, but it's no secret I thought of you as my daughter. From the moment I held you in my arms as a baby, I've loved you. I've always considered myself one of the luckiest men in the Four Sectors; I got to follow my calling, while enjoying the riches of being a father. You make me very proud, Shae, and I don't think I told you that enough. You're the most amazing person I know, and that's not just because of your gift, but because of the wonderful, thoughtful, loving person you are."

Ash leant forward and touched my knee gently.

"I was in the Brotherhood long before you came along, and it's a vocation I still believe in with all my soul. My vows are as strong today as they were when I took them back on my eighteenth birthday... but there's one order that's never sat well with me. I'm torn, Shae. I took an oath a long time ago to protect a secret – one I vowed to take to the grave unless specifically ordered to divulge it. I've never received that order, but now I find myself with a dilemma: protect the secret, or protect you. You need to be very careful, Shae. There are people out there who'll come for you if they find out who you are. The signs are clear: something bad is coming, and unless you're prepared, I fear for the future of all Humankind – no, I fear for all races. There are so many things I'd tell you if I could, but that would mean breaking my vows – something I still hold very dear. I hope that in time you will come to forgive me."

If it was at all possible, Ash's frown deepened.

"You must find out who you really are. You must find out the truth about your past to prepare for the future. You're the key, Shae. Go back to your beginning. Ever since you were old enough to understand, you've asked questions about your parent's death and why the Brotherhood adopted you – and I answered all of them as best as I was... able. But I'm just one person, and... well, the memory can play tricks on you. You used to question what the *Nakomo* was doing in that region of space in the first place, and the answer was always the same: a humanitarian mission. But you never asked what humanitarian mission we were on. What were we doing out there – just when your parents needed us? Was it just coincidence?"

"There's no such thing," Ash muttered.

"I'm in danger of saying too much, Shae. I'm truly sorry for leaving you to deal with this without me. When you don't know who else to believe in, trust Ash. He'll keep you safe. Let him see this message, but don't tell anyone else about what I've said. No-one – even though you may be tempted. Ash only. I love you. One final thing… find the Harbingers. Ask them about the Helyan Codex."

The message ended. Ash sat back, rubbing his chin before puffing out a long, slow breath. I stayed silent, giving him a moment to process.

"Something bad is coming?" he recapped, his mind racing. "And you're the Key? To what? To stopping the bad, whatever it is?" He looked at me questioningly, but I shrugged, just as confused as him. "Play it again."

We watched the message twice more.

"I can't believe Finnian lied to you about your parent's death, or more accurately that he was ordered to lie to you, to all of us, about their death." Ash stood and paced, massaging his eyes with the palms of his hands before sitting back down. "What does he mean by finding out the truth about your past to prepare for the future?"

"I've no idea," I replied honestly.

"Okay," He took a deep breath. "No wonder you've been struggling since we've been back. I'm so sorry you've had to deal with this on your own. Why didn't you show me this before? I could've helped, or at least been someone you could talk to about it."

"I know, I'm sorry. It's just been a lot to process. But Ash?"

"Yeah?"

"That's not everything."

"There's more?" he replied, the deep v-lines appearing between his eyebrows again.

"Remember that thing that happened in the catacombs under the Palace of Palavaria?"

"The one you said you couldn't tell me about?"

"Yes. The Khans weren't after the Third Seal, or some stupid ancestral painting like the King said, they were after something called the Helyan Cube—"

"Wait," Ash interrupted. "Finnian said to ask the

38

Harbingers about the Helyan Codex. That can't be a coincidence, they must be linked?"

"That's what I think. But quit interrupting or we'll be here all day. The King denied all knowledge of the cube, to the extreme that he would have sacrificed all of us, including Phina, to keep its existence a secret." Ash opened his mouth, then shut it again before mouthing 'sorry'. "What?" I asked, but he mimicked locking his lips and throwing away the key. "Just say it."

"But they didn't get it? That's why Vanze was so mad? Sorry, I really tried." He smiled apologetically.

"No. Jared and I managed to retrieve it, kind of, before the explosion. But the important thing is that I think the cube was made of the same brushed bronze material as my medallion, and it shared the same swirling writing."

"Writing?"

"Sorry, I'm getting ahead of myself; we'll get to that bit. When Vanze opened the wooden box it was in, and took it out, my insides started vibrating. It was like little bursts of energy flowed through my blood. I was totally fixated on it. Could take my eyes off it until Vanze put it back in the box, and then it all stopped. Just like that." I absentmindedly cracked my knuckles. "Jared saw the cube too, but he doesn't know about the effect it had on me. Anyway, Sebastian ordered both of us to never discuss the cube again, not even with each other. He was very insistent. Guess I've just broken about a million laws by telling you this."

Ash shrugged. "After everything else that's happened today, it's not even the most important thing. So the King has the Helyan Cube? That could be important information at some point, especially if the Harbingers help us find the Helyan Codex." He looked at me a moment and then scrunched up his nose. "There's more isn't there?"

"Oh yes," I replied with exaggeration. "If the cube isn't weird enough, Jared and I found the same markings again in the caves on Tartaros as we hunted down the Khans. I thought Vanze would be able to tell me what it all meant, maybe help me understand who I am, but he just left me with more questions. He was the one that told me the symbols were some sort of text, or writing, and he referred to something called the Amissa Telum. He also mentioned deciphering a codex. Didn't know what he was talking about at the time, but now…" I took out another small data disc from my bag and swapped out Finnian's message in the holo-projector. "I took this in the complex on Tartaros."

Ash watched the recording from the data-cam with almost child-like awe. "I can't believe you've been going through all of this by yourself?" he said after it finished.

"What choice did I have?"

"You could've told me. Who cares about Royal Orders? No wonder you've been going crazy. But there's something I don't get? If those markings are on your pendant, the cube, and Tartaros, chances are they're on this codex thing as well."

"Logical."

"Then why has the Brotherhood not been able to find reference of them before—" His mental roadblocks weren't strong enough to hold back the wave of pain that bulldozed its way through the Link, stopping him in his tracks. "Please don't tell me…" he trailed off, his expression almost pleading me to tell him he was wrong. He sat in silence as I told him what had happened during the storm, showing him the two separate pieces of the same page.

"And that's… everything," I stated when I had nothing more to say. Ash silently leant forward and pulled me into a hug.

That was when I cried.

And I cried a lot.

When I was finally done, Ash let go then got up and paced again, clearly thinking through everything I'd just dumped on him. I felt bad, but I also felt overwhelming relief. I could trust him; he knew nothing. And for the first time ever, ignorance was a blessing.

He lay down on the warm grass, squinting up at the cloudless sky. "So what now?" he said simply.

"That is the million-credit question," I replied, trying to force a smile that probably came out more of a grimace. "I never thought I'd say this, but apart from you, I don't know who else I can trust in the Brotherhood. I mean, what about Francis? If you didn't know any of this, then surely he doesn't either? Should we tell him?"

"No," Ash replied simply, turning his head towards me, and shielding his eyes with his hand.

"But—"

"Finnian said not to trust anyone, even if you're tempted."

"What say does he have?" I said, suddenly angry. "He's lied to me my entire life."

"I know, and I'm sorry," Ash soothed, sitting up again. "Look, we don't have to make a plan now—"

"Easy for you to say," I snapped back. "Sorry. I didn't mean to… Do you think this 'secret' Finnian was referring to, and the fact that I'm supposed to be some sort of key to an impending doom, is why that stupid chaperone rule was in place? And why I'm on lockdown now? I just always assumed it was to do with people wanting me for my gift…" I drew in a sharp breath and then smacked the palm of my hand against my temple. "Holy shit! This has everything to do with my gift. I can't believe I didn't make the connection before."

Ash stayed silent for a moment as I mumbled to myself about my own stupidity. "Don't beat yourself up, Shae. You've had a lot to deal with," he eventually said as diplomatically as he could.

"Well, you made the connection pretty damn quick." I rested my elbows on my knees and cupped my face in my hands, thinking. "You're right."

"I am?"

"Yes. We shouldn't make any rash decisions. Perhaps we should just ask Noah about the manuscript page? Force the truth."

The feelings seeping through the Link were muddled and unclear, but flickered between confusion, pain, and uncertainty among many others. I felt terrible. The Brotherhood was my family, and I felt utterly betrayed, but to Ash it was more than that. It was a calling. I could only imagine what he was going through, and I'd done that to him.

"Stop it," he said unexpectedly. "I know you, Shae. I know what you're thinking. This isn't your fault. None of it is." He closed his sad, grey eyes and took a deep breath. "I need time to think, to digest. Can you give me that before we decide what to do next?"

"Of course, and you're just being kind about it not being my fault."

"We can debate that later," he said, the hint of his trademark lopsided grin appearing. "Crap. Look at the time. I'm surprised Francis hasn't sent out a search party."

"We should head back," I agreed, packing everything back into my bag. "What do we say?"

"Something believable. We ran too far, challenging each other, then walked, and chatted. We talked about the Tetrad Summit and Fallen Star, and then you 'overshared' about your feelings for Jared and Jake." He nudged my arm playfully. "We lost track of time, that's all."

"Then we go back to helping clear up the library like nothing has happened?"

"Yes. For now. Until I can process all of this."

"I don't know if I can."

Ash took my hand. "You can because you're strong. You're stronger than even the Brotherhood knows. You can do this."

"I hope so," I replied quietly.

4

When we got back to the monastery, we got the usual chastising from Artimus for missing 'important' work that everyone else was taking seriously. I stayed quiet and let Ash do the talking, but after that, nobody seemed to care we'd been away far longer than usual. Apparently, Ash and I doing our own thing was considered perfectly normal.

I reluctantly left Ash's side so we could both go and shower. At first, I couldn't face leaving my room, for fear I'd do or say something I couldn't take back. Talking things through with Ash had made everything even more real, putting all the pain into sharp focus. How could I act like everything was normal? But after a while, I realised it would seem even more weird if I stayed in my room – besides, some hard graft was probably just what I needed to keep my mind off everything else.

"Hey, look who it is?" Francis scoffed as I walked into the library a few minutes later. "What kind of time do you call this?"

"It's…" I made a big show of looking at my com-pad. "Time to kick your arse time. That's what kind of time it is. I believe we had that scheduled in for about now. Am I right?" A grin exploded across his face.

"Bring it on, babyface," he taunted, followed by booming laughter. "You know I reign at arse-kicking. I'm the arse-kicking supremo," he teased. But after a few steps towards me, he stopped in his tracks, noticing Ash lingering at the entrance.

"What's the matter, Supremo?" Ash challenged, his grey eyes sparkling. "Not so confident anymore, are you? You reckon you could hold the crown taking on someone your own size?" In seconds, the two of them where on the floor, grappling and laughing until everyone was watching and cheering. I moved out the way and left them to their playfighting, and after a couple of minutes, they broke apart and lay on their backs, panting and guffawing like children.

"You two done?" I asked, holding out my hand out to Francis.

"For now. You and me, though? Not so much," he said menacingly, but he couldn't hold in the laughter, and I struggled to pull his shaking bulk of the floor. I'd just got him upright when Primus Noah appeared.

"Thought I'd stop by and pitch in," Noah said, rolling up his sleeves. "I'm impressed." He did a circle of the library, casting his eyes over every area, and I didn't miss the part where he paused momentarily at the black tarp still covering the gapping crack in the wall. "I can't believe so much progress has been made in just a day and a half."

"We could've made more if certain people had bothered to show up earlier," Francis joked. "Just sayin'," he added, with a playful punch to Ash's arm.

The thermo-vecs had done their job again overnight, and the library was thankfully declared fully dry by Adam. The tree branch and all the storm debris had been removed, and we'd finally separated all the library contents into piles by mid-afternoon.

"Simon, what's the eta on roof repairs?" Noah asked as we took a short breather.

"The carpentry workshop is just finishing the replacement rafters, but we can't fit them until the rest of the building is structurally sound – which means the window, lintel and brickwork on the east wall needs to be completed first. As does whatever is going on over there," he added, nodding his head towards the cordoned off bookcase.

"When's the window repair due?" Noah asked.

"A day, day and a half, with everyone chipping in."

"Excellent. Fantastic work, everyone," Noah added. "Unfortunately, I must leave you to it, but your dedication is admirable. My heartfelt thanks."

"What about that?" Ash asked, indicated towards the tarp.

"Beyond our skill-set, so I'm told," Noah responded casually. "Something to do with damaged foundations, isn't that right, David?"

"Yes, yes of course," he replied a little too quickly. "We have a specialist team arriving in a little over an hour."

"Really?" I blurted, unconvinced. "Surely we—"

"It's all arranged now, Shae. Not for you to worry about," Noah said, standing. "Let's leave the experts to fix it." He looked at his com-pad. "Damn, I'm late. I'll see you all at prayers later."

Noah's exit was taken as an indication our rest time was over and we went back to work, but a couple of hours later, we were interrupted.

"Hi. Umm, hey," David called above banging and hammering. "Can I… can I have everyone's attention please?" He waited for silence. "The engineers have arrived."

"So?" Francis grunted, his bald head slick with sweat. "They want an applause or something?"

David forced a laugh. "No, Francis, but they need us all to clear out so they can work."

"That's not at all suspicious," I whispered to Ash. He

seemed to be thinking the same thing from the furrows in his forehead.

"I'm sure they can do their work all the way over there, while we continue over here, without either of us getting in each other's way," Ash challenged.

"That's as maybe," replied David, wiping his brow with the back of his hand, "but the Primus has told them we'll give them space to work, and that's what we're going to do. Just embrace the chance to get out of here earlier than anticipated."

"Don't need to tell me twice," said Francis, dropping his hammer noisily on the nearest table. "Some of us have been working since the crack of dawn," he added, a distinct dig towards me and Ash.

The three of us left the library together, but Francis peeled off to get a drink as we passed the kitchen gardens. I'd spent all day wondering how Ash was handling the information I'd given him, but now we were alone again, I didn't know what to say. As we walked silently side-by-side, I glanced up at his pale face and he looked tired. Older.

"I'm okay," he said, catching me off guard. He bent his head down, a sad smile forced just for me. "It's just a lot to process. I need some more time. Can you give me that?"

"Of course." I squeezed his hand. "As much as you need."

"And you won't do anything crazy in the meantime?"

"Me? Crazy? Pah!" I exclaimed. "Never." He chuckled, and that made me feel a little better. "I mean it, Ash." I stepped in front to stop him and waited until he gave me eye contact. "I'm not a fool. I know how this impacts you and what you believe in."

"It's not—"

"Look at me," I interrupted. "And listen to what I'm saying, because this is probably the most important thing I'm going to tell you today." He raised a questioning eyebrow. "I can't ignore everything that's happened, and at some point, I'm going to do something that's going to put me at odds with the Brotherhood. With my family."

"Shae—"

"I'm not finished. Finnian kept the Brotherhood's secret, kept me from knowing who I am, and I'm not going to lie, that hurts." Ash opened his mouth, caught my look, and then shut it again. "But I don't blame him. I know how seriously he took his vows. And I won't blame you either, Ash. If you go down this path with me… well, I can't tell you where it will end, or what it will mean for either of us. But if you choose your vows, the Brotherhood, I will understand. I will love you regardless, and I need you to understand that."

"I'm your brother. The very definition means you have to love me whatever," Ash said softly. "But I hear what you're saying, and I appreciate it more than you know."

Later that night, the lounge was full, and you could hear the chatter halfway across the courtyard. "Noah thought we could use the pick-me-up," Thomas explained, passing me a mug of moonshine.

"Is that this year's batch, or last year's," asked Francis.

"Last years."

"Damn, Thomas, I thought we'd use the last of that to clean the toilets. That stuff is brutal," Ash joked, though it didn't stop him picking up a mug and taking a huge swig. "Damn," he repeated, before hiccoughing.

As the moonshine flowed, the merriment increased, and despite everything else that had happened, the tight knot in my chest loosened. "Don't drink too much," warned Ash as I finished my second. "Neither of us can afford to let go tonight." But just as he finished his sentence, Frances appeared and refilled my mug before I could object. As he ambled off to join some of the others in a rousing singalong, Ash switched out my full mug, for his almost empty one.

A while later, when things started to quieten, I yawned

and stretched, muscles aching from the morning's run and all the work I'd put in during the day. "I'm done," I said to several groans and objections. "No, honestly, I'm exhausted. And if you want me in the library bright and early…" I trailed off as newcomers arrived, dusty and sweaty.

"Hope you don't mind us crashing," the lead one said, "but as I understand it, you've got some pretty fine shine flowing in here." His smile displayed dazzling teeth, but his eyes flicked around the room, like he was tactically assessing all of us.

"Of course, come in. All of you," Thomas replied graciously, gesturing with his arm. "Help yourself."

"Just be warned," Frances chipped in. "I know you're big guys and all, but it's not for the faint-hearted."

"Yeah?" The lead guy poured a mug. "We'll take our chances and appreciate the hospitality." There was an awkward moment while the group of four got their drinks and joined us. "Brother Luke." He extended an arm to Francis. "This is half my team. I've left the others still working."

Francis watched him carefully as he took his first swig, then roared as he spluttered and turned red. "You'll get used to it, Luke," he said through the laughter, whacking the poor guy on the back. I noticed Luke's men watching the interaction closely. Something didn't seem right, but I couldn't put my finger on it.

"How are the repairs going?" Ash asked, his question more loaded than anyone else in the room realised.

"Not bad," Luke replied. "We'll have most of the tough stuff done tonight, so you guys should be able to get back in there tomorrow. Must've been one hell of a storm."

"That it was," said Thomas, his face beetroot from the alcohol. He smiled at me with genuine affection, and I felt a stab of guilt as I wondered if he knew my secret. "Would've been worse, too, if Shae hadn't warned us it was coming," he continued. "We would never have had time to prepare as much as we did if not for our girl."

"Is that so?" Luke's attention turned swiftly towards me, and Ash sat back, resting a protective arm on the back of my chair. "Sounds like you saved the day then. The monastery's lucky to have you."

"That we are," Thomas replied. "That we are."

"That bookcase held some of our most valuable positions," Luke continued, and it jarred that he'd used the word 'our' rather than 'your.' Or was I just being super-sensitive? "I understand we've also got you to thank for saving some of them," he continued.

"Me?" I questioned, realising he was still looking in my direction.

"That is true, isn't it? I understand from Brother Adam that it was you who carried a number of those priceless books and artifacts out of the library that night." I felt Ash stiffen beside me.

"Yes, that's true." My mind raced. Where was he going with this? And why didn't he just mention the hidden compartment? "In all honesty, the whole thing was a bit of a blur. The wind was whipping paper and scrolls around all over the place, and you could barely see through the rain. I just grabbed what I could, dumped it in the corridor and repeated." While I talked, I watched the other men who'd come in with Luke and realise what I couldn't put my finger on earlier: all of them sat with full mugs. Not one of them had taken a sip, and I was sure it wasn't because of Luke's initial reaction to the moonshine.

"Well, you saved a great deal. I'm sure the Brotherhood is thankful."

"You make it sound like the Brotherhood and Shae are separate entities," Ash commented, just a hint of irritation in his voice.

"Forgive me. My choice of words was… unfortunate. Your reputation precedes you, Shae, I didn't mean to imply you're not Brotherhood," Luke replied diplomatically, but an almost imperceptible change in demeaner had rippled through his men. "It must've been difficult knowing you couldn't save everything."

"It was, but I grabbed what I could."

"Are you referring to anything in particular?" Ash asked. For a moment Luke looked as surprised by his directness as me. Perhaps he was as sick of this cat and mouse game as I was.

"No, no, nothing in particular," Luke replied smoothly, fine rock-dust wafting from his dirty blond hair as he shook his head. "We're still inventorying that area and I was just curious as to whether there was anything Shae saw that might have got destroyed... or lost... before anyone was able to save it, that is."

I managed to swallow the urge to leap across the coffee table and choke him in a headlock until he told me just what the hell he was playing at, but instead, I smiled graciously. "No, I'm sorry, nothing. I grabbed what I saw. I hope you and your men don't take this the wrong way, but I was just leaving when you arrived. So, I'll say goodnight, and leave you to it. If you'll excuse me?"

Luke leaned over to the side to let me pass. "See you tomorrow," he said politely, but something in his voice made my skin prickle.

Even though I was tired, it took me a long time to get to sleep, continuously tossing and turning as I worked through everything all over again. Only this time, I'd added Luke and his team to my paranoia, as well as my fear I'd pushed Ash too far by dragging him into this as well. Should I have just kept my gods-damn mouth shut? Was it my own selfishness that led me to telling Ash so I didn't have to be in this alone? I'm sure I hadn't been asleep long when heavy pounding woke me up.

"Rise and shine, sleepyhead," Ash chanted as he entered the room. I opened my stinging eyes just long enough to register he was dressed for running. "The sun is shining, the sky is blue, and Luke's team are still working in the library."

"So?" I grumbled, pulling the covers over my head.

"So…" he yanked them down again, "we've got time for a run."

"I'm too tired."

"Get up. Get dressed. I've brought refreshments, and I'm not taking no for an answer."

I sat up and finally looked at him properly, squinting as he pulled open the curtains letting the morning sun in. "Fine," I agreed in protest. I'll meet you on the patio."

My legs we sluggish and uncooperative to begin with, but after a couple of miles I started to get into a rhythm. Ash seemed preoccupied in thought, and I didn't push him, knowing he'd say what he had to eventually. I'd told him I'd give him time, and that's what I'd do, even though I was biting my tongue the entire run. When we got to the same spot from the previous day, he slowed and then stopped, taking a moment to let me catch my breath. Ash, on the other hand, was barely puffing.

Eventually, my impatience got the better of me. "So… are we going to talk about Luke, and how he and his men are most definitely not engineers. At least, not the ones that came to the lounge last night." He opened his mouth to respond. "And did you see how he checked us all out?" I continued. "And those other guys didn't even take a sip of their drinks. I mean, even overlooking the sheer waste of Thomas's moonshine, that's weird, right?" Ash opened his mouth again. "And Luke might as well have just come outright and ask if I'd taken the manuscript page. Wait… do you think Noah knows I have it? Damn it, Ash, you must have some thoughts on this…"

He frowned and pursed his lips. "Couldn't get a word in edgeways," he said, his eyes crinkling. "You done?"

"Yeah, sure. Sorry," I offered apologetically, gesturing with my hand that he should continue.

"My thoughts? Well... you pretty much covered it. I don't know who they are, or why they're here, but it's certainly not to fix a wall. That's not why I got you out here this morning, though."

"It's not?"

He sat on the ground, rubbing his chin. "Yesterday wasn't easy for me, Shae." He held up his hand to silence me, as I slumped in front of him, guilt stabbing at my heart. "I've learnt things that worry me a great deal, and I have questions I never thought I would. After I was orphaned, the Brotherhood took me in, just like they did with you and Francis, and so many others. I'm thankful for that, and for giving me something to believe in. To some, it's a calling, to others it's a purpose or a duty. However you look at it, I vowed to spend my life protecting the unprotected, and this is something I intend to continue doing."

"I understand," I said sadly, my head dropping into my hands.

"I don't think you do." My head raised, and he took one of my hands in his. "All yesterday, I was trying to look at what had happened from every angle, including the Brotherhood's. I tried to put myself in their position, to understand why they might have lied to you about the day you were rescued, or about the manuscript page. Was it to protect you? To keep you safe? And, in all honesty, I'd pretty much decided that my advice to you would be to confront Noah."

"Really?"

"Yes. He was on the *Nakomo* when you were rescued; he must know something. I hoped it would give the clarity you would need to make an informed decision on your next steps. If he realised you knew what you did, and offered the rest, or at least acknowledged there was more, that would be one thing. And if he denied everything..."

"That would be another. How very rational of you." I couldn't help being disappointed, and I pulled my hand away. Somehow, I'd expected more from Ash.

"I haven't finished," he declared, picking it up again. "I said that was what I was going to recommend."

"What changed your mind?"

"A couple of things."

"Luke's team?"

"That's one of them, sure. I left the lounge not long after you did last night, but I couldn't sleep. I had the same nagging hunch about them as you did, so after an hour or so, I got up and tried to find out more about Luke."

"And…"

"And nothing. His file was classified."

"Even from you? A Ninth-Degree?"

"Yes. So that got me thinking more, and I pulled up the information from the day you were born. The logs clearly show the *Nakomo* was dispatched on a humanitarian mission, but they re-routed to the transporter your parents were on when after they received a distress call. The rest of the mission reports and the *Nakomo's* logs detail the rescue and their return to the monastery with you. Nothing I haven't read a hundred times before, and nothing out or the ordinary – at least to anyone not already questioning the validity of the information"

"You found something."

"Yes… no… not exactly. It's what I didn't find that concerns me. If the *Nakomo* was on its way to offer humanitarian aid, and they couldn't make it because of the distress call, another ship must've been dispatched, right? Wrong. I can't find any trace. Nor can I find any real details of what the mission was in the first place. So, I started to wonder whether the transporter and your parents were, in fact, the true mission." I sucked in a surprised breath, and he held my hand tighter.

"And was it?" I pulled in a shaky breath, waiting for his response.

"I don't know."

"What do you mean?"

"I mean, I don't know. I checked the mission logs submitted by Finnian, Noah, and Benjamin, and on the face of it, they look legit, but looking at them again, I wonder if they're not too perfect. They're so similar, and so carefully worded, they reminded me of the After Action Reports you, Jake and Ty submitted after the whole foot amputation thing. But of course, none of that is proof of anything. So, next I delved deep into the *Nakomo's* flight logs to see if they were congruent with the mission logs."

"And…?"

"They are. But again, something didn't feel right. I got dressed and went to the ship to pull the logs directly. They're gone. Deleted."

"Seriously? Another dead end then."

"Not entirely. After I left the *Nakomo*, I went to Ops to access the central computer directly."

"And you found something?"

"There's something else there. Something hidden behind the official statements and ship's log, but I couldn't read it. It's heavily encrypted and far beyond my technical expertise, but…" he pulled a data disc out of his pocket, "I downloaded the whole thing. Who do we know who's a tech-genius?"

"Ty."

"Exactly."

"But that doesn't help us. He's probably on the same super-secret mission with Jared and Jake. Besides," I absentmindedly shuffled rocks around with small flicks of my finger, "last time I checked, we were both confined to planet."

"The way I see it, if we want to know what the hell's going on, we have three options."

"I'm listening."

"One: we go with my first thought, which is to confront Noah with everything we know – cards on the table – and see what he's got to say for himself. Two: we go straight to Supreme Primus Isaiah and follow the same principles as option one. Either way, the Brotherhood knows that we know, and if they deny everything, we've tipped our hands and there will be even tighter controls levied on both of us."

"I'm not sure what tighter controls they can invoke; we already can't leave the planet. And with Jared and Jake uncontactable, we have no other allies outside of the Brotherhood. What's option three?"

"Ah yes, option three…" If it was possible, Ash looked even more uneasy. "We do what Finnian said in his message: we find the Harbingers and ask them about the Helyan Codex. And if we can track down Ty or the *Veritas* along the way, all the better."

After he'd finished there was an awkward silence while we both sat, digesting the possibilities laid out in front of us.

"Well, those are some options," I stated eventually.

"Don't give me an answer now," Ash replied. "Before we do anything we can't take back, we both need to be sure. You can't un-throw a grenade." It was a good point.

The rest of that day was a rinse and repeat of the previous one, the only difference being the addition of Luke and his men helping to repair the library. Even though I was fully aware my paranoia was cranked up to full, I couldn't shake the feeling they were more than casually interested in what everyone else was doing, especially me.

Throughout the day, I went over all the facts in my head, trying to rationally distinguish what I knew for fact that the Brotherhood were involved in. By the time Ash and I were alone again that night, there was one thing that I was sure of more than anything else.

"We should take the option that has least impact on you," I said defiantly, while he shook his head slowly. "I don't want to blow up my relationship with the

Brotherhood, they're my family, but like I said before, I may not have a choice. But you… you shouldn't risk everything for me."

He laughed unexpectedly, taking me by surprise. "You are my everything, don't you see that? The more I've thought about it, the more I think Finnian knew it might come to this. I think he encouraged our bond for this exact moment."

"What are you saying?"

"I'm saying that I will follow you, Shae. I will follow you wherever this takes us. We'll do it together." He held up a hand to silence me. "Even if that puts both of us at odds with the Brotherhood."

"They could excommunicate you, Ash. I can't be responsible for that. I won't."

"You're right, they could, and I'll deal with that if and when it happens. That's not something that should impact our decision. And also… not technically your responsibility. Mine."

"We'll if you're going to get all stubborn on me…" I tried to joke, but it came out sad and hopeless. Ash put his arms around my shoulder, and I felt his affection like a warm pulse through the Link. "I think we should give the Brotherhood the benefit of the doubt," I said eventually. "Option two; confront Isaiah. Lay it all out, see how he reacts. I thought about giving Noah the opportunity, but he might be under oath like Finnian, in which case we won't get any answers anyway. I say we go straight to the top, tomorrow, after breakfast."

"That's a fair plan," Ash conceded. "But if it fails, the only option that leaves us with is three, and that could be tricky. We'd have to find a way to get off planet, and then stay off the Brotherhood's radar. Lucky for you, I've already been thinking about just how we can do that."

5

Ever since I'd dragged Ash into this whole sorry situation, he'd practically begged me not to go off half-cocked. And I'd agreed because I trusted him, and no matter what else happened, I still wanted to believe the Brotherhood would do right when the chips were down. Our strategy was rational and thought out, weighing the pros and cons – doing what was fair to Ash, to the brotherhood, and to me, and I was ok with that.

Not anymore.

I crashed through the refectory doors, practically bowling over Thomas, as I scanned the room for the person I was looking for.

"Woah, where's the fire?" Francis joked as I pushed passed his and Ash's table without acknowledgement. Ash was up and following me in a second, but he didn't get to me before I'd made it to where I wanted to be.

Primus Noah looked perplexed, standing just as I launched my carved wooded trinket box at him. He caught it awkwardly as the lid opened mid-flight.

"Where are they?" I demanded loudly, heat burning my cheeks.

"Shae…" Ash cautioned, reaching out to me, but I brushed his arm away. "What's going on?"

"What's going on?" I laughed sarcastically. "Well, that's exactly what I'd like to know. What… the hell… is going on, Noah?" The rest of the refectory had frozen in silence.

"Shae, I'm not sure what's going on here," Noah said carefully, "but I think you should take a few minutes to calm down—"

"Calm down!" I practically shrieked. "This is me calm."

"Perhaps we should take this to my office. David, if you could—"

"I'm not going anywhere until you tell me where they are."

Noah looked confused, placing the empty box on the table before flipping the lid closed. "I don't know—"

"What I'm talking about? You don't know why I'm being so not-calm?"

"Shae, talk to me. What's going on?" Ash asked, concern and anxiety burning through the Link. I could barely think straight I was so livid. Blood rushed in my ears, and I know I must have looked like a maniac, but I couldn't help it.

"They took it, Ash."

"Took what?"

"All of it." I picked up the box, turning it upside down, the lid swinging back and forth. "The manuscript page, Finnian's message, the vid-disc from Tartaros… the whole gods-damn lot." I turned to Noah, emotions flicking between anger and betrayal. "I want it back. I want it all back now."

"I really don't know—"

"Don't say it! Don't you dare say one more time that you don't know what I'm talking about. It was locked." I waved the box before slamming it down on the table. "With a biometric sensor. You're the Primus; no one does anything at this monastery that you don't know about, so you know what was taken. What I can't believe is that one of you lot," I waved my arm wildly around the room, "did it." As I glanced around, my gaze settled on Luke and his men, who unlike everyone else in the room, were still sat at their table across the far side of the room. "Or did you leave the dirty work to outsiders," I snarled at Noah.

"Before you interrupt me again, please do me the courtesy of listening to what I have to say," he appealed.

"Be my guest," I replied over-graciously, indicating with a wave of my arm that he had the floor.

"I've never seen this box before, I don't know anything about a vid-disc, and why on Lilania would I want to take the message Finnian left you?" I notice he didn't mention the manuscript page.

"And I suppose you don't know anything about the true mission the *Nakomo* was on the day my parents died. Or why the *Nakomo's* data logs have been amended. Or the real reason why I've been restricted to planet for the last month?" I pushed, anger rising again.

"I… I…" For a moment he was lost for words, a tiny vein now prominent in his temple. He took a deep breath, rallying himself, and then he squared his shoulders. "Ash, I'm not sure what Shae thinks has happened here, or what she's hoping to achieve, but I suggest you get this situation under control."

"Me?" Ash snorted, and I quickly realised I'd dragged him into a course of action he wasn't prepared for. "Actually, I'm just as interested in hearing the answers to her questions." He stood close to me, and I appreciated the solidarity more than he would know.

"You need to think carefully about your next move, Ash," Noah cautioned as he flicked an eye in the direction of Luke's table, where the men had stood and were now edging their way around tables towards us.

I could also have also been imagining it, but for a moment Noah looked anxious – fearful even. Who were those men?

"I need you to trust me, Ash," Noah continued quickly, as the rest of the monks moved out of Luke's way. "It would be best for all concerned if you took Shae back to her room, and everyone else," he flicked a meaningful glance back in Luke's direction, "had a moment to centre themselves."

Ash was barely listening to Noah anymore, his glower now squarely aimed at Luke. The two men sized each other up for a moment, but as Ash held out his arm and shuffled me behind him, so he now stood between us, Luke held his own arms out to the side to indicate his men should stand down.

"Ash?" Noah said to pull his attention away from Luke, but mine was still very much focussed on the strangers, and I didn't like the subtle glances and micro-expressions. Did they not think we'd had exactly the same tactical training? "I think perhaps Shae's not feeling well, it would be best for her—"

"That's enough!" I shouted, almost surprising myself as much as everyone else. I stepped out from behind Ash. "I've actually had it with the Brotherhood trying to tell me how I feel, what I should be doing, and what's best for me. You have two choices, Noah. You can give me back my belongings and tell me just what the hell you've been keeping secret from me since I was a baby, or you can get the hell out of my way and let me find out for myself. Either way, there's no putting the genie back in the bottle after this. Your choice."

"Shae, I'll—"

I knew my ultimatum would have consequences, but what happened next started a chain of events no one could've predicted.

"I've had enough of this as well," stated Luke, almost sounding bored by the situation. "Primus, all due respect, but I'll take this from here."

Noah's face immediately flushed, and his fists balled at his side. "Stand down, Luke. I have everything under control."

"No, you don't. You never did. That's why I'm here."

Ash and I shared confused glances, and then I caught Francis's eye. Guilt prickled my skin as I remembered he had no idea what this was all about. I knew him. I knew he would feel left out – hurt that we hadn't shared something with him. I mouthed, 'I'm sorry,' and he mouthed back, 'what can I do?' That made me feel even worse.

"Don't do this, Luke," Noah continued. "It isn't necessary." He glanced around the room at the confused, anxious faces, then settled on mine. "Shae, you're our family. We are one. Please trust that everything we've done is to protect you; to keep you safe. To—"

"Keep her in the dark. To keep her compliant," Luke added. For a moment, he sounded like he was on my side, and that rattled me even more, but he wasn't done. "She's too important for you to screw it up now, Noah, so I'm going to take her with me."

"I'm not going anywhere with you," I replied, but Luke moved forward unexpectedly, and in an instant his team was on his heals.

The rest of what happened, was pure instinct. Without thinking, I raised my arm. A shimmering silver-blue pulse travelled down it, gathering in my hand for the briefest moment before pulsing towards Luke and his men. They flew backwards, tables and chairs with them, until they all slammed into the far wall. Realising what I'd done, I looked at Noah, and I saw fear in his eyes. My stomach turned as I remembered Ash was the only one there who knew my gift had advanced. As far as anyone else in the room was concerned, including Francis, the only thing I could do was heal people.

I couldn't read Francis's face, but I knew I'd let him down, and I wasn't sure whether this was something he could forgive. I was a terrible friend – if I even was his friend anymore.

There were so many feelings swirling around my head, I could barely think straight, and in the hushed silence of the refectory, I felt all eyes on me.

As Luke and his men started to rouse, I felt Ash grip my arm and tug it gently. "We need to leave," he said, his distress and fear scratching at the Link.

"No," Noah cried. "Please, Ash. I can fix this. Where are you even going to go? You can't get off planet. You're just making things worse."

"Worse than this," he grunted back, indicating the tears streaming down my cheeks. "If this is what we're doing to 'protect' Shae, we're doing a pretty gods-damn pitiful job at it."

"You should listen to him, Asher," Luke croaked. He slowly edged forward, arms up and palms forward in surrender, but I didn't trust him. His eyes were wide and bright, and I realised that unlike everyone else in the room, he wasn't fearful of my apparent new skills. He was excited. "Noah's right, you can't leave the planet. We can play cat and mouse for a bit, but eventually she's going to come with us."

Ash squeezed my wrist and I looked up into his weary face. "Do you trust me?" he asked quietly.

"Always."

"Then hit him again."

Without hesitation, I raised my arm and sent Luke sprawling back against the wall. The moment my arm fell, Ash turned and headed for the door, pulling me with him. We paused briefly as monks blocked our path, but then Noah nodded his head and they shuffled out of the way.

"Where are we going?" I puffed, trying to keep up with Ash, but then as realisation dawned, I slowed, forcing him to stop. "Noah's right. There's nowhere for us to go. What have I done?"

"You said you trusted me, right?" I nodded. "Then don't flake out on me now." He took my chin in his hand and lifted my head, taking my gaze from my toes to his face. He forced a lopsided grin and said, "Option three, remember? We planned for this. Come on, let's go."

"Go where? We still have the whole stuck on planet thing to…" I caught the look on his face and nodded my acceptance. "Trust you. Got it."

"Head to the *Nakomo*. I'll meet you there," he said.

"Where are you going?"

"Just something I have to do. Don't worry, I'll be right behind you. Start the flight checks."

I arrived at the *Nakomo* a couple of minutes later. Michael, who'd not been in the refectory, seemed surprised to see me.

"I wasn't aware she was going out today," he said, affectionately patting the shuttle. "And I thought you were, umm, planet-bound," he added diplomatically.

"She wasn't, and I am," I replied, releasing the *Nakomo's* docking clamps.

"Then why…? Do I even want to know?" He finished his sentence as Ash arrived on the pad with Francis hot on his heal, puffing.

Francis stared at us, his eyes moving between me and Ash, and I couldn't read him. "I told you I hate running," he grunted eventually. "Come here," he added, gathering me up into a bearhug. "I don't know what's going on," he whispered in my ear, "but I trust you and Ash." He let me go, but I pulled him into another brief hug.

"Thank you. You have no idea what that means." I let him go.

"What do you need from me?" he asked.

"I've got this," Ash said to me as he led Francis off, but he turned back and added, "Get her ready to take off."

Through the *Nakomo's* panoramic front screen, I watched Francis and Ash talking as I did the final flight checks. When I saw the line of monks nearing the landing pads, I hammed on the screen to get their attention. I couldn't hear what was being said, but I could tell the conversation sped up at that point, and I gasped as I watched Ash lamp Francis so hard, he tumbled back, falling over a create. Before I could comprehend what had happened, I heard the usual groans of the rear ramp closing, and moments later, Ash threw himself in the pilot's seat.

"Why did you hit—"

"Not now."

"But—"

"Not now, Shae," he ordered as he pressed buttons and flicked switches.

The thunder of the engines drowned out any potential pleas from Noah, and I watched them shrink to tiny ants and then disappear as the *Nakomo* climbed into atmo. Even though I had a million questions, I kept silent, watching Ash scramble to get his thoughts in order.

When we got to the cloaking field, we came to a stop, and for a moment Ash just sat there, staring out the front screen, like he was a million miles away. I chewed on my tongue, desperate to ask how we were going to get through the shield, but then Noah's voice broke Ash's reverie and he was back on the *Nakomo* with me.

"There's no harm done yet," Noah was saying. "We've got Luke and his men under control. You have nothing to fear from them."

"But what about you?" I blurted, unable to keep quiet any longer. "Should I fear you?"

"Of course not, Shae. If you come back, we'll call Supreme Primus Isaiah. Together. Find out what he wants to do about—"

"About me?" I finished for him. "I already said I'm tired of other people deciding my—" the com-link went dead, leaving me open-mouthed halfway through my sentence.

"There's no going back now," Ash said taking his finger

off the switch.

"Well, clearly, there's no going forward either," I replied, pointing out at a whole heap of nothingness. "Have faith, you said, but faith doesn't get you through a seriously death-inducing forcefield."

"True, but preparation and ingenuity does." He ducked under the console and reappeared holding a data-pad that was hard-wired to the ships control systems. "Option three," Ash explained, typing code I didn't recognise. "Didn't think we'd have to use it though." He saw my confusion. "When it became obvious that there was a chance, even a small one, we'd have to get off Lilania quickly, I knew the biggest challenge would be getting through the shield. As soon as we took the *Nakomo*, Noah would've locked out our command codes and ordered the ops room not to open the cloaking field. I would've done exactly the same thing."

"Comforting."

"So last night, after we talked," he carried on, ignoring my sarcastic interruption, "I added an override code to the central computer, allowing me to control the field from here." He indicated the tablet. "They've already figured out what I'm doing and they're trying to stop me, so as soon as the field is down, you need to take us through quickly."

"No worries," I said, sitting forward and accessing flight control.

"I mean it, Shae. Quickly. If you don't, and they close the field before or while we're going through it…"

"I got it. Besides, if I'm that important to the Brotherhood, there not exactly going to splat me with the forcefield, are they?"

"Let's hope—" The panoramic screen filled with a view of asteroids. "Go, go, go, go, go…" he shouted, and I did exactly what I was told.

To leave Lilania and get to DeadSpace, Ash would have to navigate through the deadly asteroid field. Francis was the best pilot, so he would normally do it, but Ash was the next best thing. "She's all yours," I said, transferring flight control to him."

"Not this time," he revealed, shifting it back. "You're going to have to take this one."

"Me?"

"You."

"Now's not the time to joke, Ash. You know I haven't done this run in, well, forever."

"I know. So do us both a favour and don't get us…what was the word you used? Splatted? Don't get us splatted on a rock."

"That's not funny, Ash."

"And I'm not joking, Shae," he replied seriously. "Sensors indicated they were already getting ready to launch another ship as we went through the shield. I need to disconnect the *Nakomo's* tracking module by the time we get to DeadSpace, or we might as well just wait there for them to catch up with us."

"Okay, just don't blame me if things get a little hairy."

He laughed, and it lifted my heart a little. "You could always disconnect the module, and I'll fly," he offered.

"Nope, you're okay. Do what you need to do."

About thirty minutes later, Ash returned to the flight area looking triumphant. "All done?" I asked, still concentrating hard on the path through the asteroids.

"All done. I blew it out the airlock, so it's probably splatted against an asteroid, or floating around somewhere we're not."

"Can you please stop using that word."

"It's your word."

"I used it once. And you're going to jinx us."

"No more than your flying skills."

The unexpected levity was good, and for a moment we allowed ourselves to enjoy it, but then his expression got all serious again. "Now what are you doing?" I asked as he ducked down under the console again. "Hey!" I added as he pushed my legs out of the way.

"Do you actually know how anything on the *Nakomo* works?" he asked.

"What's your point?"

"The Brotherhood uses the tracking module to, well, track our entire fleet, but that's just unique to us. All ships have a transponder beacon that tells other ships and locations who we are. And as we don't want people to know who we are—"

"We need to disconnect the transponder as well."

Ash popped his head up from under the console. "Sorry, what was that? 'We' need to disconnect the transponder?"

"Okay, Exacto. 'You' need to disconnect the doohickie. And can you stop interrupting me, I'm trying to concentrate here," I added laughing, but only half joking. "Avoiding gigantic killer rocks is tough work."

Ten minutes later we were clear into DeadSpace. "Where to?" I asked.

"Good question. Like I said, I didn't expect things to move quite so quickly."

"Yeah, about that. I'm really sorry. It's just when I saw that all the evidence had gone, I lost it. Who's going to believe us now?"

"Not all the evidence has gone."

"I guess," I replied, twisting my pendant.

"Don't forget this," Ash added, holding up the data-disc containing the encrypted information from the main computer.

"So that's where you went. I guess it's something, I suppose."

Ash set destination coordinates into the nav system, and I raised an eyebrow in curiosity. "Angel Ridge," he explained, and I snorted. "Wow, that's ladylike."

"You're kidding? Why on Lilania would we go to a

shitpit like Angel Ridge. We have no allies there."

"Exactly. We can't go to our usual sources, and we've got to get off the grid, so we go to the one place they wouldn't be expecting us to go. Besides, I can think of one person there who may be pleased to see you."

"Me? Oh, come on! You're not seriously thinking of Beck?"

"Why not? We know he's a half-way descent guy after he helped us get out of his bar alive, even though he wants to keep that a secret."

"Which bit? The fact he helped us, or the fact he's only a bad guy 'ish."

"Both. But he's enough on the murky side of grey to be able to help us out with a few things were going to need. Plus, it doesn't hurt that he likes you," he added mischievously. That lopsided grin appeared, and for the first time since this all started, it reflected in the sparkle of his eyes.

"We don't even know if Beck's still on the Ridge. After his bar got toasted, it's possible he moved on."

"True, but we'll have to take the risk."

"What exactly do we need from him anyway?"

"Well, don't freak out, but the Brotherhood are still able to track us. To a point."

"What do you mean still able to track us?" I practically screeched. "I thought you said you disconnected the transponder thingy and blew the gods-damn tracking module out the airlock. What could possibly be left?"

"Whoa, I said don't freak out." He laughed loudly and I punched him on the arm – playfully, I think, but I'm not sure. "I did do all of that, but it's a little-known fact that the *Nakomo* has some kind of a unique energy pulse built into the engine systems which allows for the ship to be tracked at shorter ranges."

"So, they can't track us long distance, but if a Brotherhood ship gets too close to us, they'll be able to find us?"

"Correct. If they know what to look for, and if they've been given the *Nakomo's* unique identifier."

"I think we can safely assume it won't be long until they all have it."

"Exactly."

"I wonder what story they'll be told for why they're looking for us."

"Try not to think about it. Anyway, that's the main reason for going to the Ridge. There has to be someone there who can help us with that particular problem."

"And you think Beck will know that someone?" I asked. Ash nodded. "If this additional tracking system is so super-secret, how do you know about it?"

"Finnian told me. Told me not to tell anyone else, that only restricted people knew about it. I didn't tell anyone, by the way – not until now – so don't get all huffy thinking you've been left out. And before you ask, I have no idea why the Supreme Primus would want a secret way to track the *Nakomo*."

"Fine," I huffed. Then realising I'd done exactly what Ash knew I would, I changed the subject. "Ash, do you think we should try to contact Jared and Jake? Or at least the Wolfpack? I know they're on some classified mission, but you said yourself, Ty's the one person we can call on to decrypt that disc, and if anyone can help us, it's them."

"I agree, but not yet. Contacting Jake and Jared is the first thing Noah will expect us to do; he'll be monitoring all the coms channels."

"How do you know?"

"It's what I would do. We can't take the risk. Let's get to the Ridge, get the *Nakomo* 100% off the grid, then use one of those shady backchannel com-links you just know they'll have lurking about… if you know the right person to ask…"

"Beck you mean," I said, catching the wink he gave me. I rolled my eyes dramatically, but I knew he was right.

During the flight to Angel Ridge, or 'the shithole' as I was now unkindly calling it, Ash and I recapped what evidence we'd lost, and what we still had. What resources we had, and what we'd need.

"So, firstly, you might find this useful," Ash said, prying up one of the floor panels in the main cabin. Underneath, there were four large canvas holdalls. He pulled one half out, checked the tag, and replaced it. "Francis's," he explained, his expression regretful for a moment. The next tag obviously had my name because he hauled it out and dumped it at my feet, and while he got the other two, I opened it up.

"You're kidding me," I marvelled, pulling out a Sentinel pistol, a fake civilian ident with my picture on it, a massive wad of credits, and various other paraphernalia. I dug around further. "I wondered what had happened to this... and these," I added, pulling out items of my own clothing. "I thought I was going crazy when these went missing. That, or one of the Brothers had a thing for women's clothing. When did you do all this?"

"I've been doing it for years," he replied. "But I update them about every six months. You never know when something's going to happen."

"Why didn't you just say something?"

"Say what? Tell you that I think something so horrible is going to happen that I'm preparing for us to be stranded on the *Nakomo* at some point? Separated from the Brotherhood? I didn't want you or Francis to worry about it, besides, Finnian told me... of course he did." He sighed heavily with recognition. "Finnian told me this was what he did when he used the *Nakomo*. The same time he told me about the extra tracking signal. He encouraged me to do the same, even showed me where the compartment was. He was the one that suggested I didn't upset you by telling you about it." He sat heavily on the floor, and I sank down beside him. "How could I not have seen it? How could I have been so blind that I didn't realise he was preparing me to be your protector all that time?"

"Because he wasn't asking you to do anything you wouldn't have done for me anyway," I said gently, putting my arm around him. "I know how you feel about me, and I've just witnessed what you'll do for me. He would have known that too."

"He took advantage. I thought he always showed interest in me because I was good, because he saw something in me. But now I wonder if it was all just because of my friendship with you?"

"No, don't think like that. Do you think if Finnian had, for a second, thought you weren't the best person, the best fighter, the best strategist, that he would've spent his time on you? He trained you because you were... you are, the best. Our friendship was a bonus, and did he take advantage of that? Maybe. But I'll tell you something Brother Asher, Ninth Degree Warrior Caste... and you better listen to me... if Finnian didn't think you were worthy of protecting his daughter, he wouldn't have treated you like a son. We're going to have to accept that in his own way, Finnian was getting us both ready for whatever we have to do next."

"I guess you're right," he conceded, resting his head on mine.

"I'm sorry, I didn't quite hear that. I'm right, did you say?"

"You had to take it too far, didn't you?"

Sitting on the cold floor of the *Nakomo's* main cabin, we both laughed, and it felt good. When I got myself under control, I noticed the extra canvas holdall. "What's in the fourth bag?"

"Thought you'd never ask," Ash replied, pulling the heavy bag over with difficulty and unzipping it.

"Now you're talking," I said, peering in at the array of rifles, guns, grenades, and other assorted ordnance.

6

During the trip to the shithole, Ash and I changed out of our Brotherhood fatigues, swapping them for the civilian clothes he'd hidden away in the emergency holdalls.

"Don't think we'll be wearing these again for a while," Ash advised as he stowed our old clothes and our Brotherhood credentials in the secret compartment before sliding the floor panel back in place.

"I'm sorry," I replied. "I don't know what else to say."

"I know." He stood and pulled me into a one-armed hug. "And that's the last time you're going to say it. This is not your fault, so you have nothing to apologise for. Whatever journey we're on now, we're on it together, okay?"

I took a deep breath. "Okay," I replied resolutely. "So would now be a good time to ask why you lamped Francis back on Lilania?"

Ash checked his feet for a moment, then looked up and shrugged remorsefully. "He wanted to come with us. He said whatever it was we were caught up in, he wanted to help."

"Of course, he did." My heart felt heavy, and I felt bad

we'd kept him in the dark. "But you said no, obviously."

"Yes, but it felt wrong. I wanted to tell him to get onboard, but I kept getting echoes of Finnian's message about trusting no one creeping into my head. Did I do the right thing?"

I felt his anguish through the link. "The right thing? I don't know. But I would've done the same. It's bad enough putting you in this position, I would hate to do it to Francis as well."

"I lied to him, and I feel terrible about it. I told him it was Guardian stuff that we'd been asked to do, but the Brotherhood didn't want us to get involved. Told him we had to do it alone. He said he understood, but I'm not sure he did. He certainly wasn't happy."

"So why'd you hit him?"

"Because we both knew Noah would've expected him to stop us from leaving, or at least try."

"And you had to make it look like he had."

"Exactly. Anyway, we need to move forward," he said, shaking off the sadness. "We need to get our heads ready for the Ridge."

"Do you think they'll recognise us? It's not been that long since we went there to meet Nyan."

"Ah, yes. The alcoholic thief who set us on a path to preventing a devastating attack on the Four Sectors. Should be okay, we were only there a few hours."

"True, but in that time, we lost Nyan to a bullet from an Agent of Death, met Jared for the first time, and got into one hell of a fight with the locals. In all honesty, I'm not exactly looking forward to going back."

"Hmm, maybe…" Ash replied with a worrying amount of vagueness. "I'm sure skirmishes like ours are an everyday occurrence. Besides, the whole thing was caused by Jared. If they did take much notice of it, hopefully they blamed it on Fleet and didn't even realise our involvement in it. I think our biggest problem's going to be getting them to let us in in the first place."

"What do you mean?"

"With our transponder down, we're going to show up on their systems as a ghost ship, and that's going to raise red flags. Though, given the Ridge's usual visitors and their occupations, hopefully they're used to it and won't blow us into oblivion as soon as we approach.

"That's comforting."

"We're going to have to blag our way in and hope those fake idents I got for us are worth the credits I paid for them."

"Fingers crossed then, or this is going to be the shortest getaway in history."

As we approached the colossal asteroid, butterflies fluttered nervously in my chest and Ash had to lean over and put his hand on my knee to stop it jiggling. Even though I was expecting it, I still jumped when the warning alarm told us we'd been weapons locked.

"Unknown vessel, this is Angel Ridge Control, we have you targeted. Power down your engines immediately and identify yourself." The voice was demanding and uncompromising. The warning light continued to flash on the console.

"Control, this is Asher Gage. I request landing authorisation."

"Gage, this is Control, state the reason for your visit and why you're running dark."

"Control, we're running dark because a few hours ago we stole this ship." I raised an eyebrow at him, and he took his hand off the coms button, turning to me. "Well, that's technically correct," he replied, adding a lopsided grin before pressing the coms button again. "We're looking for somewhere to chill for a while. Let the heat die down."

There was silence for a moment and Ash held my knee again.

"This is Control. How many souls aboard?"

"Two."

More silence. "Gage, we're going to need you to drop your shields so we can scan your ship for life signs. You also need to send us your idents."

"Of course." Ash turned to me, his face set and serious. "If this doesn't work, we're probably dead. You ready?" I nodded, passing him my fake credentials with a shaking hand. "Control, lowering now." After deactivating the shields, Ash placed both of our ident cards to the reader and sent the information.

My heart was in my throat as the minutes passed, then a single beep and an extinguished light signalled we were no longer being targeted by the Ridge.

"Gage, this is Control, you're cleared to land on Level Three. Use entrance Gamma and head to pad 348. Docking fees and taxes are payable on arrival. As a disclaimer, please be advised that Ridge Management accepts no liability for theft of property, injury, maiming, loss of limbs, hearing and or sight, or total death. Welcome to Angel Ridge, we hope you have a great stay."

"Wow. Total death. That's serious stuff," I joked as Ash powered up the engines.

"This is serious stuff, Shae," he scolded. "You know how dangerous this place is. The plan is to get in, get the *Nakomo* running fully dark, then get the hell out as quickly as possible."

Unlike the last time, which was also my first time to the shithole, I was prepared for the stench. Garbage and sewage, combined with poor air filtration, was never a good mix, but this time I remembered to breathe through my mouth. Though, to be fair, having spent some time in the creature cave on planet 758-C2, this wasn't the worst smell in the Universe. I stepped super-carefully over the rivulet of dark, stinky liquid that flowed down the side of the pathway.

More people pushed and shoved their way up and down

the vast tunnel than I remembered. I surveyed the area for threats, but there were too many to keep track of, so instead, I tried to figure out exactly where we were in relation to Finnegan's bar. The poor quality chem-lights flickered sporadically, making it difficult to see any markings. Eventually, I located an old rusting sign on the wall, partly obscured by an ARRO tag.

"West 19," I said to Ash, but he didn't hear me above the fight that had just broken out to our left. I tugged his sleeve to get his attention and pointed to the sign. "We need to head to the East tunnel," I shouted pulling him nearer to me so he could hear. He nodded an acknowledgement, took my hand, and then strode off. He walked with purpose and determination, shunting people out of the way as much as anyone else. I don't know whether he was trying to fit in, acting like the locals, or he was just keen to get us to where we needed to be. Either way, I felt suffocated as I tried to avoid contact with other people, paranoid they all knew who we were and why we were there.

The crossroads between the East and West tunnels started to look familiar. As we headed down the East passageway, filled with makeshift market stalls, memories of our last trip came flooding back.

I'm not sure whether it was because this tunnel was wider, or because there were less people maybe, but it certainly felt less claustrophobic. Ash slowed slightly, letting go of my hand, and we were able to walk side-by-side rather than me being pulled along in his wake.

"Sorry," he said. "I just didn't want us to be there longer than we needed."

"I get it. Just next time, try not to dislocate my shoulder, okay?"

He was instantly horrified and stopped dead, resting his hands on my shoulders, searching my eyes. "I didn't—"

"Relax, I was joking," I said quickly, offering an

apologetic smile.

"For the love of… Shae!" he chastised. "I thought I'd hurt you. Now's not the time to joke about things like that."

"Okay." I held up my palms in surrender. "I didn't think; I'll be more careful."

"Thank you. Let's keep going."

A few minutes later, we arrived at the location of Finnegan's Bar, owned and run by the man we were there to see.

"Bollocks," I muttered.

"Bollocks," Ash repeated. "Well, that complicates things."

Finnegan's had been one of the few structures on Level Three, but it had also taken a bit of hammering during our last visit. What used to be the bar's right-side wall, still lay in rubble following the explosion, and the rest of the bar had been razed to the ground by the fire. The main drinking area had been cleared and vendors had moved in, and more cobbled-together stalls stood on charred ground.

"I was hoping there wasn't too much damage and Beck would be back running the bar," Ash said, but I gave him my, we're never that lucky, frown. "Let's take a closer look. You never know."

We navigated the stalls, and I glanced my eye over a disturbing array of weapons. My hand dropped to my thigh, and I felt comforted by the cold handle of my Sentinel. Over the haggle and bartering, I thought I heard a voice I recognised, and I concentrated hard to home in on a direction.

"What is it," Ash asked, but I hushed him, trying to listen.

"This way." That time, it was my chance to take Ash's hand and lead him with me. We passed a couple of stalls and then turned between them towards the far wall of the bar. The large stand was heaving, heavily armed gun-thugs and mercs standing two and three deep.

I froze.

My heart pounded in my chest, and my brain fogged. I felt light-headed, and only vaguely registered that someone was leading me away from the table. A moment later, Ash sat me down, his grey eyes flashing with concern. "Shae, what happened?" I couldn't answer; I could barely breath. "Shae, it's okay, we're safe. You're okay now. Breathe. Just breathe. In... out... in..."

"Ash?"

"I'm here," he replied. I felt worry and anguish pushing on the Link and I strengthened my blocks. "You okay?"

"I don't know. What happened?"

"I should be asking you the same thing. One minute you were all, 'follow me,' the next you just went ghost white and started shaking. You didn't respond when I spoke to you. Was it something to do with your gift? Did something new happen?"

"No. No, it was nothing like that. I... I panicked."

"You don't panic, Shae," he said, followed by a laugh that stopped abruptly when he saw the fear on my face.

"I could help it. I froze."

"This situation... those men... this is child's-play for us. This isn't like you."

"I know." I was frustrated I couldn't explain it properly. "What if by following Finnian's message I get us both killed? Get you killed?"

"That's not going to happen."

"You sound like Jared now. You can't promise that."

"You're right, I can't. But what I can promise you is that we're both committed to this, yes?" I didn't answer. "Because I am. I'm one hundred percent committed to you and this journey we're on. Wherever it takes us. I know the risks, and I'm accepting them, so the sooner you realise we're in this together, the better. Besides, who better to go on some weird quest thing than with someone who has the powers you do? Quite frankly, I couldn't be with anyone safer. So, I ask you… are you committed, Shae?"

I took a deep breath, centred myself, and unlocked the part of me that knew he was right. I felt the energy in me sizzle to the point the air around me practically crackled "Yes," I replied.

"One hundred percent?" he pushed.

"One hundred a fifty percent," I confirmed.

"That's my sister. Then what are we going to do about that red-headed son-of-a-bitch?"

"Depends how much time you want to spend in this shithole."

"As little as possible. What have you got in mind?"

I ducked around the back of the bar, waited 5 minutes, and then came through what was left of the old rear entrance. I ran in shouting at the top of my voice, "Royal Earth Force! REF! There's a squad of REF Fleet troopers heading this way." I had everyone's attention, and a few people bolted, but it wasn't until Ash came from the opposite direction yelling something pretty similar, that the mass exodus ensued. A few hard-core customers remained.

As most people scattered, I got my first look at what was for sale on the stall, and it explained the popularity. When we'd last met the red-headed, skinny guy, he'd been selling stolen Fleet weapons – which is what had brought Jared and his troopers to the Ridge in the first place. This time, I was horrified to see a table full of D'Antaran weapons, equally acquired illegally, no doubt.

"Hi," I said politely, as the seller shovelled ammunition into a box. He looked at me with narrowed eyes before passing the box off to an Other in exchange for a wad or credits.

"What do you want?" he asked some meathead gun-thug who'd remained at the table, totally ignoring me.

"'Bout fuckin' time, mate. Hurry up before those Fleet fuckers get here. Give me—"

"Sorry, don't mean to interrupt, but on the clock here,"

I said, winning a glare from the ginger seller, and a gun in the face from the merc. "Whoa there," I added, taking my hands slowly out of my pockets.

"What the fuck?" he growled, taking an immediate step backwards, his eyes fixed on the thermite grenades.

"I've got no problem with you," I told him. "Unless you create one."

"You know, lady, I'm gonna fuck off if that's cool with you," the merc said, slowly holstering his gun. I nodded my agreement and he bolted.

"You, on the other hand," I swung my arm towards the seller as he tried to edge along the table, "need to answer a few questions. Starting with an easy one: what's your name?"

"Ven."

"Did I miss all the fun?" Ash asked casually as he strode up to the table.

"Nope, we were just getting started. Ven here was about to tell me where we can find Beck."

"Beck?" he replied, his eyebrows puckering into a deep V.

"Did I stutter?" I asked Ash.

"No, I thought you were quite clear," he replied. "And nice to see you back on your A-game."

"Thanks," I said, before holding a grenade nearer to Ven's head. "Do I need to ask again?"

"No, no," he said. "But I don't know anyone called—"

"Stop," I demanded, tapping the grenade against his forehead. "Before you finish that sentence, consider the fact that we already know you and Beck are acquaintances. And that you are close enough for you to know he had a hidden escape route behind his bar for when, I don't know, say Fleet Captains come looking for their stolen weapons."

"Wait, you..." He turned to Ash. "And you... you were both in the bar that day. Oh man, you guys are in big trouble. Do you know what Dax will do to you if he knows your back? He'd skin you alive."

"Yeah, well, hopefully we'll be gone long before he realises," said Ash, looking around. "And on that note, I think we should go somewhere a little more private."

"Maintenance shaft?" I asked.

"Maintenance shaft," he confirmed, grabbing Ven by his shirt, but the redhead fought his ground. "You might not want to resist," Ash suggested calmly, as I popped the caps off the thermite grenades and tossed them on to the table.

We left quickly through the rear exit, taking a side alley before reaching an access panel. Ash checked to make sure we didn't have anyone watching before we ducked inside.

"Okay, let's try this again, shall we," Ash said, unholstering his Sentinel. "I actually don't care about you at all, but Shae here thinks you might know where Beck is." He pointed his gun at Ven's head. "So, she says I can't kill you. But, well, I just don't know…"

Ven looked more confused than scared. "But you're Brotherhood. You can't just go around killing people."

"True, I suppose." He lowered the gun and fired, pouncing on Ven and covering his mouth to stifle the screams. "Relax… relax… it's just a flesh wound. You'll be fine. Breath. Breath. Give it a minute." Tears rolled down Ven's scarlet cheeks and his chest heaved. His scared eyes reminded me of Martha's before I'd punched her out during the assault on the Palace of Palavaria. "Can I let you go now?" Ash asked when Ven had calmed slightly. He nodded slowly. "You promise you won't do anything stupid?" Ven nodded again and Ash removed his hand.

"I can't believe you fuckin' did that," Ven screeched, but as Ash reached for him again, he covered his own mouth quickly before removing it long enough to mouth, 'okay'.

"Look," I said, trying to get him to focus. "Just tell us where Beck is, and we'll let you go."

"Yeah, I believe that. Not," Ven grunted though pained breaths.

"You have my word."

"Like that means shit." He pointed to the oozing wound on his leg.

"Then believe this," Ash chipped in. "Either you tell us where Beck is, or I put another hole in you – only the next one will be in a far more vital location." He pointed the Sentinel at Ven's crotch.

"Okay, okay, no need for the theatrics. I'll tell you where Beck is, but it won't do you any good. You won't be able to get to him."

"What the hell does that mean?" I asked, my patience waning.

"It means, Beck's in the Basement."

"So, he's in the basement. Big deal," Ash grunted, but Ven sighed dramatically.

"Not the basement, the Basement." He looked between our confused faces. "It's where Dax sends all the people he doesn't like. He forces them to mine the asteroid for rare minerals, which he then sells to pay for all the muscle he needs to stay in control of the Ridge. How did you think he's managed to keep his position for so long? Good looks and charm? Anyone who crosses him, causes trouble, or just plain looks at him wrong, is tried in some phoney kangaroo court then sentenced to work the mines. Once you go to the Basement, the only way you come back is in a body bag. It's heavily guarded and impossible to get to. If Beck isn't already dead, he soon will be. People don't tend to last long, especially not people like Beck."

"What do you mean by that?" I asked, my stomach churning.

"Do you even know this guy at all? Beck doesn't like to be confined or locked up—"

"Nobody likes being locked up." Ash grunted.

"No, he really doesn't like it, like pure fuckin' phobia doesn't like it. Don't know why, he never talks about it, but he won't play nice. He'll do anything to get out, even if that means getting himself dead in the process. He'll take death over being locked up."

"How did he end up down there?" I asked, already fearing the answer. Ven barked out a dry laugh.

"You really need to ask that? After what you did? You and the fuckin' REF, that is. By helping you all escape, Beck put himself squarely on Dax's shit list."

"How did he know? Beck was careful, and we obviously didn't say anything," I explained.

"Yeah? Not careful enough. I've only heard rumours, but I think he got caught on camera at some hatch you guys came out of on Level Three. So, there you have it. Congrats. You managed to get one of the good ones killed."

"You said he wasn't dead."

"I've not heard he's dead, but that doesn't make it fact. If he is still alive, it's only a matter of time."

Ash caught the look on my face. "I know, I know." He turned to Ven. "Sit," he ordered. Ven obliged, wincing in pain, as Ash took the pack of his shoulder and started rummaging through it. "This will help with the pain," he added, jabbing him with Oxytanyl before wrapping a field bandage around his leg. "How do we get to the Basement?"

Ven's laugh turned to a groan as Ash pulled the bandage tight and secured it. "You can't. Not unless you have a death wish."

"Say we do," I said. He cocked his head to the side and eyed me carefully. "You said yourself Beck was one of the good ones. Tell us how to get him back."

"So I can end up down there in his place? No thank you."

"She wasn't giving you an option," Ash explained, pointing the gun at Ven's head again. "If you can't help us, you're of no use to us. And if you're no use to us, you may as well be—"

"Fine," Ven huffed. "You're going to get dead anyway. What do I care?"

"Okay, now we're getting somewhere. Tell us everything you know."

"I take it there's just the two of you? There's no hidden army somewhere to help?"

"Just us," I confirmed. He shook his head.

"Then you are both sooooo dead." Bloody drugs. "When I said you can't get to the Basement, I meant it. There are only three ways in and out, and each one is guarded by a fuck-tonne of roaches."

"Roaches?" I asked.

"Yeah, roaches. Dax's people. The worst of the worst. If a shitstorm was to blaze its way through the Ridge, those are the fuckers who'd be left standing."

"Just tell us about the three entrances," Ash demanded.

"Okay, okay." He held up bloodied hands in submission. "One: there's a cargo access point from outside the asteroid – a way to transport the minerals out of the mines and on to the waiting transporters. The entrance is flanked by huge fuck-off railguns, and without the right access codes, you'd be blown into itty bitty pieces before you can even get close. And before you ask, I've no fuckin' clue how you'd get the codes."

I looked at Ash, who shrugged his broad shoulders. "Okay, so that's not exactly practical," I admitted. "Next – and please tell me this is internal."

"Two." Ven held up two fingers. I think he was starting to enjoy himself, though it could've been the drugs. "And internal or not, this one is just as impractical. There's an elevator from the Courtroom on Level one all the way down to the Basement."

"Okay, now we're talking," I said, but as Ven laughed hysterically, I turned to Ash and asked, "Just how much Oxytanyl did you give him?"

"Not much. Not my fault he's a lightweight."

"Let me explain," Ven said, his eyes glazing over. "The roaches are everywhere. You'll have to get passed gazillions of them on this level alone to get to one of the access shafts that go to Level One. There are five of those by the way; one at the far end of each main tunnel and one at the crossroads in the centre." His words started to slur. "Then, if you actually do manage to get into one of the elevators, you'd be met by another load of roaches when you got out at Level One. Dax is some paranoid bastard. His security is like an impenetrable wall of walking shit-stains, who will kill first and not even bother with asking the questions. Am I setting the scene for you here? Because after all of that, you've then got to somehow get from there to the Courtroom, past another army of roaches, before accessing the lift back down to the Basement. Oh, and it doesn't stop there…"

"There's a surprise," Ash interrupted, but then quickly made a continue motion with his hand as Ven started to slide sideways down the wall. I propped him back up and rubbed his cheek until he focused again.

"Yeah, well, I think I made my point," he mumbled. "There's even more security at the access point to the Basement. You're fuckin' dead, dead, dead," he almost sang. Damn drugs.

"Not exactly liking those odds," Ash agreed. "What about the third?"

"Hmm?"

"The third access point," Ash prompted.

"Oh yeah, sure, that's the easiest one." He laughed loudly, and I couldn't tell if he was joking or not. "All you've got to do is get a private audience with Dax, incapacitate him and a couple of his closest entourage, and then take his private elevator from his office. The access point for that shaft comes out behind the security and operations station in the Basement, so they'll be limited number of roaches. Easy fuckin' peasy."

"And you didn't think to start with this because…?" I asked, straightening him up again. He blinked slowly and grinned ridiculously.

"Because getting a private audience with Dax, is like trying to jerk off with your hands tied behind your back. It ain't gonna happen."

"Yeah? Well, we can be quite resourceful when we need," I replied.

"Where can we find these roaches?" Ash asked.

"They're all…" My hand left a red imprint on his cheek "Hey," he grunted, shaking his head. "Uncalled for. I was going to say, they're all over the place, but if you carry on along this tunnel, there's a roach station not too far on the left. You can't miss it."

"Great," I replied sarcastically, as Ash leant forward and jabbed him with another dose of Oxytanyl. "What was that for?"

"The dose I've given him should keep him out cold for a good ten to twelve hours. We don't want him giving us up before we have the chance to get the hell off this rock, do we? You know, it'd be a hell of a lot easier to just find someone else to help with the *Nakomo*. Yeah, yeah, you don't need to say it. We can't leave Beck down there."

7

I tried to ignore Ven's snores as Ash and I settled on our plan to get to Dax.

"And you think this will work without us getting shot as soon as we open our mouths?" I asked.

"Umm, pretty sure," Ash replied vaguely. "Only one way to find out."

"Well, I suppose there's one good thing in all this."

"What's that?" he asked, holding open the hatch door.

"If we get dead, at least we won't have to worry about all that Helyan stuff anymore."

Ash pursed his lip, shook his head, and said nothing, but I caught the small tug at the corner of his mouth.

Even though we approached the roach station with our hands raised, it didn't take long for a dozen weapons to be shoved in our faces. It was difficult to make out distinct orders through all the chaotic shouting, but we got the gist and dropped to our knees, hands behind our heads. Eventually, as the frenetic activity subsided, it was finally possible to make out who was in charge.

At least we'd made it past part one without getting shot.

"What the fuck do you want?" grunted the chief roach.

"You got a death wish or something, rocking up on us like that?" He sounded like Ven.

"We don't want any trouble," Ash said. "I can explain, but it would be a lot easier without this gun in my face." He watched the roach carefully. "Look, there's two of us and, what? Fifteen of you guys? You've just stripped us of our weapons and bound our wrists. What trouble can we cause?"

The chief roach narrowed his eyes and looked between Ash and me. After a moment, he jerked his head, and the others took a couple of steps backwards, guns still pointing at our heads.

"Thank you," Ash said graciously.

I could almost see the cogs whirring in the chief roach's head. I don't think he knew what to make of Ash. After all, Ash certainly wasn't like the meatheads, gun-thugs, and mercs they usually dealt with.

"Just shoot 'um so we can get back to our game," goaded a roach, followed by a chorus of similar requests. A moment later, one of them lurched forward and primed his weapon, but before he had a chance to fire, the chief roach had him in a headlock the Wolfpack would've been proud of. The gun clattered to the floor as the man flailed.

"Who's in charge?" the chief growled, spit dribbling on to his ear.

"You are," the man whispered as he choked.

"Sorry, I didn't hear that properly. Who... the fuck... is in charge here?" he said slowly as he twisted the guy around so his whole team could see him choking.

"You are," the main whimpered.

"You're damn fucking right, I am," the chief said, letting go so the man fell to the floor gasping for breath. When someone reached out to help him up, the chief pointed his pistol at them instead, and they backed off slowly. "And you all better remember that – coz I can guaran-damn-tee you won't like the fucking consequences otherwise. Now,

I'll ask one final time," he added, turning to Ash. "What the fuck do you want?"

"I'll tell you, but I ask you to hear me out before you do anything rash."

"Just get the hell on with it before I let the kids play with their new toys," he replied, indicating to his people.

"My name is Brother Asher—" A disbelieving snort broke his sentence. "I'm Ninth Degree Warrior Caste from the Brotherhood of the Virtuous Sun, and this is Shae, who's also affiliated with the Brotherhood. We'd like to see Dax." He waited for the jeers and laughter to subside, while the chief roach continued to eye him carefully. Then unexpectedly he broke into big booming laughter.

"Dax? Ruler of the Ridge, Dax?" he asked through draws in breath.

"Yes," Ash confirmed.

"And you want to see him?"

"Yes."

"As if," the chief replied, pistol-whipping Ash hard across the face to raucous approval from his team. I lowered my arms and tried to get to Ash, but several pairs of hands restrained me.

We'd planned for this. We knew it was unlikely one, if not both, of us would make it through this initial confrontation unharmed. But even though Ash had made me promise to protect myself and not create more of a scene, I desperately wanted to release the energy swirling in my chest and smash every one of their dumb roach heads against the tunnel wall.

"I'm okay," Ash said, holding his bound hands up towards me as if to stop me doing anything stupid. "I'm okay," he repeated, blood oozing from the gash on his cheekbone. Somebody righted him as the chief kneeled down to eye level.

"You could be the god-damn Supreme Primus for all I give a shit," he taunted. "What in the holy name of hell gives you the idea that Dax would even want to see you?"

Ash sat back on his heels. "Dax is pissed about an incident that occurred a while back involving the REF and the Brotherhood, yes?" There was a combined intake of breath and the butt of the gun raised, so Ash continued quickly. "We've been sent by Brotherhood to clear up a misunderstanding and provide… reparation."

"And why should I believe anything you say? You don't exactly look like Brotherhood."

"After what went down, if I'd turned up in robes, I'm guessing we wouldn't be having this conversation."

The chief roach thought for a moment, rubbing a filthy chin. "I'll give you that," he said eventually. "Still not proof, though."

"Check my right upper arm," Ash continued. "And hers."

The chief used the muzzle of the gun to lift the sleeve of Ash's T-shirt, revealing his Warrior Caste tattoo. He didn't bother checking mine, instead, motioning for a woman to come forward. The wings of the tattooed bird on her chest looked like they fluttered as she flexed her shoulders. "If one of them moves, shoot them both," he ordered before disappearing into the station.

"Must be your lucky day," he said, reappearing after a while. "Seems Dax wants to hear what the Brotherhood has to say. And if he doesn't like it, well, I guess it's not your lucky day after all." He turned to the woman. "Phoenix, you're in charge till I get back."

The elevator ride to Level One was painfully long and awkward as the chief roach had demanded silence from everyone. The first phase of the plan was complete, and we were still alive. And the chief roach would literally walk us straight passed all the security on Level One, right up to Dax's office, where we would start phase two. At least that's what I thought.

I was pleasantly surprised by the fragrant, freshly filtered air that filled the lift as soon as the doors opened. I stepped out into a clean, brightly-lit room, filled with more of Dax's men – and while they were still heavily armed and clearly menacing, they were also decidedly less roach-like. One of them approached, flanked by others armed with Fleet issue plasma rifles.

"Nico," the chief roach said stiffly, the tension between them palpable.

"I'll take it from here, Gerran," Nico replied, his arms folding tightly across his chest just like Jake does when he's not happy.

"Thanks, but I've got it."

Nico's men closed in around him, and Ash nudged me a few steps to our right.

"It wasn't a request, Gerran. You know the rules. You do your time on Level three, and if you survive, you can put in for a transfer. Until then, I outrank you. So, when I say I got it, I fuckin' got it." He sniffed the air towards the Level 3 roaches and gagged. "You and your mutts better get on the elevator and go back to where you belong before you stink up my crib. Understand? Or do I need to say it a bit slower for—"

Gerran launched at Nico, and in the moments it took Ash and me to get out of the way, a brawl erupted between the two groups. In a scene reminiscent of the bar brawl at Finnegan's, fists flew, and knives flashed in the bright light.

"I do not want to be here when the shooting starts," Ash said, leading me around the outside of the room, our presence forgotten.

"I'm surprised it hasn't started already," I said loudly above the grunts and shouts of the fight.

"That's because guns aren't part of the rules," a deep voice replied as if it was obvious. I looked around me for the origin, startled as a life-size hologram of a man materialised beside me.

"What the hell?" I gasped. A frown settled across my

forehead, but it cleared as I ducked to avoid a flying chem-lamp.

"The rules," the man continued, looking directly at me. "They can fight as much as they like; fists, knives, any old object lying around. But no guns. I used to allow it, but I kept losing too many people, and well, loyal staff is harder to come by nowadays." The hologram dissolved and then reformed as a chair passed through it.

"Dax?" I questioned, as he continued to fix me with weirdly hypnotic lilac eyes.

"In the flesh, so to speak. Colour me intrigued at your presence..." He paused to allow Ash to intercept a roach as he came tumbling towards me, but he seemed more amused than concerned. "Let me just deal with this," he added, waving a holo arm towards the brawl.

A siren blasted through the room, and I instinctively tried to cover my ears, but the binds dug into my wrists. The fighting ceased almost immediately and the two groups of men that were still able to, stood and backed away from each other. The noise stopped when the elevator door opened, and Gerran limped, bleeding, to the threshold, waiting there until the last of his people was dragged in.

"I look forward to the next time," Rico goaded, the door shutting on his words. He wiped his nose with the back of his hand, smearing blood across his face, before turning to his own men and throwing his fist up in the air to a chorus of cheers.

"What the fuck, Rico?" Dax grunted. "Can we not go one fucking day without a fight? Where are your manners? We have guests here," he added sarcastically before turning his long oval face back towards me. He grinned, flashing a platinum tooth. "Bring them to my office... and Rico? Try not to kill them along the way."

"Of course, sir," Rico replied, before raising another round of cheers from his roaches.

"Kinda not what I was expecting," I said a few minutes

later, as I settled myself into a surprisingly comfortable seat. The doors of the mag-train slid shut, but we lurched forward so hard, my head banged on the compartment wall behind me. "I take it back," I added, as Rico guffawed, his mood still clearly bolstered by his 'win' over Gerran.

"How far are we going?" Ash asked casually.

"Why the fuck do you want to know?" one of Rico's men asked dangerously.

"No reason, just interested," Ash replied, though I know he would be mentally working out how far we were travelling away from the *Nakomo*. It was a surprising long trip, which made me uneasy, but I should've expected it – the asteroid was, after all, colossal.

When we started to slow, I readied myself and was prepared for the jarring stop. And when we stood, Ash blocked my exit briefly, stooping to whisper in my ear. "Stay behind me. You can heal me remember, not the other way around." I nodded my understanding, but I didn't like this part of the plan.

Dax's office smelled of testosterone and sweat, even though two out of the five people that were in the room were female – I think. Rico led us to the two small plastic chairs that had been put in front of an imposing desk. I couldn't help noticing the plastic sheeting on the floor and wondered for the tenth time whether we'd made a huge mistake. Rico forced Ash into a seat, almost toppling it over with aggressive enthusiasm. I sat quickly as the thug next to me reach out for my shoulders. Our utility belts and weapons were dumped heavily on the desk.

Dax relaxed back into an oversized leather chair, his huge, scuffed boots resting casually on the desktop. But while he was the epitome of chilled, the others had hands on knives or guns. I'd hoped there'd be less people around, but there was no going back now. As if he'd read my thoughts, Dax turned to his men.

"You can go, Rico ... and take your retards with you,"

he grunted dismissively. Rico opened his mouth to respond, then thought better of it. "I've got enough muscle here to protect me from one monk and a little lady." I chewed on my tongue. "Go clean yourself up, you're a fuckin' mess. No, wait. Before you do, take your men down to Level Three and remind Gerran of his place."

"With pleasure," Rico replied, cracking his knuckles.

Dax turned towards Ash. "Can't have people thinking they can dictate what the fuck happens around here, am I right?" He nailed Ash with a warning scowl, then looked bored as he waited for people to shuffle out. As the heavy door swing shut with a deep thud, I felt better knowing that we were back to Dax, two gun-thugs who'd taken up flanking positions by the door, and the pair of women. Even though their array of weaponry was spectacular, I still felt that the odds were so much more in our favour.

"To what do I owe the pleasure of such auspicious visitors today," Dax asked eventually, his vocabulary and diction at odds with the blood-stained vest and camo's he wore.

"My name's Brother Asher—"

"So I've been told," Dax interrupted, to jeers from his people.

"We're here from the Brother—"

"Again, so I've been told," Dax interrupted, and I felt Ash's annoyance flash through the Link. "Do you want to tell me something I don't know, before I decide you're wasting my clearly valuable time."

"Well," Ash thought for a moment. "You do have a little something right there." He pointed to Dax's chin. I held my breath as thunderous storm clouds raged across Dax's face, but they cleared as he pulled a stained rag from his pocked and wiped the drying blood from his chalk-white goatee.

"Better?" he goaded. "Bit of an occupational hazard around here, I'm afraid." He lowered his feet and sat forward in the chair. "Okay, let's get down to business. You and the little miss here have got some balls coming back after the last time. You must be seriously fed up with living to walk right into the lion's den." He clocked the glance Ash and I gave each other. "What? You thought we were too hick to know it was you two and some bald brick shithouse who caused all the trouble last time?"

"Technically, we didn't start the trouble," I said, unable to keep quiet. "If you know we were here, then you know that's true."

Dax eyed me carefully with those lilac eyes, but then he stood without warning and strode around the desk to perch on the edge, right in front of me. "Go on," he said, cleaning his nails with a knife.

"We were just passing through. We weren't looking for any trouble," I explained.

"You're saying trouble just found you?"

"That's right. One minute we were enjoying a peaceful drink at Finnegan's, and the next, some arsehole Fleet Captain comes in looking for a fight. Things went downhill from there, and we had to fight our way out to make sure we weren't caught up in the middle of it. Call it self-preservation."

Dax surprised me by laughing, but as he leant forward, I recoiled. "Relax. If I wanted you dead, you would be... still might be if I change my mind." His laugh turned nasty. "Depends what's in it for me, I guess. So, if you want to walk out of here, you better pique my interest." He slipped the knife under the binds, cutting them easily, and I massaged my wrists. Ash held his hands out, but Dax just grunted before returning to his own side of the desk. He paced for a moment.

"Still doesn't explain why you're here now?" he said, putting the knife on the desk before running a dirty hand through even dirtier white hair. He pulled the chair out to sit, but as he did, I flicked my hand slightly, moving it backwards. Dax grunted as he fell to the floor, and in the split-second window that had given us, Ash launched himself over the desk, picking up the knife as he did.

A second pulse sent the two men by the door smashing against the wall, while a third took out the two women struggling to get up from the oversized sofa they'd been provocatively lounging on. When I turned back to the desk, Ash and Dax were locked together, pushing and shoving, vying for control of the knife. Ash, severely hampered by his bound wrists, was being pushed back until Dax smashed him into the wall.

I wasted no time, retrieving a weapon from one of the thugs slumped at the base of the back wall, before returning to them.

Ash and Dax were scrapping on the floor, and it was difficult to get a clear shot of Dax as they rolled around. I didn't want to hit Ash, and I didn't want the shot to draw in more unwanted goons, but when I heard Ash let out a deep throaty groan, I knew I couldn't wait.

"Get off him Dax, or I'll shoot" I ordered. He turned his head and laughed.

"I don't think so, little girl," he mocked. "Looks like your protector's a gonna, and you haven't got the balls."

"You know nothing about me." I winced as he moved away from Ash, and I saw the knife embedded in his stomach. I forced myself to ignore his moans, and turned my attention back to Dax, who was slowly moving around the table towards me.

He held out a bloodied hand. "Give me the gun, and I'll let you go. Promise."

"You're not going to let me go anywhere."

He smiled and shrugged. "Okay, you go me. You ain't leaving this rock, little lady."

It was my turn to smile. "You think you're in a position to make threats?" I waved the gun a little to remind him I had the advantage, but he took a step forward. "I don't have time for this," I said, firing two shots in quick succession – one in his shoulder and one in his thigh. He dropped to the ground, howling and I pounced on him. "Shut up," I hissed into his ear, pressing the muzzle of the pistol to his temple.

"I'm going to kill you, bitc—" The heavy blow to the side of his head cut off his words, blood puddles spreading across the plastic wrapping on the floor beneath him.

I left him where he lay and went to tend to Ash. "This is going to hurt," I said, grabbing the handle of the knife.

"It's like déjà vu but in reverse," he joked through gritted teeth. I frowned. "Last time it was you who got stabbed on Angel Ridge… and I believe I said exactly the same thing to yo— aww!" he cried. "A little warning next time." Fat blood drops fell from the blade before I threw it to the side.

"Hold still, you big baby." I lifted his wet shirt to reveal the oozing wound. Placing my hands over the neat slit, I cleared my mind. In my head, I imagined Ash whole and perfect. The usual tickling sensation began swirling in my tummy before spreading out like electricity through my veins. Pulses of silver-blue light shimmered down my arms, pooling in my hands for a moment before dancing strings arced between my fingers and Ash's skin. Both of us shimmered and sparkled as the wound knitted together. Red-raw skin turned to pink, and the slit paled to the shiny white of a new scar before disappearing all together. I wiped the blood away and inspected the skin, pressing down and then watching it pink up again.

"How do you feel?" I asked.

"I'm good… thanks to you."

"You sure? You're not in any pain? Did I get it all?"

"You did a great job, Shae, as always. I owe you… again."

"You don't owe me anything," I replied, moving out the way so he could sit up. "I owe you everything."

"Let's just agree to disagree on that one." He smiled, putting a comforting hand on my shoulder. "Where's Dax?"

"Oh, shit! He's over here," I said, getting up to quickly navigate around the desk. I dropped to my knees again next to him, checking for a pulse.

"Is he…?"

"Still alive," I announced. "I don't think the wounds are fatal, but he's a bit of a bleeder, so there's always the risk he'll bleed out if I don't do something. What do we do?" I asked, fastening my utility belt around my hips and holstering my Sentinel.

"Well…" Ash rubbed his temples and thought for a moment. "We have two options. One, we leave him injured like this, tie him up, and hope that we can get down to the Basement and back again before anyone comes in."

"Or?

"Or… you fix him a bit, just enough to get him mobile, and we take him with us to the Basement as leverage if we need it."

"I think I prefer option two. What about them?" I indicated the others.

Ash surveyed the room. "Check those." He pointed to what looked like cupboard doors. "I'll check this door."

I readied myself, then yanked the handle, gun ready. "It's full of weapons," I said, shutting it again. "You?"

Ash backed away from the door he'd opened, his nose wrinkled and a disgusted look on his face. "It's a…" he gagged, "bathroom. How much sedative do we have left?"

"Enough to keep those four under for a couple of hours each, but that's it."

We worked together to drug Dax's entourage, then stuffed them all together in the bathroom – and I use that term lightly. Once they were secure, I readied myself and healed Dax's leg enough so he'd be able to hobble. The shoulder wound, I left. It wasn't fatal, but it would hurt like a son-of-a-bitch, and it would allow us to control him better. Lastly, I healed the head-wound and concussion. He came too, moaning.

Ash clicked his fingers in front of Dax's face to get his attention. As his eye's focussed, they darkened with rage.

"We haven't got much time," explained Ash, "so I'm just going to lay everything out for you."

A look of pure evil settled in Dax's narrowed eyes. "I'm listening," he mumbled, gingerly holding his arm.

"You have someone in the Basement we want," I said. He turned to face me, his eyes taking a moment longer than they should to focus. "You're going to come with us down there to help get him without fuss. Then we're going to go back to our ship and leave, and we're never going to come back. No one will know you helped us. And when we're gone, you can go back to business as usual, with everyone else blissfully unaware."

"That is what's going to happen if you cooperate," Ash clarified.

"And if I don't?"

"Well, I could say we'd kill you, but in all honestly, that's a little too cliché, and a man of your fine reputation deserves something grander. So, we'd probably just let it be known that you were assisting the Brotherhood, sharing details of all the criminals and gun-thugs we came here looking for, and let the disgruntled employees tear you apart. A lot less messy for us. Your choice though, we're happy to go either way," Ash goaded.

Dax sighed and tried to stand. I scooped my arm under his good armpit and helped him up. He swayed silently for a moment. "Fine."

"Fine, what?" Ash asked.

"Fine. I'll help you get whoever it is out of the Basement, but after that, you have to keep your word and get the fuck off my rock – silently, without drawing any more attention. If even one of my people suspect I've helped, I'm fucking dead. And then, so are you."

"What about them?" I asked, waving a hand at the bathroom.

"You leave them to me. I'll handle it."

I knew what he meant and opened my mouth to object, but Ash shook his head in warning. I closed my mouth and picked up my pack, getting ready to leave. Ash quickly bandaged Dax's wounds, then picked up a long, dirty-grey jacket from the arm of the sofa and helped him shrug painfully into it, hiding the bloody bandages as best as he could.

The elevator doors were ornate but tired, and they creaked as they opened.

"What's your big plan?" Dax asked as we descended the incredibly long way to the Basement. I looked expectantly at Ash for the answer.

"Hell if I know. I honestly didn't think we'd make it this far," he said, but his trademark lopsided grin appeared, and I don't know if it was the meds, but even Dax conceded a dry laugh. For a guy with such a fearsome reputation, he didn't seem so bad face to face, but I knew better than to let my guard down. "Seriously though, this doesn't have to be a big drama. Dax, how do we get Beck out of the mines, without causing a fuss?"

"Beck?" He almost chocked on the word. "All of this for that traitorous piece of shit?" I kneed him in the thigh, and he cried out in pain, buckling before managing to steady himself. "That prick has been a pain in my fuckin' arse since the day he got to the Ridge. If I didn't have my rep to consider, I'd hand the fucker over to you willingly." He paused, thinking. "You know the chances of all of us living through this are about five fuckin' percent... and that's being generous."

"The odds are low, I get it," I conceded. "So, tell us how we can do this without getting dead."

"Let me tell you the dilemma," Dax responded. "If we go into the Basement, get Beck, and then I hand him over to you willingly, I'll look weak. And there are plenty of people waiting for me to show my throat so they can rip it out. But if you use me to extract Beck under duress…"

"You'll look weak, and there'll be throat ripping. We get it," I acknowledged.

"What about telling them you're taking Beck out of the mines to interrogate him and torture him for intel on something or other," I suggested.

"That could work," Dax grunted. "If I'd come down with half a dozen of my roaches instead of a monk and a little lady."

"Call me little lady one more time, I dare you," I snarled, punching him in the shoulder. He collapsed to the floor in pain, and Ash gave me a half-hearted look of annoyance. "I know, I know," I added, helping him stand again.

"Jeez, and I thought you were the one to watch," Dax aimed at Ash. "Look, let me go in there alone and get Beck, then bring him back to you."

"Not a chance in hell," Ash replied. "You think we trust you not to grab the first weapon you find? You stay with us, and if you want to survive this, you better come up with a plan quick. We're almost there."

"The plan?" Dax sneered. "The only plan that's going to work is if you kill everyone down there. You up for that, Brother?"

"Not if we can avoid it," Ash replied. "Shae, set your weapon to stun." Dax barked a dry laugh as I changed the settings on my Sentinel. "What can we expect when we get there?"

"My private elevator takes us into the Basement behind all the security measures. Unless we're fuckin' unlucky, the doors will be unguarded. Most of my men are either on the entrance, or in the mines. Apart from the control room, there's no need to have them anywhere else. To get Beck out of the mines though, you'll need to send the order from control and some of the guards will bring him to the holding room right next door. From there, it's a free run back to the elevator and up to my office. How the fuck you think you're going to get back to your ship from there, is your fuckin' business."

"So, what you're saying is, we're just going to have to wing it?" I said, looking to Ash for his thoughts, but he just shrugged. Then that damn lopsided grin appeared.

"Not the first time," he offered.

8

The lift came to a grinding halt at the bottom of the shaft, and I readied my gun as the doors opened. Thankfully, there was no one in the dimly lit tunnel, and we stepped out, pausing for Dax to indicate the way.

"Left at the end," he whispered, but as we came to the corner, we paused as voices came closer. Ash took a quick peek.

"Two," he confirmed, then before waiting for a response, he stepped out and engaged.

"You gonna help?" Dax asked.

"Ash can handle it," I replied. "I'm going to stay right here and keep an eye on you."

"Easy," he growled as I pushed the muzzle of the gun into his back.

A moment later, Ash stuck his head around the corner. "All clear," he whispered.

The two thugs lay on the ground, almost parallel, and I was surprised when Dax fell to his knee beside one of them and felt for a pulse. I thought it was kinda nice he was checking they were still alive, but before I could stop him, he grabbed the guy's head and yanked it to the side, the crack amplified by the rock walls. I grabbed the back of his jacket collar as he reached for the second, pulling him away.

"You want to survive this, little la—" Dax stopped himself short, turning to Ash. "If you want my help, this is how it has to be, or you can just kill me now. You know this to be fucking true."

I felt confliction seeping through the link, then Ash turned away, letting Dax go to the second guard. I wanted to say something. I wanted to say we couldn't possibly let this happen, but I felt the same way I knew Ash did. I re-set my Sentinel to default.

Thankfully, we got to the control room without meeting anyone else, but there were three people in there. They seemed surprised to see Dax, and even more perplexed to see us, but their expressions quickly turned dangerous when they realised our intentions. I didn't want to risk bringing more guards by using my gun, so I engaged the neared guard in hand-to-hand, quickly taking him out using a combination of Tok-ma manoeuvres.

By the time I'd checked he was actually dead, the other two guards had been despatched and Dax and Ash were in a dangerous standoff. Dax had obviously got a gun off the guard he taken down, and the two of them now stood a couple of meters apart, guns almost parallel. I pulled my Sentinel and quickly ended the standoff by tapping the back of Dax's head with it.

"Worth a try," he joked humorously, as he lowered the gun. I took it from him and kneed him in the back of the legs, dropping him to the floor. "Hands behind your back," I demanded, grabbing a pair of flexi-cuffs from one of the guards.

"What now?" Ash asked, hauling him into a chair.

"Check the prisoner log, there, on that plexi." He nodded towards one of the screens. "That will tell you what zone Beck's in. And if the fuckers down here did what I told them to, he'll be in one of the deepest, darkest fucking caves we have."

"He's in Tau," I confirmed, after checking. Dax shrugged his shoulders.

"Could've been worse," he confessed. "Use that com-panel over there and select direct line, then Tau, then add your message. And for fuck's sake, don't be all Brotherhood polite or they'll know something's the fuck up. Tell them he needs interrogating and to bring him stat to the holding room, something like that. You want me to do it?"

"I got it," Ash replied. "How long will it take?"

"Not sure. They have to find him, then get him on one of the monos to get back here. Twenty minutes maybe?"

"Well, looks like the guards in Tau got the message, they've confirmed receipt."

"Great," Dax replied sarcastically.

"How many guards will be with him?" I asked.

"Depends what condition he's in," Dax replied, and my stomach churned. "By now, I'm guessing it'll take one, maybe two, guards to subdue him."

I felt the shudder of the mono-train arriving. "Can we not just let the guards leave?" I suggested. "You could let them go and they wouldn't even need to know what's happening," I added, but as the door opened, I saw one of the guards use a stun-stick on an already subdued Beck. He spasmed in pain, unable to get away from the weapon, and his teeth clenched. Without thinking, I pulled my gun and fired, blood and grey matter peppering the walls of the train. As the other guard lifted his own weapon towards me, I fired again, his body bowling backwards over one of the benches.

"Sorry," I said, turning back towards Ash, but there was little feeling in it.

"It's okay," he replied. "Just be alert. The noise might attract some unwanted guests," he added before entering the train.

Beck groaned as Ash dragged him from the carriage. We returned to the control room and Ash laid him on the floor. He was barely conscious, no clue what was happening, and his body told a horrific story of abuse. An anger towards Dax bubbled inside of me, and I guess Ash must've felt it through the Link, because he placed a calming hand on my arm.

"So, you have the traitor," Dax goaded, reigniting my rage. "What do you think happens next? This piece of shit's mostly dead. Was it all worth—" The blast from my weapon sent him sprawling over one of the consoles before sliding off into a heap on the floor.

"Really?" Ash reprimanded.

"It was on stun," I confessed. "Besides, I need to sort Beck out, and there's no way in hell I want Dax seeing what I'm capable of."

"I'm not sure Beck knowing is much better," Ash replied. "I know, I know," he conceded. "Do your thing."

I held up my hands, stands of light dancing between my fingers, and the control room filled with a silver-blue shimmer. It dissipated suddenly.

"What's the matter?" Ash tensed. "You okay?"

"I'm fine," I said, frowning. "It's just…"

"What?"

"Should I heal the plasma scar on his arm and the one in his beard?"

"Is that all? Shae, I thought something terrible had happened." He puffed out a breath, and I felt relief through the Link. "Leave the scars, they're too obvious to disappear. People will question what happened to them."

"Sure, you're right," I replied, turning my attention back to Beck. I picked up one of his hands, callused and raw, and placed it neatly by his side. His clothes were ripped and bloodied, and he smelled terrible. The black, tribal tattoos on his arms were a stark contrast to his pallid skin, and his eyes were sunken in a wasted face.

I closed my eyes, and put my hands over his chest, remembering the man we first met at Finnigan's Bar. My stomach tingled, then my chest, and then quickly every part of me shimmered. Stands of light crossed to Beck and he started to shimmer too – first his chest, then his tummy, and then down his arms and legs. I felt the strength return to his lungs and heart, muscles and skin were restored, and bones that had broken and been left to heal without medical care, began to heal properly. Even his skin darkened to a smooth olive colour.

As I pulled my hands away, and the light disappeared. He opened hazelnut brown eyes, and blinked, adjusting to the light. He looked confused, glancing between me and Ash before noticing Dax on the floor next to him. He moved quickly, making me jump, backing away from the unconscious man before scrambling to his feet.

"It's okay, we're here to get you out," Ash said, but Beck still looked confused. He was feeling his body and face, and looking at his muscular limbs.

"What…? How…?" he eventually murmured.

"Beck?" Ash said to get his attention. "Beck, I need to you focus. Do you remember us?"

The huge barman's frown deepened as he studied me. "Shae?"

I smiled. "You remember my name."

"I told you before, we don't get many like you round here. You're kinda unforgettable." I blushed outrageously.

"I don't understand," he continued, looking towards Ash.

"We don't have much time to explain," Ash said. "We came to the Ridge looking for your help, but when we found you'd ended up in the Basement for helping us, well, we couldn't just leave you here."

"I'm certainly not going to turn down the assist," Beck replied, "but that's not what I meant." He looked down at his torso, lifting his ripped shirt to reveal muscles that rivalled Jake's.

"Oh, that," I said. "Yeah, that was me. But it's a long story, so for now, just accept that you're good, because we are still far from getting out of this alive."

He contemplated for a moment, studying his hands. "Okay. We'll save that for a later discussion. Is he dead?"

"Not yet," I said, giving him a boot in the ribs.

"Yeah, I knew I liked you," Beck said, putting his arms around me and lifting me off the floor – reminiscent of when we were in the tunnels last time we were here.

He put me down a few moments later, when Ash coughed and said, "Can we focus please. There are still a hundred roaches between us and getting off this rock. Beck, I assume you've got no problem coming with us this time?"

"Hell no," he replied without hesitation. "Are you open to suggestion on exit strategies?"

"We're all ears," Ash said.

"Open the gates."

"Huh?" I questioned.

"Open the gates and let everyone out of the Basement. The roaches will be too busy dealing with that shit to worry about us. All available security will be dispatched to subdue the escapees, and trust me, the locals will take advantage of the lack of firepower on the other levels."

"It'll be carnage," I said.

Beck smiled, the rough scar in his beard curving. "Most of the people down here don't deserve to be here. You're giving them an opportunity they've only dreamt of so far, so don't feal bad for them. And sure as shit don't feel bad for him and his roaches," he added, copying my kick to Dax's torso.

"It could work," Ash acknowledged, nodding his head slowly. "Better than our plan."

"We haven't got one," I challenged.

"Exactly," he replied grinning. "You know how to work all this stuff?" he asked Beck.

"How hard can it be?" he replied, sitting in front of one

of the consoles. "Here, I think this is the master security application. He scrolled a list of files. "Inmate profiles, utilities, weapons controls… ah, here it is: access controls." He selected the option. More files appeared on the plexi, and a map of the whole Basement complex displayed on the windows behind the console. Each door and corridor had a unique code displayed next to it.

"There," I said, a little to excitedly, leaning forward to point to a 'release all' command. Beck turned his head and kissed me on the cheek, heat instantly rising.

"Good catch," he said, a broad smile lighting up his eyes. "Shall we?"

"Do it," Ash replied.

A loud claxon broke the cloying air, and the monitors showed the doors and gates swinging open. For a moment the inmates stood, as if frozen in time, while the guards look at each other with panic. Then all hell broke loose.

"Time to go," Ash said urgently. "This place is going to get flooded with inmates and roaches in moments. "Give me a hand with Dax," he added to Beck.

"Fuck no! Leave him here."

"We need him for the biometric sensors on his private lift," Ash explained.

"Oh well, in that case… Would've helped if you'd led with that," Beck replied, crouching to grab on arm. Ash rolled his eyes.

We encountered a handful of thugs on our way to Dax's lift, but nothing I couldn't handle. It actually felt good to let off some steam with a little hand-to-hand fighting, and the mindless gun-thugs were no match for my Tok-ma training.

"Man, I think I'm in love," Beck muttered.

"Hey!" Ash replied

"What?" he asked innocently, reminding me of Jake's boyish charm. "It's not like you're going there."

I felt Ash's indignant rage bulldoze through the link. "We're here," I said, quickly intervening. We need a hand

and his eye."

"Do they still need to be attached?" Beck asked casually. "Okay, okay, I've got a hand," he said grabbing Dax's wrist and lifting his palm to the sensor. The light turned from red to amber.

"I've got the eye," Ash said, hoisting Dax up a bit before pushing his head forward. The light turned from amber to green and the doors opened.

"Get Dax inside and I'll—" I heard the gun fire at almost the same time I felt the pain rip though my back and shoulder blade. Beck grabbed me, pulling me into the lift, while Ash took out the newcomers.

The doors seemed to take an eternity to close, but once Ash was able to select Dax's office as our destination, he threw himself on the ground beside me. "Out of the way," he ordered Beck.

"If I take my hand away, she's just gonna keep bleeding," he protested.

"It's fine," Ash replied sternly. "Trust me." I felt the pressure release when Beck removed his hand, and the pain froze the air in my lungs. "What do you need?" He asked me.

"The bullet's still in there," I said through gritted teeth. "You need to get it out before I can heal."

"You sure?" Ash's face looked as white as Beck's was when we'd first seen him.

"Just do it," I ordered, a groan escaping my lips.

"You're really going to do this here?" said Beck.

"You want to know what happened to you?" replied Ash irritably. Beck nodded carefully. "Then shut up and let me do this."

Ash pulled a knife from his belt and moved behind me, as Beck took my hands. "Look at me, okay? I got you."

The pain was excruciating, and my hands clenched, crushing his. I felt warm, sticky liquid dripping down my back, but I couldn't feel any tingling or itching.

"What happened?" I asked through ragged breaths.

"I couldn't get it, it's in there too deep. We need to get you some pain meds first."

"Stop it, Ash."

"Stop what?" He sounded surprised.

"Stop mothering me." Beck laughed and I looked up, directly into his eyes. He stopped. "Anyone else and you'd have dug in and got that bullet out. You're going to need me five by five if we're going to get out of here, so just do it."

I screamed as the knife went in, searching for the bullet, and a moment later the grey tendrils of fog infiltrated my brain, and I must've passed out. I came too, curled up on the floor using Beck's lap as a pillow. He didn't seem to mind. The lift was still ascending, so I couldn't have been out long, and the last of the silver blue shimmer reflected in Beck's eyes. I sat up, stretched my arms above my head, flexing my shoulder. Good as new.

"You did that glowey thing on me? That's how I'm back to normal?" he asked, looking awestruck.

"Yup. You're welcome by the way," I replied. Ash reached down and helped me off the floor.

"But how?" Beck pushed.

"That's—"

"For a later discussion?"

"Most definitely."

"You okay?" Ash asked. I nodded. "You sure?" I nodded again. "Tired…hungry?" I nodded emphatically. "Okay, well you can eat and rest when we get out of here. We're nearly at Dax's office, and we don't know what's waiting for us. It's also a long way back to the *Nakomo*, so get ready."

Dax's office was empty when we arrived. Beck grabbed one of his boots and dragged him from the elevator, his head bouncing roughly over the door runners.

"So far, so good," he half-joked. "What are we doing

with this arsehole?"

"Leave him here," Ash said. "He's served his purpose. From now on, he's more of a hinderance than a help. Whoa," he added as Beck raised his gun a Dax's head. "No need for that. He'll be out long enou—" The gunshot stopped him mid-word. "Shae!"

"It's on stun," I said, both men looking at me. "Just making sure he stays... stunned, until we're long gone."

Beck turned to Ash and raised his arms out. "Like I said, I'm in love."

Ash chewed his tongue, and I knew what he wanted to say. I knew he'd feel my embarrassment at Beck's attention, but instead, he simply said, "Move out."

Beck had been right about all roaches being called to deal with the breakout, or the ensuing chaos on the other levels. We met a few gun-thugs on the way to the mag-train, but nothing to write home about. Once we were settled, and on our way back to the nearest station from the *Nakomo*, I took a moment to check out my shoulder in the reflection of the windows.

"You said you came here looking for me," Beck asked, breaking a silence that had settled over our group. "I'm intrigued."

"We need your help," Ash replied, looking serious. "We were hoping you'd know someone who can alter or camouflage the energy pulse built into some ship's engine systems."

"A sequencer? The tech that allows for shortrange tracking?"

"Yes, if that's what it's called."

"There's a sequencer on your shuttle?"

"Yes."

"Why?" He caught the look on my face. "Okay, another long storey. Who knew the Brotherhood had so many secrets? So basically, you came here because you think I'm shady enough to know some other shady dude, who'd fix the shady tracking device on your shuttle. And don't think I haven't noticed that neither of you are displaying Brotherhood colours or ID, which is also pretty damn shady."

"Can you please stop saying the word 'shady,'" I asked, guilt rippling under my ribcage. "It doesn't matter anyway."

"Why?" Beck looked surprised.

"Because as soon as we get back to the *Nakomo*, we're not sticking around. We're out of time," Ash explained.

"For a monk, you have very little faith," Beck replied, turning to give me an award-winning smile. "You came to me for my help and ended up orchestrating a jailbreak on the fly. You really think I'm not gonna help? Where's the *Nakomo* docked?"

"Three forty-eight. Gamma," Ash replied, a v-shaped frown settling between his eyebrows.

Beck accessed a coms panel on the arm of one of the chairs and tapped in a few numbers. A moment later, a woman's voice answered. "Who's this?" She asked, fear and intrigue in her voice.

"Tanny, it's Beck."

"Beck?"

"Yeah, seems I'm back, thanks to a couple of new friends."

"I nearly didn't answer the coms. Do you know what's going on?" She didn't wait for an answer. "It's bedlam, that's what's going on. And what the hell are you doing on Level One?"

"It's a long story…" He paused then looked at me sideways. "Yes, I get the irony."

"What was that?" Tanny asked, confusion replacing the fear.

"Sorry, that was to someone else," Beck explained. "I need a favour?"

"Now? Are you shitting me? Did you not just hear what I said?"

"Tanny, if my friends and I don't get off this rock quick, we're going to die."

The line went silent. "What do you need?" she said eventually.

"You're a legend."

"Yeah, yeah, just tell me."

"There's a shuttle on pad 348, Gamma, that needs a sequencer removed from their engine. Can you do it?"

"Of course, I can do it." She sounded indignant.

"No, I mean can you do it right now."

"Now?" she practically screeched. Silence descended and for a moment I thought she'd cut us off. "You really going to die?"

"I just broke out of the Basement, and Dax knows who broke me out. We're all dead if they find us."

"Fine. I'm ten minutes from the pad – I'll get started and meet you there. It's not a long job, but it's fiddly as fuck, so you're going to have to be patient. And Beck?"

"Yeah?"

"I'm glad you're alive." The line went dead and for a moment we all sat in silence again.

"So… Tanny…?" I said, nudging Beck's boot with my own foot. He raised his hazelnut eyes to mine. "Is that some blushing I can see there? Sounds to me like you two have got a little something going on," I teased.

"Slow your roll there, missy. That there is ancient history."

"If you say so," I teased, nudging his foot again.

"I do," he replied, trying to give me a stern look, but then the crinkles around his eyes appeared and he let out a booming laugh. "Besides, my heart has been stollen by another."

Twenty minutes later we readied ourselves for whoever we'd meet at the station, but as we disembarked, the only person there was an old geezer manning the controls. When he saw us, he lowered his weapon, and when Ash indicated he could go, he limped off as fast as he could.

The tunnels, in contrast, were pure chaos. People pushing and shoving, roaches not knowing quite what to do. Ash took my hand, striding forward, and instinctively, I grabbed Beck's – the three of us snaking through the masses. We headed up the East tunnel, turning down the west when we got the crossroads. Having healed Beck and my own wound, I felt weary, and the constant pushing and shoving on me started to take its toll. I should have objected, but the warm, firmness of Beck behind me, pushed me on. One hand curled around my waist, while the other pushed people away from me. At one point, Ash turned and scowled at him, but he must have felt my exhaustion through the link, because he didn't push further.

After what seemed like an eternity, we reached West 19, and took the tunnel to the landing pads.

"This is your shuttle?" Beck asked, squinting at the *Nakomo*. "I was expecting something…"

"Something what?" I challenged, giving him my, don't mess with the *Nakomo*, look.

"Something a little more…" He struggled to find the words as I added a raised eyebrow, but he was saved by Tanny.

"Hey," she said, waving us over. "Come here," she added to Beck, barely able to get her arms around him. He bent down and affectionately returned the hug.

"So turquoise this time?" he said, flicking her short, bright hair. "I like it. I think it suits you even better than the pink."

"Thanks, gotta keep things interesting, right? And holy-hell you smell bad." She turned to Ash and me. "This is your tub?" I nodded. "Well, she's had a bloody good overhaul recently. In excellent condition for her age. Respect to you for keeping her this good; a lot of people would just move on to something new. These older ships have way too much heart to be tossed aside."

I decided I quite liked Tanny.

"Anyway, back to business. I've removed the sequencer. Wasn't that difficult for someone of my skill."

"You're a ship-whisperer, we get it," Beck joked. "We're good to go?"

"Not quite. I need ten more minutes to reconnect the parts I had to disconnect to remove the tech."

"What are you doing hanging around here then?" he challenged jokingly. He reached for her shoulders, turned her towards the *Nakomo*, then dropped his hands and pushed her bottom in that direction. "Go and finish what you started." She raised her arm and gave him the finger.

"Sure looks like history to me," I teased. He came at me playfully but pulled up when Ash stepped between us.

The sounds coming from the tunnel worried me. What had appeared to be relatively harmless as we'd pushed through the crowd, now started to vibrate in a new mood – with a more angry, hostile undertone. While we waited for Tanny to complete the work, a few people overflowed into the hanger bay, but it only took us raising our weapons for them to quickly move on.

"Has anyone thought about how we're going to get passed the cannons without getting blasted out of existence?" Beck asked casually.

"We just ask for departure codes," Ash replied.

"And you think they're just going to let us leave?"

"I have faith."

"Oh, now that's funny," Beck mocked.

"I might be able to help with that, but it'll cost you," Tanny said, wiping her hands on her dirty overall, a smudge of something red in her hair.

"How much?" Ash asked.

"A thousand."

"Are you shitting me, Tanny?" Beck spluttered. "Whatever happened to mates-rates?"

"Well, as it's you, muscles, I'll let you have it for eight

hundred, not a credit less."

"Great! But what the hell do you have that worth that much anyway?" he asked.

"This," she replied, pulling out a silver thingy with wires coming from it. "Brought it with me; thought you might need it."

Beck scratched his dirty beard. "Is that a—"

"It sure is," she interrupted proudly. "A genuine roach transponder. Plug it in, turn it on, and as far as control is concerned, you're AR-5-27-J. Just another a roach-coach."

"Deal," Ash said, as a heavily armed group piled into the bay. "How long to fit it?"

"Five, give or take. You can do all your flight checks at the same time, so you'll be good to go when I'm done. Feel bad for asking, but you sure you're good for eight hundred?"

"Fuck, Tanny, they're Brotherhood. If they say they got it, they got it." He turned to Ash and lowered his voice. "You do got it, don't you?"

Ash ignored him. "Tanny, if you can get us up and flying in five minutes, I'll give you the full thousand in hard currency." He'd barely finished before she'd sprinted off.

While Ash did the internal flight checks, I did the outside. I think Beck just checked Tanny arse as she installed the silver gizmo under the flight console. When I was done, I took up position at the bottom of the ramp, guarding it against the increased number of people who'd spilled into the docking bay. One of the unattended shuttles further down the bay looked like it was getting stripped as people swarmed over it like ants.

"You're squared away," Tanny said as she walked down the ramp, carrying a toolbox that looked very heavy.

"You sure you're going to be okay getting all those credits out of here?" I asked.

"I'll be fine," she replied, "Thanks for asking though."

A fight broke out further down the bay. "You can come

with us, if you want."

She stopped and eyed me carefully. "You have a good soul," she said kindly, but I was too surprised by her words to answer. "You could do far worse than Beck, you know. He's got a past, who the hell hasn't, but he's a rock. One of the good ones."

"I've heard that," I replied when I got my voice back. "But my heart is elsewhere."

She laid a hand on my arm and smiled. "That's a shame."

9

When I got to the flight area, Ash was already in the pilot's chair and Beck had made himself comfortable in the navigator's. I didn't want to go back to the cabin, so instead, I sat on the floor, too tired to remain standing.

"If you want to make it out of here in one piece, let me deal with control," Beck said. Ash and I shared a glance before he nodded his agreement. "Good." He opened coms. "Yo, Control. What the fuck? We got orders to go pick up some shit for the main man fucking ages ago, and you bastards are still fannying around with departure codes. What the fuck's going on?"

"This is Angel Ridge Control. Who's this?"

"Who's this? Who's this," Beck almost shouted. "This is AR-5-27-J requesting departure from 348 Gamma. Sort yourselves the fuck out and get us off this rock, or you can be explaining to Dax why he doesn't have every fucking item from his fucking shopping list."

"AR-5-27-J, this is Control. Records show a ghost ship docked in 348 gamma."

"Do we look like a fucking ghost-ship?" Beck really was shouting now. "Check your fucking sensors, and then tell me we're a fucking ghost ship. And while you at it, slit the throat of whoever fucked up in the first place." Beck turned and smiled down at me. I think he was enjoying himself a little more than he should've been.

"AR-5-27-J, this is Control. You're clear for take-off. Have a great day."

"About fucking time, Control." Beck bellowed. "Over to you," he added to Ash, who immediately got us off the deck. "Worth every credit," he added, as if he paid himself, but as we approached the exit, Control contacted us again.

"AR-5-27-J, this is Control. Hold where you are. I repeat, hold where you are. Do not attempt to leave Angel Ridge or you'll be fired on."

"What the fuck, Control? Stop fucking around and let us on our way."

"AR-5-27-J, your designation is out of date and showing as decommissioned. Hold for further instructions."

"Shit," Beck exclaimed. "And we've got a clear view out of here. So bloody close," he added pointing out the panoramic window to the expanse of space and twinkly stars just the other side of the gate. But there was also an assortment of weapons ready to make us dead.

"Shae, what do you think would happen if we went to FTL from here?" Ash asked, not turning to look at me. I got up and stood next to him, peering through the window to see how much space there was around us."

"You're not really thinking about this seriously, are you?" Beck challenged. We both ignored him.

"I'm not the expert. Where's Francis when you need him?" I said, clearing away the sudden pangs of guilt. "Best guess, jumping to FTL from here... 50% chance we'd make it. 100% chance we'd blow the tunnel and probably a big chunk of this shithole along with it. Not that that's much of a loss. But jumping to FTL... in this tunnel... from a standing start? I'd say zero percent survival for us."

"Well, there's your answer to that completely insane

question," Beck stated.

"Have you got a better idea?" Ash challenged back, tempers flaring.

I thought for a moment, not liking our options. "We can't stay here. They're probably sending a ship as we speak to check us out."

"Or blow us the hell up," Beck interrupted.

"And, we can't go back; we'll be trapped," I continued, ignoring him.

"Please don't say what I think you're going to say." Beck shook his head.

"The only logical conclusion is that we go forward. Think about it? The weapons are there to keep people out, not in."

"So?" he questioned.

"I see where you're going with this," said Ash. "The guns are targeted away from the asteroid, so there's a dead spot between the rock and the point at which they're focussed. You think we can get enough speed and distance to be able to shift to FTL safely?"

"I don't know about safely, but it's the only idea I've got. Punch the sub-light engines as hard as you can, and pray the shields hold long enough to get us to the point we can engage FTL."

"You know this is suicide, right?" Beck said, but then his mouth broke open and a booming laugh came out. "Hell, what else have I got to do today? I'd rather die in a blaze of glory, then waste away in those mines. Just to be clear, you two… you have no idea what you've done for me today. If we die, know I die a happy, free man. Shit, that sounds melancholic."

"AR-5-27-J, this is Control. We have a ship headed your way to escort you to the nearest landing pad. Do not resist or disobey this order, or you will be fired upon."

"Now or never then," said Ash, engaging the sub-light engines with full power. We lurched forward, and I would have been thrown backwards if Beck hadn't caught me. I grabbed the back of the chair and held on tightly, but he pulled me around the arm, and I fell into his lap, his arm closed tightly around my waist.

"AR-5-27-J, this is Control. Power down your engines or you will be fired on. I repeat—" Beck cut the coms signal, but we jolted violently as the first of the weapons found their target.

"Aft shields at 87%," Beck said. "75," he added as we shook again. "68."

"Shut up, Beck," Ash demanded, but then we got hit by a volley of fire.

"I know you told me to shut up, but another round like that and the aft shield are toast. How long until FTL?"

"Fifteen seconds."

"We don't have fifteen seconds," I said, but as I did, a ship filled the front screen as it raced passed us, railguns blazing, and torpedoes firing. The bottom left-hand corner of the window displayed the rear view, and we watched the weapons turrets destroyed in blistering explosions. The ship turned and took up position behind us, shielding us from the remaining weapons fire, and an incoming coms filled part of the screen.

"No time for hellos," Jake said, rocking as they got hit. "I'm sending…" he paused, the deepest frown puckering his forehead. "Who the fuck is he? And what the fuck are you doing sat on him, Shae?"

"Uh-oh, someone's jealous," Beck mocked, but I elbowed him in the ribs.

Conner said something to Jake, thankfully distracting him, and he bent down to listen. When he righted himself, he said, "We're sending you coordinates. Get your FTL online now and we'll meet you there. It's… it's good to see you both." He turned his attention to Beck. "And you, stranger – keep your hands to yourself." The coms cut.

"I like him," said Beck, not at all ruffled. "Where's he

sending us?"

"Looks like Dennford," Ash replied. "Hold tight," he added as we jumped to FTL.

"Never heard of it. What's at Dennford?" Beck asked.

"Nothing. That's probably the point," I said, getting up. "The Khan family had a militia encampment there that's since been demolished, but other than that, the locals are mainly self-sufficient, extreme technophobes. They see themselves as independent to the crown, and don't recognise their authority, but basically, they just want to be left alone."

"They don't cause any trouble," Ash added, "so the REF doesn't bother them. The Brotherhood visits a few times a year, just to check in, make sure they're all okay, but we had nothing scheduled for the next couple of months. It was a good shout by Jake – out of the way, and not an obvious choice for us."

"Won't they distrust us when we arrive in a big hunking pile of tech," Beck asked, waving his arm around.

"The inhabitants of Dennford choose not to use any but the most basic tech, but they're also realists and know that other people do. They're okay with ships, bringing buyers and sellers, but they insist that all tech is left onboard. So, bear that in mind when we land."

"No guns? No coms?"

"Nope, but knives are okay."

"Blades it is then," he said. "I presume you have some." Ash gave him a sideways look and raised an eyebrow. A yawn surprised me, and I tried to stifle it.

"How long till we get there," I asked

"Long enough for you to rest," Ash said. "Why don't you hit your bunk, and I'll wake you up when were near? And yes, I'll have food waiting," he said, smiling. I bent down and kissed him on the forehead as I passed between the seats, swatting Beck as he made sarcastic kissy noises.

"You might want to take the opportunity to grab a

shower," I added, sniffing in his direction.

Our approach to Jake's coordinates on Dennford took us around the edge of the largest settlement. On the outskirts, a tented marketplace lit the night sky with lights the colour of jewels.

"How far?" I asked, sitting on the arm of the navigator's seat.

"Almost there. It's just a few miles west of the town," Ash replied.

"I can't believe how excited I am to see them all. I know it's only been a month, but it feels like an eternity. It's weird, but I can almost feel my chest vibrating... you know what? It's probably nothing. Just aftereffects of healing Beck and then my shoulder."

"Did I hear my name?" Beck said, entering the flight areas, his muscular, tattooed arms folded across a clean, black vest. Beck noticed me looking. "Ash gave it me. Looks a little tight, though, don't you think? You need to do some bulking up my man." Ash raised his eyes to the ceiling, then shook his head.

"We're coming into land, better take a seat," Ash said. I scooted my bum backwards and plopped down, swinging my legs around to sit properly. Beck gave me puppy-dog eyes.

"Forget it. You're not sitting on me," I told him.

"You could sit on me again, I don't mind. Or maybe that would just annoy lover boy further." I turned to glare at him. "Fine, I'll just stand."

The *Veritas* was faster than the *Nakomo* and was already powered down when we landed. I leant forward, over the console, to get a better look through the screen. They'd set up a campfire beside the ship, and it looked like Ty was already cooking, but as we landed, they all got up and headed towards us.

My chest literally buzzed when I saw them all standing

there, but I was inexplicably drawn to Jake, just like I'd been since the second we met. I broke into a run and threw myself into his arms, which closed around me. Neither of us said anything, we just stayed like that, holding each other as tightly as possible, my feet not even touching the floor. The knot in the pit of my stomach that had been there since we'd left Lilania, loosened a little.

Jake put my feet back on the grass and released me slightly so he could pull back far enough to see the stupid, happy grin on my face. He moved a strand of hair that had fallen over my eye.

"I shouldn't have let you leave," he said quietly. "I—"

"Stop hogging, boss," Ty moaned, tapping him on the shoulder. "Share the love." Jake released me and I was immediately swept up and spun around. "Where you been Little Wolfpup?"

"Wolfpup?" Beck questioned.

"None of your business, stranger," Jake answered, but before anything else was said, I was crushed by black leather.

"Hey, Kaiser," I said, giving him a kiss on his weathered cheek.

"Hey, Blue," he replied, noticeably blushing, even in the dim light.

As the others welcomed Ash, Connor gave me a shy, awkward embrace, and I thought that was everyone, until I noticed a fifth man.

"What? You too famous to give out free hugs?" I asked.

"For you, I'd give my life," he said, but the others jeered him, and Ty pounced on him until his face broke into a grin and he started laughing. "Too serious?" he joked.

"A little," I replied. "Get over her, Cal," I ordered, and he obliged.

"Okay, okay, break up the love-fest," Jake said. "Kaiser, Connor, Cal, set up a perimeter of AG42's around both ships. I know the locals aren't known for being unfriendly, but I don't want to us to get caught with our pants down. Ty, you're on dinner duty. You, stranger? You look like you know your way around an automated weapons station."

"The name's Beck," he said.

"Whatever," Jake replied. "Go help the others."

Beck stood his ground a moment. "Please," I said kindly.

"Fine," he grunted. "But I'll be back. And I expect a couple of those long stories you promised me." He jogged off after the others.

Jake led us away from everyone else. He took my hand and held it close to his chest. "The stranger? Can he be trusted?"

"Well, I guess in your words, you'd call Beck a scroat," Ash said, and Jake snorted. "But yes, he can be trusted."

"I'll take your word on that." Jake paused and looked up at the stars. "You know, I've been going out of my mind with worry," he confessed, a sudden look of unease on his face. How could he know what'd happened? "Jared, too."

"I don't understand," Ash said, mirroring my bewilderment. "The Brotherhood told the REF we'd left?"

"The Brotherhood's told us shit, that's why we've been so worried." He looked between our puzzled faces, before raking a hand through unruly hair. "Come on, you both go on some top-secret missions, and we don't hear from you, not even a goodbye, for a month. I've been worried shitless something had happened to you."

"Wait, you think we went on a mission. And that's why we were uncontactable?" I said, astounded.

Jake's eyebrows knitted together as he looked between us again. "You weren't on a mission?"

"No," Ash said simply. He rubbed his temples, and Jake gave him the moment he needed to collect his thoughts. "Jake, who told you this?"

"We knew something was up when none of our coms were being answered. After Shea's promise, I knew she wouldn't knowingly leave us hanging, so Jared and I both tried official Brotherhood channels. Eventually, they must've got tired of the harassment because Jared spoke to your Primus directly."

"Noah?" I asked.

"Yeah, evasive little fuck. Sorry," he added, shrugging his shoulders. "He said you'd been sent on a mission and couldn't be contacted. To begin with, it kinda fit, given you were recalled to the monastery so quickly. We assumed it was because they wanted you on this new mission asap, but as time went on, I couldn't help thinking something was up. I couldn't believe you'd have disappeared without some kind of notice, even if it was to let us know you were going off grid. After a couple of weeks, I tried to get answers, but by that point they were stonewalling. They wouldn't even acknowledge us. Eventually, I reached out to all my contacts, leaving instructions to let us know on the down-low if anyone sees you guys or the *Nakomo*. When we didn't hear anything… babe, I thought you were…" I touched his cheek gently. "Then, out of nowhere, I get a message from Bishop."

"Who?"

"That scroat from Angel Ridge, remember? The one who confirmed the Hawksworth was docked there when Nyan's assassination took place. Anyway, he tells me some shit's going down after a Brotherhood rep and some sweet side chick—"

"Hey," I cried, pulling my hand away and swatting him playfully on the shoulder.

"His words, babe, not mine. You want to know the rest of the story?" he teased.

"Just get on with it, Jake," Ash prompted.

"Okay, so the rest's simple. From Bishop's description, it could only have been you two, so we hauled arse to the Ridge. Only, when we get there, we find them firing on one of their own shuttles. Good job Connor recognised the

Nakomo by sight – what the hell were you doing with a roach transponder?"

"That's a very long story," Ash confessed.

"Is that one of the same long stories Beck was referring to? And does that story explain why you were sitting on his lap?"

"Yes, and yes. And it was completely innocent," I answered.

"I'll take your word for it. Is he part of your mission?"

"Jake, we're not on a mission, not a Brotherhood one anyway," Ash explained. "We've never been on a mission. We've been on Lilania since the moment we returned from Decerra."

"Now I'm the one who doesn't understand."

"Noah told us you and Jared were on a secret mission and were off the grid and uncontactable. Jake, we've been on planet lockdown all this time. We've had no coms or messages from anyone outside of the Brotherhood, and any that we've sent to you guys have been undelivered or unanswered."

"I've not had anything," Jake confirmed. "What the hell's going on?"

"It seems the Brotherhood has gone to some extreme measures to keep us apart," Ash concluded.

"So, if you're on planet lockdown, how did we find you at the Ridge." He saw the forlorn glance we shared and drew in a surprised breath. "That's what you meant? When you asked if the Brotherhood had told us you'd left? Have you both left the Brotherhood? Fuck me, this is huge. Why? What happened?"

"There's a lot to it, Jake," I said sadly. "And in all honesty, I don't think I've got the emotional strength for it tonight." I looked at his scruffy hair and three-days' worth of stubble and realised just how much I'd missed him.

"She's had a bit of a workout with her gift today," Ash explained.

"Say no more," Jake replied. "Now I have you here, right here," he took my hand again, "the rest can wait. Tonight, we celebrate we've found each other again."

As we walked back to the *Veritas*, I said, "I was surprised to see Cal."

"Good surprise?"

"Of course."

"The guys have taken to him, and he's not really got anywhere else to go."

"And you like having him around, you big softie," I teased.

"Tell anyone and I'll deny it." His hazel eyes were brown in the darkness, but they still sparkled. "Besides, you like him, so that means something. You've got good intuition about these things."

"I like you," I said, "So I wouldn't trust my intuition too much."

"She got you there," Ash added. It felt good to see him laugh.

By the time the others returned from setting up the weapons stations, Ty had stoked the fire pit and pulled some logs around it to sit on or lean against.

The heat warmed me to my bones, or it could've been the amazing stew Ty served. Either way it felt good. It wasn't long until the inevitable stories and jokes started, and it felt good to be part of something normal. As the night went on, the beer changed to hooch and the stories became more outlandish. While he was still relatively steady, Ash went to close up the *Nakomo* and Jake appeared silently at my side.

"You're smiling," he observed.

"I am? Must be the alcohol." I rested my head on his shoulder, staring into the depths of the fire pit. "Honestly though, I can't tell you how happy I am to be with the Pack again. And I'm also so happy Cal's found a new family."

"You're part of that family, you know." He placed a

light kiss on the forehead.

"Jake—"

"Right now, I'm just glad you're here, babe," he said quietly, as the Pack decided it was a good time to show off their dancing skills. Or lack thereof. "I haven't magically changed my feelings over the last month," he continued. "But I know now's not the time. I know—"

"Blue," Kaiser bellowed. "Hey, Blue! I know you can hear me." He guffawed loudly. "Put the boss down and come join us."

"Kaiser," Jake replied, his voice dropping to warning tone.

"It's good," I said, laughing. "There's no way I can be worse than that," I added, pointing towards the Pack. "I don't think they've got a rhythm between them."

"That's because you haven't seen me dance," Jake replied, taking my hand and spinning me around – though he had to grab me again to steady me. Damn that hooch was strong.

It didn't take long for all of us to end up in a big, undignified heap around the fire, and when Ash returned with pillows and blankets, Beck was explaining to the Pack how we'd met.

"I'm telling you," he said enthusiastically, "it was like an angel walked into my bar that day. Didn't think much of her entourage at the time, but that was nothing compared to the arrogant prick who caused the real trouble. I hope I never see that fucking arsehole again after he got my bar destroyed. And just to be clear, it wasn't that fucker or his troopers I was helping that night." He nodded his head towards me.

"Please tell me he's talking about Jared?" Jake asked me, trying not to laugh.

"Umm, yeah. Kind of," I replied.

"Can we keep him around, just to see what happens when they meet?"

"Stop it," I chastised half-heartedly. "Jared's changed a lot since then."

"Well, I'll give you that," he conceded, filling my glass. "Are you warm enough?"

"I'm a bit chilly."

"Here." He held out the side of his blanket and I moved closer so he could wrap it around my shoulders. The added warmth of his body and the burn of the hooch re-heated my insides and my eyes started to droop.

I felt my head explode before I'd even opened my eyes, and it took a moment to remember where I was. The early morning light seared my eyeballs, and I raised my hand to shield them. Jake stirred and tightened his arm around my waist.

"Morning," Connor whispered, carefully placing a coffee pot on the embers still glowing in the fire pit.

I moved Jake's arm and sat up, surveying the carnage. Bodies littered the ground, the snores and grunts occasionally breaking the silence. Someone farted loudly and Connor and I tried to stifle laughter, but I failed dismally.

"Now that's a sound I could get used to waking up to," Jake said, rubbing his eyes.

"What? Farting?" I joked.

"No, your laughter. You're so beautiful… I know, I'm sorry. I just can't help myself sometimes. Hey, you okay?"

"My head's pounding."

"Can't you just glowey-thing it away?" Cal asked, still half asleep. I laughed, but that just made it worse.

"Wish I could, but hangovers are something I've never been able to get a handle on. We've got something on the *Nakomo* that'll help – courtesy of Jared."

"You mean this?" Ash tossed me a hypospray. "Thought you might need it."

"Yo! If you're gonna bring sweets to class, you have to

bring enough for everyone," Beck said, swaying as he stood. He looked bilious. "I should hang out with you guys more often. You know how to throw a serious party."

"Heads up," Ash said, throwing him another hypospray. "Anyone else?"

Breakfast was a sedate affair in comparison to the night before, and there was an air of anticipation. Everyone knew there was a story to tell.

As I drank Shatokian coffee, the aroma seemed to clear my head further. Ash leant towards me so we could talk privately. "You want to do this with Beck here?"

"You don't?"

"Jake's right, he's a stranger."

"True, but…"

"What?"

"I can't help thinking meeting Beck, him saving us, us saving him, being here with the Pack now… I don't know, it just seems right somehow. Do you feel it?"

"I feel that you feel it. I don't know, maybe he's exactly where he should be."

"Is that a little bit of faith I hear there?" I joked and he laughed, nudging me with his shoulder.

When everyone was sat, and the fire pit was blazing once again, Ash started. For Beck's benefit, he gave a little background to me, how I ended up in the Brotherhood, and the missions we'd been on together. The old story. The lie. We'd come back to the truth later.

"Ah," Beck said, nodding with understanding. "That's where Little Wolfpup comes from."

"You hear all that shit, and that's the only fucking comment you make," Kaiser scoffed. "Scuse my language," he added, looking at me sheepishly.

"I've been around," Beck replied vaguely. "Apart from Shae's, what did you call it? Gift? Well, apart from that, which is pretty weird by the way, there's nothing there that surprises me. Except maybe for the fact that you ended up working with that Fleet Super-Prick."

Jake chuckled, but when I looked his way, he held his hands up innocently and mouthed, "What?"

"Come on, Ash, we know all that," Ty said impatiently, "Get to the good stuff."

"Ty," Jake said in a tone that left Ty physically recoiling.

"My bad," he apologised. "Please continue."

"It's fine," Ash said. "But to be clear, this isn't good stuff." The shift in mood was almost palpable, and a serious hush descended. Ash told them about the lockdown and the lie we'd been told about Jake and Jared. He told them about Finnian's message, and his hint that things weren't what they seemed, but he left out everything else. He didn't mention that Finnian said I was some kind of key, or that my life was in danger if people knew who I really was – and he certainly didn't mention the Harbingers or the Helyan Codex. That wasn't for general consumption yet. He mentioned finding the manuscript page, and it matching the piece I had, but stopped short of saying what was on it. Finally, he mentioned the hidden data on the central computer.

They were mostly silent, but when Ash talked about Luke arriving that first night, Jake couldn't keep quiet. "Who do you think that guy really is?" he asked.

"No idea, his file was classified."

"Do you know what his mission was?" Jake pushed.

"We know he was there to find the scroll. But he sure as hell wanted Shae as well," Ash confirmed.

"He said Noah didn't have control of the situation and that's why he was there," I added. "He told Noah to stand down and he'd deal with things."

"He ordered a Primus?" Jake marvelled. "I thought the only person above a Primus was the Supreme Primus."

"Us too. Beats me," said Ash, rubbing his temples vigorously. I felt his pain through the Link, and I knew it wasn't from the hangover.

"He wanted to take me away from the monastery," I remembered. "He said they shouldn't have tried to keep me in the dark. What was the word he used, Ash?"

"Compliant," he confirmed grimly.

"Compliant? Fuck me," Jake exclaimed. "I mean, what the hell? I'm… I'm actually speechless."

Ash finished off the story, explaining to the Pack how we'd got Beck out of the Basement, and why we'd ended up with the *Nakomo* squawking a roach coach transponder ident.

"You're running dark now, though?" Jake checked.

"Affirmative."

"Fuck me," he repeated.

10

The mood in the camp felt heavy as everyone digested the information in their own way, oblivious to the fact that Ash had left out huge chunks. Rendezvousing with Jake and the Pack and having one night of normality before dropping the bombshell this morning seemed the right thing to do, but now all I could think about was Jared.

"You don't think contacting Jared's the right thing to do?" I asked, seeing the worry-lines cross Ash's forehead.

"Honestly, I don't know," he replied, his hand resting on his belt buckle. "Jake and the Wolfpack are REF, yes, but they work as an independent unit. They're not on the same kind of leash as a captain commanding one of the Fleet's most prestigious ships."

"But we're not wanted by the REF. The Constantine Agreement goes both ways."

"That's a stretch and you know it," Ash replied. "What do you think would happen if the REF High Command knew about you and what you can do?"

"Come on, Ash, now you're stretching. Enough people have seen what I can do. It would be ridiculous, irresponsible even, for us to be that naïve. Chances are, they already know. What they're going to do about it is the unknown variable."

"Okay, I know you're right," he conceded. "But if you contact Jared and tell him what's happened, you know what'll happen next. He'll move heaven and earth to get to you."

"What's the alternative?" Jake said, appearing from the bushes. "Sorry, didn't mean to eavesdrop. Look, you know me and Captain Fantastic don't exactly see eye to eye on a lot of things, hell, most things to be honest. And I sure as shit wouldn't mind having you all to myself for a while." He smiled, and I was touch by the genuineness of his affection. "But think about it. At best, he thinks you're on a top secret, hazardous mission, with your life in danger and nothing he can do about it. At worst, he fears you're already dead, and that's why the Brotherhood have gone radio silent. I can't believe I'm actually saying this, but do you really think it's fair to keep him in the dark?"

"Don't look at me. You know how I feel about Jared," I said, the pain in my chest like a knife as I caught the wince on Jake's face. "I'm way too emotionally invested," I continued as Ash reflected on Jake's words. "I'd fly the *Nakomo* to him right this second, if I thought it was safe."

Ash laid his hand gently on my shoulder and looked purposely into my eyes. "Every part of my training tells me it's too risky to bring Jared in on—"

"But—"

"Let me finish, Shae. Every part of my training tells me that it's too risky to bring Jared in on this, for him, just as much as us. But... that feeling... I can't shake that feeling that we need him. You know what I mean, Shae, I know you do. It's just like when you knew Beck should be here, and Cal."

"I know what you mean, too," Jake said unexpectedly.

"You do?" I replied.

He sighed, looking perplexed. "Scares the crap outta me

to be honest. But ever since I met you, both of you, I just keep getting these weird, unexplainable feelings. Like it just feels right when were together. I mean, how else can you explain how much you meant to me from the second we met. Shit, even I know I sound nine kinds of crazy right now."

"You think Jared feels the same way?" I asked.

"I know he feels the same way, babe," Jake replied. "We can contact him from the *Veritas* on secured coms. It'll just look like one of our normal check-in."

"Wait, you and Jared actually talk to each other… voluntarily?" I joked, lightening the mood slightly.

"Yeah," he confirmed sheepishly. "I may not always agree with Super-Prick… Hey! And Ouch! No punching, I'm trying to be nice here." His green-flecked eyes crinkled. "But I can empathise with what he's going through because I've been there myself. And it's hell. The only difference is, I know you're safe now, and you have no idea what kinda weight that's lifted."

"Come here," I said, pulling him into a hug. "And you," I added, holding out my hand to Ash.

"Umm, really?" he replied.

"Just get in here," Jake ordered.

"Is this an 'anyone can join in' kinda thing?" Beck's voice broke the reverie, and the two men took an awkward step back.

"No," Jake grunted, and I noticed his voice had deepened. "It's a family thing. Fuck off."

"Easy, dude, I was just coming to tell you the AG42s are stowed away. The blond guy? Connor's his name?" I nodded. "He said to tell you there's a localised weather front coming in fast. It ain't gonna last long, but we don't want to be out in it. The guys are packing away the camp now."

"Acknowledged. Tell Connor to baton down the ship, we'll be there in five," Jake ordered.

"Yeah, whatever," Beck mumbled before turning on his heals.

"And tell him to ready the anchors, just in case."

"I don't work for you," he shouted back over his shoulder.

"And we can leave your arse on this rock," Jake called back.

Beck raised an arm and gave him the finger.

"Maybe he's the Super-Prick," Jake said, and I laughed, even though I knew I shouldn't. "You sure we need a scroat like that around? Don't tell me… it's feelings thing. Anyway, back to business. Are we contacting Jared or not?"

"We are," agreed Ash. He'd barely finished the words before I'd pounced on him. "Okay, okay, you can stop hugging me know. I just wanted to make sure we were making an informed choice – seen as we're making it for Jared as well."

"Great," said Jake. "Maybe you can tell both of us all the shit you left out earlier."

The only thing that gave away Ash's surprise, was a momentary squint of the eyes and the slightest tilt of his head, but it was gone quickly. "Maybe we will," he said, clapping Jake hard on the shoulder.

Dry, russet leaves were already whipping around my legs by the time we'd got back to the *Veritas*, momentarily reminding me of the storm back on Lilania. I shivered involuntarily.

"What's up? You good?" Jake asked.

"Memories," I explained. "That's all."

The camp had completely disappeared, not a sign we'd even been there except for a patch of scorched earth from the fire pit. Everyone was back on the ship except for Kaiser, who stood like a sentry at the bottom of the ramp. "Hey, boss," he said as we approached. "Connor says we can take off before the weather hits, or ride it out. He thinks it'll last a few hours maybe. And Ty said to tell you, if we stay, he'd like to do a provision run to the market we saw on the outskirts of that town we flew over. Says we could do with re-stocking the perishables while we're here."

"We don't know our next move yet, so there's no point taking off until we know where we're going," Jake said. "We'll stay here... for the moment. Lock it up, Kaiser."

The ramp was half-way raised by the time we'd got to the top, and I leant against one of the Rover's huge tyres, closing my eyes. "It's good to be back," I said listening to the gears grind to a halt and the locking bolts clank into place.

"Jake, we need Ty," Ash said, causing Jake's eyes to narrow. "If it's okay with you, we'd like to take advantage of his tech skills?" Jake looked like he was about to ask a question, then instead, he tapped his compad.

"Ty, where are you?" he asked.

"Weapon's storage," Ty replied. "You need me?"

"Yeah, meet us on the flight deck, asap."

"Sure, boss."

Jake held out his hand and let me through the hatch to the flight deck first. "You've had some upgrades," I noted, perching on the arm of the pilot's chair.

"A few since the last time you were here." He smiled, as if he were remembering some things of his own. "After Fallen Star, we were ordered to Carmare for repairs. She was in bad shape following our encounter with Fletcher, but on the upside, we got a few extra bells and whistles for our trouble."

"She looks good," I said.

"She sure does," Jake replied, not taking his eyes from me.

"Hey." Ty stuck his head through the hatch. "What can I do you for?" he added, looking a Jake.

"Fucked if I know," Jake replied, looking more intrigued by the second. He nodded to Ash, signalling for him to take over.

"We need your tech skills," Ash said.

"You mean my tech awesomeness… my tech genius… my—"

"Shut it, Ty," warned Jake.

"Sorry, boss. Carry on, Ash," he said magnanimously, a grin lighting up his face.

"We need you to decrypt this," Ash said, holding out a data-disc. "I said earlier that the data from the *Nakomo's* mission logs seem too perfect, and I found evidence of hidden data on the Monastery mainframe."

"Oh, don't tell me," Ty marvelled. "You got a copy?"

"Yes. It's heavily encrypted, way beyond my rudimentary skills, but should be a cake walk for a tech genius." He handed over the disc, but I could feel the hesitation through the Link.

"Ty," I added to get his attention. "This is serious."

"Shit, I know," he replied, looking at it with the same level of awe he regards my Cal'ret.

"No, I don't think you do," I continued. "What you're holding there is Brotherhood information. No one, and I mean no one outside the Brotherhood has access to this. Whatever you find on there… whatever," I reiterated, "you need to keep top secret. We're trusting you, Ty. You can't mention it to anyone, not even the others – our eyes only." I indicated the four people on the flight deck. "Do you understand?"

A new level of seriousness descended over Ty's face. "I understand," he said. "You guys can trust me."

"Top secret," Jake reiterated.

"Got it," Ty responded. "Should be a cake walk. I'll get back to you shortly." He left and the three of us stood in reflective silence for a moment.

"So?" Jake said after a moment. "We doing this, or what? You mind?" he said, brushing past me, and I stood to let him sink into the pilot's seat. "You don't have to move on my account," he teased. "Plenty of room for you too."

"Thanks, but I'll stand," I offered, as Ash took the navigator's seat.

It wasn't long before we were connected to the *Defender*, and I felt the butterflies fluttering in my tummy. It'd been over a month since I'd left Jared on Decerra and had imagined all sorts of horrors happening to him, and Jake, on their fictitious mission since. Now I was about to see him, I felt nervous and giddy.

"*Veritas*, this is the *Defender*, what can we do for you today?" an authoritative voice said through the speakers.

"*Defender*, this is Colonel Mitchell." It seemed strange to hear him use his rank. "Patch me through to Captain Marcos."

"Greetings, Colonel Mitchell. Please hold if you will."

"They're always so damn formal… and polite," Jake complained.

"Colonel Mitchell." The slightly melodic voice was unmistakably Commander Tel'an's. "I apologise, but the Captain's in a meeting in his Stateroom. I can ask him to contact you back when he's finished; should be in about an hour or so."

"Unacceptable, Commander," Jake replied calmly. "I need you to interrupt the meeting and inform him I need to speak to him urgently."

"Colonel, I—"

"Commander, Jared will want to take this coms." Jake's voice had taken on a seriousness even Tel'an couldn't ignore.

"Let me see what I can do," she replied.

We waited as a few minutes ticked over, then my stomach flipped as Jared's voice filled the *Veritas'* flight deck. "This better be good, Jake." His voice hinted at irritation, but also interest.

"You still in your Stateroom?"

"Yes."

"Alone?"

"Yes. What the hell's going on, Jake? This is sketchy, even for you."

"Stop being an arsehole for just one second," Jake grunted. "Can you go secure vid-coms?"

"Wait, okay, done. You want to tell me what's going…" his sentence hung and his mouth dropped open for a second before I watched a mix of relief and delight burst across his face. "Shae…" It was all he could say, but I felt my insides warm, and my cheeks pink. He stood there for a moment, his eyes on me, that boyish grin fixed in place. I was overwhelmingly happy to see him there on screen after all this time, but it was tinged with sadness, knowing I was lightyears from his touch. Ash coughed loudly and Jared blinked slowly, as if waking himself from a sleep. "Ash…"

"It's good to see you, my friend," Ash replied.

"You too, Ash. I can't tell you how relieved I am to see you both… unbroken, as Shae would say. I have a million questions. Where are you? I'll bring the *Defender* to rendezvous with—"

"No!" Jake, Ash and I all chorused together, leaving Jared looking even more perplexed, and if possible, hurt.

"Are you sure this line is secure?" asked Ash.

"Of course," Jared replied, sitting again. The worry etched on his face made him look older. "Please, will someone tell we what's going on, I'm imagining all sorts of things here."

"My apologies, Jared," Ash said, "but we really can't be too careful. You'll understand shortly." He started the story he'd told by the fire pit earlier, but when he got to the bit about Finnian's message, he said, "We'll come back to that detail later," before carrying on. Later, when he told Jared about the manuscript page, he added the details about the symbols being writing. For Jake's benefit, we discussed the Helyan Cube Jared and I had seen in the Catacombs below the Palace of Palavaria, and how the symbols matched the parchment, my pendant and the carvings on Tartaros.

"Fuck me," Jake said, rubbing his stubble. "The King is in on this, too?"

"We don't know how he's involved," I said, "but he has the cube, and he was willing to let us all die to keep it a secret."

"He also gave us a Royal Order not to discuss it with anyone, not even each other," Jared added sternly.

"Don't be a dick," hissed Jake.

"I'm not being a… I was just trying to add weight to the fact that the King was trying to keep the object secret, not chastise Shea for talking about it."

"Oh, well being a dick is kinda your default position, so I just assumed…"

"We're getting off track," Ash advised. "The point is, you're both right. By possessing the cube, and issuing an order not to discuss it, the King is indeed involved. To what extent, is yet unclear. Let's continue."

"All that's left is the data-disc?" Jared asked, still trying to digest everything.

"Yes, and this," I confirmed, pulling out the pendant from under my shirt. "But only because I was wearing it at the time. The manuscript page – both parts of it – the vid-disc from Tartaros and the message from Finnian… all gone."

"Go back over what Vanze said on Tartaros," Jake asked.

"He said the cube holds some kind of energy, and whoever controls it, has great power," I recalled.

"It makes no sense," Jared added. "That cube was maybe five by five. It'd fit in the palm of your hand. How much energy could it hold?"

"I don't know," I confessed, "but it sure made my insides vibrate."

"It did?" Jared said, ignoring Jake's childish chuckles. "You haven't mentioned that before."

"We weren't supposed to talk about it, remember? And

after we got back from Tartaros, we didn't have any time before…" I trailed off, trying not to think about the ache in my heart as we walked away on Decerra. "The point is the cube affected me on a physical level."

"This is just crazy" Jake said. "And for god's sake, will you sit down? You're making me uncomfortable." He shifted over in the seat giving me plenty of room to perch back down on the arm, but I hesitated.

"You should sit, Shae. We could be here for a while," Jared said, and I know why he did. Not that I needed his permission, but knowing he was okay with me being so close to Jake, made me more comfortable, so I sat. "What else did Vanze say?"

"He asked what my pendant does, and what it says. These swirly things are apparently some kind of writing. He mentioned a codex, and he thought I knew the location of something called the Amissa Telum."

"Just a bunch more 'what the fuck?' things to add to the growing list," Jake mumbled. "Also, let's not forget those super-scroats, the Khans, and that mysterious fucker, the Outsider, both wanted it – to the extreme they'd infiltrate a royal palace. We're not the only ones who know about it, regardless of the King's ridiculous Royal Order." He took a deep breath. "So that's everything we know so far until Ty decrypts the data-disc," Jake concluded.

"Um, not exactly," Ash said, all attention back on him.

"There's more?" Jared asked.

"How much more could there be?" added Jake, looking just as dumbfounded as Jared.

Ash told them about the full content of Finnian's message, and when he'd finished the two men sat in stunned silence. I looked down at Jake, who opened his mouth a couple of times, but couldn't find the words. In the end, he simply took my hand and held it to his chest.

"We're going to help you get to the bottom of this, babe. You're family." He swivelled the chair so he could see

Ash as well. "Both of you. If people are coming for you, me and the boys will stop them, and if finding the Harbingers is what you need to do next, then we'll be right there by your side."

"I know I speak for both of us when I thank you for your offer, Jake, but we can't put you in danger. Ty decrypting the data-disc is as much as we could ask for," Ash said, and I couldn't stop the weight of foreboding knocking down the Link. It took my breath away for a second, and Jake squeezed my hand, looking up at me, his face etched with concern.

"I'm okay, just a little Link overload," I explained. He released his grip, and I tactfully removed my hand, glancing guiltily at Jared on the screen. It pained me that he was so far away, and I knew that he'd feel helpless – a feeling he detested more than anything else.

"I meant every word. And you didn't ask," Jake continued, oblivious.

"You have no idea what that means to both of us," Ash continued. "However, I can't ask you to speak for the rest of the Pack. Even if we don't share the full details, they should know the seriousness of the situation, and that this isn't a mission sanctioned by either the REF or the Brotherhood. We could end up being hunted by both sides."

"I guess that keeps thing interesting," Jake responded, but I noticed Jared had fallen quiet.

"Ash, why don't you and Jake go and talk to the guys. It's not just our lives at stake anymore."

"That's a good idea," Ash said kindly, looked purposely between me and Jared. "Come on, Jake, there are five other souls who need to make their own choices here."

"Five?" Jared repeated.

"You two go, I'll fill him in," I pushed. Jake rose reluctantly, and when he brushed past me, it was closer than he needed to be. He stopped and kissed me on the forehead, leaning down to whisper in my ear.

"Whatever happens, I'm here for you." His breath was warm and the inevitable goose bumps skittered across my skin. He sighed and straightened up. "Remember that," he added.

Once they were out of the room, I got up and shut the hatch before sitting in the pilot's seat, still warm from Jake's arse. I'd waited so long to see Jared, to speak to him, but now we were alone, my words stuck in my throat.

"This is killing me," Jared said, opening a floodgate of tears. He sighed deeply and I felt his pain as strongly as any feeling through the Link. "Please don't cry. I wish I were there to wipe your tears away."

"If you were here, there wouldn't be any," I replied though sniffles. "I'm sorry," I said quickly, realising that just added to the pain. I rallied myself and used my sleeve to dry my cheeks, the odd rogue tear defying me.

"I need to say something," Jared told me. "But I don't want you to start crying again."

"I can't promise anything." I tried to smile. "Though, if it's anything like what I need to say to you, then I'll survive. Please say it."

"I've missed you." My breath caught. "I've missed you like I never thought I could miss anyone," he continued. "I've beaten myself up so many times for letting you go that day, I've lost count. And every day since Noah told me you were uncontactable on some top-secret mission, I've worried something would happen to you. I love you, Shae, I should never have let you go. But now, you're there... with him... and I'm here."

"I'm sorry Noah lied to you, and I'm sorry you've carried that worry." I laughed unexpectedly. "Though should remember that I'm awesome on missions, so you really had nothing to worry about." I laughed genuinely, and the boyish smile returned to his face. "I understand how you felt though, it was no different to when Noah told me you and Jake were on a mission."

Jared chuckled and it sounded beyond amazing. "There was your first clue something was up – me and Jake on an op together? Like hell!"

"Not going to lie, that did cross my mind, but rumour has it you two are kind of besties now."

His chuckle broke into full-on laughter, and it took him a while to get himself under control. "Besties? Not exactly, but we did share a common goal, and that allowed us to bury the hatchet... for a while." He was still smiling. "I'm glad he found you."

"So am I," I replied. "But Jared..."

"Yes."

"Part of me wishes you'd never let me go that day either. A very large part of me, in fact," I clarified. Emotions flicked across his face too quickly to read. "I love you too. And that doesn't change because I'm here... with him... and you're there." He opened his mouth, but I carried on quickly. "Honestly, we didn't know whether to coms you or not."

"You what?" he spluttered.

"I mean, I wanted to. I would've done it in a heartbeat, but you said it yourself. You're there, captaining one of the most prestigious ships in the Fleet, and we're here, possibly about to go up against the Brotherhood, the REF, and the Monarchy – a bloody trifecta." I laughed sadly. "You can't bring the *Defender* into this without the REF knowing. And how can I ask you to leave your ship, and possibly disobey direct orders, not to mention get yourself killed."

"Shae, just knowing you're alive and safe makes me immeasurable happy. But knowing you're going through all of this shit without me by your side pains me more than you know." He thought for a moment. "I'm glad you're with him," Jared concluded.

"You are?"

"He loves you. Clearly not as much as I do, though."

The boyish grin appeared. "I know he'll do anything to keep you safe. And so will the Pack, Little Wolfpup."

"Don't you start on that," I huffed.

"Which brings me to my next questions: Five?"

I laughed. "Cal's joined the Pack."

"I thought he might've. Jake mentioned something previously which made we wonder. And the fifth?"

"Ah yes, the fifth…"

"I know that look."

"You do?"

"Yes. It's the look you get when you need to tell me something you don't think I'm going to like. Don't tell me Beck's still with you?"

"Okay, I won't tell you, but then I'd be lying by omission."

He sighed and pinched the bridge of his nose. "So now I've got to worry about that arsehole getting his ape paws on you as well as Jake. This is hell."

"Jared, Beck's a harmless cantooa," I said, but he snorted. "He's just chancing his luck, that's all."

"So he has tried something. I swear to god if that tattooed bastard has laid a hand on you…"

"Jared, it's fine. Nothing's happened, and I can handle myself. Do you really think Ash is going to let anything happen to me? Or Jake, for that matter? That's one thing you don't need to worry about." I thought about how the conversation was going with Ash and Jake, and it was if Jared knew what I was thinking.

"I know you have to go," he said. "I need time to digest everything as well. There's so much. I'm sorry you're going through all of this."

"I know you are."

"I need to act like nothing's changed here, at least for the moment. Unfortunately, that means I have meetings and stuff going on for the rest of the day. We're picking up a D'antaran trade delegation in a few hours to take them to a conference in the Western Agricultural region near Chartreuse." I caught the shudder.

"Do me a favour and stay out of No Man's Land this time. I don't want to add another beast-hunt to the list of things I have to worry about."

"You can count on it."

"Good."

"Listen, I have to schmooze the visitors at some cocktail event tonight that Tel'an arranged. God, you know how much I hate those things. Anyway, I can coms you after if it doesn't end too late."

"I don't care how late it is, promise you'll call?"

"I will. And Shae? Stay safe, you hear?"

"I promise."

11

I just caught the tale-end of the conversation with the Pack. "So, there you have it," Ash concluded. "I'm not going to lie, things could get dangerous, and they'll probably put us at odds with your superiors. I won't think..." he saw me lurking in the hatchway, "we won't think any less of you if you want to walk away, but this is the time to do it."

Jake stepped forward. "Wolfpack, this is a decision that each one of you will need to—"

"I'm in," said Kaiser, not even waiting for Jake to finish his sentence.

"Me too," added Ty, without hesitation.

"And me." Cal raised his hand.

"It's not a Pack party without all of us," concluded Conner.

Pride radiated on Jake's face, but then it darkened. "What about you?" he practically grunted, and all eyes shifted to Beck. He remained silent, thinking.

"This isn't your fight, Beck," I said, walking around the Pack to be nearer to him. "You barely know us, and we seem to have caused you nothing but trouble since the day we first met."

"That's true enough," he replied, and I wasn't quite sure if it was said in recognition or anger. He stood and the rest of the guys eyeballed him as he paced, until he eventually stopped and crossed tattooed arms across his chest. "You're right; this ain't my fight."

"No, no, it's his decision," Ash said, trying to calm the outraged comments from the Pack. "That's what we said – no recriminations. It's Beck's decision, and we will all accept it with… grace."

"Grace, my shiny black arse," growled Ty. "No, you know what? That's the best decision. We don't even know this arsehole. Good riddance, I say. Better off without him." I guess the Pack thought Ty had said it all because they got up and dispersed after that.

"I've disappointed you," Beck said as I joined him.

"Of course not," I replied honestly, though I couldn't shake the nagging feeling we needed him. "Ash wasn't lying when he said we won't think less of you. In fact, it takes a strong person to go with his heart, even if that puts him on a different path to everyone else."

"We blew up your life on the Ridge and put you in the Basement for helping us. You owe us nothing," Ash pointed out. "We need to work out our next steps, but let us know what we can do to help you. You can stay on Dennford if you like, or we can drop you off at the next commerce planet we pass, and you can jump a ride from there to anywhere you want. Also, we can't give you much, but we can give you some credits to get you started."

"Appreciate the offer," he replied, clearly preoccupied with his thoughts. "But like I told you before, the bar ain't everything I got."

"Ash, Shae," Jake bellowed from the other side of the cabin.

"Be right there," Ash called back, then he refocussed on Beck. "Just let us know what you need, okay?"

Beck nodded, but then he reached for my arm as I

turned to join Jake. "You mind," he said to Ash, indicating that he wanted to talk to me.

"Of course," he agreed. "Don't be long," he added to me.

Beck paused long enough for Ash to walk away, then he turned his full attention to me, a look of surprising intensity on his face. "Leave with me," he said quietly, but I laughed. "I'm serious. Sack it all off and walk away." I stopped laughing. "I'll take you away, somewhere completely different, where no one knows you. I'll keep you safe."

"I can't," I replied, touched by his intentions. "There's too much at stake here. And, well, there's something I haven't exactly told you."

"Really?" he questioned sarcastically.

"Captain Marcos—"

"Super-Prick," he corrected.

"Jared," I continued, ignoring him, "and I are—"

"For fuck's sake, please don't finish that sentence. I think I vomited in my mouth a bit."

"Beck! Fact is, I can't leave. But I don't blame you for wanting to."

"Shae," Jake bellowed.

"I've got to go," I told Beck. "Like Ash said, just let us know if you want us to drop you off anywhere."

Jake shut the hatch to the flight deck. "What did Beck want? Don't tell me, he wanted you to run away with him," he joked, but I didn't laugh. "Wait, the fucker did, didn't he?"

"Relax, Jake," Ash waded in. "Beck's harmless; a chancer. He knows he's not going to get anywhere with Shae, and to him it's just banter."

"Banter? Sure. Whatever. He's off my boat first opportunity," Jake replied. "Okay, I've gotta be honest, my brain is still blown from everything you've told us. You've had more time to digest this, what do we tackle first?"

"Tartaros is destroyed, and Khans are dead," Ash

started. "The vid-disc is missing, as are both parts the manuscript and Finnian's message to Shae."

"There's also zero chance the King is going to even talk to us about the Helyan Cube, let alone let us see it," I added.

"So, the only tangible thing left then is Shae's pendant and the encrypted files from the monastery mainframe?" Jake asked.

"Yes," Ash replied grimly. "But I'm hoping Ty might be able to get something useful of the disc."

"And in reality, we also have Finnian's message," I offered. "We may not have the actual disc, but I've watched it so many times, I practically know it word for word."

"You're right," Ash conceded. "Though honestly, a lot of what he says just opens up more questions. However, the one completely clear instruction he gives, is find the Harbingers. It's the only path I can see here."

"So, that's our next step," concluded Jake. "We find the Harbingers. Just one thing... who the hell are the Harbingers?"

My shrug matched Ash's. "Do you think any of the others will have come across them on their travels?"

Jake reached over and pressed a button. "Listen up, anyone who knows anything about a group of people called the Harbingers, come to the flight deck immediately. Ty, report to me asap." He pressed the button again, before swivelling his chair back towards me. "Don't worry, babe, we've got the best people on it. We'll find them."

"And what if we do?" I asked. "What if we actually get to talk to them, and they don't know anything? Or won't share anything? What then?"

Jake opened his mouth to answer, but a knock on the hatch changed what he was going to say. "Enter."

"You yelled?" Ty said.

"Yes, where are you on the decryption?"

"I'd be further along if I didn't keep getting

interruptions," he replied, but a look from Jake wiped the grin off his face. "Sorry, boss. I'm making progress, but the encryption is far more complex than I was expecting. Not being funny, but that's some serious high-level shit, and way more than your standard Brotherhood encoding."

Ash raised an eyebrow. "I don't even want to know how you would know what Brotherhood coding looks like."

Ty looked guilty for a second. "Yeah, probably best not to ask," he confessed.

"Can you crack it or not?" Jake asked, impatience getting the best of him.

"Boss," Ty replied, wounded. "This is me you're talking to. Of course, I can crack it. It's just gonna take a little longer than I expected."

"Fine, but I've got another task for you as well. I need you searching the Data-Net for the Harbingers. Can you search REF files without it looking like us?"

"Sure. I can spoof another ships id, easy peasy. A search algorithm should—"

"I don't care how you do it, Ty. Just get it done."

"Leave it to me, boss. No problem."

"Excellent. Dismissed."

"So now we wait?" I asked.

"No," replied Jake, scratching his stubble and breaking into a smile. "Now we go shopping."

"Shopping?"

"Yup. No point in sitting here, sucking recycled O2 and twiddling our thumbs while Ty works his magic. As soon as this storm blows over, we might as well take the opportunity to get some fresh air and restock the perishables while we can."

The market seemed much bigger on the ground than it did from the air, and the tented stalls were even more vibrant. The late afternoon sun shone down through canopies, bathing the ground in reds, oranges and yellows, almost no sign a storm had blown through earlier. The air was thick with aromatic perfumes mixed with herbs and spices, and I started to breathe through my mouth as a matter of self-preservation. It wasn't a bad smell, but it was pungent, and my stomach still churned from the previous night's impromptu session with the Pack. It irritated me that Jake looked unaffected as he chatted amiably with street vendors.

Street performers played catchy music, and bright fabrics lay draped over make-shift frames. An Other chatted excitedly to a couple looking to buy a length of gaudy cloth, and I made the mistake of flicking through the colours nearest to me as something to do. His eye immediately shot in my direction, followed by a few weird clicking noises with his tongue. From nowhere a child appeared, an expectant eye wide and shimmering a magnificent shade of jade.

"Beautiful this for beautiful lady," he squeaked, tugging out the red and gold material before slinging it effortlessly over my shoulder for someone of such small size. "This just fifty," he continued as I tried to pull it off, but by that point he'd wrapped it around my waist.

"It's very nice, but—"

"Forty-five," he interrupted. His smile was sincere, and his dimples were so damn cute he was almost impossible to say no to, but what the hell was I going to do with it. Needlework wasn't exactly in my skillset.

"Really, I—"

"But beautiful lady deserve beautiful things, yes?"

"She absolutely does," replied Jake, appearing at my side. "But not today, thanks." He untangled me from the material, before smoothly wrapping his arm around my waist and leading me away. "Making more friends, I see," he joked. "Do you ever go anywhere without drawing attention?"

I thought for a moment. "Normally, wherever I go, I

end up making enemies." Jake raised an eyebrow, as he led us down a different row of stalls. "The Brotherhood's Warrior Caste isn't normally called in unless our skills are needed. It's not like we do a lot of socialising."

"Then, when this is all over, I'm going to take you somewhere." We changed direction. "Somewhere just because. No missions, no bad guys, no fighting – just relaxing, and cocktails, and dancing…"

"Dancing? I've seen your moves, remember? I've got to admit, it does sound nice, but also very far away. What is it?" Jake was still smiling, but his body had stiffened, like he was suddenly alert.

He pulled me into a full body-hug and lowered his head. "Don't react, but we're being followed," he whispered, before nuzzling my neck. Goose bumps covered my skin as he moved a hand behind my head and stroked the back of my neck.

"You sure?" I whispered back. His other hand had found its way under my top, his thump gently caressing the small of my back.

"Two of them. Damn this no tech, no weapon, rule. One male at my three – multi coloured robe, head covered, but check out the boots. The other, female, at my seven pretending to check out the raish on the plant stall." He spun me around, just like two lovers enjoying each other's company, and I saw what he had already seen. I was angry with myself for not picking up on the threat, and it's as if Jake knew what I was thinking. "They're good," he said kindly. "If I hadn't been unwrapping you from the fabric back there, I wouldn't have seen the guy's boots. After that, it was obvious when they followed us."

"So that's why we kept changing direction. Jake, I know why we're so close, but if you want me to think clearly, you need to stop what you're doing with your hands."

"Would you prefer this?" he asked, removing both hands to cup my face. His lips were warm and soft, and for a moment I was back in the *Veritas* on Decerra, and my insides tingled. Before I could stop myself, I kissed him back. I tried to tell myself it was to keep up the ruse, but the truth was, I liked it. Jake pulled away, looking deeply into my eyes for a moment before pulling me back into a full body hug. I felt his sigh on my skin. "No tech equals no coms, so we've got no way of telling the others what's happening. We need to get back to the rover, without making it too obvious."

We separated from our hug and Jake slipped his arm around my waist again while pretending to look at some earthenware on the nearest stall. "Where should we go now?" I asked, loud enough for others to hear.

"Me? Well, you know where I'd like to take you right now, babe," he replied laughing, while squeezing my backside gently.

"Jake I—"

This time when Jake spun me, it wasn't gentle, and I stumbled into a stall, knocking henta fruit tumbling to the floor. The bullet just missed me, a large, ripe hemlon exploding next to my head. I heard a second shot, but it was the third that hit my left shoulder, the pain so excruciating I thought I was going to black out. I tried to push myself off the stall, but my left arm wouldn't cooperate, and my vision blurred from tears of agony. There was a fourth and fifth shot in quick succession, but all I could do was slump to the floor, and when I was able to wipe my eyes, I saw Jake grappling with the woman. The man lay in a pool of blood, already soaking into the earth.

Most of the locals had scattered, but a few had remained, watching the fight with a mix of fear and intrigue. As guns weren't allowed on Dennford, the scene was a rarity. My shoulder tingled and started to itch, but even through the fog of pain, I could tell there was something very wrong. With a wound this severe, I would normally be glowing bright enough for everyone to see, but nothing had distracted the locals from the fight.

I watched Jake land a formidable punch to the side of the woman's head, and she fell, hitting it again on the corner of the plant stall. He didn't pause for a second. He quickly came to me and pulled me off the floor, supporting my weight as my legs collapsed. "I'm sorry, but we've gotta go," he said apologetically, dragging me along. "I think there are more of them." His voice was distant and muddled as I tried to stay conscious through the pain.

When I came too, it took a moment to focus on the room around me. Jake was hunkered down by a window, peering out through a small slat. But when he heard me groan, he came straight over, helping me sit up. I was in agony.

"Babe, what's going on? You're not healing." He paused as a wave of pain ran through me. "What can I do? Shit." He ran his hand through shaggy hair before placing it on my cheek. "You're burning up, and you've lost too much blood. Why aren't you healing?"

"I think... I think there's something still in my shoulder," I said through gritted teeth.

"How can that be? I thought your body expelled foreign objects."

"It does, but—" The pain stopped me mid-sentence and Jake's eyes burned with fear. It took a moment for me to be able to talk again. "It feels like there's... Jake, you've got to get it out, please. Please," I begged. "It feels like it's getting deeper. You have to... get it—"

I knew I was supposed to be quiet, but I couldn't hold the scream in. It literally felt like someone was drilling into my soul before everything went black.

The next thing I felt was a gentle stroking of my forehead, and it felt comforting... calming. I still hurt, but it wasn't nearly as bad as before, and when I opened my eyes, the room was bathed in silver blue.

"What happened?" I asked, noticing that as my light

disappeared, the room darkened into soft shadow.

"Shit, Shae, don't frighten me like that," Jake ordered. "I haven't been that scared since Tartaros."

"I'm sorry," I replied.

"Hey, it's okay, I didn't mean it." He pulled me gently closer, and I rested my head on his shoulder. "It wasn't your fault. God damn it, I should've been more vigilant."

"It wasn't your fault either," I said.

"No? I told you I'd keep you safe. Great fucking job I did."

It wasn't long before I was able to clearly focus, and the wound was completely healed not long after that. I rotated my arm, checking for any lingering pain.

"Where are we?"

"Someone's house. Looked empty, so I took a chance. We needed to get off the street."

"What happened out there?" I asked again, brushing bits of hemlon fruit off my clothes. "Why didn't I heal? And what the hell did they shoot us with on a so-say weapons free planet?"

"I hate to tell you this, but it wasn't me they were after, babe. They were after you. I was just in their way. And this is what was in your shoulder." He carefully held up a mangled, large-gauge bullet, the small, pointed spikes covering the outer surface, still trying to rotate.

"I've never seen anything like it."

"Me neither," he confessed, looking even more concerned. "As our resident weapons expert, I'll get Connor to look at it when we get back. We've just got to get to the Rover without running into any more of those merc bastards."

"Who were they?" I asked.

"No clue. But they've sure got a hard-on for you."

"You really think I was the target?"

"Yes." He didn't need to say anything further.

I sat heavily in a nearby chair as my legs threatened to

give way. Jake was kneeling in front of me in a second. "But why?" I asked, looking deep into his dark, worried eyes.

"I don't know," he replied quietly. "But you can guarantee, where there's two of those fuckers, there'll be more. Hey," he touched my cheek gently with the back of his fingers, "look at it this way, we've got through worse situations than this, babe."

"True," I conceded. "What's the plan?"

"Well, thanks to the whole 'no tech' deal on this backwards planet, we've no weapons other than a blade each, and no coms. So we can't call in reinforcements."

"Those mercs sure as shit had weapons," I challenged, flexing my shoulder as if to make a point. "How did they get those into the marketplace?"

Jake scraped a hand though his hair. "No clue. But we have to assume, if they did, others could've as well." He pulled the curtain back slightly and peered outside. "The sun's almost down. At this point I don't know whether that's going to help or hinder us. What I do know, is we're going to miss the rendezvous back at the Rover if we don't move soon."

"What are you looking for?"

"Something for us to wear," he replied, rummaging through a wardrobe before pulling out an ankle-length, hooded shawl. "Put this on. It'll help you blend in."

"What about you?" I asked, wrapping the brightly coloured garment around me.

He rummaged a bit more before huffing with disgust. "You think this suits me?" he grumbled, holding a smock the colour of raish-yellow up against himself to check sizing. I couldn't help laughing. "One word," he warned. "Not one word, you hear."

"My lips are sealed," I said, but my shoulders shook as I tried to stifle a laugh.

Just before he opened the front door, he stopped and looked deep into my eyes to make sure he had my attention.

"It's almost dark, and the alleyways are in shadow, but we're going to have to go back through the market to get to the Rover. We don't know who, if anyone, is still out there trying to get to you, so at this point, we have to assume that everyone is." I nodded my understanding. "But we also can't draw attention to ourselves, so we're going to have to act as naturally as possible. Like just a normal couple out for a stroll through the market. You okay with that?" I nodded again. "Okay. Keep your eyes open, but try not to make it too obvious, yeah?"

"Jake?"

"Yes."

"You do remember I'm a trained field operative, don't you?"

Jake smiled and shook his head. "Sorry, babe. I just can't have anything happen to you. It makes me a little crazy. I didn't mean to…" It was my turn to smile.

"It's alright, I understand. Let's get it over and done with, shall we. Then you can take off that truly ridiculous shirt and I can start taking you seriously again."

"You had to go there, didn't you?" Jake grumbled as we walked out into the back street.

When we reached the edge of the market, there was a line along the ground where the darkness of the ally reached the bright lights from the stalls. Jake took my hand and paused us in the last bit of shadow. "You ready?" he asked.

"Let's do it," I replied.

"Okay. Game face on," he said as we both stepped into the light. The smile on his lips wasn't mirrored in his alert eyes, and although he looked relaxed, I knew he was anything but. After a few minutes, he pulled me closer, bending his head so he could whisper in my ear. "You alright?"

"All good," I replied, but I had a knot in the pit of my tummy I couldn't ignore.

I was anxious to get back to the Rover, back to Beck

and Ash who I knew would be waiting, but Jake tightened his grip, slowing me down. He steered me towards a table to rummage through some crockery before continuing. All the while, we small-talked about beautiful patterns or freshness of the produce, but we kept our eyes on the people around us.

About two thirds of the way through the marketplace, we came to an open arena, where street performers played cheerful music, and a mass of locals danced and twirled in a frenzy of blurred colour.

The place was heaving – happy, carefree people flowing to the rhythm – so packed it was difficult to move. We carefully navigated our way through the crowd, but there were so many people, it was difficult to watch all of them for threats. It was also impossible for us to remain walking side by side, so Jake took the lead.

"Stay close," he said loudly over the music, but as he did, his hand was torn from mine. I watch in cold fear as he was bundled away by two or three people, it was difficult to tell through the crowd. I tried to follow, pushing people out of the way so I could see him, but it was like the crowd had swallowed them up.

Through a brief gap, I saw Jake being pulled up a side ally, the coloured lights glinting off knife steel.

I tried again to get to him, but by that point the tide of people had swept me along with them. I managed to turn, but at the same time I felt a punch to the guts, followed by a hot sting deep in my stomach. I looked up into the face of a hooded woman, but then she was gone, disappearing into the melee of people.

At first, I didn't understand what'd happened, but as I moved the shawl out of the way, a red patch seeped through my shirt. My hand covered the wound, deep crimson running between my fingers, but the pain was so much deeper. No longer able to fight the crowd, I got swept along, stumbling and grasping out at people to keep my balance. I didn't see the threat coming again, but I felt the second wound worse than the first – this one on my side, just under the ribcage.

I floundered, my legs giving way, but then there was a gap in the wall of people, and I reached out for the edge of a stall. I'd clamped a hand to my stomach, the other to my side, but it still felt like white-hot pokers were twisting my insides. Deep red oozed from the hole in my tummy as I took my hand away long enough to assess the wound. A faint silver-blue glow tinged the raw skin around the edge, but I wasn't healing. My legs buckled from the excruciating pain, and I fought to stay conscious.

The stall-owner immediately came to my aid, calling to others as she did. Within seconds, I was surrounded by people, all fussing and trying to figure out what'd happened. Through my tears, I watched two hooded men step out of the crowd, and head towards me. I tried to stand, asking the stall owner for her help, but she seemed confused and kept trying to get me to sit back down again. The pain took over, and I couldn't resist her.

When the men were only steps away, I closed my eyes and waited for the inevitable, but then I heard muffled grunts and the shuffling of feet on earth. I finally managed to open my eyes, grateful to see Ash and Beck, but fearful for them at the same time. I tried to stand again, only this time it was easy, too easy, and my head swam again.

"I've got you," Jake said as he lifted my feet off the floor and carried me quickly from the fight. Over his shoulder, I tried to watch the others, but the gap closed as people flocked to see what was going on. I turned to look at Jake, registering the black eye already turning a quite beautiful shade of deep purple. My head swam.

I think I was in and out of consciousness, but I certainly felt it as Jake hoisted me into the back seats of the Rover and I cried out.

"I'm sorry, I'm sorry," he repeated quickly, searching for

a light. He tried to move my hand out the way, but I fought him. I knew it was irrational. I knew he was trying to help, but I couldn't take my hand away. "I'm sorry," he said again as he grabbed my wrist. "What happened?"

"I don't…"

"Shae," He rubbed my cheek and I forced open my eyes again. "What happened? What weapon did they use?"

"I don't know… a knife I think… it was so quick. I thought you'd… where's Ash?"

"Shh, don't talk." He tried to climb over the back of the seat to the rear of the Rover, but I held out my arm and grabbed his shirt.

"Don't leave me."

Jake stopped and bent down, giving me a brief kiss on the forehead. "I'm not going anywhere, babe, but I need to get the med-kit, okay?"

"Okay," I said weekly, closing my eyes again.

It only seemed like a second later that I opened them again, but it must've been longer. Ash and Beck scrambled onto the back of the Rover, ducking bullets, and Jake tossed them weapons to return fire, the noise deafening as I lay on the back seat. I looked down. My shirt had been ripped and field dressings had been stuck to my side and stomach, but it wasn't the puncture wound that worried me. It was the weapon still drilling into my insides.

"They're still in me," I cried, as Jake threw himself back over the seats towards the front. He looked confused. "Like the bullet… still in…" He held the side of my face in his palm for a second, fear aging him.

"We need to get you back. Hold on."

The roar of the engine momentarily drowned out the weapons, but then it seemed distant, like it was far away from me.

The Rover bucked and bounced as Jake raced us back towards the *Veritas*, and I tried not to cry out. He kept turning to check on me, or to make sure I was still alive, his face telling me how bad it was. I held up a hand to reassure him I was okay, but it was slick with blood, so I don't think I did a very good job.

Jake's voice was loud and urgent as he spoke into the vehicle's coms. "No, I haven't got time to explain, Con. Just do what I fucking told you to do: prep the *Veritas* for emergency dust-off and tell Ty to get the med-bed ready."

12

My eyes felt heavy and uncooperative, my whole mouth dry like sandpaper. I felt someone shift beside me and take my hand, but as much as I tried, I couldn't get my eyelids to open. Ash picked up my hand, intertwining our fingers and it felt warm and comforting. I finally managed to open my eyes.

"Hey, Ash," I croaked. He opened a flask and passed it to me, and in the dim light I saw his worry.

"Careful. Not too fast," he said, as water spilled down my chin from gulping it back. "And before you ask, you've been out for a while. Everyone's safe. And Jake is currently talking to Jared."

"Jared? Have I been out that long?"

"Long enough."

I moved the blanket out of the way and lifted my top, looking down at my tummy. Nothing but smooth skin with not a blemish in sight. The same with my side. My eyes narrowed as I watched Ash's face. "What aren't you telling me? And, where are we? Where's the *Nakomo*?"

Ash smiled, but it was tinged with concern. "So many questions," he tried to joke. I gave him my serious look and he held up his palms in surrender. "We're on the *Veritas*."

"I know that, Mr Obvious, I meant…"

"I know what you meant." Ash sighed. "We're in space, heading…well, I'm not quite sure where – I'm not even sure Jake knows. And the *Nakomo* is still on Dennford." I gasped, surprised we'd left her behind. "Don't give me that look, Shae. We didn't have time to get her ready to fly. I got Kaiser to grab our stuff and lock her up tight. We barely made it back here in time."

"I don't understand."

"Thankfully."

"What does that mean?"

"It means you nearly didn't make it. Whoever was after you at the market, chased us all the way back to the ship."

"Is everyone okay?' I asked, sliding off the med-bed, noticing the large black holdalls lined up on the floor.

"Nothing for you to worry about," Ash replied too causally, causing me to stop checking the tags on the bags and turn to look at him.

"Ash…?" It sounded like a warning. "Tell me."

"Beck got winged – nothing too serious. He'll live. And Jake took a pretty bad beating when they, whoever they are, dragged him away from you."

"Jake thinks it was me they were after the first time, when I got shot by whatever the hell that thing was. You don't agree with him, do you?" I challenged, pulling on a fresh top.

"Actually, I do," he replied after a pause, but as he was about to say more, Jake appeared through the hatch.

'Thank god you're awake," he said drawing me into a careful hug – which was more to do with his pain than him being worried about mine. "It was pretty hairy there for a few minutes."

"Jake," Ash warned.

"What? She deserves to know. I bet you haven't told her, have you?"

"I haven't had the opportunity," Ash replied.

"You can't keep protecting her, Ash. She deserves to know. If you keep her in the dark, you're no better than the Brotherhood."

"Whoa now, dial it back, Jake," I waded in. "It's not like—"

"He's right," Ash butted in, surprising me. "My default position has always been to protect you... but I won't keep you in the dark," he added purposely, glaring at Jake. "You need to know. I really just hadn't had the opportunity to say anything." I looked between the pair of them and huffed, trying to ignore Jake's mashed up face and the fact he was holding his ribs gingerly.

"Okay, so spill," I suggested. "Now's your opportunity."

"I'll start," Jake said. He picked up a tray from the side and slid it on to the bed next to where I'd perched. He used tongs to hold up one of the objects so we could all see it. "You told me your body expels foreign objects, right?" I nodded. "This is the bullet I dug out of your shoulder after the first attack." I looked closer and nodded again. "You see these tiny little spines?"

"They were moving last time. Rotating," I said.

"You're right, they were. We think these tiny spikes are designed to keep the projectile burying into you so you can't expel it. I had to use a knife to get this one out. Thankfully, you'd already passed out by that point, because it took some digging." I flinched and he returned the bullet back to the tray.

"What about those two?" I asked, pointing to the long thin objects on the cloth.

"The same type of thing," Ash said. "Same barbs, same function, only these were delivered by some kind of knife that left the... I don't even know what to call them."

"Shafts... sticks...rods?" Jake offered.

"All of the above? Anyway, you were stabbed with something that then left these spiked rods inside you."

"As quickly as we tried to remove them, they seemed to bury in further," Jake explained. "It's like once they were in, the spikes stuck out inside you, tearing up your insides as we tried to pull them out. If it wasn't for your ability to heal, we would've lost you for sure." He ran his hands through messy hair as silence filled the room. "And there's more. If that wasn't bad enough, they also excreted some kind of neurotoxin we haven't been able to identify."

"And you still think I was the target, Jake?" I asked.

"Babe, I'm sorry, but without doubt. And that's not the most worrying thing..."

"What? Tell me. You were the one that said not to keep me in the dark.'

"We think the weapons were designed specifically for you," Ash said, causing me to suck in air which made me choke.

"I'm okay,' I spluttered as Jake tapped my back. "Keep going."

"Connor's our weapons specialist, as you know," Jake said. "What he doesn't know about weapons isn't worth knowing, at least until now."

"What does that mean?" I asked.

"Connor's not seen anything like these, and he's up on all the latest weapon designs. He says it's like whoever designed these knew about your abilities," Jake continued, his hand now drawing calming circles on my back. "Like they knew how you healed, and then tried to make a weapon that would specifically combat your ability to do just that. If we hadn't been there to help you…"

"I could've died. Really died. As in dead dead," I finished for him. I looked between Ash and Jake, and they shared the same worried expression. "Well, I didn't die. I'm okay. But you're not, Jake. Hold still," I said, reaching out to him, but he backed away.

"I think you've done enough for today," he said gently, taking my hand in his.

"Since when has that been your decision to make? You know the rule: no more business until everyone's fixed. And that means you… and Beck. So, hold still." I placed one hand on his cheek and the other felt his muscles stiffen as I slipped it under his T-shirt and rested it on is ribs. A couple of minutes later, he was totally healed, and I tried my hardest to hide how weary I felt.

We found Beck in the main cabin, sporting an un-impressive field bandage. I knew Wolfpack was capable of doing so much better and wondered if this was some sort of retribution for him not coming on the journey with us. It didn't really matter, there was no need for it after I'd healed the wound. I stood back to inspect my work, but in an instant Beck had drawn me into one of his now legendary vice-like hugs, complete with arse squeeze as he put me down.

"Okay, okay, that's enough," Jake grunted, but Beck just laughed. He let me go and Jake stepped between us, chest puffed out and a deep frown lingering. "The only reason I don't have you thrown out an airlock right this second, is because you helped back on the planet. But don't for a second think that gives you a free fucking pass to do whatever the hell you want on my ship. You read me?"

"Sure, whatever," Beck replied. "I'll be out of your hair the next decent planet we come across."

"I suggest we get back to business," Ash said as the two men continued to scowl at each other.

"Of course," Jake said, sitting casually by my side. "Where do you want to start?"

"Probably with who those fuckers were," Beck replied, winning himself another glare. "You don't happen to know, do you Jake?"

"Why the fuck would I know?" he replied.

"Well, from what I saw, you got closer to them than any of us did… while you were getting your arse handed to you."

"You li—"

"That's enough!" Ash bellowed, causing everyone to stop in their tracks. Jake seated himself again, and the rest of the Pack backed away from Beck – who's bravado looked a little shaken. "Beck, stop being antagonistic arsehole, and remember you're here by Jake's good graces." Jake smirked silently. "And the rest of you should remember, as Jake has already acknowledged, Beck did help back at the planet." A few mumbles accompanied some reticent nods. "Good. So, does anyone know who we were dealing with back there?"

"I didn't see much," I offered. "But if I had to guess, I'd say the woman who first stabbed me was Ethileron, or possibly an Other with a fair amount of Ethileron genes."

"Ethileron? Don't see too many of them this deep in sector," Kaiser said. "Those guys give me the willies." He shuddered for effect. "Hey, don't laugh at me until you've had to fight one of those devious, grey, ninja-fuckers," he warned as Ty and Connor sniggered.

It was actually good to laugh, and the banter settled the room into a more conducive atmosphere. When the Pack had stopped teasing Kaiser, Jake asked, "What was the woman like, babe? The more you can tell us the better."

"Like I said, I didn't see much. It all happened so quickly, and my focus was trying to get to you. People were pushing and shoving all over the place. I guess I felt the knife first, though it felt more like a punch followed by a stinging deep inside my tummy, and then another in my side a bit later. I only really saw her face for a second. She wore a long, hooded cloak that came low over her face, to her eyes." I showed on my own face with a hand that shook slightly. "Her eyes were black, soulless. That's the thing I remember most. And her skin – that chalky, white-grey colour stretched over a thin, almost skeletal face." It was my turn to shudder, lost in the memory.

"Did she have any tattoos?" Jake asked. "Babe?"

"Huh?"

"You zoned out for a second."

"I'm sorry."

"You have no need to be sorry." Jake's voice was soft and calming. "You look exhausted." He touched my forehead with the back of his fingers. "And you feel hot. Maybe we should finish this in the morning." I caught the anxious glance he gave Ash.

"I concur," added Ash, his own eyes searching my face. "Tomorr—"

"I'm okay," I said, taking his hand in mine. "I'd rather get this finished. Jake?" I turned and took his hand in my free one, feeling his anxiety lesson slightly. "I'm sorry, you asked a question?"

"Did she have any tattoos?"

I paused, thinking, and I felt like I was wading through treacle to find the answer. "Possibly," I said eventually.

"You don't sound too sure, Blue," Kaiser said.

"She had something... markings under her eyes, which ran towards her temples and then up over the top of her eyebrows. I thought they were part of her makeup, but... I guess they could've been tattoos."

"Can you describe them?" Jake asked, now rubbing the back of my hand gently with his thumb.

"Sure, they were..." It was harder to remember than it should've been, and Jake was right, I felt exhausted. I took strength from the warmth of Ash and Jake's hands and dredged up her face from my memory. "They were strange, silvery in colour, but now I think about it, they were raised slightly, like keloid scars."

"Was each marking similar lines and dots, but in different designs," Jake offered.

"Yes, how did you know?"

"Because the two that shot you during the first attack, and the group that pulled me away from you during the second, all had the same type of markings. One was definitely part Rhinorian," he rubbed his ribs, "one was Santian, another, Human, and the rest were a mixed bag. But the one thing all of them have in common, were the tattoos – or scars – or scar tattoos. Put your hand down, Connor, this isn't the fucking academy. What is it?"

"From what you've all said, there were at least six people who managed to get never-before-seen weaponry into a strictly no-weapons-allowed community, right?" We nodded. "And all six were different races or mixed Others?"

"Is that a statement or a question, Con?" Jake said.

"Ethilerons loath Santians," he continued. "They look on them as animals, insects even. Humans feel the same way about Rhinorians, and Others don't tend to have any affiliation other than what will benefit their needs at the time. Yet they not only shared a similar branding, but they also worked together, as a team, to try and kill Shae. Don't you think that's significant."

"He ain't wrong," added Beck.

"I'm not done," replied Connor, not even trying to hide the animosity in his tone. Beck sat back and motioned with his hand that Connor should continue.

"Just ignore the loser, Con. What are you getting at?" Ty asked.

"Like I said, whoever it was who came after Shae at the market, was organised enough to get weapons in. And I think we can all agree they weren't locals, so—"

"Whoa, oh, oh, oh, I see where you're going with this C-man," Ty interrupted, looking triumphant, like he'd just solved a thousand-year-old puzzle. But then his grin disappeared just as quick.

"Am I the only one who doesn't understand what's going on here?" I asked, too tired to be annoyed.

"Someone explain. It's too late for this shit," Jake barked.

"Sorry, boss," Connor said, taking control of the

conversation again. "But I think we've got a problem."

"Of course, we've got a problem, Con. Someone's trying to kill Shae, just as she's managed to escape the clutches of the bloody Brotherhood. No offence," he added to Ash.

"None taken," Ash replied graciously.

"That's not the problem Connor's referring to," Ty offered.

"Then for fuck's sake, Conner, just tell us what's put a bug up your arse," Beck interjected.

"Fine," Conner replied, taking offence. "If the rest of you would just stop fucking interrupting, I might be able to get there." He took a breath while everyone waited with bated breath.

"This better be worth it," Beck whispered loudly.

"When the *Nakomo* left Angel Ridge, she had the transponder of a Roach Coach," Conner stated. "Ash had previously removed and discarded the tracking module, and Beck's mate had re-modified the sequencer in the engine so it would no longer show up on any Brotherhood scans. So do the maths. If the *Nakomo* was completely off the grid, how did the bad guys find Shae on Dennford so quick?"

"They must've followed us from the Ridge," I suggested.

Connor shook his head. "Did you see anyone with scar tattoos there?"

"Can't say I noticed anyone fitting the description," Ash said.

"And even if they were there, there's no way they followed you out," Connor continued. "You only just made it through the defence grid in one piece, and when you jumped to FTL, there was no way anyone would be able to follow... So how did they find you on Dennford, when you got there via a completely untraceable shuttle?" It wasn't lost on me that he emphasised the word 'you'.

"What you're saying is impossible," Jake said, letting go of my hand to run his hand through his hair. He stood and paced while everyone else watched silently – even Beck. "You're saying it's us who's being tracked? We have the transponder of a trade ship that randomly modulates to stop this exact thing. You really think it's us?" he asked Connor.

"Only explanation I can think of."

"Okay, here's what we're going to do: Connor, cut the engines. I'm not going another light year without knowing for definite if it's us. Then I want you to check for any rogue transmission coming from the flight deck, engine, and propulsion areas. Ty and Kaiser, check upper areas including the cabin, kitchen, upper storage areas and weapons locker. Cal and Beck, you've got main cargo bay and lower storage lockers. Ash and I will check living quarters and all the other areas not allocated. And Shae, for the love of God, please go to bed. You can barely keep your eyes open."

I was going to object, but to be honest, I didn't have the energy. He held out his hand and pulled me off the seat and I yawned, using his muscular body as a resting post.

"What are you all waiting for? A formal fucking invitation?" Jake bellowed, causing a blur of instant activity.

It was Jake who pulled up the sheets and tucked me in, but Ash stood at the end of my bed, on guard.

"I really feel like I should be helping," I said, but I wasn't sure if I could get up again once I was cosy. "And I really don't want to take your bed from you, Jake."

"I think you've helped enough today," Ash said kindly, and I let my mental barriers down just enough to let his love warm my insides.

"And I'm not getting into an argument about bunk allocation," Jake said.

I could have argued, but in all honesty, I'm not sure I stayed awake long enough to even see them leave the room.

I woke naturally, no alarm or wakeup call. Jake's room was still in darkness, and though I listened hard, I couldn't hear anything either. I was tempted to close my eyes, as sleep was only moments away, so I checked the time to see how long I could realistically have before the rest of the Pack would be up.

"Oh shit. Shit, shit, shit," I said to myself, sitting up and rubbing my eyes. "Lights." The time on my compad almost mocked me as I jumped out of bed before grabbing a towel and heading to Jake's private washroom.

"Look who's awake," Ty said as I entered the main cabin, my hair still damp, and my skin glowing from the shower – which had two settings: ice cold and lava hot.

"Why didn't someone wake me?"

Kaiser strolled passed. "Seemed like you needed to recharge the batteries, Blue," he said. "Jake told us to wake you up for lunch. I was just about to head down now."

"Where is he?" I asked, looking around. "And Ash?"

"They're both on the flight deck," Ty replied. "They've been holed up in there all morning. I managed to do that thing you wanted me to do. I think they're looking at it now… and she's gone," I heard him say as I left the cabin, heading for the flight deck. Unusually, the hatch was shut, and when I tried the handle, it didn't budge. I knocked, and when I say knocked, it was more like hammering.

"Who is it?" Jake's voice sounded scratchy through the intercom.

"Who the hell do you think it is?"

The bolts clunked as they retracted, and the hatch creaked as it opened. "Afternoon," Jake quipped. I'm sure he thought he was being charming – he wasn't.

"Ash, I can't believe you're looking at the *Nakomo's* mission logs without me," I huffed, looking between the two of them as they both shared the same enigmatic smile. Then Ash's smile broadened.

"That's 50 credits you owe me, Jake," he said before laughing. "And you thought she wouldn't be pissed if we took a look at the data without her." Jake shrugged as an acceptance of his defeat, but then his laughed mirroring Ash's. The whole thing just made me even more annoyed.

"So?" I demanded.

"So, what, babe?" Jake replied unwisely.

"So… did you look at it or not?"

"Of course, we didn't," Ash said, probably feeling the blast wave about to head his way through the Link. "Did you really think I'd do that to you? After everything we've been through."

I thought for a moment, cold logic replacing fiery assumption. "No," I conceded. "So, what have you been up to all this time? Ty says you've been in here all morning."

"We've been looking for these Harbingers Finnian told you to find," Jake said, sitting back in the pilot's seat and swivelling it to face the console. He pressed a few buttons and a series of pages appeared one at a time on the front screen. There were so many, they overlapped each other to the point the whole screen was covered in multiple layers of pages stacked on top of each other.

"These all mention the Harbingers?" I gasped. "All of them?"

"Actually, all of them and none of them… not exactly," Ash clarified, but it just made me feel more confused. I turned to look at him, searching his face for clues to whatever it was he meant. "This is what you get if you search the Data-Net for the Harbingers." He waved his hand at the screen. "The search brings up anything from omens to portents to… well, anything that sounds like a prediction across all species."

"Which is just about everything to some extent," clarified Jake. "Hence the massive data-dump you see on the screen. We've tried to narrow it down, making the assumption were looking for two or more people, from any race, who have been around for a while."

"Why those criteria?"

"Finnian refers to finding the Harbingers, plural, hence

the two or more people," Jake explained.

"And these people, and I'll use people in the loosest term, as we actually don't know what they are," Ash chipped in, "must've been around for a while, as all the data and evidence we've seen goes back a long, long way. You just have to look at the carvings on Tartaros to know that."

"So, what do you get with those criteria?" I asked.

"This," replied Jake, pressing a button. The front screen momentarily cleared of data, then a second later, filled up with thousands of documents again. "From what we've sifted through so far—"

"Which is a minute fraction," Ash added.

Jake continued as if he hadn't been interrupted. "There's references to lore and folk tales, children's stories and rumours – across many species, religions and customs. Some refer to Harbingers as great seers, others as evil, used to scare children into being good. It's impossible to tie our search down to the one specific group we're looking for. I hate to say it, but it's a damn shame we don't have the *Defender's* Oracle."

"Could we?" I asked. "Is it feasible to ask Jared to do the search for us?"

"I'd love to say yes, and technically that's the correct answer," said Jake, scratching the stubble on his chin. "But if we ask Jared to do anything, or use any of the resources at his disposal, there will be an audit trail and the REF will find out."

"Is that a bad thing?" I challenged. "I mean, the REF isn't after us, just the..." I trailed of catching the unmistakable glance of unease between the two men. "What?"

"It was us," Jake said cryptically.

"What was us?"

"Not you; the *Nakomo* was clean. It was us." He held up a piece of tech I didn't recognise, his expression flicking through anger, betrayal, and pain. "We brought those merc bastards to you on Dennford. I couldn't protect you in the market, and now I find it was us that made it possible for them to find you in the first place." He slammed the tech on the console.

"Jake, it's okay. I'm—"

"It's not ok!" he snapped. "I'm sorry, I'm sorry, I didn't mean that. Please, I didn't mean to…"

"Stand up, Jake," I said. He looked confused. "Stand up." He looked to Ash, who shrugged his shoulders. "Do I have to ask again?" I said gently. He stood and I held both his hands in mine. The little crinkles around his concerned eyes looked slightly less tanned than the rest of his face. "This is not your—" He opened his mouth and I let go of one of his hands to cover it before he could say anything. "This is not your fault." He gently took hold of my hand and removed it from his mouth.

"We brought them to you," Jake replied, his tone now gentle. "If anything had happened to you…"

"It didn't. Well, it did, but I'm okay – thanks to you and Ash, and the Pack."

"But—"

"But nothing, Jake. No harm's been done, and the way I see it, we have more insight into what's going on now than we did before Dennford."

"What do you mean?" Ash asked, concern seeping through the Link.

"Well, we know that someone was able to get a tracker onboard the *Veritas* without Jake or the Pack knowing."

"Rub it in why don't you?" Jake commented, but when I turned to chastise him again, is eyes sparked.

"And that tracker," I said, carrying on regardless, "was to alert a group of mercs – all of whom share the same weird scar tattoos – to my doorstep. If we are still assuming they were there for me and not you, Jake."

"They weren't after me, babe," he admitted. "I wish they were."

"Okay, so Shae's right," Ash said. "This is all new information. The *Veritas* was tracked, seemingly to find and kill Shae. And there's a group of people, from all races, coordinated enough to carry out an armed attack using weapons in a tech-free zone."

"And those weapons seem to be specifically designed for Shae's unique physiology," added Jake. We all fell silent, digesting the information.

"I take it that thing isn't working anymore," I asked to break the silence, nodding towards the tracker.

"No. Ty's had a look at it, and it's some pretty damn sophisticated shit," Jake explained. "Want to guess which sadistic bastard we know made it?"

"I'm going to go with Jesper," I replied, shaking my head.

"Bingo. That guy's still screwing with us, even though he's a kebab."

"So, we know who made it," Ash stressed, bringing us back on track. "But how did it get onto the *Veritas*?"

"That, my friend, is a damn good question," Jake said, his anger flaring again.

13

Ash and I sat quietly, waiting for Jake's anger to subside. I couldn't blame him for his fury, after all, I'd felt the same way when Jared bugged the *Nakomo*. Like it was a violation.

When he'd calmed himself sufficiently, he said, "As part of our security protocols, we sweep the ship at random intervals. A deep-sweep is also done on any ship entering REF facilities to make sure we're not bringing in any computer viruses, trackers, data-bombs – that kinda thing. The *Veritas* was swept just before docking at Carmare for repairs. I saw the results myself; we were clean. So, either the tracker was onboard already, and someone faked the results, or, more likely, the tracker was attached to the *Veritas* while we were on shore leave waiting for the repairs to be completed."

"But you said Carmare is an REF repair station," I challenged.

"I know."

"But that means…"

"I know," Jake repeated, sitting heavily back in the pilot's chair. "Just what the hell is going on? The Brotherhood is lying, and clearly knows more than it's letting on, and the REF is keeping secret tabs on us, that results in an attack on Shae by unknown assailants. All this since Fallen Star. Did we do something on that mission? Something that has led to this?"

"Actually, I think something was going on before that mission," Ash commented. I looked to Jake, but he seemed as confused as me. "When did we first meet Jared?"

"Angel Ridge," I replied. "He was there with his troopers to round up some stolen weaponry. You're not trying to tell me he's in on whatever the hell is going on, are you?"

"No, at least not intentionally," Ash said, but I felt more confused. "The meeting on the Ridge was chance, I believe that to be true. But meeting up with him on GalaxyBase 4 was coincidence?"

"We know it wasn't," I declared, probably angrier than I had a right to be, but I felt like Jared was on trial. "He was sent there to find out what we were doing, why we were on the Ridge, and who Nyan was. Jared said they wanted to know what was going on as an Agent of Death was involved."

"And that didn't seem strange?" Jake questioned. "That the REF would be interested in a drunk, who could've really just been spouting alcohol infused nonsense."

"A drunk that led us to saving the Four Sectors as we know them," I challenged back.

"But they didn't know that then. And it wasn't just about the drunk. You told me Jared found you on GB4 because he'd bugged the *Nakomo*."

"You don't know what your—"

"He's right, Shae," interrupted Ash. I glared at him, not knowing whether I was more angry or more hurt. "You've told me before that Jared didn't understand the orders he was given after Angel Ridge. He was ordered to bug the *Nakomo* and follow us."

"You're saying you think Jared is in on this – whatever

the hell this is?" I felt hot and angry, and sad and hurt all at the same time.

Ash stood abruptly and put his hands on my shoulders, waiting until I gave him eye contact. "Listen to me, Shae. I don't think Jared is in on whatever the hell this is. I think he was used, just as Jake has with the tracker here. I don't think he has a clue what's going on and is in the dark like we are. Come here," he said, wrapping a comforting arm around my shoulder. "All I was trying to say, is that it's now clear the REF has had an interest in you since that first mission report Jared sent in after the Angel Ridge fiasco."

"But what could've piqued their interest?" I asked, rubbing my eyes. "What could he have possible reported other than he recovered the weapons, lost the seller he was looking for, and then got into the mother of all fights with the locals. Oh, and a drunk was killed by an Agent of Death. I'm not sure what the REF could've possibly been interested in, unless they were intrigued by the fact there was a member of the Assassin Elite there?"

"You're missing one important fact," Jake said.

"And what's that?"

"You. You were there with two Warrior caste from the Brotherhood. You said Jared even had your ID scanned."

"So?"

"So, they knew you were there."

"I understand that. What I don't understand is why they'd be interested. They have my ident, it's not like they don't know I'm part of the Brotherhood."

Jake shook his head and rubbed his temples. "Honestly, I don't know, Shae. I'm clutching at straws, just like you. The REF knows of you, but up until that day, have you ever been idented?"

I thought back, wracking my brains. "No, I don't think I have."

"Then maybe that was the moment. Like you said, they know about you, but this was the first time you would have been on their radar."

"You understand what you're saying, don't you, Jake?" asked Ash.

He rubbed his temples again. "Yes. Yes, unfortunately I do." He tapped his com-pad. "Connor, please come to the flight deck immediately."

"What's going on, Jake?" I asked. "I don't understand."

"Give me a moment," he asked as he stepped around me to unlock and open the hatch. A moment later Connor appeared. "Con, I need you to do something that will cause you to have a lot of questions – which I don't have time to answer right now – but I will."

"Sure, boss, what do you need?" he replied, scanning his eyes around the group. "Discreet is my middle name."

"It better be," Jake said. "I need the *Veritas* to run dark as soon as possible."

Connor looked confused. "The tracker's been disabled, and we've checked and double checked – there are no other signals coming from us," he explained.

"There are two."

"Boss, I can guarantee, the only signals we're giving off are the rotating transponder and the REF tracker." Conner still looked perplexed. "There's nothing…" realisation cleared his forehead of creases, but his eyes widened. "You mean dark, dark?"

"Yes, Con, that's what I mean. Can you do it?"

"Of course. The transponder signal's easy – I've picked up a number in the past that the REF doesn't know about." He shrugged. "Never know when you're gonna need one."

"Good lad, Con. Knew I could count on you," Jake said, slapping him on the shoulder. "How soon can she be dark?"

"Like I said, the transponder's not too difficult – maybe thirty minutes. But the REF tracker? That's a completely different story. They're specifically designed to be tamper-proof in the case of pirates and hijackers. That little beauty's going to be a bitch. I can do it, but it's going to take a few hours. With Ty's help, I can probably half that."

"Get Ty to help. I need this done ASAP."

"I don't think you understand, boss. We need the engines off, so we'll be dead in the water."

"And…?"

"Once we start the process of removal, it will automatically send out a distress call – that's something I can't avoid. Any REF ship in the vicinity will home in on that beacon, and us. If we haven't finished removing it and started up our engines by the time they arrive, you'll be left answering some pretty awkward questions."

"Understood. I trust you Con. You and Ty. Do it and do it quick."

"On it."

Jake shut the hatch again and sighed deeply, rubbing his eyes. "Let's hope there aren't too many REF ships close by."

"We should leave, Jake," Ash said, standing. "This isn't your fight – yours or the Packs."

"Ash," Jake replied, placing a hand on his shoulder. "This has always been our fight since the moment we met on GB4. I guess we just didn't realise that until now."

"It's all my fault," I said, overwhelmed by the new information, but both men shook their heads. Jake placed his free hand on my shoulder and Ash did the same. We stood in a triangle for a moment until Jake let go and rubbed his head vigorously.

"Let's get one thing clear," he said. "That's the last time I want to hear anyone say this is their fault. You hear me?" he added pointedly as I opened my mouth. "You hear me?" he repeated, and I reluctantly nodded my head. "Good."

"This day is shaping up to be a day of revelations," Ash said. "The Brotherhood has purposely kept Shae isolated from everyone else, and in Luke's words, compliant. And I'm pretty certain they're doing everything in their means to get her back. Now we find out that the REF has been keeping tabs on Shae since that first meeting on the Ridge – to the extreme that they violated the Constantine Agreement by ordering Jared to track the *Nakomo*. And now we find out someone within the REF has also placed a tracker on the *Veritas*."

"Don't forget the fact that King Sebastian has at least some knowledge of what's going on," I stressed. "Why else would he be willing to sacrifice himself and Phina for that cube?"

"Shit just gets crazier," said Jake, pacing the flight deck, which was no more than a few steps wide. "Is it time to add even more craziness?" he asked Ash, flicking his eyes towards the data-disc sitting on the navigation panel.

"Why not?" said Ash. "Now Shae's here." He grinned unexpectedly. "You still owe me that 50 credits, Jake. I've not forgotten."

"Yeah, yeah, whatever. I'll wait outside."

"Where do you think you're going?" I said, catching the back of his T-shirt to stop him in his tracks.

"I thought you'd want to see it alone. Well, together, but alone. Just—"

"I want you here," I confirmed.

"You sure?

"Yes, I'm sure. Your family, remember?"

Ash slotted the data-disc into the reader, and all three of us seemed to hold our breath while data filled the screen.

"What are we expecting to find," Jake asked, skim reading the documents.

"We're looking for anything that relates to the *Nakomo's* true mission on the day that Shae was born," explained Ash. "The official reports say that the *Nakomo* was on a humanitarian mission when it picked up a distress call and was redirected to a transporter."

"That was the ship you were on?" Jake asked.

"Yes, well not exactly," I replied. "My mother and father

were passengers – the only people the Brotherhood were able to save." My voice wavered slightly. "My dad died on the *Nakomo*, my mother too, but only after giving birth to me. Finnian was there. He always told me they never knew the reason for the transporter's engine overload leading to its destruction. The ship was obliterated in the explosion and all data was destroyed. Finnian told me I was a miracle, being the only one who survived. But all data was lost in the explosion, so they didn't know who my parents were."

"I'm sorry," Jake said kindly.

"Thanks. I appreciate it, but," I shook off the sadness, "we're about to find out what really happened. Though, there's a large part of me hopes there's nothing to find."

It took some time to scroll through layers of data and information, but eventually Ash made me jump by saying, "Found it." I looked over and we locked eyes for a moment. "Last chance, Shae. We can close everything down and destroy the disc – no one would blame you."

"Or we can open it and find the truth, no matter how hard it is."

"Are you sure?"

I thought for the briefest moment, my heart pounding in my chest. "Do it," I confirmed.

It seemed like a lifetime later that Ash closed down all the logs and removed the disc. The flight desk had been eerily silent since Ash had opened the file, and now it was closed, we still sat there, not saying a word. I felt tears fall on hot cheeks, and when Ash leant towards me, I held up my hand to stop him. Jake sat on the floor, hands resting on bent knees. I sniffed and wiped my eyes. "Could I… could I have a moment alone?"

"Are you sure you're—"

"I'll be okay, Ash" I said, interrupting. "I just need a few minutes to myself. I need…" I trailed off, hurt and betrayal confusing my thoughts. I vaguely registered Ash stand up, and when he passed between the navigator and pilot's chairs, he touched my shoulder gently. I heard the hatch close, and I glanced around to make sure they'd both gone.

I was alone.

I cried. I cried hard. It was like a veil had lifted and I could see things more clearly. The years of lies and manipulation now revealed in the logs we'd just reviewed. It felt like I'd been physically wounded, only it wasn't a wound my gift could heal. I was broken and sad, and then I was angry. A swirling mass of energy roiled inside me, my skin glowed silver-blue, and the flight deck glittered as specks of blue and silver energy sparked in the air, some appearing and disappearing, others bouncing off the floor and walls. It wasn't until one landed on the nav-panel, overloading it and adding orange sparks to the blue, that I realised what was happening.

I concentrated on my heartbeat; it was way too fast. Deep breaths in. Deep breaths out. In… out… in… out. After a few moments, the light show dissipated, and the swirling mass settled to a sad churn in the pit of my stomach.

I don't know how long I sat there, other than it was a long time, but eventually the pain in my tummy came from hunger rather than betrayal, and I realised I hadn't eaten anything all day. I stood and stretched and wondered how much Ash and Jake had told the others. Somehow, I felt it was inevitable that I would learn the truth, though now I had, I was left with even more questions.

I left the flight deck and returned to the main cabin, surprised to see it empty. A noise from the small galley prompted me detour that way, and as I expected to see Ty, I was surprised to see Ash bent down with his head in a food locker. "Where is everyone?" I asked, making him jump. He hit his head on the locker as he stood up. "Ouch, that looked like it hurt."

"It's okay, it didn't," Ash replied with obvious bravado. He rubbed the back of his head gingerly and gave me lopsided grin which seemed tinged with sadness. "I'm not going to ask if you're okay, that would be a ridiculous thing to do, but… I'm here. I'll be here whenever you're ready to talk. Whenever you need me." Tears started to well, but I got myself under control. I appreciated that Ash tactfully ignored the few strays that managed to slip down my cheek. "You missed dinner. Sorry, I told the guys not to bother you. I hope that was the right thing."

"It was. Exactly right."

"Are you hungry?"

I smiled at him and nodded. "Starving."

"Ty plated you up some dinner. He said he's never known a time you've gone this long without either drinking coffee or eating ice cream."

"I used to think there were only two people in the entire universe that know me as well as you. Knew me, in Finnian's case. Seems that number might be expanding."

"Francis loves you like a sister."

"I know, which makes all this, this… shit, worse because we left him behind."

"You think we should've told him – not left him on Lilania?"

"No, we did the right thing. I feel bad enough I've thrown your life into chaos. I don't want that for him as well."

"You're not going to start blaming yourself for me again are you, because I seem to recall a conversation that very clearly laid out my position on that matter."

"I didn't say a word." I mimed zipping my lips and throwing the key over my shoulder, and he smiled as he put the hugest pile of rice something in front of me.

"It tastes amazing," he said. "But I think Ty got a bit carried away with portion control. You want me to stay, or be alone?"

"Stay, please." He sat and I leant over the table to touch his hand gently before attempting to make a dent in the mountain of food in front of me. "Where's everyone else?" I asked between mouthfuls.

"In the hold, training."

"What do they know?"

"They know our mission is to find the Harbingers. They must be out there. Somewhere. Finnian wouldn't have pointed us in their direction otherwise."

"Agreed. What else?"

"Jake told them about us running dark. Gave them all the same offer."

"What offer?"

"To be allowed to leave with Beck at the next commerce planet we get too."

"What did they say?"

"They said they were all in. To be fair, I think they would've agreed to it without knowing about the tracker, but when Jake told them it could only have been attached at Carmare, they were even more in. They want answers as much as we do."

"And Beck?" I still felt it was important he stay, but I would never make him, or guilt him into it.

"He stayed quiet. I don't think his plans have changed."

"That's a shame. Hey, I know we're moving, did Connor and Ty fix the REF tracker?"

"Yes, it's all good. We're off the grid."

I swallowed another spoonful of rice. Ash hadn't oversold the meal, it was delicious, and Ty was a culinary mastermind. "Do you think he's in the wrong business?"

Ash sat back, stretching until his shoulder cracked. "Who?"

"Ty. He could be a chef, have his own place. Cater for the rich and famous."

"I agree, he is a food genius. Anyone who can turn military rations into a decent meal is a magician, but I think he enjoys the day job more."

"Fair enough." It felt like a million questions were

swirling around my head, but one came to the fore. "Jared!"

"I don't think he wants to open a restaurant either."

I gave him my best reproaching frown. "I know that, dumb-arse. Last night, when I woke up, Jake wasn't there. You said he was talking to Jared. What's happened? Is Jared okay"

"He's fine as can be," Ash replied, covering the still significant amount of dinner that I'd left untouched. He popped it in the cooler and then opened another door, pulling out the unmistakable pink and cream ice cream tub.

"Chocamel?"

"Yeah, no, sorry – nuts about vanilla. Guess you won't be wanting any then," he said, leaning back towards the chiller.

"Don't you dare."

"Dare what?" Jake said, and I practically fell of my stool turning to see him. He lent against the bulkhead, arms crossed lightly, head tilted slightly to one side. He seemed uncomfortable, reluctant to step forward.

"I was just about to put the ice cream away," Ash said.

"No, he most definitely wasn't," I corrected. "Will you join us?"

"You sure? I don't want to interrupt."

"Please. Come sit. We were just talking about Jared," Ash said.

"Whoa, if we're going down that road, I'm outta here," Jake joked, pretending to leave the galley, but I caught his hand.

"Don't even think about it," I said, patting the stool next to me. Ash sat and slid the open tub in front of me, followed by a spoon for everyone.

"You know, I don't just share ice cream with anyone," I said, "But family's family." I slid the tub towards Jake.

"Shae was just asking about your vid-call with Jared last night," Ash explained.

"He called to speak to you," Jake replied, his eyes

flicking towards me. "Said you'd agreed to it."

"I did. He said he'd call for a sit-rep after he finished schmoozing the D'Antaran trade delegation."

"Yes, I'm sure it was a sit-rep he was after," Jake replied, his voice dripping with sarcasm. "Anyway, as you weren't able to speak to him, I told him what had happened."

"Everything?" I asked.

"Everything. At least everything I knew at the time. The tracker and Carmare, and the decrypted disc came later."

"So, he doesn't know about any of those things."

"Not exactly," Jake said cryptically. "I called him this afternoon. Once we disconnected the tracker, there was no way we could communicate with him without putting ourselves, and him, in jeopardy. I called him briefly before to explain what was happening, to tell him why we couldn't remain in contact."

My first reaction was of anger. Jake should've told me, given me the opportunity to have that last conversation, but I knew he was right to do what he did and leave me to digest the data-disc's information. "How was he?"

"Same old Super-Prick. I know, I know," he said, deflecting a punch that went his way. "He was as you'd expect."

"And the data-disc information," I asked with trepidation.

"I told him Ty had decrypted it."

"Not the content?" Ash asked.

"That's not my story to tell," he said, sadness creeping into his voice.

For a moment, nobody said anything, but I broke the silence. "Do we have a destination, Jake? We're obviously going somewhere."

"We are, and I do," he replied, the mood lifting. "We're going to Santorra."

"Santorra?" Ash and I chorused. Jake laughed.

"Yes, Santorra," he confirmed.

"Please don't tell me we're going anywhere near those lava pits," I practically begged. "You can smell that stink halfway around the bloody planet."

"Then you'll be happy to know we're going to the opposite side of the planet. To Vorden."

"Oh yes, that's so much better," I replied.

"Sarcasm aside, Shae's right. Why are we headed to a backwater shithole like Vorden?" asked Ash.

"Because that's where we'll find Glitch."

"Glitch?" I scoffed. "Is that a person or a phenomenon?"

"A person," Jake replied patiently.

"Who exactly is this Glitch?"

"He's a data scrubber. Buys and sells information to the highest bidder – the more classified or confidential, the higher the price."

"And you think he'll know who the Harbingers are?" I asked.

"It's as good a place to start as any," Jake said. "He's the next best thing after the Oracle on the *Defender*. Unfortunately, he's also got extreme agoraphobia and hasn't been seen outside of his citadel in years."

"Citadel? That's a bit excessive, isn't it?" Ash asked.

"Originally, Vorden was built by a faction of Scientia Corp for some kind of research project, but they left decades ago. Like a virus, the shit-sticks of the universe moved in, taking over. He who is richest, rules the city."

"He doesn't seem so bad," I said. "Considering the rest of the city's inhabitants."

"Glitch himself would probably shit a brick if any one of us got within the same room as him, but he is also off-the-charts wealthy and values his privacy. He's got a large contingent of well-armed and highly trained muscle, paid very handsomely to make sure people like us don't interrupt him."

"That's the beauty of data hoarding," Ash said. "You

can do it all from the comfort of your own self-imposed prison."

"Could Elliott and Reston get to him? Those aliases worked well on Independence and Genesis," I asked.

"Not even that would work with Glitch. We have two options as far as I see it. Option one is to walk in there and pay for the info, option two is a tactical assault to force the information on the Harbingers. If he has any. And just to help you with that choice, unless you've got a shit-ton of credits in those holdalls you brought with you, option one is off the table. As soon as we went dark, we lost all REF support – which includes access to discretionary funds."

"We've got credits, but not as much as you suggest we'd need," Ash said.

"Guess it's a tactical assault then. The guys are going to love this," Jake confirmed. At first, I thought he was being sarcastic, but one look at his face told me he meant exactly what he'd said. "Don't worry, babe, this is exactly what the Pack trains for. Plus, we've got Cal and Ash, and I seem to remember you're not too shabby yourself." He nudged me with his shoulder.

"I notice you didn't add Beck's name to the list," Ash commented.

"Yeah, well, I didn't ask him. He's made it clear he wants out. He's off my boat at Santorra whether he likes it or not. After that, it's up to him to get wherever the hell he wants to go. You got any different thoughts? He's already said he's not coming on our journey, so let him go, I say. Sooner the better – he already knows too much."

"It's your ship, Jake," I replied.

"But… you don't think it's the right call?"

"I don't know. Honestly, I don't think I know anything anymore."

"Hey," he said gently, putting an arm around my shoulder. "I get you like him, but if he wants to go…"

"I know," I replied, but that knot in the bottom of my

stomach tightened again.

14

On the way to the planet, Jake gathered us all in the main cabin. He seemed unusually serious as he waited for everyone to give him their full attention. "Before we start, has anyone other than me been to Santorra before?" There were a few noes, everyone else shook their heads. It reminded me of the briefing I'd given about Genesis during our last mission, and a cold shiver ran down my spine.

"Okay, listen up," Jake continued. "Santorra is the planet version of Angel Ridge, only worse. One half's covered in volcanoes and lava pits, where the air is toxic at worst, stinking like rotting corpses at best. The other half is scarred and pitted volcanic rock. This is where Vorden sits. Make no mistake, one side of the planet will try to kill you with fire and poison, the other side… well, it'll be the people trying to kill you – who, to make it clear, will cut off your head just for looking at them wrong."

"Well, that's as close to hell as you can get," I commented. "Why were you at Vorden?"

"Mission," Jake said before pausing. "Seems like a lifetime away." The way he said it told me not to question him further, at least, not then.

"If I may ask, Jake," Ash said, tactfully moving the briefing on. "Minus the volcanoes, it does sound very much like the Ridge. Why do you say it's worse?"

"As much as Angel Ridge is a shithole, it does have a level of order and authority provided by Dax and the Roaches—"

"Did," Beck interrupted.

"What?" Jake snapped.

"Did. It did have some order," Beck clarified. "Thanks to our friends here, I would say it's probably in absolute chaos right now."

Jake was annoyed at the interruption, but it was Kaiser who stepped in. "Who the fuck cares what you've got to say, fuck-monkey? You've made it quite fucking clear that you're not part of this, so shut the fuck up before I come over there and kick you in the nut-sack." He turned and caught my eye. "Scuse my language," he added, which just made me smile more.

"Kaiser, you really don't have to keep apologising. It's not like I haven't heard that and worse before," I said. His weathered cheeks pinked slightly, and he nodded his head briefly as an acknowledgement. Jake huffed.

"What I was trying to explain to Ash," he continued loudly, all attention back on him. "Is that Vorden has no rules, no ruler, and no sense of structure at all. It's a trading outpost for the dregs of the Sector – mercs, gun-thugs, criminals, and arseholes. The only respect on offer here is based on size of your—"

"Cock?" Ty suggested, to a round of raucous laughter.

Jake waited for them to calm, but I could almost feel the anger rippling under the surface. "I was going to say weapons or bank balance, but you could whip out your cock if you want and see what happens." Laughter again, and I couldn't help joining in. I looked down at my feet to hide it, but I'm sure my shaking shoulders gave me away. "I'm serious," he said, his voice grave. "I wasn't joking when I said they'd cut your head off – no order or structure means no consequence. There's only two ways you survive long-term on the planet, and that's by being the toughest or the richest. The city is carved up into factions, with each gang-lord trying to take over one of the others. This isn't going to be a cakewalk and we all need to be prepared. We can't pay for the information we need, so we're going to have to take it, and I'm not losing anyone on this mission. Understand?"

"Yeah, sorry, boss," Ty replied.

"That goes for everyone," Jake clarified.

"Jake, you're the only one who's been to the planet," Ash said, and his tone matched Jake's seriousness. "Have you been to the citadel?"

"Yes, but only as far as the main hall and Glitch may have made alterations since then. The building itself is reminiscent of old-Earth cathedral architecture, only bigger, and it's made from black volcanic rock, which makes it pretty damn intimidating to look at. It was built as a place of worship for the staff of Scientia. There's a layout of the city, tunnels and the citadel from those old days on Hermes, but as we know, we lost access to the REF's classified data-net when we went dark."

"I could get it," Ty said, "They wouldn't even know I was there."

"It's too much of a risk," Jake replied. "Anyway, we don't need to worry about the map, we need to concentrate on getting to Glitch."

"Are you sure," Ty pushed. "Won't take—"

"We concentrate on the tactical assault," Jake said as a holo appeared above the table in the middle of the group. You could almost feel the heat from the lava pits, and I scrunched up my nose. "This is the best image we have from the open Data-Net." He spun the planet with a flick of his hand and then stretched the image until Vorden was clearly visible. He wiped away the rest of the holo and settled the image of the city horizontally on the table. "This is where we're going to land, Connor." He pointed to a landing zone in the southern district of the city. "It will be a drop and dash."

"Seriously?" Connor moaned. "Again?"

"Sorry, Con, but I need you with the ship, and we can't leave it on the ground."

"But…"

"Have you ever seen a colony of fruit ants decimate a hemlon in, like, 30 seconds?"

"Okay, okay, I get it – you want to have a ship to come back to. Doesn't mean I have to be happy being left out again."

"Next one, I promise," Jake compromised.

"So, we've got boots on the ground. Then what?" Beck asked.

"Again, why the fuck do you care?" Kaiser challenged as Ty stopped him from getting up. He settled himself again. "You're not even part of this mission. You're gone as soon as we're down."

"Yeah, well, about that… can't say Santorra sounds like a peachy place to visit," Beck said, relaxing back once Kaiser was sat and no longer a threat. "If it's all the same to you, I'd rather ditch somewhere a bit more savoury."

"That's not your fucking decision, fuck-turd," Kaiser scoffed.

"What is your malfunction, Kaiser? You seem to have a real bug up your arse about me."

"Enough!" Jake bellowed as they both got to their feet. "Sit… the fuck… down. Not another word from either of you unless it's going to benefit this briefing. What? This better be good," he added as Beck indicated he wanted to say something.

"I meant what I said about not wanting to stay on the planet, and I'd be most grateful to stay on to the next. For my passage, I'll play my part in the mission. An extra gun can't be a bad thing, right?"

Jake raised his hand to stop Kaiser from saying his next sentence, so instead, he closed his mouth and sat back, crossing his arms.

"From what you've said, Jake, it sounds like we're going to need all the help we can get," Ash said rationally. "If Beck's offering, I think we should consider it."

Jake picked at a thread on his combats, and we waited. "Agreed," he determined. "But no more of this." He waved his hand between the Pack and Beck. "I want no bullshit on the mission. If Beck comes, he comes as part of the team. End of."

"Sure, Jake," Kaiser mumbled.

"Good. Can we get back to the briefing now?" He didn't wait for an answer. "From the landing pad, we'll move out in pairs. Any more than that and we'll draw attention and be seen as a threat. Assuming nothing's changed since this map was done, we'll take three different routes towards the citadel. Shae, you'll come with me." He paused as Ash looked like he was going to say something, but he simply nodded his agreement. "Cal, you're with Ash, Ty, I want you to stay with Connor, and—"

"Really?" Kaiser moaned.

"And you two can work together," Jake said, looking between Kaiser and Beck. When he turned back to me, it was impossible to miss the sparkle in his eyes and the devious grin on his lips. "Serves them both right," he whispered.

"And why do I have to stay with Conner," Ty grumbled.

"Because I god-damn assigned you to," Jake ordered, his patience running thin. "So, all of you, listen the fuck up, and only say something if it's useful to the mission. Am I clear? Good."

Jake took each of us through our designated routes through the city, and I momentarily wondered why the directions for him and me took us around the edge, a fair bit further than the other two paths. It was forgotten seconds later as he started to talk about the building.

"There's only one main entrance, and as you can see, there's like a no-man zone around the front building as part of their defences. There used to be barricades and weapons stations, so we've got to assume they're still there – and possibly more advanced. It was a long time ago."

"You said that's the main entrance. Are there any other ways in?" asked Ash.

"There are two further entry points. One at the rear, which I believe is like a service entrance for provisions and shit. It's heavily guarded and surrounded by natural rock formations. The only way to get to it, is through the front defences and then skirting around the building." He drew the line on the holo with his finger.

"And the other?" I asked.

"It's about halfway down the south wall here." He pointed. "But it's blocked both inside and out. By the time we could blast our way through, Glitch's army of goons would be on us. And if all of that wasn't bad enough, you can bet your shit they'll have roving guards. And I'm not even finished. In addition to the front defences, there's also heavy automatic armaments on the ramparts, and surface to air tactical smart missiles to dissuade any airborne attacks."

"What about amenities?" I asked. "They must have access points to power, water, waste drainage, at the very least."

"You're absolutely right, babe. Their water comes from a natural spring under the building, and their waste is the same – filtered back through the volcanic rocks in some sort of drainage system built by the Scientia Corp. Power, however, is a different animal. I can pretty much guarantee Glitch will have increased his data-mining ability since I was last here, so the immense power requirements he needs is going to be his weakness."

"How?" Ash asked.

"Scientia built a series of tunnels under the city so their people could move around easily when the winds carried volcanic ash and stench. Last time I was here, each of the gang-lords had carved up the tunnels to match the land they occupied above. Thanks to them, the tunnels have been blocked, blown up, or boobytrapped as the turf wars continued."

"So the tunnels are out then?" I said.

"Not necessarily. I said the power is the key weakness here. Glitch has a series of massive dishes along the ridge line to the west of the of the city, here." He pointed to the map. "They link to a vast network of satellites in orbit and are heavily guarded with a powerful defence shield and automated weapons stations, plus about fifty guards. But he's got to get power to the dishes, and data back to the Citadel."

"More tunnels," Ash commented.

"Yes, and I can guarantee you those tunnels will be in good shape – and patrolled."

"Don't want to be a Debbie Downer here," Beck said, causing Kaiser to bristle. "But what you're saying, is that there's a passageway that leads from an impenetrable satellite farm to an impenetrable citadel that sounds like something out of a kid's nightmare. Oh, and not forgetting the random arseholes on patrol. And this is Glitch's weakness?"

"Yup. Pretty much," agreed Jake. "On the face of it," he added cryptically.

"This is where it gets interesting, I can tell," Cal said, sitting forward.

"How did you get in last time, Jake? Did you go in through the front door?" I asked.

"Actually, I didn't," he replied. "As part of the pre-mission intel gathering, the REF requested all of Scientia's intel on the city.

"I bet that was like getting blood out of a lava rock," Ty

said. "Their data's air-gapped and runs on their own coding. Not even Glitch could get hold of it – unless he has someone on the inside. Jeez, did he have someone in Scientia?"

"No, Ty," Jake confirmed. "But, on this occasion, they decided to be magnanimous. You know what they're like – once they leave, they never look back. Normally because they leave a desolate planet in their wake. They provided the REF with the files, which included all the tunnels under the city. The sub-structure of the city is like a goddamn maze, and the tunnels are huge, branching out way further than the city. I guess the new occupants claimed what they found, but it's what they didn't find that will help us."

"Now we're talking," said Cal.

"There's a power relay station about halfway between the city and the satellite dishes," Jake continued, pointing to the map again. "That's where the guards are based, with some going east towards the dishes, and some patrolling west, back towards the citadel. But here," he pointed to a patch of dilapidated buildings on the outskirts of the city, "is where it gets interesting. Somewhere in this area, is the access point for long-forgotten, underground barracks, where the workmen who built the tunnels used to bunk. It was bricked up after they no longer needed workers down there, but I was able to break through quite easily once I knew it was there."

"You said 'somewhere'?" Ash questioned.

"Yeah, well, it's been a long time since I was there, and the buildings look a bit different now. It's not a problem," Jake said confidently. "We'll rendezvous by this intersection, enter through the barracks, and follow the main tunnel to Glitch. Con, Ty, this is where you come in. Ty, you'll need to hack their radio traffic and let us know if there are any patrols in our area. Con, you need to get him close enough to do that, but if we run into trouble, we might need you buzz the citadel to take some of the attention off us."

"Oh yeah," Con replied, smiling and nodding his agreement.

"Get close enough to get their interest, but not so close that you get my ship scratched. Remember, it comes out of your pay packet."

"Sure thing, boss."

"The tunnel will bring us into the building here." Jake closed in on the citadel and the holo morphed into a floorplan.

"Why's all this blank?" asked Kaiser, leaning forward to take a closer look.

"This is the most you can get on the open data-net" Jake replied. "It was all detailed by Scientia in the data-package I had for the last mission. I can remember most of it."

"That's reassuring," Beck replied, and that time it was me who nailed him with a glare.

"The map's not important," Jake continued. "All of the firepower and security is on the outside to stop unwanted people getting in. Once we're in, there shouldn't be too many scroats to worry about, unless any one of us trips an alarm. There are sensor jammers, so Ty? You'll need to hack those as well. We won't be able to tell the difference between the gun-thugs and Glitch on sensors, but we're going in at night, so that would suggest he'll be in his personal quarters. That said, Glitch isn't your average geek, so it's possible he won't be tucked up in bed. If that's the case, he'll likely be in the main hall. When we're in, we'll split into two groups, with one group taking Glitch's personal quarters, and the other, taking the main hall, just in case. Ash, you're with me and Shae. We'll go east, towards the back of the building, using these stairs here towards the private quarters. Cal, you're with Kaiser and Beck. The three of you go south towards the front and take these stairs. You'll check the main hall for Glitch, but it's likely there'll be bad guys, even at night, so stay frosty."

"I'd feel happier with a better map," Kaiser said.

"Don't worry about the god-damn map. It'll be fine," Jake assured.

"So, one of us gets Glitch, then what?" Beck asked.

"Depends how we take him. If we're quiet, we may be able to get the info we need there and then. If it gets noisy though, we'll fall back to the tunnels and get the hell out of dodge," Jake replied. "We get Glitch back to the ship, get the information we need, and then drop his arse off at the nearest REF outpost. Any questions?"

"Just to confirm," Cal said, "We're going to a hostile planet, filled with hostile people, to break into an impenetrable fortress, to find some geeky little shite, who may or may not have information to help our bigger mission?"

Jake looked at him for a moment, then a smile tugged his lips. "Yup"

"Sounds awesome," Cal replied, tying his hair back. "Count me in."

When we arrived in Santorra's orbit, Jake took us through the plan again, such that it was. My insides knotted and I couldn't shake the feeling I was putting everyone's life in danger for potentially nothing. I took Jake to one side.

"I'm worried," I said.

"Hey, don't be. This is what we do best."

"What if Glitch has nothing on the Harbingers? What if someone gets dead, dead? I won't forgive myself if—"

Jake pulled me closer and bent his head so he could whisper, his breath sending goose bumps skittering over my skin. "Everyone on this ship would die for you, Shae. But that's not going to happen today. You hear?"

"But—"

"But nothing. Trust us. Trust yourself. This is the best option we have for finding the Harbingers, we all know that. Besides, the guys have been cooped up for too long, they could do with letting off some steam."

I pulled back and looked up into his hazel eyes, searching for any reticence, but they sparkled greeny-brown, the lighter lines around his eyes crinkling as he smiled. "We got this, babe."

"I still don't understand why the four of us have to hang at the drop point for twenty minutes while you and Shae take off," said Beck, and for once, I think he was asking the question the others wanted to ask. After all, I'd wondered the same question myself.

"I told you, our route is longer," Jake said vaguely. "Just do what I've asked."

Connor's version of drop and dash was to lower the ramp as we were descending, and then close it again, just as we were stepping off. I don't think the *Veritas* even touched the ground. "Sorry, I should've warned you about that," Jake said, brushing dirt off my sleeve. He waited a moment for my eyes to adjust to the darkness of the night. "Ready?"

I nodded, though my stomach churned.

"The key is not to look too conspicuous," Jake said, slipping his hand into mine as we walked down a narrow street.

"Really?" I replied. "I would never have guessed that."

"Ah, we're going with sarcasm now, are we?"

"If the shoe fits." Then the randomness of my brain linked that sentence to Jake's boots, and then to the horrific moment I had to re-attach his foot after the last time we'd got caught in a boobytrap. I laughed. I shouldn't have, because it really wasn't funny, but the memory of Jake being doped up on pain meds, was certainly a sight to see.

"What's so amusing?"

"You."

"Me?"

I explained my thought logic, and for a moment he faked offence that I'd laughed at his misfortune, but then he put his arm around me, and pulled me close. We followed our route, skirting around the side of the city. My hand fell to the grip of my Sentinel a few times, but Jake's glare was sufficient to keep most people away. A couple of times we had to fend off an attack by one of two people, but they were no match for us on our own, let alone together. To be fair, it didn't look like they'd eaten in a week.

At the very edge of the city, we came to a small square, and Jake stopped us. He led me to one of the buildings and flattened us against the wall. In the shadow of the awning, I could barely make out his face.

"What's going on?"

"Shh."

"Jake, I'm not going to shh," I whispered. "This wasn't part of the plan."

"Actually, it was," he whispered back, checking his compad for the time. "Just wait."

Five minutes passed, and it dawned on me that this, whatever this was, was why we had left before the others.

Jake checked the time again. His eyes darted around the square, and I wondered what he was looking for. "Wha—"

"Shh."

"Don't shh me. What's going on?"

He put his finger to my lips and silently shh'd me again, which was even more infuriating. Another five minutes passed, and I didn't need the Link to tell me he was getting agitated. He checked the time again.

"Damn it. We can't wait any longer."

"Wait for what?" I asked, but he ignored my question, his eyes still searching the square and the alleyways.

"We need to go," Jake instructed, taking my elbow to lead me back into the square, but as we moved, a hooded figure stepped out of a side street opposite. Both Jake and I dropped our hands to our guns, but the stranger held his out to show he was unarmed.

"You're late," Jake grunted. "We were about to leave.

Did you bring what I asked for?"

"Of course," the stranger replied, lowering the hood of his cloak, but I didn't need to see him to recognise that voice. I literally threw myself at him, and his arms closed around me.

When I finally let him go, I turned to Jake. "You knew he was coming all along?"

"Yeah, umm, surprise!"

"Why didn't you tell me?"

"We weren't sure he'd make it," Jake explained. "I didn't want to get your hopes up."

"I can't believe it. But how? Why? What are you doing here?"

"Well, that's a nice greeting," Jared said, the boyish grin just visible in the darkness. He surveyed the square and the few people who seemed to be interested in our reunion.

"We should go. We've lost too much time," Jake added pointedly towards Jared. "You can catch up on the way."

Jared took my hand, but for a moment I was rooted to the spot. I couldn't believe he was there, in front of me. All I wanted to do was hug him and never let go, but the mission was priority, and after all, it was my fault that everyone was there. Instead, I squeezed his hand and he looked down and smiled. My insides flipped and I'm sure I blushed – thankful that it wouldn't be noticed in the darkness.

"Don't get me wrong, I love that you're here. I still can't get over it," I gushed, hugging him again. "But why? How? It's too risky for you. What are you doing?" I turned to Jake. "Didn't you tell him it's too risky for him to be caught up in this?"

"I told him," Jake confirmed. "I told him I've got it covered, but you know what he's like. Want's to be the boss of everything."

"I'm standing right here," Jared said. "And you know me being here has nothing to do with anyone's ability to handle the situation."

"Yeah well… you said you had what we needed?"

"Sure." Jared tapped his com-pad, searching for something, then a moment later, my own com-pad received a couple of data-files. "One's the map of the tunnels and the exact location of the barracks entrance, the other's a full map of the citadel."

"Now I know why you kept telling us not to worry about the distinct lack of data at the briefing," I recalled.

"Like I said, it wasn't a done deal Captain Fantastic here would make it."

I caught an odd look on Jared's face I couldn't quite read. "What have you done? Tell me you haven't jeopardised your career."

"Shae, please don't worry." He stopped us and held both my hands against his chest. "I'll tell you all about it later, but in the meantime, in your words, we have to get our heads in the game. Yes?"

Jake looked at his watch again. "Okay, okay," I conceded. "Let's go and meet the others before Beck and Kaiser kill each other."

"For the love of all things, please don't tell me he's here as well," grunted Jared. "I thought you were going to bounce him at the earliest possibility," he added to Jake, who broke into a mischievous grin.

"He likes you so much, I thought I'd keep him around for a reunion between the two of you."

"You're an arsehole."

"Yeah, but I'm a lovable arsehole," Jake replied, before striding off.

15

We arrived at the intersection a few minutes behind schedule. The other four were huddled together, scrutinising the tunnel and citadel layouts Jake had obviously forwarded on. Without turning, Ash said, "Nice to have you with us, Captain."

"How...?" Jared replied.

Ash turned and held out his hand, smiling. "Sometimes, when Shae's surprised, she forgets to strengthen those mental blocks of hers. I got that hit loud and clear."

"I thought he was having some kind of fit till he explained it," added Cal.

"I'm so sorry, Ash," I apologised, blushing again.

"No harm done," he replied, laughing.

I noticed Jake standing a couple of steps back, arms folded, watching Beck. I knew what he was waiting for.

Jared greeted Cal and Kaiser, finally coming to Beck. "Well, look who it is," Beck said. "Nobody said Super Pr—"

"Should we move on?" I said, cutting Beck off. Jake stepped forward, clearing the smile from his lips.

"Is this going to be a problem?" he said, waving a hand

between Jared and Beck.

"No problem here," Jared said, holding out his hand.

"Nope, me neither," Beck added, but he left Jared's hand hanging.

"Good. Then let's get going. Thanks to the new data, the entrance we're looking for is this way," Jake said, leading the group. The buildings were old, and crumbling. In the darkness they looked like the skeletons of giant creatures, just the bones left of an area that was once thriving with Scientia Corp's employees. I inexplicably felt sad for a moment, but it passed quickly.

We entered one of the buildings, checking foot placement on disintegrating floors. "There's a door to the basement somewhere behind all this junk," Jake said.

Beck passed behind me, giving my arse a squeeze as he did.

"Hey!" I protested, louder than I should have. Everyone else froze. "Sorry," I whispered, noticing Jared moving closer to me.

"You okay?" he asked.

"Yes, it was nothing."

"You sure?"

"Come on man, she said it was nothing," Beck said, squaring up. "Shae can handle herself. She sure as shit doesn't need you to wade in."

"That's enough," Jake hissed. "You're walking a thin line, Beck," he continued. "And if it comes to a choice between you and anyone else here, including Captain Annoying, it will be you we ditch. Do I make myself clear?"

Beck nodded, but he didn't seem fazed by the ultimatum.

"Found it," Cal said, carefully trying to move a collapsing shelf unit. I helped to catch falling wood, carefully putting it quietly on the ground. When the door was accessible, Cal pulled on the handle, but the wood was so rotten, the metal plate pulled away and he staggard back.

"Thanks," he said as I steadied him until he found his feet again.

"Kaiser, check the street," Jake ordered.

"All clear. Wait, hold," he said as Ash was about to put his full weight to the door. "Okay, all clear."

The wood gave way easily, making little noise. Ash pointed a torch down the stairs and took a cautious step. As the light disappeared downwards, Jake followed. I was halfway down behind him, when he stopped and turned, pointing his light to one side of the stairs. "Stay to the left," he whispered. I relayed the message to Jared behind me.

The basement wasn't large and felt a little claustrophobic with all of us, plus the left belongings of whoever lived in the house. "We need to clear this corner," Jake instructed, picking up junk and passing it along to be stacked up on the other side. When the floor was cleared, he checked the map, measuring the floor for an exact position. He tapped his com-pad. "We still clear outside, Kaiser."

"Affirmative," he replied.

"Okay, come join us. Stand back folks," Jake added, popping the cap off a thermite grenade. I covered my eyes as the blinding light filled the room.

The passageway below was narrow, and we had to shuffle along as the next person dropped through the hole made with the grenade. I followed Jake for a while, eventually wondering if he'd lost his way, and was just about to ask when I practically ran into him. The screeching of metal on metal filled the tunnel and I put my hands to my ears. A moment later, he was gone.

"Be careful of the drop," he said pointing his torch back to show me the tunnel entered the barracks about two thirds of the way up the wall. Kaiser was the last person through, and a moment later the room lightened as Jake turned on some of the ancient chem-lights. Rows of dusty bunks were made with perfectly folded sheets.

"Am I the only on getting the creeps?" Cal said. "Reminds me of Tartaros."

I squeezed his arm as I walked past to indicate I knew what he was feeling. "Where now, Jake?" I asked.

He studied the map again. "Through the mess hall and then then down another shaft for about a hundred meters."

"Great, another frickin' tunnel I'll have to squeeze through," moaned Kaiser, flexing his muscles.

"Don't worry, big guy," Jake continued. "After that we'll be in the main tunnel, and you never know, you might even get the opportunity to punch a bad guy or two." Kaiser smiled and cracked his knuckles.

At the end of the passageway was another hatch, and we paused for Jake to contact Ty. "Sit-rep?" he said succinctly.

"You're five by five," Ty replied. "No one in the vicinity. You've got two hostiles approaching the citadel. They'll turn and come back your way, and by the speed and heat signatures, they're travelling by some kind of buggy or rail system. You'll either need to stay put until they pass or hope there's some cover in the tunnels."

"ETA on them passing us on the way back?"

"Ten, maybe fifteen minutes travel time, but it depends on whether they stop for a break before coming back."

"So basically, you don't know. Keep us updated. I'll let you know if Connor needs to buzz the building."

"Received loud and clear, boss."

Jake opened the hatch carefully, the dim light from the tunnel seeping into the shaft. He lent in and looked each way before raising himself back up.

"There are power nodes along the route," he explained. "If the guards don't stop at the citadel and come straight back, we'll cross paths in maybe ten minutes, but Ty will be our eyes and ears. We should be able to find cover and let them sail on by. If we wait, and they stop for refreshments, we'd be wasting valuable time."

"It's your mission, Jake," Jared said. "What do you want

to do?"

"I say we go," he replied, and that was the decision made. "You'll need to lower me down with a rope so I can access the ladder controls."

I was surprised it took so much rope to get Jake to the tunnel floor, but just after he was down, I heard the tired motor straining to lower the ladder. Jared was halfway down when the gears slipped, and ladder dropped slightly. He took the remaining steps carefully, as did the rest of us who followed.

"Wow," I commented looking around me as the ladder disappeared back into the ceiling. "This must be what... eight meters high?"

"About that," Jake confirmed. "Scientia used to move heavy machinery through here. Now, as you can see," he pointed to the walls and ceiling, "it just cables, cables, and more cables. Ty, what's going on with those guards?"

"They're still at the citadel," came the reply.

"Okay, let us know when they move."

We headed down the tunnel, weapons raised. We'd got about two thirds of the way when Ty informed us the guards were leaving. Thanks to the cabling and data nodes, we were able to find shadowed cover before they were on us. Even though Kaiser was quite ready for a fight, they sailed past, not even on alert.

Just before we got to the end, Jake indicated for us to hold where we were. He crept forward on his own and then returned, silently indicated three bad guys ahead. Jared and Kaiser went ahead with Jake, and by the time we were notified of the all-clear, Kaiser and Jared were stuffing bodies into a side room. Jake righted a couple of chairs, checking the scene for any indication we'd been there.

"You know the plan," Jake whispered. "Coms open at all times. If Glitch is in his quarters, Kaiser, you get your team back here and wait for the evac. If he's in the hall, we'll converge on your location. Got it? This needs to be quick and quiet, but if things go sideways, or anyone gets separated, we meet here and fall back together."

I followed Jake east, through the winding black corridors in the bowels of the building, Ash and Jared right behind me. I'd expected we'd come across someone – goons, thugs, staff – but we were alone, and somehow that unnerved me more. We found the first signs of life at the bottom of the stairs we needed to use. We got the warning from Ty, so even though the targets were heavily armed, they didn't even have time to draw before Jake and I dispatched them. Quick, clean, and most of all, quiet.

Our boots made muffled thuds as we ascended as quickly as the noise would allow. Ty continued to warn us of roving guards, which we were able to avoid or deal with, but I couldn't shake the feeling something didn't feel right.

Jake indicated we were going to turn right at the next junction, but just before we got there, Ty was trying to tell us something. His voice crackled in my ear, and I thought it was just my coms fritzing out at first, but one glance around the group told me it was all of us. "Ty?" Jake said. Nothing but static. "Ty, come in. Connor?"

"Ty?" I repeated. "Nothing."

"Kaiser," Jake said. "Cal? Beck? If anyone can hear me, check in." Still nothing but static.

"I don't like this, Jake," I said. "Maybe we should abort?"

"How close are we?" Ash asked.

"Literally at the end of the next corridor. Through the door there's a lounge, and then a second door leads to his personal quarters. Last check in with Ty had three heat signatures in the lounge and one in the quarters. We've got to assume that's Glitch. We're so close."

"I say we continue," said Jared, "But this is your party, Jake." It was weird to see them playing so nicely.

"I agree," Jake concurred. "We haven't got this far to turn back now. Nothing changes – we take out the guys in the lounge, get to Glitch, and make him help us."

The first part of that equation was accomplished easily enough; the element of surprise in our favour. Ash stayed at the door, closing it to a gap so he could still see down the hall. "I think we're good," he said. "Doesn't look like we sent out an invite to the party."

"Good," said Jake. "Because it's going to take me a moment to get through this lock."

I went over to look.

"Is anyone else wondering why there's a heavy-duty lock on the outside of Glitch's quarters," Jared said.

"Really? I hadn't noticed, Captain Obvious. What do you think this frowny-face is for?"

"Sorry, I thought that was your natural default look."

"Funny," Jake grunted. The lock clicked and Jared immediate raised his gun. "Ready?" he asked. Jared nodded. "Remember we need him alive," he added, but Jared just rolled his eyes.

Jake pulled back the door letting me and Jared through, but by the time he'd followed us in, Glitch was already babbling. "Thank you, thank you, thank you," he repeated, sobbing. He'd fallen to his knees openly weeping at Jared's feet. He wiped the string of snot from his nose and stood, my gun still trained on him. "I can't believe you're finally here. You took your time, but no bother now you're here. I only sent out the message like forever ago."

Jared cautiously lowered his weapon, and Glitch grabbed his hand, shaking it furiously. He stepped towards me, but I backed off, my gun still pointed centre chest. Instead, he turned to Jake, who was equally having none of it.

"Umm, what's going on?" I asked to no one in particular.

"Not a clue," Jake replied, the frown lines deepening. He pulled up a chair. "Sit," he ordered Glitch. "And for fuck's sake, stop snivelling. Ash, what's it looking like out there?"

"All clear."

"Good." He turned to Glitch. "Talk. And it better make sense. What the hell is going on here?"

"I explained everything in my message," Glitch babbled, but Jared and I exchanged confused glances. "You did get the message, didn't you?" He continued, his eyes now showing the same confusion as us.

"What fucking message?" Jake asked, raising his gun.

"But if you didn't get the message..." he trailed off, thinking. "Are you not here to rescue me?"

"No, arsehole, we're not," Jake confirmed.

"Well don't think you're getting the four million credits then," Glitch stated defensively.

"What four million credits? And rescue you from whom?" Jared asked.

"From the..." he waved his arm towards the door. "You know. From the same jacked up retards I paid very handsomely to protect me. It was all going great until that son-of-a-bitch, Luther, decided I could work for him instead of the other way around."

"You just can't rely on a good bad-guy anymore," Jake quipped. "But you're in luck."

"This look lucky to you?" He pointed at my gun.

"Call it insurance," I said.

"If you didn't come here to rescue me, why are you here?"

"We need some information," Jared replied.

"Well, now you're in luck," Glitch replied. "Because information is all I've got. You get me out of here, and I'll give you whatever you want."

"We could just put holes in you here until you give us what we want," suggested Jake.

"Really?" I questioned. He shrugged his shoulders and grinned.

"Okay, get up," said Jared, tying his hands behind his

back with flexi-cuffs. "We're leaving. I don't like that our coms are down."

"Of course, they are, genius. We're on an encrypted channel here – no outside coms work," explained Glitch.

"We hijacked that signal before we even came in," Jake replied.

"So, your coms went off since you've been in the building?"

"About ten minutes ago."

"No, no, no. This is not good. It either means they found out about the hack, or…"

"Or what?" I asked apprehensively.

"You got anyone else in the building?" he asked, wiping sweat from his brow.

"A second team, heading for the hall," Jake confirmed.

"That's your 'or what.' Luther's either found the hack, or he found your people. Either way, it makes getting out of here ten times harder. So, we better leave, yes? If you want that precious data, that is. I'm no good to you dead."

Jake thought for a moment. "We fall back to the rendezvous point," he concluded. "We've lost coms and sensor info, so we're going out the hard way. Shae, it's your job to get Glitch out alive, Jared, you've got the rear. Ash, you're up front with me. If we've lost the element of surprise, we're likely to encounter more hostiles. But on the positive, there's no reason to keep it quiet anymore. They can't know how we came in, so they won't be able to predict where we're going. That gives us a slight edge, but not much. We do this fast, but safe."

I slung my TK70 over my shoulder and pulled out my Sentinel, leading Glitch back through the lounge, as agreed. Ash and Jake led the way, but it wasn't long before we were engaged in a firefight. Bullets careered off stone walls, ricocheting randomly, but it was all over quickly, and everything was quiet again. We stepped around bleeding bodies, getting to the staircase moments later.

We couldn't have been more than halfway down when weapons fire behind made me spin. I momentarily took my hand off Glitch to help Jared clear the rear, but when I turned back, Glitch had already taken the opportunity to bolt ahead. I don't know what made Ash stop and turn, but Glitch careered straight into him. Jake's arm shot out and grabbed Ash's jacket, steadying him, but with Glitch's arms still tied behind his back, his momentum carried him forward. If the situation wasn't so serious, it would've been funny to watch as he bounced all the way to the next landing.

"I'm so sorry," I said as we raced after him, visions of Nyan dead on the table at Finnigan's bar clouding my thoughts. "I know, I should've kept hold of him."

"You were protecting all of us," Jared said kindly. Ash checked on Glitch, who's loud moaning indicated he was still alive. "There's no way I could have taken out all those hostiles on my own," he continued.

"I think you're exaggerating. You had it," I replied.

Jake knelt; his rifle pointed down the stairs. Jared's pointed up the stairs.

"What's the damage?" I asked as Ash stabbed him with some Oxytanyl. The moans decreased in decibel.

"Head lac, probably concussion. A few broken ribs, maybe a fractured ulna. But it's the open tib-fib break that's the issue."

"Do we have time for me to fix him?" I asked, but my answer came in a volley of gunfire.

"Help me," Jake said to Ash, as the two lifted Glitch on to his shoulders. "Fuck me, this guy's heavy."

I holstered my Sentinel and pulled the TK70 over my shoulder. We continued down the stairs to the basement, gunfire still echoing off stone walls, but when every hostile had been taken care of, I could still hear the muffled sound of weapons.

"Kaiser," I said, fear chilling my insides.

"I know," Jake puffed. "We've got to get this sorry sack of shit back to the rendezvous point, then we can deal with the next issue." I nodded my understanding as gunfire started again, but a second later, Ash spun, blood splattering my jacket. I took out the shooters before turning to him.

"What's hit?" I asked urgently.

"It's nothing," he replied.

"What's hit," I repeated, unabated.

"It's just my arm, Shae. Through and through."

"You sure?" My eyes searched for other injuries.

"Eyes front, Shae," Jake ordered. "Time for that later."

When we arrived at the rendezvous point, Cal appeared from behind a crate so quickly, I'd raised my gun before I realised who it was.

"Whoa, easy! Good guy here," he said quickly.

"My bad," I replied, lowering my weapon.

"At least you'd be able to fix any hole you put in me," he said, smiling. "Here, let me help," he added, supporting a still whimpering Glitch while Jake dumped him on a crate.

"Where are the others?" Jake asked as he pulled a field dressing from his backpack, throwing at Jared. "Please don't tell me they've actually gone and killed each other."

"Not yet. We made it to the hall in good time. Not exactly the empty room you'd expect at this time of night. Some guy was holding court, and by that, I mean executing some dude for taking something that didn't belong to him." I listened while watching Jared wrap the field bandage around Ash's arm. "Then I guess something had happened. Coms went dead, and everyone got very loud and excitable. We hunkered down in an alcove to avoid detection, but then some arseholes decided they wanted to camp out right there. We waited, but had no idea what your situation was, so Kaiser told me to bolt back here as soon as he and Beck caused a distraction."

"Were they captured?" Jake asked.

"Not when I left," Cal replied. "But there was some serious gunfire going on as I bolted. If it's ok with you, Jake, I'd really like to go get our guys now."

"Hold," Jake instructed, causing Cal to stop in his tracks. "Ash, Cal, Shae, take that hefty bastard back to the shaft. It'll probably take all of you to get him up the ladder."

"Hang on," I started, but Jake ignored me.

"Jared, you and I will head back to the hall to get our men." He went to pick up his rifle, but I put my hand on it.

"No," I said in my sternest voice.

"Don't do this, babe. I haven't got the time to argue with you."

"Then don't," I replied. Jake turned to Ash for support, but he just shrugged his shoulders and then winced in pain. "Kaiser and Beck are here because of me, and you can be damn sure I'm not leaving without them."

"You can be really infuriating, you know that?"

"Yes, I do," I replied.

"Just you and me then, Cal," said Ash. "And as you've got young legs, you can carry dough-boy here."

"Thanks, old man," replied Cal, grunting as Jake helped lift Glitch onto his shoulders.

"Watch out for those roving patrols," Jake said. "We haven't got Ty helping this time."

"Wait," Jared said, as if Jake's words had given him an idea. He lifted Glitch's head. "Where's the sensor jammer located?"

"Huh?" Glitch slurred.

"The jammer? How can we get our coms back on?"

"Huh?"

"Never mind," Jared commented. "Get him out of here."

"What's the plan, Jake," I asked, refocussing my attention on the task ahead.

"Make our way to the hall, taking out everyone who tries

to stop us, grab Kaiser and Beck, and get the hell back to the *Veritas*," he replied.

"Sounds like a plan to me," said Jared, readying his weapon.

"Same rule applies as before," Jake continued. "If anyone gets separated, or if things go south, we meet back here."

"Got it," Jared confirmed.

"Shae?"

"I understand," I said over my shoulder, already heading for the door.

It wasn't long before we were pinned down, weapons fire coming from multiple directions. I lobbed a stun grenade down the corridor, clearing out some of the hostiles, leaving Jake and Jared to take out the rest.

"Keep moving," Jake yelled, ducking a volley of plasma shots. I took him at his word, bowling into the gun-thugs shaking off the stun grenade. I got into a fist fight with one of them, who managed to get in a face punch before I put him down. The usual tickling sensation was brief, and I wiped away the blood.

We paused at the t-junction of two passages, hunkering down while we got our breath back. "About fifteen meters down the next corridor, we'll come out on balcony that goes all around the hall. It's open, not much cover, but it'll let us see what's going on. Cal said Beck and Kaiser are in this general location. Jared, go clockwise, Shae and I will go anti. If we meet up and haven't found them, we'll reassess at that time. Jared, if you find them during your sweep, you know what to do."

"Retreat to the rendezvous point," he replied.

"Not so keen on the word retreat there, Jared," Jake decided. "Call it strategic redeployment to the tunnels. Sound much more…"

"Manly," I offered. Jake laughed.

"Yeah, babe, that sounds about right."

We split up, moving quietly in the shadows, checking alcoves and shadowed area for any sign of Kaiser and Beck. I stepped carefully, trying to avoid the bullet casings littered the floor and Jake pointed out the scorched walls from plasma weapons – probably from TK70s.

When we got to the balcony, there were several hostiles leaning over the balustrade to get a better view. Waves of cheers erupted from them and the people below, or where they jeers? It was difficult to tell. Jake signalled to move right, so I followed silently behind him. My stomach churned, knowing that whatever was going on in the hall was way more important and interesting to those thugs than looking for us. I was confused when Jake veered away from the balcony, but his motives became clear as he very carefully opened a service door that took us to a higher level. More importantly, there were no bad guys there.

My breath caught as I got my first look into the hall. A stage had been erected at one end, and I assumed the man draped lazily over the oversized throne, was Luther. He seemed bored as several other thugs swarmed around something I couldn't see on the floor in front.

"Enough!" Luther shouted, jumping to his feet. "They're no good to me dead." He pulled away a couple of men, sending them sprawling across the floor, grunting and shouting until they saw who'd done it. They cowered back, offering apologies, and for the first time we could clearly see what was happening.

Beck and Kaiser we're pulled to their knees in front of Luther.

16

Flaming torches lit up the dark red banners draping the walls, the grenade and snake emblem ominous in black. I felt the heat from the fires, but my insides were ice. I scanned the balcony, looking for Jared, disappointed but not surprised I couldn't see him.

Jake looked murderous in the shadows as he worked through options. We both took a knee as he puffed out a long breath. "Gotta say, babe, this doesn't look great. We've got no contact with Jared, or the *Veritas*, and there's way more of them than there is of us, even if you do include Captain Courageous. They know the building and have home-turf advantage. Chances of getting those two out before we all die, are slim to no fucking chance... so why the hell are you smiling?"

"Because I know that no matter what you say, we're doing nothing other than raining holy fucking hell on those arseholes."

"Whoa, babe!" he replied, surprised.

"Come on, Jake, you can't tell me I'm wrong."

"It's not that," he said, his lips breaking into a smile.

"Then what?"

"I don't think I've ever heard you swear before."

It was my turn to be surprised. "Sure, you have," I replied. Jake thought for a moment.

"Umm, nope. Damn, shit, maybe a bollocks here and there, but never the fuck word."

"Guess the situation warrants it."

"Or perhaps you're starting to pick up my bad habits."

"Perhaps. So, are we doing this, or what?"

"You know damn straight I am. I'm not going to be able to talk you in to going straight to the rendezvous point, am I?" My scowl gave him his answer. "Worth a try."

"This would be easier if we knew where Jared was."

"I can't believe I'm saying this, but I agree with you. As it stands, it's just you and me."

"Have you got a plan?"

"Other than raising holy fucking hell?" Jake replied, and I swatted him on the arm. "Options are limited with just the two of us, but… you think you could skirt around the hall, and create a diversion at the back?" I nodded. "There's an access point behind the throne. I'll come in from there and see if I can take out this Luther guy. Maybe without their gang-lord, the rest will be more compliant."

"Maybe," I said, but we both knew it was a long shot. I got up to move, but he grabbed my arm.

"Be safe," he whispered.

"Don't get dead, dead," I replied.

It was relatively easy to navigate the gantry without coming across anyone, but as I crept down the service stairs to the balcony, I heard at least three separate voices, but probably more. The occasional cheer roared through the crowd, and I tried hard not to think what had caused them. The only saving grace was that their attention was almost exclusively on activities occurring below in the hall.

I was able to slip out of the service door and carefully make my way down to the back of the hall, ducking behind grotesque, black statues to avoid being seen. There were a few gun-thugs milling around the foyer, but most looked to be squeezed around the entrance, the people at the back pushing and shoving to get a better look. A few men, a term I use lightly, broke into a fist fight, but when a couple of them pulled knives, someone else barked orders and they separated, still throwing dangerous glances at each other.

I paused behind a statue, planning my next moves based on the weapons I had with me. Jake had wanted a distraction, and that's what I was going to give. I popped the cap off a couple of grenades, sliding them across the floor in different direction before ducking back down to avoid the blast. I came out shooting, firing at anyone still standing. Part of the wall had collapsed, the railings of the balcony twisted metal in the debris.

Between the rubble and the bodies, the hostiles had difficulty getting out of the hall, but it didn't stop them trying, and they just kept coming. A plasma bullet hit my shoulder sending me sprawling back, the TK70 clattering across the smooth black rock. The stench of burning material and skin made me momentarily nauseous. I reached for my Sentinel while trying to stand, but the kick to my back sent waves of pain through my body. I managed to get to my feet, my gun drawn, but there were already way too many gun-thugs eager to pull the trigger.

I hoped Jake had used the advantage to get to Luther, because no matter how hard I tried, I couldn't see me getting out of this situation unscathed.

"Well, ain't you in ten shades of shit," said someone I couldn't see until he cleared himself a path through the goons. "Now why did a pretty little thing like you want to go ahead and blow my shit up, not to mention, make corpses of these fine, upstanding citizens here?"

I let out an involuntary laugh, and he scowled. "I don't suppose there's any chance you're going to let me walk out of here, is there?" I asked.

"Yeah, you know, not really," Luther said. "But if you

pass that there gun to Si, and don't do anything stupid," he looked at the damage from the grenades, "stupider, you might live another thirty minutes or so. But I warn you, these men are kinda on the twitchy side. And by the level of drool, I can say with some level of certainty, it's not your weapons they're interested in."

I was outgunned twenty to one and didn't have my Cal'ret. The close, solid walls also made my use of a pulse wave unadvisable. Doing the maths, I figured living another thirty minutes was a better option than getting dead, dead right there in that scarred lobby. I reluctantly handed off my gun, but as soon as I had, I felt the full force of a blow from a gun butt. I wasn't too dazed to notice the fury in Luther's steel-grey eyes, or the sound of gunfire that followed. The man who'd hit me, crumpled to the floor, his dead eyes frozen in shock.

"Did I ask this bastard to hit my guest," he bellowed, turning to address everyone in the foyer. "Well, did I?" he shouted, to shakes of heads and mumbled answers. "No one, and I mean no fuckin' one of you does anything unless I order it. Is that clear?" This time the answers were a little louder. "Don't fuck with me," he continued to the assembled bad guys, "and I won't shoot you in your fuckin' melon heads. It's that simple even a child could get it."

A couple of people dragged the dead guy away, a blood stain following the body.

"You know the rule," Luther continued. "This is my house, and nobody, I mean nobody," he repeated loudly, "does anything in my house that I haven't approved."

"But, bo—" The sound of the bullet halted the young guy mid-sentence.

"Now look what the fuck you've made me fucking do," Luther yelled, pointing his gun at the blood seeping along the floor, barely visible against the black. "Really?" Turning to address me, he lowered his voice, "I'm surrounded by fucking idiots. This is what I have to deal with every day.

It's exhausting. Do you see how exhausting it is?" He waved his arm around the assembled group. "Do you have this problem? I bet you don't have this problem. I bet you're surrounded by hard arses, not the incompetents I have to deal with. Are you? I reckon so. Let's see, shall we?"

By the time Luther had dragged me to my feet, the damage to my back had mended, as had the plasma wound. The burnt-edged hole in my top was still there, but I hoped no one would look too closely. I felt extremely uncomfortable as he put his arm around my shoulders, leading me carefully through the rubble and into the hall.

I scanned the room quickly looking for Jake or Jared, but nothing. I guess my distraction had helped a bit, as I would guess about half of the people who'd been in the hall when Jake and I were on the gantry, had cleared out – either on orders to sweep the building, or just because I'd blown one end of the hall to pieces. Unfortunately, it wasn't the distraction Jake needed to get Beck and Kaiser.

The two men were still on their knees not too far in front of the makeshift throne, though it was clear Beck was buckling to one side.

They were both disappointed to see me as a kick to the back of my leg left me dropping to my knees beside them. If I had to guess, I'd say Beck was nursing some broken ribs and maybe some internal bleeding to go with the dark blue bruise covering half his face, and the swollen shut eye. Kaiser didn't look much better.

"Hey, guys," I said. "Fancy meeting you here."

"Hey, Blue," Kaiser replied. "Well, ain't this a shit-ton of fucked up."

"Not going to lie, big guy, it's not the best situation I've been in," I replied, mentally calculating whether it would be easier to get the metal cuffs off their wrists or go for the links chaining them to o-rings in the floor.

"Now this is what I'm talking about," said Luther,

sliding into his throne, one leg casually hanging over an arm. "See this?" he shouted to the people left in the room. "This is what I'm talking about. She blew up half my goddamn hall to get her crew back. You guys would stab your mam in the back for taking the last fuckin' bullet in the rack." He looked back at us. "It's a shame I'm going to have to kill you all. I don't want to, but what's a gang-lord supposed to do when someone tries to take his shit. I mean, you guys look kinda cute together, but how am I gonna keep everyone in line if I let you continue breathing." He stood to address the room. "Am I right? You know what? I don't know why I'm asking you sorry sacks of shit. I know I'm fuckin' right."

I think I knew what he was going to do, before he did it. I was halfway to my feet in front of Kaiser when I heard the gun. For a split second, it felt like a gut punch, then the pain hit. I know I crumpled to the floor, but everything else was a blur. I curled up in a ball, my arms tightly across my stomach. I already felt the tingling in the wound, but I knew it was bad. I sucked in ragged breaths, sweat trickling down my forehead. It seemed like a lifetime, but I'm sure it was only a couple of minutes before the pain subsided. A few minutes more until I was able to uncurl myself.

Luther sat cross-legged less than a meter away from me, his eyes wide, his breathing quick and shallow. It was like looking at an excitable kid. He leant forward and I recoiled, but when he pointed his gun at my head, I let him inspect the hole on my shirt.

Kaiser was practically growling so I reached out a hand and touched his knee. "I'm okay," I confirmed.

"Holy mother-fucking, mother fucks," Luther said, rubbing his eye and practically dancing on the spot. "Whoo whee," he added before dropping down beside me again. "You don't see that every god-damn day of the week."

"I don't know what you're talking about?" I said, knowing it was going to be useless trying to talk this away.

"Oh now, baby girl, you're not gonna go get all fibby on me now, are ya? That would be such a shame now we're getting on so well an' all."

"That obvious?" I asked Kaiser. His nod was my answer, but then he pulled on his chains, trying to get up. Luther seemed unimpressed.

"I'm going to kill you," he scowled, but Luther's answer was a raised weapon pointing straight at Kaiser's face.

"There's no need for all this… negativity," Luther concluded, unconcerned. "This little side-show trick might just keep you all alive – for a bit anyway." He crouched back down, the gun resting easily on his thigh. "Colour me intrigued," he said, touching my face gently with his fingers. This time it was Beck who objected, but Luther didn't even flinch or take his eyes from mine. "Does this… is this… how?" he asked.

"Not a clue," I replied honestly, though this was the last conversation I wanted to have with a sociopathic gang-lord. At least we were still alive, and I had to hope that Jake and Jared were both still out there.

"So, if I like, blew a hole through your brains," Luther continued, but Kaiser started growling again, so he moved the gun from my head to Kaiser's.

"No," I replied quickly, trying to get his focus back on me. It worked.

"No?"

"You shoot me in the head, and I'll die, just like shooting anyone else in the head."

"But you healed when I shot you in the guts."

"Dead's, dead," I replied. Not the greatest thing to say when you've got the muzzle of a gun against your temple, but I had to hope that every second I could stall for, was a second longer for Jared and Jake. "But I heal from anything that doesn't kill me."

He seemed genuinely interested, asking more and more questions, until he said, "Show me again," and before I could react, a bullet tore through my thigh, a dark stain spreading across the fabric.

"What the hell?" I blasted, only just getting it in before the onslaught from Beck and Kaiser.

"This is interesting," Luther said, studying my face. "You're in pain."

"Of course, I am," I growled through gritted teeth. "You just shot me in the leg." The silvery-blue glow danced in his eyes, until it dissipated, and the pain subsided.

"You know, I knew today was gonna be a hella good day," he said. "Didn't I tell you it was gonna be a good day?" He asked one of his minions. "Never mind, I don't care what you think. Fuck off." He waved the person away with a dismissive hand. "Again," he ordered, the bullet ripping through my other thigh.

Tears of pain rolled down my cheeks and I found it difficult to breathe.

"Do that one more time and I'll rip your head off," Kaiser grunted, but it was like he was completely off Luther's radar. It took a little longer for me to heal, the pain lingering. The scarred skin barely had time to flatten out when the next bullet went through my arm. In the haze of pain and exhaustion, I heard Luther laughing.

"You're killing her," Beck shouted, earning himself a backhander. "Look at her, man," he continued unabated. "You keep this up and you will kill her."

"Well, we wouldn't want that now, would we?" Luther replied, this time allowing me to sit up, watching me carefully as I struggled. I rested my head in my hands, waiting for the next bullet, so I was completely unprepared for the knife stabbed mercilessly into my leg. I barely had the energy to cry out in pain. I lay on the floor, shaking, telling myself to keep it together. I didn't even bother to try and sit up, but I heard footsteps, so I forced my eyes open. A pair of boots approached, and I tried to look up to see who they belonged to. A woman with long black hair had her back to me, whispering to Luther.

I tried to listen to what she said, but I couldn't hear until Luther blurted out, "How much?" The woman whispered again. "Others?" he asked. "You sure?" She nodded, and I knew what was coming next. I forced myself off the floor as the bullet hit Beck. The force pushed him back, but the chains stopped him, almost bouncing him back before he fell beside me. He hadn't cried out, but I knew all too well what pain he was in. I tried to ignore his ashen face and grimace as my attempt to roll him on to his back, was made more difficult by the chains.

If I healed him, chances were Luther would keep putting holes in him and Kaiser, just for kicks, causing more and more pain, just like he had with me. But if I didn't, he was going to die for sure.

"Don't," he groaned. "You don't have to."

"You know I do," I replied, placing my hands gently over the hole in his stomach. He tried to protest further, but I ignored him, thoughts of my own blocking him out. I tried to concentrate, ignoring all the people who'd gathered round for the show. It was hard, and for a moment I wondered if I could, but then the energy swirled in my chest before spreading down my arms. Flickering strands of fine silver-blue arced from my hands to Beck, lighting up the area around us. It took longer than it should've, but I didn't stop at the bullet wound, healing all his other injuries at the same time. When I'd finished, it was Beck's turn to help me back up to kneeling position.

Luther was awestruck, his eye's flickering back and forth between me and Beck. "You reckon they'll pay that much," he asked the woman.

"No doubt," she replied, turning to face me for the first time. An exhausted laugh escaped my lips, but it wasn't from humour. In the flickering light from the flames, the silver scar tattoos around her right eye almost glowed.

"What's funny," Luther asked.

"Nothing," I replied, "Not a god-damn thing."

"Again," Luther cried, this time raising his gun towards Kaiser, but I was surprised to hear the woman interject.

"My people can be here in a matter of hours," she said, stepping between Luther and Kaiser. "And they'll pay what I've said... but not if she's dead."

"You know what?" Luther asked, standing to pace the floor. "What if I was to keep her? I'm beginning to think she'd be a pretty good pet to keep around."

"Take the money, Luther, and hand her over when my people arrive," she said, the hardening of her voice, and the change in her stance barely noticeable. Luther didn't pick up on it, anyway.

"Yeah, no, I don't think so," he replied before saying something I missed, too distracted by the crackle in my earpiece.

"Coms are back on-line. Kinda," Ty said, his voice breaking up in parts. The next voice was Jake's, and I let out a relived breath. I glanced carefully at Kaiser, who's nod was almost imperceptible, but it was enough to tell me he'd heard it too.

"You don't need to keep these two chained to the floor," I said, more to Jake and the others, than to Luther. I already knew what his answer would be, but at least Jake would know there was a problem to factor into any rescue op.

"I don't need them chained?" He sounded surprised. "What? You think I should let them just wander freely around?" He came closer, the gun still in his hand. "Truth be told, my little miracle, I don't really need them alive. You? You on the other hand, I think I'll keep as my pet."

"Oh, for fuck's sake," sighed the tattooed woman. "Couldn't you just take the money." The plasma blast exploded Luther's head like a ripe hemlon, splattering the throne behind him. "Dead's dead, right?" she added blandly, but I was too preoccupied listening to Jake's instruction than be concerned with how Luther's thugs were going to react to his death.

The citadel shook as the missiles from the *Veritas* hit the shield, fine black dust floating down from the ceiling. It didn't take long for the military-grade weapons to overwhelm the citadel's defences and take out the surface to air weapons located around the ramparts. With Luther dead, and the building disintegrating, most of the people in the room were more concerned with self-preservation, than punishing the woman who'd killed their leader. In fact, I wondered if they were relived, given that some had bolted even before the attack.

Beck and Kaiser pulled at their chains, and I tried to help, but the woman grabbed my hair, trying to pull me along the floor. I tried to reach for her, but in my weakened state, she swatted me off easily. Then she was gone. I picked myself up as I watched Jared bundle her away from me. "Wait, we need... never mind," I said as he broke her neck. A heartbeat later, I was in his arms, too tired to object.

Jake knelt by Beck, cutting the chains with a laser saw. Kaiser stood by, rubbing his chafed wrists before accepting a weapon from Jared. "Thanks," he said, but his next words were drowned out by weapons fire. Thugs were starting to come into the hall, perhaps unaware of their gang-lord's death, but Kaiser had it under control.

When Jake stood, so did Beck. "You good?" Jake asked, picking up Luther's gun.

"Am now," Beck replied, accepting it from him. "How are we getting out of here?"

"The way we came in," Jake replied. "Con, you know what to do. Wait five then rain holy hell on this building."

"Got you loud and clear," Connor replied. "Five and counting."

We headed out of the hall and found the nearest steps leading down. Anyone we encountered was taken out. "You can put me down now," I said, feeling guilty that Jared was still carrying me."

"You sure?" He searched my eyes and I blinked slowly before nodding. He lowered my feet to the floor and steadied me as I swayed.

"Unless you want to be pancaked, we need to move," Jake ordered, and I put one foot in front of the other. Jared pulled his TK70 off his back but stayed close to me.

"Ain't this a strike of luck," Kaiser commented, starting up one of the buggies at the entrance to the tunnel. Jake jumped on behind him, holding out his hand to help me up. With Jared and Beck on, it was cosy, and the buggy objected to the weight as we drove off.

"I think I can run faster than this shitty thing," Beck grumbled.

"You're more than welcome to get off any time you want," Kaiser replied.

"You wish I'd—"

"Enough." Jake stopped the conversation dead.

In the silence that followed, a had a thought. "If Connor blows the citadel, won't that destroy the information we need as well? I can't believe I've put you all in danger for nothing."

"Don't worry, babe," Jake said. "Glitch has got to have back-up somewhere."

"But—"

"Trust me," he replied, putting a hand on my bloodied leg, feeling one of the holes made by Luther. That reminded me.

"Kaiser?"

"Yeah, Blue," he said, turning gingerly from the front seat to look at me.

"I'm a little knackered right now, but when I get my strength back, I'm going to heal you. Okay?" The genuine smile lit up his weathered face.

"No worries, Blue. You just get yourself better. To be

honest, Luther was a bit of a pussy – I've had worse injuries sparring with the Pack."

"I just want you to know I haven't forgotten about you."

"I know, Blue."

When we got to the hatch in the ceiling, I was glad I couldn't see Ash of Cal. It meant they'd already gone ahead. The gears groaned as the ladder descended, and a clunk told me it was locked in place.

"Beck, go first. Open the hatch and check the passageway. Shae, you're next," Jake said.

Beck did as asked, but as he climbed the ladder he called back over his shoulder, "I still don't work for you."

"You're on my ship, taking part in my operation. I'd say that was the definition of working for me," Jake replied.

"Whatever," Beck said casually, his middle finger clearly raised as he reached for the next rung.

"Arsehole," Jake mumbled.

When Beck called the all-clear, I lifted my foot onto the bottom rung with difficulty. Jared took a step forward. "I'm okay," I added, not sure if that was his or my benefit.

Kaiser came next, the ladder creaking in protest to his bulk.

Jared had just started his ascent when Connor's destruction of the citadel began. Explosions rocked the tunnel, the ladder finally giving up. Jared jumped down and rolled out the way as the fatigued metal landed heavily on the tunnel floor.

"You okay?" Jake asked as Jared dusted himself off. He nodded, then looked up at the hatch, frowning. The explosions subsided and everything was quiet for a moment. Kaiser started to lower a rope, but as he did, a louder, closer explosion knocked Jake and Jared off their feet, and Kaiser almost fell through the hatch. An ominous rumble filled the tunnel.

"That sounded like the basement generators," Jake said,

waving his arm for the rope.

"But if they blow…" replied Jared.

"I know. The explosion is going to roll straight through this tunnel. You go first," Jake said, handing him the end of the rope. Jared paused. "My mission, my rules. Just don't hang around, I'd rather not be here when—"

The final explosion drowned out the words, but when Jared looked up, I saw the fear in his eyes. "Close the hatch, close the hatch," he shouted, but instead I stuck my head through, the tunnel filled with an orange glow at the end that was getting brighter and brighter. There was no time.

"Anchor the rope," I practically screamed at Kaiser before throwing myself through the hatch, the rope burning my palms as I slid down. I hit the ground hard, ignoring the barrage of objections from Jake and Jared. I'm not really sure I knew what I was doing, but I told them to get behind me as the fire raced down the tunnel.

I put my hands up, a mass of energy twisting and balling in my chest. The release of energy filled the tunnel like a shield, and as the flames bowled into us, I turned my head away from the blinding light. The shield turned our side silver blue, while the other side raged in orange and red.

I struggled to keep it going, dropping to my knees. It seemed like forever until the explosion subsided, and when the flames dissipated, so did the shield. I vaguely felt the pain in my hands and lifted them to see the raw, burnt flesh.

The smell was the last thing I remembered.

17

I turned over, almost falling out of bed. It was dark and quiet, just the low hum of the engines for background noise. I contemplated getting up, but it seemed like hard work, so instead I pulled the blankets up and went back to sleep. When I woke up again, the room was still dark and quiet. I checked my com-pad to get the time, but my wrist was bare. My hand jumped to my chest in panic, but my pendants were still there.

I sat up, bones protesting, and swung my legs over the edge of the bed. "Lights," I said, still not sure where I was at first. My brain felt muddled, even my hair hurt. I stood, carefully getting my balance, heat rushing to my cheeks when I finally figured out where I was. I crossed Jake's quarters to his private washroom, trying not to think about what happened the first time I'd been in the room.

The bathroom was modest, but the shower was decent, and I chose the lava-hot water rather than stone cold. On the counter next to the sink, someone – probably Ash – had placed clean clothes from my holdall. I stood under the stream of water, letting it run over my face. My mind worked its way back through the mission, my hand tracing the skin on my thigh where Luther had shot me.

The memory continued right up to those last seconds in the tunnel. I wiped the water out of my eyes and studies the palms of my hands. Like the skin on my thighs, there was no evidence of burns, from the rope or the fire. I sighed and put my head back under the shower jets.

By the time I got out and dressed, I'd been warmed to the core. My joints felt better, but they still protested when I bent over to put my feet through the holes of my trousers. My holdall had been left at the end of the bed, my com-pad, earpiece, and Sentinel had been placed on top. I pulled up the sheets before sitting on the edge of the bunk.

I allowed a moment to feel sorry for myself. Well, not strictly for myself, but for the danger I'd put the others in. How could I be so selfish? It wasn't fair of me to ask so many people to put my existential crises ahead of their own lives. My hands started to shake as I thought about how Ash had turned against the Brotherhood, and now Jake and Jared. Not to mention the Pack and Beck. At what point do you say it's not worth it?

A knock at the door pulled me out of my reflections. "Who is it?"

"It's me," was the reply. "Can I come in?"

"Of course." I stood and took a few steps towards the hatch, inexplicably panicking over what was going to happen.

"Come here," Jared said, wrapping me up in his arms. So many emotions filtered through me – love, fear, pain, anguish, love. He held me tight, not letting go, and I did the one thing I was told not to do. I tried to apologise, but it was muffled as I sobbed into his chest. "It's okay," he said, moving one hand behind my head. "It's okay," he repeated. "I've waited too long to have you in my arms, I'm not about to let you go just yet." If it was possible, he held me even closer.

When I finally finished crying, he released me and

passed me a tissue. He didn't say anything as we sat side-by-side on the bunk, waiting for me to lead the conversation. He held out his hand and I took it, intertwining our fingers.

"I assume Ash and Cal got Glitch back here okay. I can feel Ash through the Link; is Cal okay? What about Kaiser, I said I'd heal him."

I didn't understand Jared's smile. "It's all sorted, Shae. You don't need to worry about it."

"But what if Glitch—"

"Like I said it's all sorted." He gave my hand a reassuring squeeze. "Glitch gave us what info he had days ago, not that it was much."

"Days? How long have I been asleep?"

"A long time."

"How long, Jared?"

"Three days 'ish, give or take a few hours."

"That long?" I marvelled. "What happened? After the explosion?"

"Perhaps Ash should…" He said starting to rise, but I pulled him pack down.

"Tell me," I persisted.

"If you're sure…" He saw the look on my face and continued. "Once the flames died down you collapsed." His eyes showed me his pain. "I thought you were dead, Jake did too. You barely had a pulse, and you just…" He cleared his throat. "You were so limp in my arms. We got out of the tunnels through the barracks and back up into the old house where Ash and Cal were waiting with Glitch. Connor deserves a medal for the way he put the *Veritas* down amongst all that debris, without even a scratch he kept saying to Jake." I laughed quietly, and I think that made Jared smile.

"Then what?"

"When everyone was safe onboard and we broke atmo, Jake started… well, Jake started being Jake again." I could picture it in my head. "He started getting his arse off about the amount of… excess baggage I think was the word he used. Anyway, with the Pack expanding from four to five, then adding Beck, you, Ash, and now me. I think he felt like the *Veritas* had been invaded."

"That makes no sense. I'm here in the biggest room on my own. You can get three in here easy."

"Jake was adamant you had this space to yourself, with the private washroom. Which I think he cleaned specially for you while you were out. To be fair, I've seen the other shower, and trust me, you're better off here."

"Yeah, I probably won't disagree on that one. Hey, how did you know I was up?"

"Ash's ESP Link. He felt when you were awake, told me to give it a while before heading down. I waited as long as I could."

"And now you're here, I can barely believe it." I touched his face, healing the graze that was still there from the fight in the citadel.

"You shouldn't," he said, gently removing my hand, but it was too late, he was already fixed. "Not after…"

"After being shot three times, no, four, stabbed once, and then healing Beck completely? He better not have got himself broken again on the way out."

"He's fine. He's even stopped calling me Super-Prick after the rescue." Jared's sparkling blue eyes captivated me the same way they had when we'd first met.

"He called you that, huh?"

"Only once." Jared's smile was mischievous. "To be fair, he held his own in the citadel." His eyes searched my face.

"What?"

"You have no idea how much I want to kiss you right now."

I'm sure I blushed outrageously, the heat in my cheeks giving me away. My stomach flipped. "What's stopping you?" I asked, my voice more airy than usual.

"Me." I must've looked confused, so he continued. "If I

kiss you, I'll want to kiss you again, and again. And I'm not blind to the fact that we're literally sitting on a bed. It would be so easy too… and that is why I'm stopping myself from kissing you, and why this is so god-damn hard," he concluded, the boyish grin I loved on his soft, dark pink lips. "When we're alone, when we have time, things will be different, I promise."

I loved Jared, and I had missed him more than he would ever know, but I knew he was right. I couldn't help pulling him towards me for one, quick kiss.

"That's my ration for today, is it?" he joked.

"Something like that," I replied, still blushing hard. "Okay, so back to the worky stuff. What happened after we left Santorra?"

"Ash had already given Glitch some medical treatment while they waited for us, but obviously the good stuff was on the *Veritas*. I guess he was just so relived to be out of Luther's control, he didn't even seem to be bothered by the injuries. It probably helped that Ash doubled the dose of Oxytanyl."

"Yeah, that'll do it," I said, laughing.

"What's so funny?"

"Jake. I gave him a double dose of Oxytanyl when he got his foot cut off. He hates me talking about it, says it dents his tough image, but he was funny as hell."

Jared smiled, but I knew it wasn't because of Jake, it was because I was laughing.

"Anyway," he continued. "You can imagine what Glitch was like. He accessed the main data source, which was never actually in the citadel, or even on the planet. Held duplicates of the whole thing on the ring of satellites in orbit. He also said he had a backup somewhere, but he wasn't sharing that location, even if he was doped up. We dropped him on some random planet in the middle of nowhere, which is more than he deserves. Both Jake and I agreed it was too dangerous to take the *Veritas* close to any

REF bases."

"Are you two friends now?"

"Not friends. I guess we tolerate each other," he replied, grinning playfully, and I really wanted to kiss him again.

"Fair enough," I replied, having given up on trying to make them friends. "What info did Glitch give before you booted him?"

"Something. Nothing. We're trying to piece together bits of data still, but I'll be honest, Shae, I'm not sure it going to get us anywhere."

"So, all this was for nothing." I stood and started to pace, but Jared stepped in my way, sitting me on a cold metal chair. He pulled up another and sat facing me.

"Not for nothing." He took my hand again and I leant forward, resting my head on his chest for a moment before sitting up again. His eyes narrowed with concern. "What?"

"How did you get here," I asked seriously. "I can't be responsible for you losing your career."

"I'm not going to," he assured me. "After we dropped the D'antaran trade delegation off for the agricultural conference near Chartreuse, we were ordered to stick around. It was no more than diplomatic optics – something Commander Tel'an could do in her sleep. I contacted High Command and requested to take some leave, which seemed plausible given it's my birthday in—"

"Your birthday! Jared, I'm so sorry, I completely forgot."

"It's alright. I don't think I actually told you what day it is anyway."

"Well?"

"It's not important given everything else that's going on."

"It's important because everything else is going on," I replied, trying to give him a serious look and failing dismally. "A little bit of normality is what we need in all this chaos."

"I can't see Jake of the others being fussed about it."

"But I am. I don't care about anyone else. So, are you going to tell me?"

"Okay, okay," Jared said, giving up. "If I tell you, can I get back to my debrief.

"Yes," I said simply.

"Then it's seven days from now. Can we move on?"

"Yes, in one second." I leant forward and kissed him, longer than I should have. "Happy birthday for seven days' time. You can continue now."

"How do you expect me to concentrate after that?" he asked, leaning forward to kiss me back, but I playfully scolded him. "This is so much harder than I thought it was going to be."

"Concentrate on something less pleasant," I suggested. "Like Glitch in the nude."

"Eww, gross," Jared spluttered. "I guess that's done it. Okay, so where were we?"

"Taking vacation time for your birthday."

"Oh yes, well I've not had any time off since way before taking the chair of the *Defender*, and with nothing urgent coming up on the roster, they agreed."

"How long?"

"Two weeks as a starter."

"How did you end up on Santorra with us?"

"Jake called me to say they were taking the *Veritas* offline, and you were all going on a mission to Santorra. He may have mentioned that there were files in the archives that would help, and he may have given me the case access codes. After that, I hopped a shuttle that was on its way to a commerce planet to re-stock, and from there I bought a clapped-out old Scimitar to get me to Santorra."

"I'm in shock," I said playfully, sitting back in my chair.

"I know, me too. That Scimitar was so old, I didn't hold out much hope it would actually get me there."

"That's not why I'm shocked."

Jared looked confused. "Then what?"

"I'm surprised you can actually pilot anything, let alone an old colonial attack ship."

"I'm wounded," he said, pulling a sad face and placing one hand over his heart. "You do know that everyone in Fleet has to pass at least a rudimentary piloting class at the academy?"

"You do know I'm just playing with you?"

"I know. I promise you I can fly most tubs. Did you know that the Vanguard Class cruisers, like the *Defender*, are designed so that in emergencies, one person can keep the ship operational? Basic, but moving."

"I didn't know that," I said, genuinely interested.

"Well, the upshot is the Scimitar got me to you, and because it so old, there was no way to track it. Plus, I paid in credits. Totally untraceable."

"You sure you're not going to get in trouble."

"Depends on what you mean by trouble. But as far as the REF is concerned, I've taken genuine shore leave that's long overdue. I actually think they were glad I was taking a break – especially after Fallen Star."

"Well, I for one am very glad you're here."

"And yours is the only opinion I care about… and maybe Ash… possibly Jake at a push. Definitely not Beck," he teased. I leant forward and hugged him, breathing in the sandalwood and musk that seemed homely somehow, but then my stomach grumbled so loudly we both laughed.

"I suppose we should join the others?" I suggested reluctantly.

"That depends." Jared sounded serious.

"On what?"

"On whether you want to talk about the decrypted Brotherhood data-logs." He saw the sudden change in my demeanour and continued quickly. "You don't have to. Not if you don't want to. It's really okay. I know it's personal, and I could tell from Jake's reaction it was hard to look at. I just want you to know I'm here. If you need me."

I thought for a moment, the coldness of betrayal chilling my insides. "Her name was Mia," I said.

"Who's was?"

"My mother's. My father's name was William."

Jared sucked in a surprised breath. "The Brotherhood knew who your parents were all the time, and they didn't tell you? Shit, Shae, I'm so sorry. You don't need to do this now."

"I do, Jared. I want you to know everything, but this hurts so bad. I just need to get it all out in one go. Is that okay?"

"If you're sure." He took both my hands in his and waited patiently while I composed myself.

"The Brotherhood sent Finnian and the *Nakomo* to rendezvous with the transporter. There was no humanitarian mission or distress call, that was all made up. The real mission was for Finnian to meet the transporter at pre-agreed coordinates near the edge of Sector Three and pick up my..." I paused, trying to swallow a lump in my throat. "Pick up Mia and William, and obviously me as a bump onboard, but they never refer to me as the baby, only the key."

"What does that mean?"

"I've no idea, but Finnian used the same word in his message to me. Anyway, there was no surname in the log, so I guess I stay as just Shae, and definitely not 'the key'. The logs then go on to say that when the *Nakomo* got near the transporter, a ship unlike anything the Brotherhood had seen before, or seen since, fired on the transporter's FTL engines. There's a lot of telemetry information after that, that means nothing now, but the log shows that while Benjamin stayed on the *Nakomo*, Finnian and Noah transferred to the disintegrating transporter, returning with just William and Mia."

"Just?"

"There were 97 souls on the ships manifest. I guess the Brotherhood felt safe sharing part of the information. I knew my father had died as they got him on board, my mother slightly later, after I was born. But here's the real kicker… Finnian and Mia knew each other prior to that meeting."

Jared removed a hand to wipe over his mouth, digesting the information I was sharing. "How?"

"The logs don't say. Finnian told me Mia had asked for the Brotherhood to look after me, that I'd be safe with them, and the data corroborates that, but what Finnian left out of that story was that the mission was already to get Mia and William to the monastery with the key. Me."

"Outsiders? I thought there was a strict rule that only members of the Brotherhood could know the whereabouts of the monastery."

"That's true, hence the *Nakomo* planned to meet with the transporter and bring just my mother and father to the monastery. But you're right, they were still outsiders."

"And you."

"Right, and me. In fact, it was all about me. There were plans on that data disk, plans for me to be born safety at the monastery, and then we'd all be moved to a secure location, where we were to be protected, and I was to be trained."

"Trained for what?"

"I thought it meant training with the Warrior Caste, but now I'm not so sure. When Ash and I… when I threw a fit at Noah for taking my stuff, looking back, he seemed genuinely confused. Then Luke, the monk that turned up to so-say rebuild a fricking wall, seemed pissed that the Brotherhood had kept me in the dark, and 'compliant' of all things. So now I wonder if it was some other kind of training I was supposed to get."

"What else was on the disc," Jared asked quietly.

"A few bits and pieces, some stuff I knew, some that wasn't important. But they knew my parents, Jared. They knew their names, yet all my life they've told me they didn't know anything about them, about me. And now I find out that it was all because of me. My parents died bringing me to the Brotherhood." Tears fell freely and Jared wrapped his arms around me, letting me cry into his chest for a second time.

"I'm here, I'm not going anywhere until we find out what this is all about," he said when he let me go.

"What were they supposed to get me ready for? Why am I the key? My mother was called Mia, Jared. Mia and William. They were real people. They were my parents. What would have been the issue with sharing that information with me?"

"I don't know, Shae, but we're going to find out together, okay?" He lifted my chin and gave me the briefest, softest kiss. "Together."

"I can't tell you how much that means to me," I said, sniffing. "Because I'm lost, and I'm afraid with every new piece of information we find, I'm just drifting further away."

"I won't let that happen," Jared said, cupping my face with his hands. "I'll be your rock, your anchor, whatever you need me to be to stop that from happening. Okay?"

"Okay," I said sniffing again. The mood was depressing, and I didn't want to spend my first time with Jared to end on a downer. "If nothing else," I said, forcing a bit of a smile, "I get to spend your birthday with you."

"And that is precisely one of the many reasons I love you," Jared replied, and my insides warmed a little.

"Do you think we should go meet the others now?" I asked.

"Not looking like that," he replied cheekily. "I think you ought to freshen up first."

"I look that bad, huh?"

"A little pale, a little streaky," he said. "And your eyes are a little bloodshot." He paused like the words had unlocked a memory. "Your eyes."

"Yeah, I know, bloodshot. There's some drops in my bag that will solve that."

"That's not what I meant."

The way he said it made me stop routing around in the holdall. "What did you mean?" I asked carefully, not sure if I wanted to know the answer.

"Back in the tunnel, you created a shield that held back a massive explosion."

"I know, I was there," I said, trying to make light of it, and failing.

"I've never seen you do that before."

"I've never done that before."

"Then you jumped back into the tunnel not knowing whether you'd be able to save any of us?"

"Seemed like the right thing to do at the time. I agree, it doesn't make sense, I just knew I had to do it."

Jared followed me to the washroom, stopping at the door to laze casually against the wall. I was beginning to wonder if that's a move they teach at the academy given Jake does the same thing. I washed my face with cold water, drying it with a simple towel that was a million light years from the plush loveliness of the ones in my quarters on the *Defender*.

"Since I've known you, you've gone from healing yourself, to healing others, then from a blast wave to full on shield, powerful enough to hold back a generator explosion."

"Okay," I said slowly, dropping liquid into my eyes before blinking like a crazy lady. "What's that got to do with my eyes?"

"They turned blue."

"I always shimmer silvery blue, you know that. You've seen it enough times."

"No, this was different. When you sparked up that shield, yes there was the usual silver-blue light, but your eyes… your eyes turned blue."

I was confused. "Are you sure? What kind of blue?"

"I don't know. Blue, blue – like cobalt blue."

I was too tired to be shocked at my power having another quirk of evolution. "Well, that's new, I guess. They look okay now, though," I said, going on tip toes so he could have a good look. "What?"

"Is it wrong to want to keep you here and have you all to myself?"

"Umm, no," I concluded kissing him quickly on the lips before ducking around him back into Jake's quarters. "But needs must, etcetera etcetera."

"I suppose you're right," he agreed. "It's just…"

"Nice to spend some time together, alone?"

"Yes."

"I know. I feel the same way. Did my eyes really turn blue?" I asked, pulling on my boots.

"No word of a lie."

"Did I look good with blue eyes?" I teased, pulling my damp hair back into a ponytail. "I bet they looked a lot better than bloodshot red."

"I don't care what colour eyes you have, as long as we're together."

"I bet you say that to all the girls."

"Just you," he replied, pulling me into a tight hug. "But you're right, we really should join the others. They may have found something in Glitch's data."

"Are you trying to convince me, or you?" I said into his chest.

"Both of us, I think."

18

When Jared and I entered the main cabin, Kaiser and Beck were mid-argument, and it made me smile because it felt normal. All attention was on them, but somehow it didn't feel like they were hating on each other, more like a disagreement. A rather loud disagreement. Ash was the first to see us, maybe triggered by the Link.

"Nice of you to join us," he said, crossing the distance quickly, but when he got up close, his forehead creased. He held out an arm, and I thought he was going to hug me, but instead he felt my forehead with the back of his hand. "You okay?" he added quietly, searching my eyes. I nodded as Jared diplomatically let go of my hand and joined the others.

"I'm okay," I replied.

"No, you're not. You look tired… and pale."

"I'm always pale, but honestly, you're right. I am tired. And every time I remember being shot or stabbed, it's like there's an ache still lingering where the wound was. That's new."

"So is creating a force shield."

"They told you? Of course, they told you. Another step

on the evolutionary ladder." I tried to smile. Over Ash's shoulder, I saw the others gathering around the holo-projector. "Did they tell you my eyes changed colour?"

"They were worried about you," Ash replied, which meant they had. "I'm worried about you. We should talk more, but if you're up for it, we should join the others to go over Glitch's data. Ty's managed to piece together some semblance of order to the files, but it still doesn't make any sense."

"Is that what Beck and Kaiser are beefing over?"

Ash laughed; his eyes truly sparkling. "Would you believe that was just sparring?" I raised my eyebrows. "Whatever happened to them at the citadel seems to have cleared the animosity. They're actually getting on quite well now."

"Will wonders never cease," I joked, looping my arm through Ash's as he led me back to the now very much extended Pack.

The hello's and hi's took a couple of minutes, during which time Jake disappeared before returning with a steaming cup of Shatokian coffee, which he placed on the table in front of me. I breathed in the aroma, instantly smiling.

"What about ours," Ty grumbled.

"Yeah, thanks, boss," added Connor. "Don't worry, everyone, I'll get them."

I took a sip and felt the warmth flow down to my stomach, closing my eyes to savour the moment.

"Okay, so let's start," Jake announced, but I held up my hand.

"You know the rule, Jake. No work, until everyone's fixed," I replied, looking purposely at Kaiser, who immediately turned to Jake.

"What?" Jake asked him. "You think anything I say is going to stop her from doing what she's going to do?"

"Welcome to my world," Ash stated, and everyone

laughed.

Connor returned with more coffee, just as the silver-blue light waned. "Perfect timing," I said, trying not to let my voice betray the nausea churning deep down inside. I drank some more coffee and graciously accepted the chair Jared had pulled over for me. "What have I missed?"

"To start with, not a lot," Ty said. "Glitch accessed the data and downloaded anything that referred to the Harbingers, but unfortunately, most of it was a shit-ton of useless crap."

"I don't understand."

"The word harbinger, especially in human dialects, is commonly used to define something or someone who foresees or anticipates an event or change," Jared explained.

"It can also refer to any old bastard who's just giving bad news," Jake added.

"The info from Glitch included data going back as far as the original archives," Ty said, taking back the conversation. "The files referred to harbinger lore, as well as groups of people who, over time, have sold themselves as seers or Readers. There's also information on individuals who had a lucky guess at what was going to happen and were branded as a Harbinger by uneducated idiots as a result. And like I said, that's just from our own archives."

"When you start to include data from other species, who have their own word for someone, or group of someones, who make predictions or warnings, the information increases exponentially," Jake continued, causing Ty to huff.

"So," Ty said loudly getting the focus back on him again, "you can see our problem."

"I put you all at risk for nothing," I stated.

"Not nothing," Ty offered. "I've spent..." he caught the look Jake threw at him. "We've spent," he clarified, "the last couple of days filtering out all the crap – and like I said, there was shit-ton of it."

"Get to the good part, Ty," Jake ordered. "Or I will."

Ty continued quickly, not giving Jake the opportunity. "Once you filter everything out, there are some interesting, current references, but they're just snippets. Like vague shadows left after the main data's been scrubbed. Whoever these Harbingers are, they're going to extreme lengths not to be found."

"Explain in simple terms," I said, my head starting to ache.

"It means, I'm seeing gaps in the data. Where info was, but has now been deleted. This level of data manipulation across every data-net, is unheard of. I've never seen a redaction or deletion on such a comprehensive scale."

"How is that even possible?" asked Ash.

"Beats me," Ty answered.

"I still don't see how this was worth putting everyone's life in danger," I said, rubbing my forehead.

I hadn't noticed Jake leave the group, but when he returned, he was holding something in his hand. "Give me your arm," he said, and I did without hesitation. He pushed up my sleeve, the hypospray stinging a little. He gently rubbed the small patch of red skin on my forearm. "Better?"

"Yes. Thanks, Jake."

"Anytime," he replied, using the opportunity to stay close. There was a moment of awkward silence. "Carry on Ty," he instructed. "But let's have the abridged version, shall we?"

"Sure, boss. I designed an algorithm that just studied the shadow data, trying to find any kind of connection, or corroborating data. What we found isn't much, but I... we," he corrected, "feel it's something."

"And that is...?" I asked.

"Trying to find our Harbingers with all this data redaction, plus all the other references muddying the water, is like trying to find a needle in a stack of needles, on a planet full of needles."

"We get it, Ty," Jake grunted. "Now move the fuck on."

"Some of the current data refers to harbingers as reliquaries. So, we cross referenced harbingers plus reliquaries against the shadow data, and two locations came up in multiple sources."

"And they are?"

"One is the planet Phrayton, the other is the Trinity Planets," Jared confirmed.

"It's a stretch," Ash said. "But without anything else to go on, we think it's the next best step to take."

I studied the group surrounding the holo-table. Except for Ash, these were men I'd only known months. What right did I have to keep putting their lives in danger? "Ash—"

"Nope," Jake said.

"No chance," Jared added.

"Fuck it," Beck grumbled, handing 20 credits to Kaiser, who smiled triumphantly.

"What's going on?" I asked, totally confused.

"You're going to say to Ash that you don't want to put anyone in further danger," Jake said.

"And then you're going to ask Jake to take you back to Dennford to pick up the *Nakomo* so you can go off on your own," Jared added.

"And I won that bet against Beck," said Kaiser.

I stood opened mouth, before turning to Ash. "Don't look at me," he said innocently. "I never said a word. Guess they just know you too well." He nudged me with his shoulder and winked.

"I'm that predictable, huh?" I replied, not knowing whether to feel frustrated or happy.

"Anyway, to wrap up this briefing, I'm not going to take you to the *Nakomo*, so you're stuck with us," Jake concluded. "And as Phrayton is practically on the way to the Trinity Planets, that's where we're heading first. Eta mid-morning tomorrow, give or take. I'm confident we're running dark, but it's going to take longer as we're avoiding normal shipping lanes. Okay, that's it, end of briefing. Kaiser, work with Ty; I want a tactical mission proposal based on the little intel we have."

As we stood to leave, Beck coughed loudly. "Aren't we forgetting something?"

"What? Like how you're still here regardless of how hard we try to get rid of you?" Jake replied.

"No, actually, though comments like that can really hurt a guy's feeling, you know?" Beck said, not the least bit phased. "Ignoring the fact my future wife, here," he paused for objection from both Jake and Jared, "can create her own, self-generated force shield, I'm talking about that woman back in the hall."

"We don't need to do this now," Ash said, attempting to lead me away from the table, but I wanted to know what he meant.

"What about her?" I asked.

"You saw them, right?" Beck said, not taking Ash's hint.

"Saw what? I was kind of out of it at that point."

Beck glanced at Kaiser for support. "You saw them? I know you did, don't leave me hanging here."

Kaiser thought for a moment, but I think that was more to torment Beck than anything else. "I did," he finally agreed.

"Does someone want to clue me in?" I asked, my interest piqued.

"The tattoos," Beck continued, ignoring the daggers Jake was sending his way. "She had those silver scar tattoo things."

"Not now," Ash repeated ominously, but I was already searching my memories, forcing myself to relive the moments from her arrival. It didn't take long to dredge up an image of the woman's face.

"I remember," I said. "I'd forgotten, but now I can see her." Ash sighed heavily. "What's so special about her, other than she's just another tattooed person trying to kill me."

"But that's it," said Beck, winning another glare, this time from Jared. "She wasn't trying to kill you. She had opportunity, but instead she told Luther her people would pay for you. She was the one who stopped him from torturing you anymore. She was the one who wanted to keep you alive."

"I don't understand," I replied, my knees starting to buckle. Everything seemed so hard, so confusing. I blinked slowly, not sure if my eyes would open again, the weight of exhaustion pressing down on my shoulders. "Why did she want me alive, when all the others wanted me dead, and had weapons seemingly designed specifically to do that?" I felt lightheaded as the room span.

"That's enough," someone said, but I couldn't tell who it was until Jake added, "Or I'll blow you out a fucking airlock myself."

I felt Ash pick me up, aware we were on the move, and then nothing until he pulled up the blankets and kissed my forehead. "Everything will be okay," he said as I drifted off again.

I woke up in a panic, leaning over the side of the bed to grab my com-pad. But after checking the time, I laid back on the bed, my pulse slowing once I knew I hadn't missed the mission to Phrayton. Though I still didn't know what we were hoping to find.

"Hey," Ash said in the darkness, my pulse quickening again.

"You practically scared me to death," I replied.

"Don't be so dramatic. Lights." The cot he'd been sleeping on looked uncomfortable as hell, and he practically had to roll out of it to stand up. His shoulder cracked loudly as he stretched, his hands almost touching the ceiling. "How do you feel?" he asked.

"Better, thanks. Quit staring at me, you're giving me a complex."

"You look better," he decided. "Hope you don't mind, but after everything, I thought it prudent that I bunk in here."

"When have I ever minded?"

"Yeah, well, when have you ever had three people vying for your attention?"

"Three?" I questioned, sitting up in bed and rubbing my eye vigorously with the balls of my hands.

"I'm not sure whether Beck has got a legitimate death wish, or he just enjoys causing a ruckus, but I don't think he's winning any favours by calling you his intended."

An involuntary laugh made choke, but I held up my hand to stop Ash's advance. "I'm okay," I said, hiccoughing quietly. "He's certainly a character, I'll give him that."

"You mind?" Ash said, pointing to Jake's private washroom.

"The other one that bad?"

"No, not really. At least there's no queue for this one."

"Just me," I replied. "Don't use all the hot water."

Ash was already dressed by the time I'd finished in the washroom, but he was towel drying his light brown hair, which was so short it was almost dry already.

"Ash?" I said slowly.

"Yes?" he said in the same way, mocking me.

"Hear me out before you say anything..."

"Uh-oh. I can already tell I'm not going to like this," he said, sitting.

"Do you think the cost of this is worth it?" I asked, but he stayed quiet. "I'm just one person. And because of me, you're putting your oath to the Brotherhood at risk, not to mention all the others putting their careers on the line. For what? Is finding out who I am, and why I keep being referred to as some key, worth risking eight other people. Everyone jokes about it, but yesterday I was right to challenge their involvement." Ash sat in silence. "Don't get me wrong, I don't want to seem ungrateful…" A sudden well of panic spread through my bones. "They don't think I'm ungrateful, do they? I appreciate everything each and every one of them has done, is doing, to help me. I'm just not sure I can be the reason something awful happens to them."

Ash waited a moment before he spoke, and when he did, he chose his words carefully. "I can't explain what's happened to you, or why. I wish I could, so I could take some of that burden from you and help heal some of the wounds I know you carry around inside. I've done a lot of soul-searching these last few days, and one thing I can say with absolute certainty is that our lives have been inexplicably intertwined since the first day we met. I felt something back then, and over the years that bond has strengthened. And that's not just about the Link we share. I am on this journey with you till the end, my sister. And you have to believe that," he added in a lighter tone. "Because I've never lied to you."

"I know, but—"

"But nothing. You've always said you had a similar connection with Jake and Jared. Some feeling that was there, but you couldn't understand why. Well, they feel the same way. I've had enough conversations with them while you've been sleeping to know they both have those same genuine feelings since meeting you. For better or worse, I think the three of us need to be on the journey with you. And the rest? To them we're part of the family. Honestly, you've given all of them an out on several occasions, and they're still here."

"Even Beck?" I said, feeling better.

"Even Beck. Jake hasn't spaced him yet, but if he calls you his future wife again, I think Jared might do it. It's good to hear you laugh."

"You always know the right things to say."

"That's because I'm the best big brother in the Sector," he joked, throwing the wet towel at me. "Get dressed and I'll see you upstairs for breakfast." As he got to the hatch though, he paused and turned, giving me his serious face. "I think this may become a tough road to travel, Shae, but the one thing you don't need to waste energy worrying about, is us. All of us. We're doing this because we want to. Okay?"

"Okey," I replied, throwing the wet towel back at him.

Once the hatch was closed, I sat on the edge of the bed, digesting his words. Maybe he was right. We had given them all an option to get out of this situation, and they'd stayed – except Beck, and I couldn't blame him for that. I dressed quickly, my stomach now rumbling loudly.

By the time I got to the main cabin, the smell of fresh coffee and cooked bacon made me practically dribble. I was ravenous, digging into bacon rolls unashamedly. After my second roll, two sausages and third cup of coffee, I sat back contentedly.

"You done?" Ty asked sarcastically. "There's still a couple of sausages left."

"It was an amazing breakfast, thanks, Ty. I honestly couldn't eat another thing, but I don't think you need to worry about the sausages," I said as Beck and Kaiser helped them to disappear.

"You know, with food like this, I might never leave," Beck quipped.

"Thought you were bolting the next planet we get to," Jake sneered.

"Yeah, well, a man's gotta hold out for decent planet, and so far… not so pleasant. But while I am onboard, I'll pay my way by helping on the missions."

"He's like a god-damn bad penny," Jake said to Ash as he stood to help clear the table. "Connor. Eta for Phrayton?" he asked back over his shoulder.

"As long as we don't get held up by flight control, and they have a spare landing pad, we're talking two and a half hours, approximately."

"Phrayton's a small planet," noted Jared, "There's a couple of larger cities, one in the norther hemisphere and one in the south. But there are hundreds of smaller settlements. What's the plan?"

"Glad you asked," Jake said, returning to the table and giving him a slap on the shoulder which even I could tell was harder than it needed to be.

"I've reviewed mission options from Ty and Kaiser, and this is what we're going to do."

I loved watching Jake at work. He had command of the group completely, even Jared and Beck. He was almost ruthlessly efficient on his brief, clearly using everyone to their strengths. There was no room for confusion or challenge, and by the end, there was a level of confidence around the group I hadn't seen for a while.

Jared was mostly silent, but he chipped in occasionally, checking his understanding, or challenging a mission parameter, but he was professional, polite, and well within his rights to do so. They were actually playing nice together, and that made me all kinds of happy inside.

"What we don't know," Jake concluded, "is how people are going to take to us asking about the Harbingers or reliquaries. Don't start anything, but stay vigilant, and make sure you've always got a way out of any situation. We're going to be split fairly thin to allow us to hit North City and South City at the same time. What's funny?" he asked as Connor and Ty tried to control their sniggering.

"It's the names, boss," Connor explained. "Like Independence and Wishbone creek. It's like all these colonials are on drugs. It's like…" he adopted a dopers voice. "I know, dude… we're gonna put a city in the north… and a city in the south. Can't be fucked to think of an original name, so let's just call them North City and South city? Great, motion approved, let's hit the booty-bars."

Even Jake couldn't help cracking a smile.

Getting landing authorisation was trickier than Connor had predicted. Apparently, the fucking retards, Connor's words, couldn't get their head around the fact that he just wanted to drop and dash, not actually rent the landing pad. Eventually they sorted the miss-understanding and we landed briefly in North City around lunchtime.

Connor didn't hesitate to raise the ramp, but that time I was ready for it. I pulled my jacket around me for warmth, checking my Sentinel was holstered at my thigh for about the tenth time. "You good?" Ash asked and I nodded. "Ty, Kaiser? You good?"

"Five by five," Ty replied, syncing all our com-pads.

"I'm good too," huffed Beck. "Just in case you care."

"We don't," Kaiser grunted, but then he stopped and turned. "Are you coming or what?"

The port was busy and loud, but we navigated through it with ease. It didn't escape me that Ash kept close by my side, and I was glad to have him there. After the likes of Genesis, Angel Ridge and Santorra, Phrayton seemed normal, dull even, but there was a fair amount of local law enforcement around the port. As we moved further into North City, their presence dwindled.

"Dude," Beck said, catching up with Ash. "Am I the only one who picked up on some major friction between Super-Prick and our fearless leader?"

"First of all," Kaiser butted in. "Never disrespect Jake like that if you want to keep your bollocks attached to your body. Secondly, I'm getting sick tired of the fucking attitude. This is a half-way decent planet, so why don't you just fuck off out of here, and let the adults do the real work."

"Just stating a fact," Beck replied. "No need to get a bug up your arse about it."

"That's enough," I barked, rubbing my temples.

"Another headache?" Ash asked, studying my face.

"Yeah. It's not so bad, I guess."

"You should've said something. I'm sure there's somewhere here we can get something."

"I'll be alright," I replied, forcing a smile, but I felt his worry through the Link.

Not getting the hint from anyone, Beck continued, "It is weird though, is all I'm saying. Both the Colonel and the Captain going to South City?"

"Not really," Ty replied, and although I was feigning indifference about the conversation, I was interested in hearing what he was going to come up with. "Ash won't leave Shae's side, not after what happened on Dennford and Santorra. Jake won't let Jared be on the same mission as Shae if he's not there with him… and vice versa. So, based on that, you'd have Ash, Shae, Jared, and Jake all on the same mission, leaving the rest of us to deal with you, without killing you," he aimed squarely at Beck. "The way I see it, this is the best split. Except you. Kaiser's right – you can fuck off whenever you like."

"Sooner the better," Kaiser called back over his shoulder.

"Hey! That's enough," Ash snapped, but then he lowered his voice to speak to me. "Ty's not wrong about Dennford and Santorra. You do seem to be attracting even more than your normal share of danger. I want you stay close to me this mission, okay?"

Normally, I'd argue that all the big brother over-protection stuff wasn't necessary, but after recent events, I couldn't argue with his threat assessment. Instead, I nodded my compliance and we carried on walking, eventually arriving at the mag-train station.

"Okay, you know the plan," Ash said, taking charge. "Kaiser, Ty and Beck, you'll travel to the Upper East Quad, heading over to the South Santian area. Shae and I will start Upper West, heading South. Jake wants check-ins on the hour. Questions?"

"I've got one," Kaiser said.

"What is it?"

"Why the fuck do we have to take Beck with us?"

I sighed as the bickering flared up again. "You know what? Beck, you're with us. I can't be dealing with this bullshit anymore. My decision's final," I added to stop the arguments. "Kaiser, your train's about to leave. Let Jake know what's happened."

"Sure thing, Blue. But now I kinda feel guilty that you have to put up with him."

"Go!" I replied, pointing at the train.

The mag-train heading West pulled into the station about ten minutes later. The lunchtime rush was at an end, and it was easy to get seats together.

"I definitely got the right team in the end. Just like old times," Beck said, sounding genuine. The antagonistic and disagreeable bravado gone. Mostly. "What's the plan, boss?"

Ash scrutinised Beck's face, and I guessed he was trying to figure out if he was being genuine or sarcastic, because that's what I was trying to decide.

"Honestly," Ash started, "I don't know if there is a plan for something like this. We don't know how the locals are going to react to us asking about Harbingers, and we don't even know who the right people are to ask. Based on my experience, every Earth-colonised planet brings with it some form of religion derived from the lore of magic or spirits. And while there may not be a direct link between the spiritual arts and the foreshadowing of future events, they do often complement each other. So, the plan, such that it is, is to locate any local practitioners, and ask for their help. What we don't know, is how open they are to outsiders."

"Well, I guess it is a plan, of sorts," Beck replied.

19

I stared out of the window, watching the colourful blur as buildings and parks whipped by, my headache making the task ahead seem even more challenging. It wasn't long before we reached our destination, but when we got to the station concourse, Ash told Beck and me to stay put while he went off to do something. Beck droned on about something to do with Angel Ridge, and while I tried to give him my full attention, I just didn't have the energy. Or, if I was being brutally honest, I just didn't care. I sat on a bench and rested my pounding head in my hands.

"Arm," Ash said when he returned. I held it out, not even bothering to look up. "That should make you feel better in a few minutes," he added, tossing the empty hypospray in a nearby trashcan.

"I thought you can heal yourself," Beck said.

"Not something that should be broadcasted," Ash commented, looking around to see if anyone was nearby.

"Sorry, my bad. It's just all so incredible," Beck replied in a much quieter voice. "Guess you guys are used to it."

"Not exactly," I said, surprised at how quickly the meds were making me feel better. "Shall we get going?"

Outside the station, the wind had picked up, and even though the sky was a cloudless shade of bright blue, the temperature was dropping rapidly. I blew onto my cold hands before stuffing them in my pockets.

"The pharmacist gave me directions to one of the more mainstream spiritualists," Ash explained as we walked quickly. "He said they may be able to steer us in a more unconventional direction, but he was pretty vague. I don't think he was comfortable being asked such questions. Hey, we're almost on the hour," he added. We moved out of the way of the afternoon shoppers and tourists, and updated Jake before carrying on.

I don't know what I was expecting, but the place we'd been sent to looked more like an upmarket tavern than the house of spiritualists. We were welcomed warmly at the door, though we had to check our weapons before heading down into the warm comfort of the waiting lounge. The dim atmospheric lighting, gentle music and soft woody aroma had my eyes closing, and I felt the weightlessness of sleep envelop me. When I came around, my head was on a pillow, which, to my blushes, was on Beck's lap. I sat up quickly.

"Sorry," I offered.

"No need to be."

"I didn't dribble on you, or snore or anything, did I?"

"No, but you do have this rather cute sigh you do every so often." I wasn't sure if he was teasing.

"Where's Ash?"

"Speaking to the owner, I think. He told me to stay with you, so he must be starting to trust me."

"How long was I out?"

"Not long. We've got our next check-in in about five minutes, so he better... talk of the devil," Beck said as Ash came out of a door opposite. He crossed the floor quickly.

"Time to go," he said, helping me off the couch before ushering me back up the stairs to the weapons lockers. As we retrieved our combined arsenal, Ash looked pensive, like he did when he was working through a problem.

After the warmth inside, it felt even colder on the street. "Well?" Beck asked.

"Let's put it this way," Ash replied. "I don't think we'll get an invitation to return any time soon."

"A bust then." Beck huffed loudly, his breath freezing on the air.

"Yes and no. I spoke to the owner, who was sceptical of my questioning. She laughed when I mentioned Harbingers, explaining that anyone and everyone can be a harbinger of sorts, just by predicting something that may come to pass if they have luck on their side. She said she'd never heard of a group of people called the Harbingers and suggested someone was playing tricks on us. She did, however, change her opinion when I mentioned reliquaries. At first, she tried to brush it off, telling me reliquaries are merely containers for artifacts – actual things rather than people."

"Finnian said, find the Harbingers and ask them about the codex," I said. "That's an actual person, right? It must be."

"I agree," Ash replied. "And in any case, just because lore suggests a reliquary is an actual place or container that holds actual objects, doesn't mean it has to be that literal. A person is a vessel, and the information held within just as important and priceless as an object."

"I'm still waiting for the part where you tell us how this wasn't a complete bust," said Beck.

"Like I said," explained Ash patiently, "the owner tried to brush off my questions, but the longer we spoke, the more confidence I have that we're on the right path. I'm just not sure if that path ends here, on Phrayton, or carries on to the Trinity Planets. She did give me the names and addresses of a couple of more extremist places."

Ash updated the others during our check-in, and we listened to remarkably similar stories from all the other parties. We all had other places to try, so the plan was to continue.

Many hours later, the sun had long gone down, and the temperature dropped even further. I stamped my feet and blew on my hands as the first flakes of snow fell. Every check-in up to that point had been a bust, and you could tell from their voices that everyone was getting despondent.

"Hey," Ash said, taking my hands in his to try and warm them. "We knew this wasn't going to be easy. The way our luck goes, we weren't going to rock up on the first planet and get all the information we need, were we. We know more now than we did earlier."

"We do?" Beck moaned hugging himself. "Don't look at me like that. I'm used to working in the stuffy, smelly, warm air of an asteroid, not freezing my nuts off in the snow."

Day workers had finished their shift ages ago, and now the streets were filled with joy and revery, despite the cold. Bright strands of beads were draped over our shoulders by tourist and locals alike, and the lanes filled with music and laughter.

"Why would anyone want to come out in this cold… never mind," Beck concluded as heaters turned on all over the square, their orangey-red light brightening the darkness as well as heating the air. I stood below one, trying to feel my toes as the snow melted.

"This last place on the list is pretty far off the normal routes," Ash explained. It'll take a bit to walk there and back, but I wouldn't want to leave without checking everywhere."

"Then we check it out," I agreed. "No stone unturned, remember?" I added for Beck's benefit as I dragged him away from the heater.

The first few streets were filled with people heading for the square, street players and food vendors lining the sides. My tummy rumbled at the smell, and we stopped briefly for something to eat. The further from the square we got, the thinner the crowd, and the more dubious the businesses looked. Neon windows offered services for all, and street hustlers earned their living off unsuspecting tourists that had strayed too far, or those who'd purposely strayed that far.

Ahead, the large windows of a bar lit the way, people spilling out onto the street. Tables opposite were draped with brightly coloured material and blazing candles, occupied by Readers – fortune tellers of all persuasions. Their customers listened intently to their futures, and I smiled, hearing the same vague rubbish as we passed each one.

As we approached the last table, I watched the Reader shake her hands before dropping marked tetrahedrons onto aquamarine cloth. She started talking to her customer, her eyes fixed of the table, but as we passed, her head lifted, and we locked eyes for a moment. It was just for a second, and then we were passed. Unnerved, I looked back over my shoulder, but her attention had returned to the table.

"Did you see that?" I asked.

"What?" Ash replied.

"That woman. The one on the end table. She looked up when we passed."

"Didn't notice," Beck said.

"Why?" Ash added.

"I don't know." I tried to smooth the frown lines. "The way she looked at me, and then…"

"Then?" Ash pushed.

"It looked like she was scared."

"You sure you didn't just imagine it?" Beck questioned.

"Maybe," I replied, already questioning myself. "Forget it, probably nothing," I concluded.

The last place on our list was another dead end, though this establishment said they would literally bury us if we ever returned there again. We checked in with the others, who were still having similar luck, and Jake made the decision that we would return to the *Veritas*. Connor had agreed with Flight Control that he could land briefly to pick us up and we headed back the way we'd come to meet up with Ty and Kaiser.

"I know you're disappointed, Shae," Ash said as we walked. "It's just a setback."

"I know, it just feels like another wasted day."

"Not completely wasted," Beck chipped in. "We know now that the Harbingers aren't on Phrayton."

"I appreciate you're trying to cheer me up, Beck, but just because we haven't found them, doesn't mean they're not here."

"True. But doesn't it sound a lot better than saying it's been a wasted day?

"When did you get so philosophical?" Ash asked.

"Oh, it's always been there. I just like to hide it, so people underestimate me." He smiled and I gave him a hug. He used the opportunity to squeeze my backside again, and I was mid-chastise when excruciating pain dropped me to my knees.

The Reader's bony fingers tightly gripped my wrist, her touch like five hot pokers searing into my skin. I looked up into her pale, wrinkled face, only the whites of her eyes showing.

"You're the key," she croaked, as tears of pain rolled down my cheeks. I looked around, registering that Ash had dropped to his knees, holding his head. The pain intensified and I cried out, but I still tried to push Beck's gun away from the old woman. "They're waiting for you," she continued. Someone shouted, more than someone, maybe. It was difficult to concentrate, and all my attention was on her.

"Who?" I cried, but she didn't answer.

"You will be betrayed," she said before her eyes rolled back into focus. She let go of my hand, collapsing into a heap. I sat on the floor next to her, panting from the pain, glad it was decreasing. A couple of locals helped the woman back on her chair, as Beck pulled me to my feet. My knees felt like jelly – like I'd been hit by a freight train – and I sank into a chair next to her. Ash brushed off Beck's attempts to help him as he got unsteadily to his feet.

A young man, early twenties maybe, passed me a steaming glass of something vibrant red, but I hesitated. "It's just tea; henta flowers, mixed with nectar and hot water. Very good for you," he explained, handing another glass to the Reader. "Help you get your energy back. Help you feel right again, so people say."

"This shit happens a lot, then?" Beck asked, looking just as concerned as Ash now did.

"Not much… sometimes, maybe?"

I pulled my arm back as the old woman reached forward to take my hand, and I waved off Ash's advance. "Please," she croaked. "Please forgive an old Reader."

"What do you know about me?" I asked, confused and scared. We'd come to the planet looking for something, but this something had blindsided me.

"Oh, my dear," she said, kindness creeping into her voice. "I don't remember anything."

"You said I was the key," I prompted. "And that someone was waiting for me." She shrugged and I started to get desperate. "Who is?" I pushed. "Who's waiting for me?"

Her eyes turned sad. "I don't know."

"You must do," I said, grabbing her hand this time as she tried to pull away, but Ash gently pulled me back. "Who's going to betray me?"

"I'm sorry," said the young man to Ash. "It's rare this happens, but when it does, she never remembers." He turned to me. "Please, drink. It will help."

I cautiously sipped the tea, instantly feeling the sweet warmth travelling all the way to my tummy. By the time I'd finished, I did feel better. The old lady, on the other hand, was too exhausted even after drink.

"I must go now," she said as the young man helped her to her feet. "I'm truly sorry I can't give you the information you want." But as she got to the doorway, she paused and turned. "There are no answers for you on this planet, girl. You must continue on your path."

"Wait," I said standing, but she was already gone.

"Are you okay," Ash asked as he checked my wrist. "I mean, physically? I only felt a fraction of your pain through the Link. I can't imagine what it was like for you."

"Not going to lie, it was pretty intense," I replied, accepting a hug from him that healed better than any stupid red tea.

"Umm, am I the only one who saw the eye thing?" Beck queried.

"What eye thing," I replied, my forehead creasing.

"It's nothing," Ash said, trying to brush off Beck's comment, but Beck wasn't getting the hint.

"If Shae's eyes turning a cool shade of sexy blue is nothing, then sure, it was nothing."

"Again?" I asked.

"Briefly," Ash confirmed, giving Beck daggers. "I know I was pretty out of it as well, but I think it was just while that old woman had hold of your wrist."

"Perfect," I grumbled.

"We need to go now," he added.

"Can I just…" I replied trying to sit back at the table, but he wouldn't let me.

"Now," he said, leading me down the ally.

"What is it?" Beck asked, the sudden alertness in his voice made me turn to look behind me. Nothing looked strange, well, stranger than what we'd just gone though.

"I'm not sure," Ash replied. "More of a feeling."

When we got to the station, the mag-train we wanted was already there, and due to depart in fifteen or so minutes. We found an empty carriage away from other people and I was happy to be seated again. "What?" I asked, noticing Ash staring at me.

"You're pale."

"I'm always pale."

"Paler than usual."

"And you've got massive dark bags," Beck added.

I laughed humourlessly, not sure if he was being serious or not. "Way to make a girl feel special," I grumbled.

"He's right," Ash said. "You look terrible. And I know what you're going to say, so save your energy."

"What? What was I going to say?" I challenged, more forcefully than I meant.

Ash sighed. "You were going to say that I'd look pale, and have bags, and look like shit, if I'd just gone through what you've just gone through. And you're fine. Quit asking."

I paused, thinking, then smiled. "Yeah, that was pretty much what I was going to say," I admitted.

"I know you too—" He froze, staring out the window. "Duck."

"Duck? Why?" I replied, by which time he'd pulled me off the chair and onto the floor at Beck's feet.

"Umm, should I be ducking too?" Beck asked, looking part bewildered, part amused.

"No, you're okay," replied Ash. "Look out of the window. There's a mag-train that's come in a couple of platforms down."

"Yeah, I saw it pull in."

"Check out the people getting off. There's a group of four or five that got off towards the rear of the train. You see them?"

"There's loads of groups, you're going to have to be more specific."

"They look like merc arseholes, centred around a guy with dirty blond hair."

"Luke?" I said, trying to sit up to look, but Ash kept me

down.

"Yeah, I see them. Walking like they own the place."

"That's them. What are they doing?"

"Walking."

"Beck, this is serious."

"Alright, don't have a conniption. They've had a good old nosey round, and now they're headed towards the concourse.

"They're leaving?"

"I think that's what I just said," he replied. Ash helped me off the floor, while Beck took the advantage to help brush the dust off me. We sat cautiously as Ash stared out the window again.

"Could you be mistaken?" I asked. "Please say you were mistaken," I added, unable to deal with any more challenges.

"I wish I could, but it was Luke, for sure," Ash replied.

"Just great," I sighed.

"There is some good news," Ash continued, as the train lurched into motion. "At least he's going in the opposite direction to us."

"If that's what we have to accept as good news, we're totally screwed," I replied, my headache returning with a vengeance.

I covered my eyes as the *Veritas* whipped up snow and debris as it came down to land. Like always, Conner's impatient piloting had the ramp closing as we were still walking up it, and it made me lightheaded. I reached out to one of the Rover's huge tyres for support, trying not to let my weariness show to the others.

Kaiser and Beck were already bickering, but I was only half listening, trying to work out if the uneasiness swirling in my chest was mine or coming through the Link from Ash – probably both. He held his arm out and I took it gratefully before he led me upstairs, an emotional support as well as physical.

My head still pounded, so I didn't argue when Ash deposited me on one end of the sofa in the lounge area before going off to get another hypospray. For a moment, I was the only one there, the quiet peace somewhat soothing, but it didn't last long.

"Seriously, why are you even still here?" Kaiser grumbled as he, Beck and Ty entered from the rear of the cabin.

"Don't be a hater, man."

"Bite me," Kaiser replied.

"Get your shit together you two," Jake barked as he and Jared entered from the front. "I'm sick of this attitude." He turned to Beck. "Are you in with us on this, or still just biding time till you jump ship? Because if you're all in, this shit has to stop… from both of you," he added. "But if you still want out, you're out. Next stop. I don't care if it's the butt-crack of nowhere, you get me?"

"You know what?" Beck said after a moment's contemplation. "This is the most fun I've had in ages. I'm in."

"You sure, Beck?" I asked as Jared sat next to me.

"Yeah, I'm sure."

"Great," Kaiser, Jake and Jared chorused, and I couldn't help laughing.

Jared took one of my hands. "You're freezing," he said, taking the other and lifting them both up to his mouth to blow on them.

"Here," Ash added. I leant forward so he could wrap the blanket around me, then held out my arm for the hypospray. "It's late. Maybe you should turn in?" he suggested.

"No, I'm okay." He looked at me sceptically. "We'll do the debrief, and then I'll go," I negotiated.

"Let's make this quick then," Jake suggested. "Shouldn't take long, given the fact that most of us had an extremely uneventful day."

Jared tried to tuck my hands under the blanket, but I compromised by burying one, and leaving the other holding his. He didn't seem to mind too much.

"I'll start then," Jake said, taking the lead as he casually slumped into a chair. "Nothing to report, followed by a whole lot of nothing. Then we had a bit of excitement when one of the locals took a liking to Cal." He paused for some laughing, during which time Cal turned crimson. "Then nothing, nothing and more nothing. Brief over."

"Okay, me next," said Kaiser, then nodding towards Jake, he added, "What he said."

"Guess I was with the best team after all," Beck joked, then copying Kaiser, he nodded towards me and Ash. "Adventure seems to follow those two around like a bad smell."

"Hey!" I protested. "Less of the bad smell."

"He is right though, babe," Jake said, and I felt Jared's grip on my hand tighten. "You do seem to be a danger-magnet."

"Not through choice," I replied. "Ash? I nominate you to do our brief."

"Kind of expected that," he replied, his lopsided grin appearing briefly. "Okay, let's just say our day was a rinse and repeat of yours, right up until the point we were heading back to the mag-train station." He paused momentarily to accept a mug of Goldflower tea from Connor, before telling everyone about the old lady.

"Are we really going to take that batty old fortune teller's words seriously?" Beck scoffed, but everyone else ignored him.

"According to the old woman, you're a key?" Ty asked, and I realised we hadn't previously shared the contents of Finnian's message with the Pack.

"Not 'a' key," Ash explained. "'The' key." He looked at me for permission, and I nodded, so he went on to disclose the full content of the message. "And before you ask," he said quickly as Ty's mouth opened, "we don't know anything more about Shae being the key than you've just heard. Though, now we have two independent sources referencing the exact thing, we must conclude that whatever it is, it's important."

"And, at this point, we can't assume that she was referring to the Harbingers waiting for Shae," Jared added. "She could've also been referring to the Brotherhood, or those tattooed assassins, or even the REF… anyone really."

"And are we really going to take her word that there's nothing further for us to learn on Phrayton?" Beck asked, unabated.

"Yes," I said bluntly, all eyes on me. "I don't know why, but I believe her. As for her comment about me being betrayed…" abruptly all eyes swivelled to Beck, "I just don't know. Not something I want to dwell on."

"But—" Ty started, but Jake shut him down.

"Not tonight," he said simply, but the message was well and truly received.

"What about this Luke character?" Kaiser asked. "How the hell did he even know we were there?"

"That's a good question," Jake acknowledged. "We're definitely running dark, double and triple checked it. So even if Captain Amazing picked up a tail in that old junker he flew to Santorra, there's no way the REF or Brotherhood could've traced us to Phrayton."

"I have no explanation for it," Ash said, shrugging his broad shoulders. "Perhaps we should stop and ask him next time – when we have more back-up?"

"Just say the word," Jake confirmed.

"What's the matter?" Jared said, looking down into my eyes. "I know that look."

"Finnian's message said not to trust anyone but Ash," I explained. "No, no that's not what I meant," I added quickly, seeing a sea of wounded faces in front of me. "It was in his message, but what I was going to say was that I'm glad you all know. You're just as much family as the Brotherhood is… was… is… maybe?"

"I think what Shae's trying to say is that we trust you. All of you, even Beck." He paused for laughter. "We wouldn't have told you any of this if we didn't. And Shae's right, you are family."

"But we haven't told all of you everything, and it's time you know fully what you've signed up for," I explained.

"Everything?" Ash said, his surprise thrumming at the Link. "Including the data disc Ty decrypted?"

"Everything," I clarified. "No secrets. Cards on the table, and all that. But if you'll all forgive me, I don't have the energy to go through it all again tonight. Ash, can you do the honours?"

"Of course," he replied. "Why don't you head to bed? You look exhausted."

"I think that's a good idea," I said, placing my empty tea mug on the table before standing and surveying the group. "But I need you to promise me one thing. Tomorrow is just business as usual. I don't want anyone treating me any differently, okay?" Agreements were given. "Good. Then I'm off to bed."

Jared stood, and I realised he was aiming to come with me, but Ash had other ideas. "Jared, your input would be beneficial," he said, his tone suggesting it wasn't a request.

"Will you be okay?" Jared asked me, and I nodded reluctantly. As I walked away, part of me wished I'd shaken my head and he was there beside me, but the other, much larger part of me, was exhausted. He was here, on the *Veritas*, and he'd still be here in the morning. That was enough for the moment.

20

I woke the following morning feeling more rested than I had in weeks. Jake's room was in pitch darkness, but I didn't need to see to know I was snuggled into the side of a firm, warm body. I felt relaxed, peaceful even as I listened to Jared's slow steady breathing, feeling the rise and fall of his chest under my arm. The slight sent of sandalwood and musk was comforting.

I moved carefully, so I could snuggle further into his side, and his arm closed tighter around me. "Going somewhere?" he asked in the darkness.

"Nope, just trying to get closer."

"I think that's something I can help with," he replied, rolling slightly so he could hold me with both arms. I felt protected lying there next to him – like everything else had dissolved into shadows and been swallowed up into the darkness. Like it had never been. He stroked my face and kissed me ever so gently on the forehead. I could've stayed like that for hours.

"Why didn't you wake me?" I asked. "And why are you still dressed?"

"I didn't want to disturb you. You barely even moved

when I got in next to you. And call me old fashioned, but I don't want Jake's bed to be the place we properly sleep together, if that makes sense."

"It does."

"But I'm also deeply in love with you," he continued. "And lying next to you might've been just too damn tempting. Clothes stayed on as a precaution. Plus, it was late."

"How late is late?"

"Later than it needed to be. I think Jake was just trying to keep it going – he knew I'd come to you first opportunity I had. I'm sure if I wasn't here, he'd have had the exact same idea."

"I'm glad it was you. Might have been a tad awkward otherwise," I joked. He laughed quietly and pulled me even closer. "Though any tighter and I'm going to need resuscitation."

"Really?" he said. "Because I'm pretty good at the whole mouth to mouth thing."

"That's good to kno—" My words were silenced by his lips gently pressing against mine.

"See?" he said.

"You know, I'm not sure," I replied, shrugging in the darkness. "I think you might need some more practice."

His lips were soft and warm, and tiny embers ignited deep in the pit of my tummy. His hands began to wander, and we shuffled positions until he was on top of me. He dropped is head and kissed me again, his stubble brushing against my chin. I didn't care.

When he pulled away, sighing, I didn't blame him, and if I was being honest, I'm glad he did. I don't think I would've had the will power to. He lay on his back, breathing heavily.

"I guess clothes weren't that much of a precaution after all," I said, and he laughed as I shuffled back up beside him.

"I believe it was all your fault."

"Mine?" I mock protested.

"If I remember correctly, you were the one that said in needed more mouth-to-mouth practice."

"Okay, you maybe got me on that one. It was kinda cheesy, but kind of nice though," I said, gently kissing him on the lips again.

"See, you're definitely the bad influence here," he replied before kissing me back. "Seriously, it's all you. I've—" Banging on the hatch stopped him mid-sentence.

"Hope you're decent," Jake yelled. "Coming in anyway."

Jake was silhouetted by the light streaming through the hatch as he unashamedly strolled straight in, not waiting for an answer. The sudden room lights seared my eyes and I put my hand up to protect them.

"A little notice on the lights would've been nice," I said, sitting up and blinking until I acclimatised to the brightness.

Jared stayed put, one arm behind his head, the other around my waist. "What do you want, Jake," he asked casually.

"Need some clean clothes," he replied nonchalantly. "This is still my room, remember."

"Of course, it is," I said, climbing over Jared and practically falling out of the bed as I got caught up in the blankets. "And you should have it back, Jake. This is your boat; I feel bad I've put you out already."

"No, it's fine, babe. You should have it," Jake said, clear emphasis on 'you' singular. He seemed momentarily surprised by Jared's clothing situation as he got up and stretched. "You could probably do with some clean clothes as well, if you're going to sleep in them, Jared."

"You're probably right. And I definitely need a shower," he replied.

"Briefing over breakfast in twenty," Jake said, shrugging out of his cargos. "Shae can use my facilities…" The shirt came off too. "You and I can use the communal facilities," he added to Jared. One more item of clothing and Jake would've been naked, a thought that had clearly crossed

Jared's mind as he bustled Jake, and his clean set of clothes, out the hatch.

"See you in a few," he said, leaning back into the room. Then he looked me up and down and sighed dramatically. I laughed and threw the pillow, but he'd already closed the hatch behind him.

Jake had said briefing in twenty, but as I stood in the shower, the hot water running over my skin, I decided I wasn't going to make it in time. I knew I should get out and get moving, but I just couldn't face it. I turned up the heat to as hot as I could stand, and just stood there, water pooling at my feet before running off.

When Ash and I had left Lilania and the Brotherhood, I thought I knew everything I didn't know, but in chasing down those answers, new questions had arisen. I absentmindedly rubbed my hand over my stomach where I'd been impaled by one of the spined knives. New weapons and new tattooed adversaries… and Luke on Phrayton? I shivered, even in the heat. What the hell was going on?

Even though I got to the brief late, I felt better after my shower. Clean, hair washed, and a fresh set of clothes, was just what I needed to set the day up right. But as I climbed the stairs, I started to worry how the guys would react to me, now they knew everything. As I entered the lounge, a sudden silence descended, like the flip of a switch.

"Hey, Blue," Kaiser said, approaching. I surveyed the group, beginning to panic, and then suddenly Kaiser was squishing me in the kind of vice-like hug Francis would normally ambush me with. He kissed me on the temple and then let go. "Enough said. From all of us," he added, before the room abruptly carried on conversations from before my arrival.

"You look better," Ash said, giving me a quick once over. "Well, rested," he added, the corner of his mouth twitching.

"Nothing happened," I replied, swatting him on the arm.

"I know."

"Gods, do I really want to know how you know that?"

"Let's just say, when you and Jared decide to… you know… get intimate, please, for the love of the gods, make sure I'm not within Link radius. You should see the look on your face," he added, guffawing, and it was such genuine, happy laughing, that I couldn't help but join in.

"What's so funny," Jake asked, handing me a sausage sandwich.

"Umm… you had to be there, I guess," Ash said diplomatically, while I got my breath back. Though I could tell by the heat, my cheeks were still scarlet.

"Jake, I'm sorry, I was longer than twenty. Did I miss anything?" I asked.

"No, we waited. Seemed like you needed the time, and it would've been wrong to go on without you." His words were kind and sincere, and I felt guilty about sharing his bed with Jared. I reached up and pulled him into a hug and his arms closed around me.

"Thanks, Jake," I said quietly.

"For what?" he whispered back.

"For everything. For helping me, despite all the danger. For staying with me, even though I know things can't be easy. For… for just being you."

"Stop, you'll make me blush."

"I mean it," I said, letting him out of the hug so I could pull back and get eye contact.

"I know," he replied seriously, then he pulled me closer and whispered, "I love you," before letting me go to join the Pack in devouring the last of the breakfast. I stood rooted to the spot until Jared walked over and said something.

"Huh?" my thoughts scrambling.

"Jake. I asked what he wanted – whether you were okay?

Looked pretty intense for a moment."

"I… I thanked him for helping with everything. Given the circumstances, he could've turned Ash and me away, and I wouldn't have blamed him."

"But then he wouldn't be Jake, would he?" Jared said.

"That's exactly what I said."

"We may never be best buddies, but that doesn't mean I wouldn't want Jake at my side in a fight. And let's not beat around the bush, this is turning in to one hell of a battle." He looked into my eyes. "But that's not what you meant, is it?"

"Yes, and no. You know it's complicated. And I don't want you and me to make things more difficult for him. That wouldn't be fair. It looks like we're all stuck on this tub for a bit, and I can't believe I'm saying this, but I don't want to rub his nose in our relationship. I'm sorry, Jared, I know—"

"It's okay, I agree with you."

"You do?"

"Of course. This isn't the place I want us to get closer either, and I don't want to make it more difficult for anyone. So, I know it will be difficult for you to keep your hands off me…" I swatted him playfully on the arm and he laughed. "In all seriousness, let's just take it as it comes, but I think you should sleep solo in Jake's bed from now on. It's the honourable thing to do."

I was just finishing my second mug of coffee when Jake called us together for the brief. "Okay, so everyone is completely up to speed after last night, and for Shae's benefit, every man in this room has voluntarily opted into this mission." I felt my eyes well up and Ash passed me a tissue. "We're going to assume that the old Reader on Phrayton wasn't totally bat-shit crazy, and the path Shae should continue on, takes us to the Trinity Planets. We have lots of questions, and very few answers at this point, so we're not losing anything by following crazy lady's advice."

"To recap," Ash said as a hollow screen projected documents, lists and photos with connections joining bits together by different coloured lines. "Finnian's message said that people will come after Shae if they learn who she is and what she can do." A list of the key points from Finnian's message was highlighted front and centre. "I think it's fair to say that our scar-tattooed friends fit this category. And they have weapons that look like they're specifically designed to kill her." The holo automatically showed the links from Finnian's message to the scar-tattoo info, and from there to the new weaponry. "The message also said that she should find out who she is – to learn about the past, to prepare for the future. We now know some of that past from the decrypted data-disc, but there's still a lot more to learn." I frowned as a big question mark appeared.

"As you know, Finnian told Shae to find the Harbingers, but that's proving trickier than first thought," Jake said, taking over the brief. "Rather than having very little info on them, there's literally billions of records to sift through, and we're still in the dark about who they are, where they are, and what they even know."

"But what we do know about them, is that they know about the Helyan Codex," I added. "According to Finnian, at least."

"Plus, we're also assuming the Helyan Codex, King Sebastian's Helyan Cube, the patterns carved into the walls on Tartaros, the manuscript page, and the pendant Shae has, are all linked," Jared said while connections between data sources continued to map out our journey.

"Additionally, we should add the supposed signs that 'something's coming,' and Shae being some mystical key, to the 'no fucking clue' list," concluded Jake, and I chuckled as an actual list entitled, 'No Fucking Clue,' appeared on screen. "And that brings us right up to this point here."

"Where do we start?" Kaiser asked. "At least Phrayton was one planet. And with the Trinity Planets, well, the clue's kind of in the name."

"Kaiser's right," Ash agreed. "And that's what this session's all about."

"We've got a couple of days until we get to the planets," Jake said. "Between now and then I want everyone on research duty. We need to know everything about them; the good, the bad, and the ugly. Cal and Connor, you're on Paradisum. Kaiser and Beck, you're on Arboribus – and I'm warning you guys, no shenanigans, or I'll toss you both out the airlock. Got it?" They looked at each other and then nodded reluctantly. "Ty, make a start on Infernum. The rest of us need to catch up on a few things, then we'll join the fun. Not a stone unturned, people. I want a full update at seventeen hundred. Let's get on it."

The relatively sedate briefing quickly became a hive of activity, with everyone breaking off in different directions until only the Guardians remained.

"Okay, so let's talk about the elephant in the room," Ash said to start the conversation.

"Which elephant?" Jake replied. "There are so many, it's getting pretty damn crowded in here." He didn't wait for a response. "Are you talking about the fact we just told everyone about the Helyan Cube, against Royal orders – which I'm okay with, to be honest – or the fact that people are trying to kill Shae for some reason, which we can only guess is to stop her, and us, finding out any more about her past, or that damn codex."

"Jake," Jared warned.

"He's right," Ash added to Jared's surprise.

"There's more," Jake continued, bolstered on by Ash's affirmation. "We only have Finnian's word about the Harbingers, though the rest of his message is on point, so we can assume it to be correct. And that brings me to my last point. What if we do find them? What then?"

"There are far too many guesses and assumptions for my liking," Ash said. "I think it's safe to say we don't really know why a mismatched group of tattooed gun-thugs would want Shae dead. Yes, we can assume that they want to stop her from getting answers to the many questions we have, but honestly, it could be anything. They may not like the fact that she has gifts, or that she lives in a monastery with the Brotherhood…"

"I think your reaching," Jared said.

"Maybe, but the alternative is they know exactly who Shae is and what she can do, and they know what we're trying to achieve by finding the Harbingers. And that, gentleman, scares me more than anything else put together."

"I hate to add to the list of things we don't know," I said, breaking the silence that had descended, "but we haven't mentioned the guy Vanze was supposedly working with."

"The Outsider?" Jake asked.

"Whoa, Shae's right," Jared confirmed. "Vanze said the Outsider was looking for the same Helyan cube he was, that their interests we're aligned and that Vanze was going to double-cross him and keep the cube for himself."

"Vanze also knew about the codex, so it stands to reason that the Outsider knows about it too," I concluded. Jake added the name to his 'No Fucking Clue' list, with links to both the cube and the codex, and the Khan brothers.

Ash massaged his eyes before looking around the group. "We can continue to sit and debate what we know and what we don't know, but I think we've done that to death," he said. "The best thing we can do now is concentrate on the next part of the puzzle – the Harbingers – while making sure those tattooed arseholes don't get anywhere near Shae."

"Agreed," Jake said.

"Agreed," Jared repeated. "I already know the response I'm going to get to this, but I have to say it… the best way to keep Shae safe, is for her to stay on the *Veritas* when we hit the Trinity Planets."

Surprisingly, Ash and Jake remained tight-lipped, and while I didn't disagree with Jared's safety protocol, I smiled. "Never going to happen," I said, getting up to go help Ty with his assessment of Infernum.

Seventeen hundred hours came on us quickly, and I felt we'd only just scratched the surface. We met in the lounge, as per Jake's orders, and he started by asking if anyone had found anything definitive on the Harbingers. Unsurprisingly, he was met by deafening silence and several head shakes. "Anything at all? Even a vague reference?" More silence. "Okay, so let's talk about the planets."

"I joined Cal and Connor on Paradisum," Jared offered. "But the guys did the heavy lifting. Connor?"

"Guess that's my cue," Connor said, standing and moving to the holo-screen. "We've waded through a lot of material, but nothing specific on the Harbingers. As you already know, the Trinity Planets, or the Pleasure Planets as they're known in some areas, is the top holiday destination for the rich and shameless. The starting price for a week on any one of the planets is more than our annual wages combined."

"Not difficult when you don't get paid," I said casually.

"You're shitting me?" Ty blurted in disbelief. "What about you?" he added turning to Ash, who shook his head. "Really? How do you even live? How do you buy things you need? No offence, but how do you get rewarded for putting your life on the line time and time again?"

"No offence taken, and the Brotherhood provides everything we need," Ash replied. "But I think we're getting a little off-topic."

"Thank you, Ash," Connor said purposely, while the data-pad he'd flung caught Ty on the shoulder. "As I was saying, you've got to be minted to holiday there. Each of the planets boast multiple luxury hotels, which are designed to cater for a range of vacation types and activities. They also provide shuttles between the planets so you can stay on one, but still go to the others for whatever activity blows your skirt up."

"You got fucking shares in the place, or what?" Beck grunted.

Connor looked to Jake. "I could take him out if you want. Wouldn't be a bother. You know I'm the explosives expert – it'd only take a small detonation, and I can make it look like an accident. No one would even know."

"Tempting," Jake replied, pretending to think through it. "But not right now."

"What do you mean, not now? You mean not ever," Beck protested, but Jake wasn't biting.

"That's enough. From everyone," he clarified. "Anyone who's not Connor, shut the fuck up. And can we please behave like the hardened bad arses we are, and not some bickering pre-schoolers? This is fucking embarrassing," he concluded.

"Paradisum," Connor continued, thankfully breaking the awkward silence, "is the water planet. The majority of the surface is ocean, punctuated by atolls and islands of varying sizes. And again, for thoroughness, the islands have some of the best beaches in the sector. Activities include scuba diving, snorkelling, fishing…" Jake coughed. "You get the drift." Connor concluded.

"There are several resorts on the planet," Cal said, not bothering to stand. "The biggest one is in the northern hemisphere and floats on the surface of the water, tethered to the seabed by heavy duty cables. There's a lift shaft that goes from the centre of the surface resort to a hub on the seafloor, with connecting tunnels spoking outwards to five smaller, boutique resorts. There's also a circular tunnel that connects all the satellite resorts on the seafloor."

"We've raked through everything we could find on the

planet, boss," said Connor. "And there's nothing that would even hint at our mystery group or reliquaries, but some of the resorts list Readers as an available service."

"Tactical analysis?" asked Jared.

"No direct threats we could detect," offered Cal. "Like Connor said, the whole planet is designed for high-end luxury. Apart from the usual unremarkable security detail you'd find at any posh hotel resort, there's nothing to write home about. But physically getting boots on the ground at any of the planets… now, that's a completely different matter. We'll swing back to that at the end of the brief."

"The only real threat on the planet is the sea life," Ash said. "There are certain areas of the ocean that have some more… aggressive, shall I say, sea creatures."

"But again, that's one of the reasons some of these rich arsehole thrill seekers go there in the first place," Connor added.

"Shouldn't be an issue for us," Ash concluded. "If we end up going to Paradisum, we should start at the floating resort, and head down if we need to, splitting into groups to take a look at the five on the seabed."

"Okay, so that's Paradisum in a nutshell," Connor concluded. "Not much to go on, I'm afraid. Next?" he asked, sitting down.

"I helped with Arboribus," said Jake, "But again, nothing much to say. Kaiser?"

"Take everything the guys have already said, and switch water for forest. There's lots and lots of trees. And lot's more, just in case I wasn't making myself clear. There are a few small resorts at ground level, but the majority are built high up into the trees and canopies, joined together by walkways and trams. It's aimed more at adventure holidaying rather than the relaxation of Paradisum. Activities range from walking and nature watching, to archery and shooting, to extreme ziplining – which I gotta say sounds kinda awesome by the way – and spelunking."

"What the fuck's spunking?" Ty said.

"Not spunking, fucktard," Beck grunted. "Get your mind out the gutter. Sper-lunking."

"Okay, so what's sper-lunking?"

"It's the exploration of caves and underground tunnel systems," Kaiser explained.

"Sounds amazing," Ty replied, not hiding the sarcasm. "Think I preferred it better the other way."

"Anyway," Kaiser said, getting back on path, "it's all pretty similar to Con's brief."

"Tactical analysis?" This time it was Ash asking.

"Same as," Jake replied. "There are hunting trips to a few areas, for the brain dead, morally devoid trophy hunters, but again nothing spectacular. Unlike the water planet, there's no primary resort that leads to others, but we've identified two or three worth concentrating on. Over to you guys," he added, looking between me and Ash.

"Shae and I joined Ty on Infernum, but to be honest," Ash said, "Ty did most of the work. Over to you, Ty."

"Not wanting to totally bore the shit out of everyone, but not much to say that hasn't already been said," Ty explained. "Out of the three planets, I'd say Infernum is for the more hardcore adventurer, but everything's still wrapped up in top-of-the-line luxury. So maybe not that hardcore," he mused. "The planet is mostly rock, rock and more fucking rock, with some volcanoes – that aren't nearly as nasty and disgusting as the ones on Santorra. There's more underground tunnels and caves for Kaiser's sper-lunking." He exaggerated to word to get a rise, but Kaiser chewed his tongue, taking the hint from Jake's expression. "Activities also include a suicidal activity called lava surfing, which you won't find me within a mile of. Tactical is the same as the others – resort security is about as trained as it gets. And still no direct link between the planets and Shae's Harbingers."

Jake stood and paced, hands behind his head, fingers

interlaced. "So, we know nothing more now than we did this morning."

"We have a workup and tactical analysis of all three planets," I offered, trying to lighten the mood. "Plus, we know Ty's never going lava-surfing, and Kaiser's hitting the extreme zip-lining when all this is over." Jake turned and smiled.

"And Ty would rather go spunking than spelunking," Beck added, causing Jake's smile to disappear, replaced by a wearily shake of the head.

"Cal, what's the problem with getting on the planets?" Jake asked, changing the subject.

"When Connor and I were checking out Paradisum, we noticed there were several landing zones in the main resort, but nothing big enough to hold more than a shuttle or two. And nowhere near the amount needed for all the tourists."

"Plus, it's pretty unusual not to have a shit-tonne of security when you're that wealthy," Connor added.

Cal continued. "Turns out, the richy rich don't like having security, even their own, watching their every move of their vacation. And on top of that, they like their privacy – which is one reason they're called the Pleasure Planets and explains the extortionate prices."

Connor took over. "The reason why the planets have little security, and few landing zones, is that you have to pass an extremely rigorous security check-point in orbit. There's literally a docking station close to each planet, and on top of that, there's orbital defence drones – again, around each planet. You have to pass a security check, just to dock at the orbital station, then you have to pass through another security checkpoint to gain access to the shuttle lounge – where you wait till the next shuttle run down to the planet. There's more security to get to the Trinity Planets than there is landing on Decerra. Again, I draw you back to the ridiculously high cost of vacationing there."

"Well, this is going to be a problem," Jared said.

"I might have an idea," offered Ty. "Part of an idea, anyway." He paused while everyone looked at him. "Maybe just a spark of an idea," he clarified, sounding more unsure by the word. "Let me look into it more tomorrow."

"Okay, fill us in when you have a full plan, and that's the same for everyone – we need to get on the planets, so pursue any ideas, no matter how bizarre or out there," Jake said.

"Sure, boss," Ty replied.

"That's it for today," continued Jake, and I was thankful. I can kick-arse all day and still feel amazing at the end, but research? Definitely not my bag. "As there doesn't seem to be one planet that leaps out as a place to start, tomorrow we go back over everything, and this time, I want each group to define a tactical plan for their Planet: where to start, where to go next, how we split the group to cover more area, tasks... everything. Just because these planets are filled with the richest of the rich, doesn't mean we can sit back and not expect trouble. We can't rock up as REF or Brotherhood, and we sure as shit aren't going to be welcomed the way we look now without raising alarm bells. So, as I said, I want you all to think about the security they have, the dangers each planet poses, and how we even get boots on the ground in the first place. Got it? Outstanding. Ty, Cal, you're on dinner duty."

21

That night, without undue fuss, Ash and Jared diplomatically switched sleeping arrangements, with Ash using the cot that was still made up in Jake's quarters. Part of me missed having Jared close, but the other part didn't want to make things difficult for Jake.

The following morning repeated the previous, and the friction between certain people was pushing Jake's patience to the limit. Around early afternoon, a flurry of activity in the main cabin was a welcome distraction.

"What's going on?" Jake asked.

"No idea. We just got here," I replied, indicating to Ash. I was also conscious Jake had taken up position by my side; a centimetre closer and we'd be touching. "Looks like Kaiser's trying to referee some kind of disagreement between Connor and Ty."

Jake laughed quietly and bent his head down, so his face was closer to mine. "Just another day on the *Veritas*," he said before striding forward to break up the argument.

"Guess this is normal then," Jared said, replacing Jake's vacant space next to me.

"I've not seen a disagreement between them quite this

bad before," I replied, watching Jake wade in.

"If this shit isn't directly related to the mission, you'll all be cleaning the inside of the slurry tank within fifteen minutes. Do I make myself clear? Kaiser, what the fuck's going on?"

"Ty has an idea to get us on to one of the planets. Connor says it won't work, and it'll probably get us arrested at best, or dead at worst."

"Okay," Jake said, physically relaxing. "This we can work with. Gather round." He indicated to the rest of us. "If we've got even the possibility of plan, I want everyone's input. Let's see if we can't make this work. Ty, you had an idea yesterday, right?"

"A spark of an idea," Connor corrected. "And a pretty shitty spark at that."

"Stow it, Con," Jake snapped. "If you're not helping, you're hindering."

"Sure, boss. Sorry," he said, taking a seat.

"Ty, what's the plan? And after all this, it better be more than a spark," warned Jake.

"The way I see it, whichever planet we go to first, we have two problems. One is to pass the stringent security checks to even dock the *Veritas* at the orbital station. The second is to get all of us through the security checkpoint on the station to access a shuttle down to the planet. Once we've achieved that, we can move unchallenged around the planet, and have easy access to the shuttle service between the three."

"Those are two pretty big problems," Ash said. "How do you suggest we can overcome them?"

Ty cracked his knuckles before he began. "Let's start with docking. None of the Pleasure Planets accept walk-ins. That means, the first thing we'll need is accommodation bookings for the first planet we go to. And on that, Connor and I do agree." Ty magnanimously passed the batten to Connor.

"Given that none of the planets have any clear indication of the Harbingers, the one that seems most likely is Paradisum. It's the only planet that specifically advertises Readers of all types, and it seems to be the hub for vacationers. Visitors mostly stay on one of the six sea resorts and then add short excursions to the other two planets."

"Anybody disagree, or have any better ideas?" Jake asked.

"It does seem logical," Ash admitted.

"Then we go to Paradisum first," confirmed Jake. "See, that wasn't so difficult. Then what?"

"This is where my technical awesomeness comes in," Ty boasted. Beck groaned. "Their booking system is just as secure as everything else, and there's no way I can hack it before we arrive."

"I'm beginning to think I was a bit harsh on Con," Jake said.

"Stay with me, boss," Ty said quickly. "I'm nowhere near finished. I can't hack it before we get there, but if we can get the *Veritas* between the orbital station and the planet, I should be able to force a line-of-sight hack into their systems."

"I'm not keen on the word 'should' in there," Jared commented. "Let me get this straight… you need Connor to literally put the ship between the station and the planet for you to maybe hack the system and get us accommodation bookings, but we need accommodation bookings to get even near to the station?"

"See?" blurted Connor. "Even the Captain gets it."

"You need the full plan," Ty said quickly. "I get that each part has it's issues but hear me out. The last thing I want to do is drop Connor in the shit, but…" He looked apologetically at his teammate.

"For fuck's sake," Connor grumbled, as all eyes moved to him. "You all know I collect transponder codes when I can. It's no secret. You never know when they're going to come in handy."

"What did you do, Con?" asked Jake, sighing. "I'm not going to like this am I?"

"Umm, possibly not," he replied shrugging. "But if I hadn't, I wouldn't be able to offer help now… so, I guess you can kinda justify it as a good thing, maybe."

"What did you do?" Jake repeated slowly.

"I might have, possibly, boosted a royal transponder code or two during the Khan's incursion on the Palace a little while back."

"Fucking hell, Connor," Kaiser bellowed. "Are you trying to get us all arrested?"

I thought Jake might have been mad, but he turned away from the group so only I could see him trying not to laugh. He winked at me before settling his face into a frown and turning back to the group. "That's reprehensible, Connor," he chastised. "Consider this a warning and all that. Don't do it again, or there'll be consequences. Got it?"

Connor nodded, trying ridiculously hard to keep a straight face.

"That's some hard-core discipline you got there, Jake," Jared observed, rubbing his mouth to hide the grin. "Great work."

"Back to me," Ty said, getting the briefing on track again. "We can use one of those transponder codes to squawk our ident as a House of Palavaria royal shuttle. And this is where Connor and I disagree. I think the royal transponder code and Con's awesome flying will get us enough time for me to do the hack. Then between a royal shuttle and vacation accommodation booking, they'll let us dock at the orbital station."

"You can blow smoke up my arse about my flying skills all you like, Ty," said Connor. "It doesn't change the fact we have to persuade the station and orbital defence system not to blow us to hell and back while you 'might' get a hack into their systems."

"But—" Jake cut off Ty's response.

"We all understand the problem," he began. "How can we buy Connor and Ty more time?"

"That's linked to the next part of my plan," Ty explained.

"Which is about as iffy as the first part," Connor said before holding up his hands and sitting back in his chair.

"Connor's not wrong," Ty surprised us by admitting. Connor more so that the rest of us. "But the way I see it, no one's got a better one, so I'm going to say it anyway. Like Connor said yesterday, the Trinity Planets are the top destination for the richest of the rich, but they've never been frequented by royalty – I'm guessing for several reasons. One of which is probably the whole security angle, and another is, the last thing you want on your royal vacation is to have a bunch of rich muckity mucks trying to schmooze with you every second of the day. Not exactly relaxing," he concluded.

"How does that help us?" asked Ash.

"Well…" Ty paused for effect. "There are four members of the royal family right in front of me."

Jared, Jake, Ash, and I all shared glances, while Ty sat back smugly.

"You think the orbital station will hesitate to fire on a royal shuttle, transporting four royals, while you have the time to do the hack?" Ash mused. "They'd have to confirm our status with the palace, which may take some time. Could work… or, like Connor said, it could get us dead."

"And just to lob in another grenade," I added. "If the station does check our status with the palace, the four of us would have to go in as us – no alternate identities to hide behind. Isn't that an open invitation for Luke and the Brotherhood, or the REF, or those scar-tattooed freaks to come find us?"

"It's a risk," said Ty. "Look, at this point it's the only

option we have. The security at the three orbital stations is insane. But I'm betting they're going to be so happy to have royals visiting, we can do some negotiation over your anonymity."

"Agree to let them advertise our stay post-vacation, if they keep our visit on the down-low while we're there?" I said.

"Exactly that," Ty agreed. "I can hack the system and book us all accommodation under aliases but using your royal status might give us that time Connor and I need to do the hack. I'm guessing the planets will fall over themselves to allow us access, but the House of Palavaria, not so sure."

"What the fuck does that mean," Beck spoke for the first time.

"Station security will contact the palace to confirm our identity," Jake explained, more patiently that I'd expected. "While the Pleasure Planets will have a vested interest in supporting our anonymity, the palace? Not so much. We can't exactly call them up and ask them to secure the info, without raising a bazillion flags."

"Unless they know of our Guardianship," I offered. "The four of us together? They may just think we're on a mission."

"Or the Brotherhood may have already contacted the palace asking them to alert the Primus if Shae and I pop up on their radar," Ash replied. "Either way, I don't think we have a choice."

"Well," Jake announced, stretching, "I can understand the heated debate you two were having." He looked between Ty and Connor. "Correct me if I'm wrong, but the plan as I see it is this: Connor switches our transponder to that of a royal Palavarian shuttle. As we approach the docking station for Paradisum, we fake some technical difficulties, get across who we are, and hope they don't blow us into hell while Ty hacks the booking system. By the time our idents have been checked with the palace, Ty will have booked us all accommodation: four royals and an entourage of an additional five, which is enough for us to dock."

"What about our identities?" asked Cal. "Be who we are, or fake it till we make it?"

"Let's keep it simple," Jared suggested. "Stay as you are, and we'll negotiate your anonymity along with ours. At the end of the day, four of you are highly decorated Marines."

"What about me," Beck huffed.

"Like the Captain said, four of us are highly decorated marines," Connor stated.

"And there's always one weird uncle at the family party," Kaiser scoffed.

"Ahh, you see me as family," Beck teased.

"Not in a million lifetimes."

"Fuck you, old man."

"That's enough," Jake intervened, but Beck clearly didn't get the hint.

"You know, I could be Shae's personal bodyguard," he offered. "I'd be happy to guard that body anytime."

I don't know whose objections were louder – Jared's, Jake's or Ash's, but it was Ash's fist that landed the punch.

"Fucking hell, I think you broke my nose," Beck moaned, pinching it to stem the bleeding.

"You're lucky that's all I broke."

When the heat had settled, I tried to get the conversation back on point. "We're really going to do this?"

"Of course, Blue," said Kaiser, smiling broadly. "We haven't had this much fun since Tartaros."

"Hey, speak for yourself," Cal said. "Not one of my top ten destinations, I gotta say."

"Yeah, sorry dude," Kaiser apologised. "Still was an awesome mission though," he said, breaking into booming laughter, which was infectious after the heavy conversation we'd just had.

"I do have another question," I said. "Exactly what are we expected to wear on the planets?"

"As little as—" Beck started but in an instant Jake had his gun pointed at his face.

"Why don't you try finishing that sentence?" he growled.

Beck kept quiet, sitting back in his chair, and touching his nose gingerly.

"I would suggest," Ty said loudly, "we get through the checkpoint, then do a bit of emergency shopping while waiting for the shuttle. Not like any of us can walk around Paradisum wearing worn cargos and boots. And big fella," he paused to get Kaiser's attention, "I know how much you're attached, but the leather jacket is a definite no."

"Oh man," Kaiser replied.

"And how are we paying for all this shopping, Ty?" Jake asked.

"It's easy, you just put it all on the rooms."

"And how are we paying for the rooms?"

Ty paused, thinking. "You know how you didn't really get mad at Connor for boosting the palace transponders…"

"Here it comes," Jake said, running a hand through unruly hair.

"Remember when we took down that warlord about a year ago? Well, when I was cleansing his data files for evidence, I might have stumbled across his personal bank account while I was at it."

"Please tell me you didn't," Jake said, shaking his head.

"It was just sat there, Jake. The warlord was already dead, his men also dead, or heading towards incarceration. The money would've just sat there in one of those shadow accounts."

"What's a shadow account?" I asked.

"It's when a person has set up a bank account in secret, then dies, and because their account is secret, no one knows it's there, and the Bank just assumes the owner doesn't need it yet. So, it just sits there until there's been no activity on the account for 50 years, then the bank claims it. Come on, Jake," he pleaded. "Better to have as an emergency slush fund for doing good, than just let it sit there for those greedy fucking bank managers, who probably pocket it themselves."

Jake sighed deeply. "I guess we all have contingencies," he said cryptically. "Okay, this mission is officially bank-rolled by a dead warlord. What's the budget, Ty?"

"I filtered three quarters of the amount anonymously back to the people the warlord stole it from, then moved the remaining quarter to a separate account under my Reston alias. But let's put it this way, I can pretty much guarantee that the nine of us couldn't spend enough to hit that quarter limit, even if we tried."

"Ty?"

"Yeah, boss,"

"Good work. Just tell me next time. In fact, all of you tell me next time you start any shenanigans. This unit works because we're tight. Let's keep it that way."

The rest of the afternoon was spent discussing how we'd investigate once we were wardrobe appropriate. As a collective, we worked on the assumption we wouldn't be blown to shit in orbit and agreed the plan for each planet – starting with Paradisum, as Ty and Connor had suggested.

Later that evening, the Guardians met in Jake's quarters.

"I'm still uncomfortable we won't have weapons after we leave the *Veritas*," Jared said.

"We didn't have weapons when we went to the Palace's post-Tetrad party, and we survived that," I said, thinking I was helping.

"We also didn't have weapons on Dennford, and remember what happened there?" Jake said.

"I get your point, Jake, but if the four of us – Guardians, and members of the Royal family – have to blag and buy our way onto Paradisum, do you really think those people with the scar tattoos will be there?"

"I know, you're right," he said, looking tired. "I just can't bear to see you go through that pain again."

"It's not something I want to repeat either," I replied, leaning forward to touch his leg. "But you know what we do?" I waited for his eye contact. "We survive, and we get shit done."

He laughed; fine wrinkles appeared around his hazel eyes. "You've been hanging with Kaiser to long."

"Nah," I replied. "He'd have said: we survive, we get stuff done, and we blow shit up."

"That's true," he said, stopping himself from leaning towards me.

Ash stood and yawned. "You got anything stronger than a beer on this tub?"

"You really have to ask?" Jake replied. "Kitchen. Far left, top locker. Pick your poison."

"I'm up for some of that," Jared advised, standing. "Shae?"

I looked at Jake, then back to Jared. "I just need a few minutes with Jake, then I'll join you."

"Sure, take whatever time you need," he replied, dropping his head to give me a quick kiss.

After they'd left the room, Jake and I sat in silence for a moment.

"Can I tell you something?" I asked. Jake looked up from his boots, his forehead crinkled.

"Of course, you can, babe. You can tell me anything you want."

I smiled weakly. "I know. Which is why you're the only one I feel I can really be honest with about this."

"Hey, what is it? Whatever it is can't be that bad?" He leant forward to take my hand and I looked up into his eyes.

"I'm scared, Jake," I admitted. "Not so much for me, but for everyone else. I'm scared I'm going to get you all killed, or worse, watch one or more of you get hurt and not be able to do anything about it. I'm scared that Ty will die before he gets to share his mam's pasta recipe with the woman he will fall in love with. I'm scared Cal will have survived torture and pain, just to die for me to find out who I am, and the Pack, who've brought me in as one of their own. I'm scared I've dragged an almost complete stranger into this after already wrecking his life. I'm scared Jared and you will die, or get court-martialled at the very least. And I'm scared that Ash's love for me has threatened everything he holds dear. And most of all, I'm scared of letting them all see how scared I am. Them… you… if it wasn't for me, none of you would be in danger."

"Of course, we'd be in danger, babe," he said softly as he touched my face. "It's what we do. I can guarantee all of us… with maybe the exception of Captain Amazing… would be arse deep in some other dangerous mission. And Beck? Well, he'd still be locked up tight in the Basement of Angel Ridge."

"Yes, but—"

"But what? You know I'm right," he said lifting my chin so he could look into my eyes. "Every single person onboard knows everything about this mission. You gave us all an out, and not one person took it – though I'm still not totally sure whether Beck's in or out, or just biding time until he can whisk you away to one of those quicky marriage ships." He smiled, and I returned it.

"I can assure you I'm not a quicky-marriage type of girl."

"Nor are you a huge wedding and big floofy dress type of girl."

"How do you know?" I teased.

"Because I know you."

"How do you know I don't want masses of flowers and finery and champagne and a massive dress, and a venue to die for?"

"Because I know you," he repeated, sighing quietly. "And it's also why I know you could only talk to me about how you're feeling."

My smile disappeared as the whimsical discussion on weddings faded away. "I could tell you because you're the same as me, Jake. I know you play the lone wolf, pardon the pun, but you care. You care more about the Pack than you do about you. The Wolfpack is the remarkable team they are because of you. Cal joined the Pack because of you. And Kaiser had a fair amount to say on how you gave him a second chance."

"Really?" Jake seemed surprised. "He told you about…"

"The court martial? Yeah, he told me everything."

Jake seemed lost for words. "When?" was all he managed.

"It was back on the Planet of Souls. Gods that feels like forever ago."

"I'm actually speechless."

"Why? What's the big deal?"

"The Planet of Souls was not long after we met. Kaiser barely acknowledges his life pre-Pack; I'm just surprised he talked to you about it. Guess he must've really taken you."

"Well, he has made me an honorary addition of the Pack, so you're kind of stuck with me through thick and thin."

"Shae?" Jake said, helping me to stand. "I'm glad you felt you could talk to me about this. And I want you to know that you can talk to me about anything, any time. And don't get all huffy, but I'm going to say it… I love you. I will do anything for you. If you want to talk, I'm here. If you just need company to sit in silence, I'm here. Need a sparring partner, here. If you need a hug," he pulled me in tight, "I'm here. And…" he let me go and stepped back so he could look into my eyes again, "when you realise it's me you love and not Captain Super-Prick, I'll be here." His face lit up as he smiled, and he pulled me into another hug.

"Thanks, Jake," I said after kissing him on the cheek. "Thanks for listening to my crazy ramblings."

"Didn't you know? Crazy ramblings are my thing."

"That's because you more than a little crazy yourself. But I feel better, just being able to talk about it. I've been holding all that in since the first time I told Ash about Finnian's message back on the monastery."

"We're all in this together. You're not alone," he said, wiping the tear track from my cheeks with his thumb. "How about you splash some water on your face and we join the others for a drink?"

"Now that sounds like a good plan," I replied, kissing him on the cheek again.

By the time we joined Ash and Jared, a party had formed. Music was playing, drinks were flowing, and bowls of Nikolov olives had been almost decimated.

"Hate to be the buzz-kill, but we have a mission tomorrow," Jake announced loudly over the music. "That means moderate the alcohol and get a good night's rest. I want your A game tomorrow. This isn't a vacation, it's a mission."

I accepted a glass of Fire Whisky from Jared. "This brings back memories," I said, resting my head on his shoulder.

"Good or bad?"

"Umm," I thought for a moment.

"That doesn't bode well." His arm closed around my waist.

"Both," I eventually decided. "I think it's the first time we had a proper conversation. It was nice to hear about your parents and about you growing up."

"If I remember rightly, you told me I was arrogant."

"You remember that, huh?" My tone was apologetic. "I remember thinking you were going to kiss me outside my quarters."

"I remember wanting to kiss you."

"But you didn't. Instead, you tried to get classified intel from me while I was drunk."

"Hence the bad part," Jared said.

"Yes, I guess. And the fact that I was also keeping a lot of stuff from you. I think, looking back on it, we both added to the bad. But the good? The good was nice. I think that's when I really saw you for the first time."

"I guess I felt the same," Jared said. "I felt comfortable with you. I still don't know why. We barely knew each other then. But there was definitely something that drew me to you. And Ash. And even Jake, though if you tell I'm that, I'll deny everything."

I thought for a moment. "Thank you, Jared."

"For what?" His eyebrows puckered. "For saying that I have some crazy connection to Jake that I don't understand? Because I mean it; I'll deny I said it," he teased.

"Not that."

"Then what?"

"For not asking." I looked up into his captivating eyes; intense blue around the outside, a gorgeous shade of icy silver-blue on the inside. "For not asking about my conversation with Jake just now."

"I trust you," he replied. "Though, I've got to admit, it was hell being on the *Defender* knowing you were with Jake, and that arsehole, Beck."

"You didn't need to worry."

"About Beck? No. He's a pretender. He just likes getting a rise out of the others, especially Kaiser."

"Not Beck."

"Ahh, yes. Jake." He blinked, and I was close enough to focus on the small black dot in his left eye, just below the pupil. "He claims he loves you, and you have... history together," he added diplomatically. "And you love him, just not in the way he wants. So, do I worry? Yes, of course. I worry that he'll do or say something to make you question your feelings for me." He put his fingers to my lips to stop what I was about to say. "But, like I said, I trust you. When and if you want to tell me what you were talking to Jake about, that's completely up to you. No pressure." I hugged him tightly and when I let him go, he dropped his head and his soft lips met mine, but a boisterous roar from the Pack left me blushing.

I was comfortable standing in front of Jared, resting against him while the guys started their usual banter. I felt safe with his left arm around my waist, but after my third glass of whisky, I decided I'd call it a night.

"I wish I could come with you," Jared whispered, his breath hot on my neck. "It's hard knowing you're so close."

"I feel the same way, but it's not the right time."

"I know," he concluded, kissing me on my neck. "I'll see you in the morning."

I discreetly said good night to Ash, and mouthed the words to Jake, who'd taken to propping up the bulkhead on the far side of the room.

"Blue?" Kaiser called, drawing out the word. "Where you going?"

"To bed," I called back. "Tomorrow's going to be a busy day."

"Tomorrow could be our last day, so why not enjoy the night?"

"As much as I love the gallows' humour, Kaiser, I'd like to think we all have many days ahead of us yet. See you all tomorrow; bright and early. No hangovers – I can't cure those."

"Hey, wait up," Jake said, jogging the short distance. "I just wanted to say that I'm touched you talked to me this evening. Remember what I said: we're all in this together. And you can spend as much time with me as you like." He shrugged, his eyes turning mischievous. "And that includes my bunk, just in case you fancied it."

"Stop it," I chastised half-heartedly. "I'm going to my own bed."

"Which is technically my bed," Jake said. "I could always turf Ash out and reclaim it?"

"You could… but you won't."

"How can you be so sure?"

"Because I know you."

"Touché."

22

Breakfast the following day was quite as everyone prepared for the day ahead.

"Hey, Blue?" Kaiser said across the table. "I've been thinking about what that freaky old bat on Phrayton said."

"And?" Jake questioned, causing Kaiser to look between me and him.

"She said 'they're waiting,' right?"

"Right." Ash joined the conversation.

"So… we've been assuming that these Harbingers are going to be hard to locate. But what if the old girl was right, and they are waiting for Shae? Maybe it'll be easier than we think."

"I like your optimism, Kaiser, but let's assume they're not walking around with a Harbinger sign attached to them," Jake responded.

"We also don't know who she was referring to," reminded Ash. "It could have been the Harbingers, but she could've equally been talking about the tattooed group."

"True, I suppose. She also said Shae would be betra—"

"Nope, no way, most definitely no," I interrupted loudly. "And in case I wasn't clear: no. We're not even touching that subject today. This is not the day to open that can of worms, understand?"

"Sure, Blue. Sorry, I didn't mean to offend."

"No offence taken," I said honestly. "It's a valid point to raise, just not today, okay?"

"Okay," he repeated.

"Con, eta on Paradisum?" asked Jake.

Connor looked at the plexi on the wall next to him, scrolling through the data. "I'd say ninety minutes until we're close enough to be of interest to the orbital security station. Another ten until we can get between the station and the planet. After that, it's all up to Ty."

"How long will you need, Ty?" asked Jared.

"Depends on the level of decryption needed. The transfer of data between the orbital platform and the planet is where data security is at its thinnest. The hack could take anything from thirty seconds to never."

"Great," Beck groaned.

"Best guess?" Jake pushed.

"If I had to, based on what I think their firewalls will look like, I'd say two to ten minutes."

"Make it two," Jake ordered. "Not sure we're going to be around for ten."

"No pressure then," Ty joked, but he was on his own.

The next hour seemed like a lifetime, but as we approached the platform, the tension was palpable. "I think it's time," Connor said, and I looked up to see Jake nod his agreement.

As Connor disappeared towards the flight deck, I asked, "Time for what?"

"Connor's going to mess up our coms a bit. Not so much to take them offline, but enough to hopefully buy some time once we become of interest to the orbital platform." He saw my frown and held out his hand to tuck an unruly strand of hair behind my ear. "It'll be ok," he stressed. "We do this—"

"For a living," I finished for him. "I know," I added smiling.

"You can really fall out with some people, you know," he joked, still holding my hand. "It's a good job I lov—"

That time it was Jared's voice over coms that interrupted him. "Game faces, people. We've just been hailed."

When we got to the flight deck, it was packed, prompting Jake to order Cal and Kaiser back to the lounge. He tapped the internal coms. "Ty? You good to go?"

"Affirmative," came the response.

"Connor, you know the plan," Jake continued. "Over to you now."

"Okay," he replied. "Let's do this." He pressed a couple of buttons and then hailed the platform. "Paradisum station, this is royal transport shuttle six one alpha from the House of Palavaria, requesting docking codes." It was a moment before we got a reply.

"Unknown shuttle approaching on vector 172, repeat your last, your coms are on the fritz."

"Sounded okay to me," Ash said.

"It does at our end, the station will have got a lot of static," Connor explained before accessing external coms again. "Apologies Paradisum station, we've had some issues with communications after a small electrical fire. We are royal transport shuttle six one alpha from the House of Palavaria, requesting docking codes."

"This is station control to approaching shuttle, you're still breaking up, but we have picked up your ident as six one alpha from the House of Palavaria. Please confirm."

"Station control, that is correct. We're royal shuttle six one alpha out of Decerra."

Silence filled the flight deck, and I held my breath.

"Six one alpha, this is Matt Buchanan, Commander of Paradisum orbital station. I'm told you have some coms issues, but for our safety and yours, I must ask you to cut your engines and hold fast while we can clear you for docking." The commander's voice was tinged with excitement, but not enough to clear us a path.

"Commander Buchanan," continued Connor, while not following the instructions to hold. "I'm transporting four members of the royal family. To repeat, I have four members of the Palavarian royal family onboard. We have reservations for them and their entourage on Paradisum for the next week. We request immediate docking codes."

"Six one alpha, say again. We have no bookings for any member of the royal family. Cut your engines and hold your position."

"Perhaps you haven't looked hard enough," Connor said, prompting Jake to kick the back of his chair. He turned and shrugged apologetically. "My apologies, Commander. Please could you review your bookings again."

"Six one alpha, either provide reservation codes, or cut your engines. If you continue on your approach without providing the information requested, we will fire on you."

"Commander, we're having problems due to the electrical fire and can't retrieve the reservation codes at this time."

We were close enough to the station to see it through the front screen.

"Tell them who we are, Conner," Jake said. "Don't think we have any choice," he added, crossing his arms.

"Commander, this is six one alpha. If it helps calm your nerves," Jake kicked the back of Connor's chair again, "we're transporting Colonel Jake Mitchell, Captain Jared Marcos, Brother Asher, and Lady Shae." The name sounded so ridiculous I snorted a laugh and then covered my mouth.

"Six one alpha repeat, you're still breaking up. Cut your engines immediately."

"Con, clean up the message, they need to get our names so they don't fire a missile up our arse," instructed Jake. Connor immediately dipped under the console before sitting back in his seat.

"Commander Buchanan, this is six one alpha, are coms better now?"

"Affirmative."

"Then I repeat, we're transporting Colonel Jake Mitchell, Captain Jared Marcos, Brother Asher, and Lady Shae. They've recently been awarded Royal status by King Sebastian himself and are taking their first vacation since. You can verify this by contacting the House of Palavaria."

Buchanan's voice was tinged with excitement again. "Six one alpha, if you can't provide reservations, you must hold your position while we verify your passengers."

"I have no intention of cutting my engines for security reasons, Commander. I'm sure you can understand it would be against Royal protocol for a shuttle carrying members of the Royal family to be dead in space. That's a security risk I will not put my passengers in, and I don't intend on losing my job over it. Do you?" Connor barked. Silence followed.

The station loomed closer and darker against the glorious blue hews of the planet below, and as the seconds ticked on, I felt my hand warm as Jared took it in his.

"How long until we're between the station and the planet?" Jake asked.

"Two minutes tops," replied Connor, "but the station's just target locked us." He opened coms to the station again. "Commander Buchanan, unless you want to spend the remainder of your days cleaning shitters on a Max-4 penal complex, I suggest you remove weapons lock immediately. You're literally committing treason right now." He paused and turned to face us. "Too much?" he asked, but Jake just smiled.

"Ty, look sharp," Jake said, "We're going to be in place in about thirty seconds. You better be awesome at this hack," he warned.

As Connor navigated us into position, Buchanan came back online. "Six one alpha, this is Commander Buchanan."

His voice was clipped and frosty. Clearly, he hadn't appreciated Connor's threat. "You are too close to the station. We're still waiting conformation of your passengers' identities and in the meantime, without being able to supply reservation codes, we will continue to lock weapons on you. You will manoeuvre away from the station immediately, or we will fire. I repeat, we will fire. You have one minute to comply."

"Sorry, orbital station, you're breaking up again," Conner replied. "Request you repeat your last." He looked at Jake and raised a concerned eyebrow, and while Buchanan was going through his spiel again, Jake spoke to Ty.

"How long?" Jake grunted.

"Sooner if you stop bothering me," Ty tried to joke, but Jake wasn't in the mood.

"I said, how long?" he growled.

"A minute. Maybe ninety seconds."

"Get it done, Ty," he ordered.

Tension between Connor and Buchanan was rising, until the Commander had clearly had enough. "This is your last warning six one alpha, if you don't retreat to your designated holding coordinates, or supply your reservation codes, we will fire in thirty seconds."

"Ty?" Jake said, the name sounding like a warning.

"Nearly there."

"They're charging their cannons," Connor advised. "Shit just got serious."

"Ty?" Jake said again.

"We need to retreat," Ash said. "Survive to fight another day."

Out the front screen I saw the plasma cannons swivel towards us.

"I agree," Jake said. "Connor, take—"

"Got it," Ty bellowed through the coms. "Just sent the station our reservation codes and apologised for the electrical issues."

The movement of the plasma cannons caught my eye and I watched them reset back into their docks. The weapons lock indicator stopped flashing, and I think we all breathed out simultaneously.

When Commander Buchanan spoke next, he was full of remorse, apologising and hoping we would understand the need for caution. Even turning it around to say we should be happy that their guest's safety is paramount, something he was sure we would understand and appreciate. He continued to gush over how welcome the royal family was when Jake reached over Connor and disconnected the com-link.

"Give him a second to calm down," Jake said to Connor, "then tell him our anonymity is paramount. No special treatment. Nothing that would make us stand out from any other holiday makers. Understand?"

"No problem, boss," Connor replied as we left the flight deck.

The underbelly of the ship creaked and groaned as it lowered, the nine of us descending like a delegation. The *Veritas* looked immediately out of place amongst the obscenely grotesque lavishness. And so did we.

"What the fuck, Con?" growled Jake. "I told you we didn't want special treatment."

"And I told them that," Conner replied. "Not my fault Commander Shitbrains is a shitbrain."

Jake shook his head. "Sorry, Con. You didn't get us dead, so good job." Jake clapped him hard on the shoulder and they both grinned.

It looked like the Commander had thrown his blazer on in a hurry, and he smelled like he'd splashed half the contents of a cologne bottle over himself. Jared stepped forward, arm extended.

"A thousand apologies, Captain Marcos," Buchanan

spluttered, struggling to hold back his excitement. "I'm so sorry about that little altercation, but it really was necessary."

"It really wasn't," Jake replied, coolly, causing Buchanan to blush fiercely.

"I... I hope you won't hold it against us when you share stories of your visit with your fellow royals."

"Commander," Jared ignored the shameless sales promo, "I thought we asked for no special treatment."

Buchanan looked confused, turning to check the army of stewards, officers, and flower girls lined up. His frowned continued as he retuned back to Jared, but then lines on his forehead cleared. "With all due respect, I think you misunderstand, Your Grace. This," he waved his arm behind him, "is our standard greeting for all our holiday makers. Nothing special, exactly what was requested. This is Pax, our Chief Steward." He gestured wildly to the impeccably dressed Other. Pax stepped forward and as he bowed deeply, Jared nudged my arm to stop me laughing. I tried to hide it behind a stifled cough.

If Pax had notice, he didn't show it. "Your Highnesses, it would be just the greatest pleasure to transport your luggage to the planet. Your holiday starts here, and you will want for nothing during your time with us. Thank you for choosing the Pleasure Planets as your destination of choice – we're extremely honoured."

"Suckup," Beck said in cough, and I wasn't the only one trying to hide a snigger.

Ash threw him a half-hearted glance before stepped forward. "Commander Buchanan, Pax," Ash said, ever the diplomate. "We've come directly from a mission, so I hope you'll forgive our attire."

"Well, I was..." Buchanan replied, but he stopped himself, gesturing for Ash to continue.

"And we have no luggage for your stewards to collect."

Pax's smile slipped as a reaction to that information, but

it was pasted back in place within seconds. "No luggage?" Ash shook his head. "None at all?" he continued, looking between us. I didn't need a Link connection to tell me Jake had had enough.

"Look," he said, taking the last step off the ramp onto the station. "Fact is, as Ash said, we've come straight from a mission. And we were so keen to get our vacation started, that we didn't have time to go back to our respective homes to pack."

Buchanan nodded his head, like he understood our decision.

"Plus, your brochures show a number of wonderful stores for us to shop at," I added, just to complete the ruse.

"Oh yes," Pax said, "Both on the station and each of the Trinity Planets."

"As we've previously stated, our price for coming here is our total anonymity," Ash continued. "You provide us with that, and we'd be happy to… shall we say, promote this as a high-end holiday destination after."

Buchanan's face lit up like a sun – I thought he was about to bust something. "You have my word," he said, though he could barely get the actual words out he was so breathy with excitement.

"Great. Then onwards," suggested Ash. "What happens next?"

While the stewards disappeared at the wave of Pax's hand, the flower girls adorned us with garlands of beautiful smelling, colourful flowers, and leaves in so many shades of green. The solid metallic clunking confirmed the ramp had locked in place as we were ushered out of the hanger.

"So that's really it," Buchanan was advising Ash as we caught them up. "All you have to do is go through our security checkpoint, and then the station, and all it offers, is yours. When you're ready, make your way to the departure lounge and take the next shuttle to Paradisum." He paused for a moment. "Are you sure you wouldn't like some stewards to help you shop? I can get you some personal shopping assistance."

"We are very self-sufficient," Ash advised him.

"In that case, we hope you have an amazing stay here at the Pleasure Planets. The security checkpoint is right ahead." He waved his arm towards the grandest looking security point I'd ever seen. "If you don't mind, I'll excuse myself." He took a few steps and then stopped and turned back. "In all the excitement, I almost forgot… congratulations on your marriage, My Lady." I looked up. "I'm sure you and Colonel Mitchell will not be disappointed with our deluxe honeymoon package." With that he was gone, leaving me with my mouth open.

In a moment that would seem comic under any other circumstance, we all swivelled towards Ty.

"I, um… yeah, well… happy honeymoon," he stuttered. "What? I was under pressure and panicked, okay? They were really booked up and the only way to get us all bookings, was to book the honeymoon package which came with a villa for the newly-weds and a bunch of separate huts for guests."

Beck couldn't control his laughter. "And you booked Shae and Jake as the bride and groom? This is priceless," he said, clearly looking at Jared.

"Like I said, I panicked," Ty tried explaining again, but now Jake was smiling.

"No harm, no foul," Jared said, trying not to look pissed off. "It's just names on a booking sheet."

"Of course," Jake said, failing to hide his amusement. "You're absolutely correct, Jared."

After that, it was pretty plain sailing. We breezed through the checkpoint and split up to do some shopping before agreeing to meet later in the departure lounge. Even though both Jared and Jake had said it wasn't safe for me to be on my own, I was glad when Ash argued the station was secure enough.

My standard go-to when faced with shopping was that it's driven by necessity, and the appropriateness of my job. Cargo pants, tees and shirts in varieties of green, beige and black. I see the task as a chore rather than fun – and this was no exception. It was a task that had to be completed to allow us to go un-noticed down on the planet. Clothes that wouldn't draw attention.

At least that's how it started.

By the time I left my first store, I'd ditched the old clothes I'd been wearing and replaced them with a tasteful blouse, capri pants, and pretty sandals that I'd also be able to run in – I couldn't completely move away from 'appropriateness'. The time flew by as I shopped, and the more places I went into, the more I realised I'd been missing out. Not on these gaudy, overpriced monstrosities, but just the ability to do something solely for me, and for a little while, I was able to feel normal – whatever normal was.

I was so engrossed that I completely lost track of time, and it took Ash to coms me to remind me it was time to meet the others at the departure lounge.

"Wow, babe," Jake said, grabbing my hand and wheeling me around in circles, before stopping to steady me. "Got everything you needed?"

"Yes, it's all being delivered to the villa."

"You mean your honeymoon villa," Beck taunted.

"Shut it, fuckface," Kaiser threatened.

"Whatever," he replied, not looking remotely bothered.

We were the only group on the shuttle, and like everything else, it was money personified, but I can't say I minded having a couple of cocktails on the way to the planet.

"Here," Jared said, allowing me the seat next to the window to watch the staggeringly beautiful blue planet get closer. He took my free hand, the one without a cocktail in it, and it felt comfortable.

"Are you okay?" I asked quietly.

"Me? Shouldn't I be asking you that same question?"

"Maybe. But right now, it's about you."

"I'm okay."

"Are you though? It's been non-stop since the square on Santorra, and I know you've put yourself in jeopardy just being with us."

"You," he replied.

"Huh?"

"I did this for you. And I'd do it again in a heartbeat." He squeezed my hand. "And maybe Ash," he added, smiling boyishly. "At a push, the Pack. But definitely not Beck."

"Yeah, you would."

"How can you be so sure?"

"Because you're a good man, Jared." I looked out the window. "It's so beautiful. I've never seen anything like it." Jared smiled, lighting up his eyes, so similar to the sea in colour. "What?"

"I forget how isolated you've been. And I don't mean that as a criticism," he added quickly, clearly seeing the look on my face. "You know what I mean. Amongst all the shit that's going on at the moment, you can still appreciate the little things a lot of us take for granted. You… you see the beauty in things. You're literally glowing at the sight a planet. Not going to lie, it is very stunning, but to you it's a new adventure – and that's one of the things I love about you." He lifted our hands and kissed the back of mine.

The shuttle descended until we were flying just above the waves. For a long while, all we could see was water, and the odd creature breaching. Pods of aquatic animals I couldn't recognise raced alongside us. We approached the large floating resort with the sun behind us, the glare from the white buildings almost blinding. We ascended a bit, allowing us to look down on the floating snowflake, before landed on the grounds of the honeymoon villa.

Before we disembarked, one of the stewards approached Jake. "On behalf of our captain and crew, I wish you all an amazing stay on Paradisum. I know you've opted not to have waiting staff while you're here, however, if you change your mind, or simply want the villa cleaned, just ask. There's a direct com to guest services in each of the rooms and we can have people here immediately."

"Thanks," Jake said, "but I think we're okay for now."

"Of course. Then I'll leave you be."

"Just one thing," Jake said, stopping the man in his tracks. "I hear you have extensive Reader services here. My wife's a big fan of the crafts," he added, pulling me to his side and kissing my cheek.

"Why yes, yes we do. Some of the best in the Sector," he gloated. "There's a hollo-directory in the lounge that will display everything available to meet our guests' desires – however exotic they may be. I believe you will find the list… extensive."

"What does that mean?" I asked.

"I'll explain," Jake replied, leading me away from the shuttle.

"Go on then?"

"What?" he teased.

"Explain what he meant," I said. Jake, who still had his arm around my waist, bent down to whisper in my ear. "Oh," I said as he finished. "Oh!" I repeated louder, blushing ridiculously.

I don't know why I was surprised after everything that had come before, but the villa was opulent. Fresh, exotic flowers covered almost every surface, their scent filling the air like sweet perfume. Gifts – chocolates, alcohol, nibbles, fruits – lay everywhere, and when I went to the master bedroom to freshen up, there were shampoos, shower gels, make-up, and fragrances.

The balcony of the bedroom had a clear view of the sea, the soft curls in my hair ruffled by the warm breeze.

The plush carpet was so thick I didn't hear him come in until he closed his arms around me. I relaxed into him, my back against his strong chest, my arms holding his. "I'm sorry about the honeymoon thing," I said, still staring out at the horizon.

"It's not a problem," Jared replied. "It's just a name on the booking form."

"I know. But that won't stop Jake rubbing it in."

"I'm not worried," he said quietly. "Because I'm the one here with you now. The one sharing this amazing scenery with you. He's—"

Ash stopped his sentence with a polite cough.

"Everything alright?" I asked.

"All good," he replied. "Ty pulled the directory for Readers – there's more than I thought there'd be. We've got a few hours left today and Jake wants to split up to cover more ground. You good to go?"

"Of course," Jared replied.

Half an hour later, we were still arguing over assignments. The majority of Readers were located in the centre of the floating snowflake, which was also where the departure lounge was to the underwater resorts. However, there were also some Readers who were located at the ends of the resort 'arms'.

"Look," Jake said for the tenth time. "It's going to seem odd if my 'wife' is wondering around with another man."

"No one is going to know or care," Jared repeated on a loop.

While the two continued debating, Ash pulled everyone else together. "We're at the end of the North arm. Connor, Ty, take the Upper East arm. Kaiser and Cal, take the South. If you don't have any joy, converge on the central hub. Beck, you'll come with me and Shae to the hub."

"What about them?" Beck looked over his shoulder.

"They can take Upper West," Ash confirmed. "Remember, we don't know what threats we might encounter, so stay vigilant and on task. If anything looks wrong, back off and we'll re-group here. If anything looks promising, send out the coms and we'll converge on you. Questions? No? Good, then get going – we've only got a few work hours left in the day."

We left a note for Jake and Jared, unwilling to get between them, and headed off.

23

Jared and Jake just managed to squeeze through the closing door of the mag-train. With Ash already sat beside me, and the rest of the guys around us, they stood – apart. There was barely any movement as the train moved forward, but Jared held on to the back of my seat anyway.

"What's the plan," Jake asked. "I mean, I assume there is one as you all headed out without us."

"Yes, there's a plan, Jake." Ash's tone was clipped with annoyance. "You and Jared have got Upper West. If you have no luck there, meet back at the hub."

"Really?" Jared asked. Ash sighed. "You're putting the two of us together?" He raised an eyebrow and nodded towards Jake.

"Figured you two needed to sort some stuff out," replied Ash, while his frown gave a clear message to Beck, who wasn't hiding his sniggering.

"Fine," Jared acquiesced.

It wasn't long until the mag-train slowed and pulled into the central terminal. As the others separated off, some more grudgingly than others, Ash, Beck and I headed towards the promenade.

The sun was setting low, and shadows crept across walkways and parks. We passed other holiday makers, some friendly and chatty, others just plain rude. We walked through streets with expensive stores and places to eat. "Remind you of anywhere?" Ash asked.

"GB4," I replied, knowing exactly where he meant. "Only this place is way more…"

"Spectacular?" Ash offered.

"I was going to say over the top, or gaudy, but I guess that works too. Plus, I didn't have to jump out of this train, and there's nobody shooting at me either, which is an added bonus."

"This sounds like an interesting story," Beck offered. "Seems trouble really does follow you around like flies on shit."

"Hey! Rude," I replied.

"But not entirely wrong," added Ash, and even though I was reluctant to admit it, both had a good point.

We continued walking until we reached the edge of the promenade, alive with the hustle and bustle of guests and performers, stalls and shops. Perfumes mixed with the gentle wafts of salt on the sea breeze, and I was inexplicably overcome with weariness. Ash's grey eyes darkened and flashed with immediate concern.

"You okay?" he asked, turning me to face him. My eyes brimmed with tears, but I had no real idea why. "Shae? What's the matter?"

"I'm alright," I said, clearing away whatever it was that had hit me. "Just tired, I think. The last few days have been full-on."

"Beck, can you take Shae back to the—"

"No, I'll be okay, Ash, I promise. But if you want to make yourself useful, Beck, why don't you get us all a coffee from that stall over them." I was surprised when he wondered off without question.

"I think that's the first time he's done what someone's

asked him without argument," Ash reflected.

"Well, we did save him from a life in the Basement," I said, sitting on one of the marble benches.

"True, but don't forget, it was helping us that put him in the Basement in the first place."

"True," I said, copying him. "How do you think they keep this thing floating?"

"Well, that's random."

"Just wondering if I should be concerned about us sinking."

"In the grand scheme of things, I think that's the very last thing you need to worry about."

"What don't we need to worry about," Beck asked.

"Us sinking," I replied.

"We're sinking?" Beck exclaimed, looking around.

"We're not sinking," Ash stated. "Calm down, Beck, you're drawing attention."

"Well, now I know we're not actually going to be fish food, I'm calm. See? This is me being calm," he added, sitting beside me on the bench.

We took a moment to drink and plan a route through the promenade that would take us past the Readers, but as we were about to head off, I wasn't able to move.

"What is it?" Ash asked.

"I don't know."

Ash squatted in front of me, his hands on my knees. "Talk to me."

"When that old woman grabbed my arm on Phrayton, it felt like... it was like hot pokers searing into my skin. I know you felt it through the Link. But more than that, it was like the pain was digging right into my core."

"Why didn't you say something?"

"There wasn't anything you could do, Ash, or you, Beck. And it went when she let go. I'm just not eager for it to happen again."

"I'm here. I won't let anything happen to you," Ash

replied, and I let my mental roadblocks down just enough for his love to warm my insides.

"And, for what it's worth," Beck added, "I'm here too."

"Thank you," I said, nudging his knee with mine. "And for what it's worth, I'm glad you're here too. Okay," I said, rallying myself. "We're not going to find any Harbinger sat here, are we?" I downed the last of my coffee and stood, feeling protected between the two of them.

As it turned out, no one had any intel we could work with. Each Reader we saw either shrugged, or straight out denied knowing anything. At one point, a young Reader appeared straight in front of me, and at first glance I thought her eyes had rolled into the back of her head. But after that brief moment of panic, I realised her eyes were just really pale – almost translucent. And as it turned out, that was the most excitement we saw all evening.

It was late by the time the others rendezvoused with us on the Promenade, and everyone's story was the same – ranging between being thrown out of establishments, to stonewalling, to simply not knowing anything. Rather than staying out to eat on the promenade, we decided to go back to the Villa and order in – allowing us to talk freely and minimise the risk of any more attention.

The sun had gone below the horizon and the stars shone like pinpricks in the dark sky. Coloured streetlights cast mesmerising patterns on the white marble, and if you could look beyond the flagrantly obscene decadence, it was a most beautiful place to visit.

The wind picked up as we made our way back towards the terminal, but as we left the seafront and headed towards the centre of the resort, I began to notice people moving along with us in the shadows.

"Ash?"

"I see them."

"Me too," added Jared as he moved closer.

"What do you want to do," Jake asked quietly, as we

continued to amble on like we hadn't noticed.

"Nothing we can do here," Ash replied. "Keep moving. Don't look suspicious."

I laughed. I actually laughed out loud.

"What?" Ash nailed me with a well-practiced, 'this isn't the time,' look.

"Have you seen us?" Beck replied, obviously on the same wavelength as me. "We're the epitome of suspicious. I mean, you can't get more sketchy-looking than us."

"We get your point," Jared conceded. "Though it's not exactly helpful."

"You've not exactly been helpful since the day you came aboard the *Veritas*," Kaiser grumbled. "I don't even know why you're still here."

"Not the time, Kaiser," Jake replied. "Stow it for a less volatile time and place."

By the time we entered the station and found the platform we wanted, I could count at least four, maybe five people lurking in corners, watching.

"What now?" Ash asked. "If we get on that train, we're boxed in with nowhere to go. And we've got no weapons."

"We've got Kaiser's breath. That's surely a weapon of mass destruction," Beck suggested while ducking a punch.

"That's enough!" A woman stepped out of the darkness, followed by the others we'd counted around us. "Camille White, head of resort security," she said, tapping the insignia on her jacket, now visible in the lights. "We don't accept this kind of behaviour on Paradisum. I'm issuing a first offence warning to your group for aggressive behaviour. One more, and you'll be removed from the planet and returned to your ship – forfeiting all holiday costs. You signed that agreement when you came through security."

"Great," Kaiser mumbled, "We've attracted the fun police."

The head of security ignored him and opened a coms to

somewhere I could only guess would be her headquarters. "This is White, I need you to log a first offence warning against the party staying at the honeymoon villa, north arm. Uh-huh, yes, that's correct. North arm honeymoon villa." Her forehead puckered. "Sure, I'll hold."

"Problem?" Ash asked politely.

"Nothing for you to worry about. Just stay where you are," she replied. "And while we wait, why doesn't one of you tell me why your group has been systematically checking out our Readers."

"Is that also an offense?" Beck mocked, stepping out from behind Ash. "Coz I feel like you should've made some of these rules a little more obvious to guests before they pay a shit-tonne of money to visit."

White stared at him a moment, then looked him up and down. "Becker? Andrew Becker?" she asked.

"Wait, Andrew?" Kaiser mocked. "And Becker? Oh, this is priceless." He couldn't contain the guffaws, and in a moment the rest of us were laughing. Except Beck.

"Do I know you?" he asked, looking at her sideways and squinting. "Wait… I do, don't I? Cam Hutchinson? It's been, what? Fifteen years?"

"Twenty, give or take," she said, visibly relaxing.

"You got married then? It's good to see you," he added before picking her up in his signature move.

"Put your weapons down," Camille directed once she was on her feet again. "I know this guy – he's rough around the edges, and all shades of murky, but he's not a bad guy."

"Told you," I whispered to Jake.

Lines furrowed her forehead "That's right. I do know you," she stated, studying his face. "And I also know a two-bit street rat like you couldn't afford this place. Are you—" She indicated a coms and stepped back a few paces. "Can you repeat that? Are you sure? Of course, Sir. Upmost discretion and confidentiality. Yes, sir. Thanks." Hands on hips, she studied the floor for moment before turning back to us. She remained silent as she studied first Beck and then the rest of us. She shook her head and turned to her people. "That'll be all. Return to your stations," she ordered, but no one moved. "I said, that will be all," she repeated. Her team looked confused but did what was asked and disappeared back into the shadows.

"Everything okay?" Beck asked. She ignored his question.

"My apologies, Your Highnesses," she said politely and quietly. "You're free to go. Please pardon my behaviour, I... I have no excuses. My superiors have asked me to advise you that should you wish to log a complaint against my actions, they could have someone meet you at your accommodation."

"That won't be necessary," Ash replied. "You did your job admirably. We've kept our stay here in the strictest of confidence, so how where you to know? We're sorry that we," he waved his arm around the group, "caused you concern."

"And thank you," Kaiser added. "Thank you for Andrew Becker." He placed amused emphasis on the name. "That's been the best moment of the day. Say, you wouldn't happen to have any more stories about Andrew you'd like to share, do you?"

"No, she doesn't," Beck said vehemently, but Camille smiled.

"As much as I would love to tell you all about Baby Becker, I value my job too much. Sharing about a guest, to other guests is a definite no-no. As is asking how a street rat ended up in the company of Royals."

"We understand," Ash said. "And that story is too long to go into. If you'll forgive us, we should be heading off."

"Of course," she replied. "But would I be overstepping if I asked why you were checking out our Readers? Two or three I could understand, getting the right fit's important, but all of them?"

The question was followed by silence, as if no one really know whether to say anything, but then Beck stepped forward. "We're looking for the Harbingers," he said succinctly, and while everyone else's attention shifted to him, I studied her.

"Let him go, Kaiser. You too, Ty," I said, as the pair had wrestled Beck to the floor. Jake, who was just about to wade in, stopped and turned. He must've seen something on my face because he broke the men apart, holding out his hand, somewhat reluctantly, to help Beck up.

"What is it," Jared asked, taking my hand.

"She knows something. Don't you," I added turning towards her. She seemed conflicted. "It's okay. Whatever it is, you can tell us. If it helps, don't think of us as Royals. We're just a group of holiday makers asking for direction."

"But, I…"

"No buts, Camille," Beck said. "You can trust us." She raised an eyebrow. "Okay, you can trust them," he clarified.

"We don't want to cause you any trouble, but we need to find the Harbingers. And we've reason to believe they're on one of the Trinity Planets," I said. "And from your reaction to the name, I think you know who we're talking about."

Camille White shuffled her weight from one foot to another, and then back again. She looked between our expectant faces before turning back to me. "I don't know about the Harbingers, exactly," she said, "but…" She looked conflicted again. "But I've heard things. Bits of information here and there. Some of the staff think they're an urban myth, but I think… I think…"

"There's no smoke without fire," I offered.

"Exactly," she replied. "I honestly don't know anything factually, but anecdotally, I think there's something to the rumours. But it would be highly inappropriate and unprofessional of me to share anything with you. I could lose my job"

"Come on, Cam," begged Beck. "Are you really going to pull that card with a member of the Palavarian Royal Family?"

"It's okay," Ash said. "We understand your predicament."

"Thanks," Camille replied followed by a moment of silence. "I should let you get on your way. I'm sorry I took time out of your vacation. Just some friendly advice: you really should visit the underwater ring. The resorts on the sea floor are stunning, especially Jade."

"Jade? Over all the other resorts?" Jake clarified.

"Yes," She replied. "I can't be sure, but I think it may have what you're looking for in terms of holiday activities. There are a number of bars and beauty salons, various shops and activities, and there's even an indoor aquarium. You should maybe try there first. It opens at 10am, with the Aquatica show starting at 11. I highly recommend it."

"Thanks," I replied. "We appreciate your help."

"That we do," said Ash. "But now, I think we should be leaving."

"Of course. Enjoy the rest of your stay and thank you for choosing the Trinity Planets as your luxury destination of choice." She started to walk away, then stopped and turned. "Just out of interest, how long did you know we were tailing you?" she called out.

"Right from the beginning," Jake said over his shoulder.

"Thought so," she said before being swallowed up by the shadows.

By the time we got to the mag-train, there were a number of other guests occupying the carriage. We sat in silence, unable to talk business, but collectively too tired and too hungry to make small talk. Even when the train cleared and it was just us left, no one seemed willing to talk.

The villa was cool compared to the warm mugginess of the night air. We headed to the lounge en masse, and while Cal ordered through an extensive list of dishes to be delivered, I wondered if I even had the energy to eat.

"So, I'm just going to say it," Beck said. "I think Cam was trying to tell us the Harbingers are in the Jade Underwater Resort."

"Really?" Kaiser gasped sarcastically. "None of us got that. But thanks for bringing it to our attention."

"Fuck you."

"Enough," Jake said loudly, flopping onto the sofa beside me and stretching his arm along the back behind my head. "Today was a bust, but we have a plan for what comes next. And there's no point worrying about that tonight. Food then sleep. We need to have our game faces on tomorrow. This is the best lead we have so far and we're not going to blow it. Understand? So, from now on, the shit's got to stop. I can't believe I'm saying this, but Beck's here, like it or not. He's part of the mission, so whatever is going on between you all stops now." A murmur of agreement rippled through the Pack. "Do you understand?" Jake continued, his voice firm and resolute. "Kaiser, can I count on you?"

"Yeah, boss," he replied, nodding his head slowly.

"The rest of you?" Jake added, to a round of agreement from the Pack. "And Beck?"

"Me?" he said innocently.

"Yes, you," Jake clarified. "This is a two-way street here, Andrew." He emphasised the name, and I watched Kaiser chew his tongue to stop himself from saying anything. "You're part of the mission, and you need to behave like part of it. Not some dip-shit groupie who's just biding time until the right moment comes along to ditch. If you're in, you're in. If not, there's the door. You can leave now."

Beck studied the group silently before his gaze came to me. "I'm in." he said.

"All the way in?" Jake pushed.

"All the way in," he replied. "Jeez, do you want me to write it in blood? Okay, okay, no need for the death stare, I get it. I'm in."

"Good," replied Jake before looking around and frowning. "Where's Captain Clingy?" he asked me.

"Checking in with Commander Tel'an," I explained.

"Really?"

"Of course. You know what he's like. It would seem odder to Tel'an if he didn't check in to make sure everything was okay."

"True. Perhaps Captain Control-Freak would be a better name."

"Stop it," I chastised, punching him gently on the leg, but he slipped his arm around my shoulders and pulled me into his side. For a moment, I rested my head on his shoulder and closed my eyes.

The honeymoon villa slept six, and there were at least four huts in the grounds, so when I opened my eyes again, I was amazed to see our entire group asleep in the lounge. Empty food containers littered the floor and my tummy rumbled. The lights were off, and a cool breeze drifted in off the ocean, swirling up the beautiful aroma from the exotic flora covering almost ever surface. I didn't know how long I'd been asleep, long enough to miss dinner, but once I was awake, I couldn't settle my mind.

I carefully extricated myself from under Jake's arm, freezing as he shifted, before stepping over bodies. The large bifold doors onto the patio were wide open, and I picked up a folded shawl from the basket, wrapping it around my shoulders. The sea twinkled in the waning moon.

"Hey," Jake said quietly.

"I'm sorry I woke you."

"You didn't. But when I realised you were gone, I thought this is where you'd be." He rested his arms on the railing, gazing out to sea. "Are you worried about today?"

"Mildly apprehensive maybe. I mean, what if this is another dead end?"

"That's not what's worrying you."

"It's not?"

"No," he said simply.

"Then what is it?"

"You know what is."

"Enlighten me," I replied, turning to search his face for clues.

"Not finding the Harbingers is not what's bothering you. It's finding them that scares you."

"I don't…" I started, ready to deny his claim, but truth was, he was right. I smiled weakly. "When did you become so smart?"

"One of us has to be."

"Well, that's just rude," I said, but it just made him grin even more.

"I mean," he continued, "you still think you're better off with Captain Fantastic rather than me, so your smarts are seriously questionable."

"Stop it," I chastised, but I knew there was nothing I could say I hadn't said before. "You're right, though."

"About Captain Annoying?" he replied quickly, his eyes turning serious.

"No, not about that. About me being scared of finding the Harbingers. I think you're right… I've put so many people through hell to get to this point – to help me get to this point – what if the whole thing's a big mistake? What if there's no big conspiracy theory, and it's just one huge misunderstanding?"

"And what if it isn't?"

I thought for a moment. "I'm not sure which is worse."

"You want my opinion?"

"Always."

"I can't speak for Beck or Jared, but the Pack… we'd stick with you through this journey a thousand times. Regardless of the outcome."

I wanted to reply, to tell him how much that meant to

me, but the lump in my throat wouldn't let me get a single word out. Instead, I pulled him into a hug, and he wrapped his muscular arms around me, holding me to his chest.

I loved Jake. I always had. And I'd convinced myself that I loved him as a friend, as family even, but the more time we spent together, the more cracks appeared in my logic. My feelings for Jared hadn't changed, but now I felt guilt as I stood in Jake's arms, feeling safe and comfortable.

The sky lightened as Jake released his hold, and we both wordlessly stared out to sea. I don't know what was going through Jake's mind right then, but mine was scrambling to find some justification for the guilt.

"It's okay, you know," he said after a while.

"What's okay?"

"To have feelings for two people at the same time. I know you love Jared, I'm smart enough to know that," he half joked, but it was like he was reading my mind. He turned to face me. "But I know you love me too. And not just as a friend." I opened my mouth to reply, but he put a finger to my lips. "All I ask is that you admit that to yourself. That you're honest with yourself about how you feel, that you—"

"What's occurring, honeymooners," Beck said loudly, and I wasn't sure whose benefit that was for until Ash and Jared followed him out. I let down my mental roadblocks for a moment, feeling Ash's utter frustration, and it made me smile.

"Good morning, Andrew," Jake said, not taking the bait.

"Beck will do just fine," he replied huffily.

"Do we have a plan yet for today," Ash asked, looking between me and Jake, but I didn't have the opportunity to reply, as Jared took my hand and led me further down the patio and around the corner of the villa, away from the group.

"What's wrong? Is everything okay?" I ask, searching his stunning blue eyes.

"Nothing's wrong," he said quietly. "It's just…"

"Just what?"

"I wanted a moment alone with you." I instantly felt guilty, again. "I know how chaotic things are at the moment, and I don't want to be 'that guy,' but I just wanted the briefest moment."

I touched his cheek with my hand and stood on tiptoes to kiss him. I'd intended it to be a short kiss before apologising for sleeping on Jake, but his lips were soft, and he responded so passionately, that I melted into him. For a moment, everything else fell away, and it was just him and me, together. The tiny embers in the pit of my stomach caught fire as my hands wandered under his shirt, but after a moment he pulled away.

"What's the matter?" I asked, panicked. "Did I do something wrong?"

"No. No," he said quickly, his voice breathier than normal. "You're perfect." Panic switched to confusion. "Hey, don't worry," he added, cupping my face with his hands, before lowering his head to kiss me again. "It's just there's no privacy here, and well…" He took my hand and lowered it, letting me feel the hardness under his trousers. "See what you do to me?" I giggled nervously, and his lips broke into a smile. "There's a huge bed upstairs no one's using, and I really want to carry you there and have my wicked way—" My laugh interrupted him. "What?"

"How do you know it wouldn't be me having my wicked way with you?"

He thought for a moment, his boyish grin widening. "I would kill to have it either way right now."

"Then why don't we?" I said, almost surprising me as much as Jared.

He remained silent for a moment, as if he was weighing up options. "Because," he said eventually. "Because when we do this, I want it to be special – for you. Not snatching a few minutes, while everyone else is only a few meters away.

Does that make sense? Because, right now, I can't believe I'm turning down the opportunity to explore every centimetre of you with my hands and lips. To hold you, to kiss you, to—" My lips silenced him as I pulled him closer to me. My hand folded behind his neck, running over the short, military haircut, while the other found its way back to his bulge.

A second later, he'd lifted me up and my legs automatically wrapped around him. The railing felt hard under my arse, but I didn't care. His tongue found mine, and he kissed me more deeply and passionately than he'd ever done before. "Are you sure?" he asked. I nodded. "Are you really sure?"

"Yes," I replied, and I was.

He picked me up off the railings and carried me into the villa towards the stairs, my arms and legs coiling around him. We were halfway up the stairs when we met Ash coming the opposite way.

"Jared," he said calmly. "Shae. I was just looking for you."

"Upstairs?" Jared replied.

"Seems I wasn't wrong... just a little premature," Ash replied. "We've got a plan for today, but we need to go through it with everyone there."

Jared placed my feet gently back on the stairs, and I knew he'd stayed behind me so Ash couldn't see what I could feel in the small of my back.

"Can I tell Jake you'll be with us imminently?"

"Two minutes," Jared said, sighing as Ash continued down the stairs and across the lounge through to the patio.

"Better to be interrupted here than down the line," I said, trying to be pragmatic, but it was a stretch.

"It was my fault," admitted Jared. "I knew this was going to happen. I should've been stronger."

"It takes two to tango," I replied, trying to make him feel better.

"Tango?" he frowned.

"It's an old Earth saying. Tango was a couple's dance. It means we were both involved in the moment. I learnt that in Earth History class, in one of the rare moments I wasn't bored to tears."

"Oh. Well, in that case, I'm glad we were both 'in the moment' as you put it." The boyish smile returned. "I guess we'll just have to wait for another moment."

"Promise?"

"Promise," he replied.

24

I'd never been anywhere before where the elevator had a tour guide – or stop quiet so regularly to watch the marine life go past. I nervously held on to Ash's shirt sleeve as the guide continued to tell us more about the whale-type creature that had just swam way too close to our tiny little elevator for my liking. It wasn't so much the round shaped car itself that caused my anxiety levels to peak, but the fact that the floor and ninety percent of the walls were glass.

"We're totally safe," Ash told me as my grip tightened.

"You know that for a fact?"

"Yes," he replied. "The resort wouldn't risk losing any of its rich customers. There are probably safety features on top of safety features on top of—"

"Okay, I get it," I replied, only slightly mollified. "You made your point." Having said that, though, I felt relief when we made it to the seafloor.

"So, you're okay here, under all the weight of the sea, but not in the elevator? Sounds a little weird to me," said Beck.

"That noticeable, huh?"

"Umm," he pretended to think, "yup."

"Well, it's not that I'm 'okay' here, it's that I can't see the ocean." I waved my arm around the deluxe arrivals lounge, filled with shops and eateries.

"It's this way to the Jade resort," Connor announced, having downloaded the map to his com-pad. I was relieved with the distraction.

"Lead the way, Con," replied Jake, taking up a position between Beck and me. Jared appeared silently at my other side.

We were ahead of schedule, so the Pack decided we should walk the glass tunnel leading to the Jade resort, which was connected to all the others by an outer ring. I wasn't impressed.

"What's the matter little wolfpup? It's just a bit of water," Kaiser teased before breaking into guffaws. The other tourists weren't enthralled by the behaviour, but he didn't care. After thirty minutes of walking, though, I think the novelty was wearing off for them, but I was just starting to enjoy watching the marine life. Especially the cute little neon jellyfish babies trying to follow behind their parent like drunk old men – disappearing off at all angles and having to be corralled back in line. It made me think of our group, and I smiled.

At the entrance to the Jade resort, we were adorned with more flower garlands, and even Kaiser seemed receptive, getting into an argument with Ty over who's flowers were better.

"Camille's advice was to come to Jade and go to the aquarium," Ash said. "And here we are." We stopped to view the living coral entrance. "But the resort map shows a few Readers are set up throughout the resort, so this is where our plan starts."

"Ty, Connor?" said Jake.

"Visit the three Readers on the west side of the resort, then rendezvous back here if no luck," replied Ty.

"Kaiser, Cal, Beck?"

"Take the four Readers on the east side, then rendezvous back here," Kaiser replied. Although I know he was pissed that Beck had been assigned with them, he managed to hold it back.

"Ash, Shae?"

"Do a clockwise loop of the aquarium and then attend the main show," replied Ash.

"And Jake and I'll do the same, but in the other direction," Jared added

"Outstanding," Jake replied. "This is the best lead we've had, so no stone unturned. Why are you all still here? Let's hustle."

It seemed ironic to me to have indoor lagoons and water-filled displays this far under the ocean, but I guess most of the people we mingled with would never consider actually visiting them in their natural habitat. I forget sometimes that not everyone is like us.

"Does everyone with money act this entitled?" I whispered to Ash after being barged out of the way for the third time so someone else could get a better look at whatever we were pretending to be interested in.

"Not everyone," he replied. "Phina and Frederick are Royal, but can you imagine either of them behaving like this?"

"Not at all."

"Having money doesn't entitle people, nor does it make them any better than... than those young kids who cleaned up the *Nakomo* on GB4 as an example. Unfortunately, ignorance and entitlement are more prevalent in the wealthy."

"I feel sorry for the staff who take the brunt of things." I nodded my head towards a steward being yelled at by two people at once. I found myself automatically heading that way, but Ash steered me back towards the main stadium, where the morning extravaganza was about to start.

We took our seats towards the front of the vast

auditorium, before us, an unoccupied deep pool of water. The backdrop was the ocean itself, the sea life creating their own show while we waited. I scanned the half-filled benches behind us looking for something out of the ordinary, but nothing – except spotting Jake and Jared sitting towards the back on the other side from us.

The loudspeakers introduced the show, and moments later, a stream of animals jumped and flipped into the main tank. Three trainers appeared from behind a curtain, smiling and waving with forced enthusiasm. One of them dived straight in, his gills allowing him to remain underwater. He appeared in one of the underwater portholes where kids were waiting, and they shrieked with delight. It was difficult to track him through the water as his blue hued skin camouflaged him well.

A second trainer, an Other with a fair few Ethileron genes, climbed to a higher stage, while the third, human trainer, started the show. Nothing seemed out of the ordinary, and there wasn't anything that screamed Harbinger, but I found myself drawn to the show in front of me.

Towards the end and highlight of the show, the young Human trainer, who'd introduced herself as Marla, rode on top of one of the animals around the tank before hopping off onto a small platform at the front, not far from where we sat. She continued with the show, the bright house lights dimming and the music changing for dramatic effect. Marla warned us all that what came next might be unsuitable for sensitive visitors and discretion was advised for the children in the hall. A few people stood and left while I scanned for any clues to the Harbingers.

The music, low and heartbeat like, foreshadowed something ominous, and I was drawn in as much as anyone else.

"In a moment," Marla continued, "we're going to turn the lights down completely, and raise the outside floodlights. What you're about to witness, must never be attempted by untrained individuals. The divers are highly trained and are putting themselves in mortal danger just by being in the cages. The sea creatures you're about to see are one of the most unique predators in the known worlds. They're able to live at great depths, but can also survive for anything up to thirty minutes in an oxygen rich environment. Their teeth are like knives, but it's their olfactory senses that make them deadly… that's their smell to you and me." The audience laughed nervously. "Most of the time they're relatively harmless, but once they get the scent of blood, even a drop, they relentlessly track their prey through water and land, and they never ever give up until they catch it. Once one of these catches the scent of your blood, you best leave the planet." She said it like a joke, but I don't think it was. "I need you to be very quiet," she carried on in a hushed voice. "Because now it's time to meet the Goralite."

A hushed murmur rippled around the auditorium as the lights went out, and we sat in complete darkness for a few seconds before the outside lights lit up the ocean. The two divers floated motionless in see through cages, with two live creatures suspended separately by chains right in front of the glass. They looked a bit like the Mantra sharks on Lilania, and at first, I wondered if they were the Goralite, but as we waited, the trainer continued to give us hushed information on the creatures and I realised they weren't. She was halfway through a sentence when she stopped. "They're here," she announced ominously. "Remember, no loud noises."

They were difficult to make out to begin with, but as they got closer, I could see more, and they reminded me of an aquatic version of the cave creatures Jared and I had encounter previously. I turned to make sure he was safe, which was ridiculous, but I couldn't see him in the dark room.

Eventually, I could make out three or four swimming in and out of the lit area, but they didn't seem remotely interested in the chained creatures, and only went to check out the divers, nudging the cages lightly.

"They look fierce, huh?" Marla continued. "But not acting very fierce-like at the moment, are they?" The audience quietly agreed. "So, what the trainers are about to do, is release a small amount of blood from each of the two chained sharks. And as I've already mentioned, this will send them into a blood frenzy. Watch carefully as this will be quick."

I thought the rod the divers had been holding was some kind of shock-stick should the creatures get to close for them, but on Marla's authorisation, they fed the stick through a hole in the cage. They were too far away to see any blood, but in an instant, the Goralight attacked the sharks, two, three creatures on each one – ripping and thrashing. It was a chaotic feeding with chunks of flesh being torn from the sharks.

I turned away. "And this is entertainment? It's barbaric."

As if Marla could hear my words, she said, "I want to assure you the sharks we use in these shows are very old and frail and going to die imminently anyway."

"I'm sure that makes the shark feel better," I said loudly over the cheering and clapping. "Being torn apart is far better than dying peacefully in old age. You're being quiet, Ash," I observed.

"I think I saw something."

"What?" My pulse quickened.

"Something. I don't know, maybe I'm mistaken. We're so desperate to find the Harbingers, I'm not sure if I can trust my own instincts anymore."

"You may not be able to, but I can. Even under extreme pressure, I'd trust your gut over anything or anyone else."

"That's kind of you to say, but you're biased."

"It's not kind, it's fact. And biased or not, you know I'm

right. So, what is it?"

"Marla."

"Marla? What about her?"

"When she came to the front of the stage, she was engaging with everyone wasn't she?"

"I don't know, I was looking and around and checking on Jake and Jared."

"I know. Which is why I can't tell if it was real or I'm stretching."

"Just tell me," I said, covering my eyes as the house lights came up.

"Marla was consistent, the routine done a thousand times before, but when she was engaging with this side, it was like something happened. For the briefest moment, her smile slipped, and the tone of her voice changed. But a second later it was like nothing happened. Like I said, it could've been anything, but I really think she was looking at you."

"Then let's go and talk to her," I suggested.

"Talk to who?" Jared asked.

"Marla," I replied. "Ash thinks she was surprised to see me, or something."

"Then let's go talk to her," Jake said. "Why are you smiling?"

"Because you literally just said the same thing as me."

"Must be a good idea then," he replied.

"But what if I'm wrong. What if it's just another dead end?" Ash said.

"Emotional second-guessing is my job, Ash," I replied. "You're the steadfast realist, so stop trying to hog my limelight. I mean, the show's finished, what else have we got to do?" I started up the steps, but Jared put his hand out to stop me. "What?"

"Talk of the devil," he explained, nodding to the stairs behind me. Marla had switched her wetsuit for a tracksuit, her damp hair soaking into her top.

"Great show," Jake said, but she ignored him.

"You need to come with me now," she ordered. "Whatever it is, not here," she added as Ash started to say something. "Come with me, now." She grabbed my wrist, as Jared grabbed hers.

"Let her go," he growled, tightening his grip. She obliged reluctantly.

"It's too dangerous for you to be out in the open like this. What the hell is the Brotherhood playing at?"

"Do you know who the Harbingers are?" I asked, butterflies swirling in my chest.

"Do I know who the…" she stuttered, and I couldn't tell if the look on her face was amazement, or disbelief. "I'll answer your questions, just not here." She looked nervously around. "Please, come with me."

We followed her down the stairs, through a staff-only door, and through another door with her name on it. Her changing room felt claustrophobic with us all in there.

"You recognised Shae in the audience, didn't you?" Ash asked.

"Yes. Why are you here?" she added, looking at me.

"We're looking for the Harbingers," I replied.

"Why? What can the Harbingers offer you?"

"I need them to tell me who I am. What I am." I replied. Jake, Jared and Ash stood silently against the wall.

Marla looked confused. "Is this a joke?"

"I don't understand. You said you'd answer all my questions."

"This is beyond belief," she said, sitting for a second before standing up again. "Are you seriously telling me you don't know who you are?"

"I think that was made clear when Shae told you that's what she's looking for the Harbingers for," Jake said, crossing his arms.

She looked between me and the three men a couple of times, lingering on the men. "Three," she said. "There's three of you."

"Last time we checked," Jake replied.

"That's not helping, Jake," Jared snapped, but Marla stepped right up to him, studying his face and his eyes, before looking back at me. She smiled.

"What's so funny?" Jake said, ignoring Jared, but Marla moved in front of him, studying him like she had Jared. Then she turned to Ash.

"There's three of you," she repeated,

"You said that already," Ash said, and I could feel his anxiety pressing against the Link. Marla put her hand on Ash's chest, holding it there for a couple of heartbeats before removing it and smiling again.

"You are family," she said to him – a statement not a question – like she already knew. "She will need you the most."

"Look, lady," Jake began, but she ignored him, not taking her gaze from Ash.

"You are Brotherhood, yes?"

"Yes," he replied.

"Then you have prepared her, right?"

"For what?"

"No, no, no. This isn't what's supposed to happen. Why are you looking for the Harbingers if you don't know what's going on? How do you even know about them?" She turned to me. "Sit. Please. Tell me what you know."

"No," Jake answered for me. "What we have is for the Harbingers only. Can you tell us where we can find them, or not?"

"Who are you?" she asked, catching him off guard. "Why are you here… with her?"

"That's none of your business. But what I will tell you is that I'll protect her till the end of time, and that includes protecting her from you if I need to."

As she had with Ash, she placed a hand on his chest and he immediately looked uncomfortable, shifting his weight from foot to foot. She smiled again. "You're a courageous protector. She's in good hands."

"I'm sorry, but—" Marla held up her hand to shush me as she turned to Jared

"And you?" she asked, placing her hand on his chest. "Are you willing to do whatever it takes to protect her?"

"Of course," he replied. "Shae comes before everything."

"No, no I don't," I replied, my cheeks getting hotter. "I don't come before any of you. I hate that you're all suffering because of me."

Jared put his arm on my shoulder, gently raising my head with the other. "I love you. What kind or a man would I be if I didn't protect the person I loved above all else?"

"And that's what makes you such an honourable man," said Marla.

"So, are you going to help us?" Ash asked.

She studied my face and her smile slipped as she became serious. "I will try, but I fear we may be too late."

"You'll tell us where the Harbingers are?" Ash asked.

"Yes, and no."

I don't know whose frustrated huff was loudest.

"So impatient," she remarked. "Give me a moment to change."

I almost fell over the chair as I jumped back in surprise. Marla's skin rippled – soft, human skin replaced by pinky-white scales. A stunning pattern of darker ruby scales on her cheekbones and temples contrasted against her pale face, and as the delicate decoration of pink and ruby spread down her neck and chest, her hair changed from dark brown to white at the roots, spreading along the length to the ends. She was… magnificent.

"You're a Harbinger," I stammered.

"Yes," she replied, her voice smoother, more melodic. "My real name is Yana."

"And you're not human." I wasn't sure if it was a

question or a statement.

"No," she laughed softly, placing a hand on my cheek. I took it in mine, surprised that the scales were soft and warm, not hard and cold as I'd expected. I stroked her forearm before realising what I was doing.

"I'm so sorry," I said, horrified. "That was rude."

"It's fine," she replied kindly. "We've been waiting for you."

"We? How many Harbingers are there?"

"Three," she replied. "There have been more in the past, and we have people who help keep our secret, but now we are all that's left."

"You're not at all was I was expecting," Jake said, studying her intensely.

"And what was that?" she asked, turning her ruby eyes on him. "A wizened old harpy in some cold, damp cave?"

"No, nothing like that," he replied, but she cocked her head and blinked slowly. "Okay, something exactly like that," he admitted, and it was the first time I'd seen Jake blush.

"We must get down to business. You're not safe here," she said, turning back to me. "Sit. Please. All of you. I'm not sure how long this is going to take, but we must be quick."

"What do you mean?" Ash asked, sitting as requested.

"It means you should all have been more prepared by the time you came to us. Tell me what you know, and I'll fill in what I can, but I'm only one of three."

Yana settled herself into an armchair and listened patiently while I – we – filled her in on everything that had happened up to that point. When we were done, she stood and paced in the small room, muttering in a language I didn't recognise, but I can guarantee most of it was profanity.

"Curse the Brotherhood," she eventually said, seating herself again. She looked and Ash. "My apologies for the outburst."

"There's no need," Ash replied. "I think we've all gathered by the conversation so far that the Brotherhood of the Virtuous Sun has failed in preparing Shae for something that's coming."

"I am so very sorry to hear about Finnian," she continued. "He was very kind to us when we met him just after your birth."

"How? When? You're too…"

"Young?" she offered. "I'm older than you think. A lot older. You don't remember meeting me when Finnian brought you here, to the Trinity Planets?"

"I remember the visit, but I'm sorry, I don't remember you."

"I'm not surprised," she reflected. "You must've only been about nine or ten, I'd guess, and our meeting was very short."

"Why did he bring me?"

"To check that you were actually the key, of course."

"And what did that entail?" Ash asked.

"Don't worry, we'll get to that," she said vaguely.

"Okay, so let's just accept I'm not as prepared as I should be and move on," I said, getting more frustrated by the second. "And please tell me you can help. I don't think I can go through another failure."

"I can give you some, enough at this point, but as I said, I'm but one of three – you'll need to find Lana and Kana for everything you need. I—"

The hammering at the door put us all on alert. "Hey, Marla," someone yelled. "You coming to Mac's for a quick lunch before this afternoon's show?"

"Thanks for the invite, Stan, but go without me. I'm not that hungry." Her voice switched to her 'human' voice.

"Okay, your loss," Stan replied, but we remained silent until we couldn't hear people in the corridor anymore.

"Who's Stan?" I asked.

"The guy from the show; the blue one with the gills. We call him Stan because nobody can pronounce his actual name. He's good people."

"Getting back to it then, I'm assuming Lana and Kana are the other two Harbingers," Jared said, starting the conversation up again.

"That would be a correct assumption," she replied, her voice back to matching her appearance.

"Please tell me you know where they are," added Jake.

"I do, and I don't."

"What the hell does that mean?" His frustration simmered right under the surface, and I knew if I couldn't move along, he was going to blow.

"Tell us what you know," I asked Marla diplomatically.

"To avoid detection before you came to us, we decided to split up amongst the planets."

"One of you on each one?" Ash asked.

"Yes. Of course, this was long before they became the Pleasure Planets." She saw the frown on my face. "I did say I was much older than I look. We agreed to stay, to take the form of someone understated. Blend in. Don't cause trouble. But now you're here, it feels... liberating."

"Okay, you know they're on the other planets, but you don't know who they are?"

"Exactly," she confirmed.

"How did you recognise Shae?" Ash asked.

"I didn't. Not at first. For me, it was like she just glowed from the inside out. Radiant... magnificent."

"Am I still glowing?" I asked, examining my arms.

"Just a little," she replied. "Are your eyes always sapphire blue?"

"No, they're hazel... have been all my life."

"To me, they shine blue and bright. A beacon in the dark times to come. But listen to me getting off track. There are things I can tell you, some bits will help, some may just add to your questions. You can walk away from this, Shae. Just get up, leave, and go back to your old life."

"That's not an option," I confirmed. "We've all come so far."

"Okay then. There's just one small test I need to do," Yana said, opening the desk drawer next to her. "I think you know what it is. May I?"

"Of course." I held out my hand, wincing as the knife pulled through my skin. Yana grabbed a tissue and wiped the blood off my arm as it healed, and a blurred memory came into focus.

"We've done this before," I said.

"Yes, when Finnian brought you." She tossed the tissue in the bin under her desk. "No turning back?"

"No turning back," I replied.

"Okay then. Let's start with the Brotherhood. They…" she paused, turning to Ash. "I'm sorry, this may be difficult to hear."

"It's alright," Ash replied. "I think it's fair to say the Brotherhood isn't what I thought it was."

"In part," she replied, her voice soft and comforting. "Finnian's message was correct, and the things he said, though cryptic, were completely true. The Brotherhood of the Virtuous Sun had three tasks: keep you safe, train you, and prepare you for what's coming."

"I guess two out of three isn't bad," Jake joked, but his eyes showed no sign of humour.

"I'm truly sorry, but the Brotherhood has failed you, Shae," Yana continued. "Let's start at the beginning and I'll try to add what I can. You've correctly deduced that Finnian and the *Nakomo* were sent to rendezvous with your parent's transporter, but it was attacked before they could get there. We suspected a group we call the Vex attacked the ship to stop your parents from getting to the Brotherhood. And I believe the tattooed people you've recently encountered are the same people Finnian said would come for you if they knew who you were."

"The Vex?" Jared asked.

"Precisely," she responded. "Finnian's message told you to find us." My pulse quickened. "But the Brotherhood's responsibility was to prepare you for what's to come, for your responsibility. Not to come here blind to your purpose."

"My purpose? Are you saying that I have to do something?"

"Yes, child."

"What?" Ash asked before I could.

"That I can't answer. What I can tell you is that whatever it is, it will have ramifications across all of space."

I sat on the edge of my chair, mouth open, unable to get out a single word.

"That's a joke, right?" said Jake. "An exaggeration?"

"It must be," I added, finding my voice. "I mean, I'm a nobody with a neat party trick." I held up my hand, strands of silver-blue sparkling.

"For the love of… I thought you might… I hoped you were testing me, but you really don't know anything, do you?"

"That's what I've been telling you all along." My voice sounded loud and frustrated in the small room, causing Yana to make hushing noises.

"Okay, okay, I get it," she replied, "I hope you're ready for this. Based on what you've said, we need to start at the beginning with a crash course. Many, many, many—"

"We get it," Jared said.

"Fine, grumpy pants." I saw Jake snigger out of the corner of my eye. "A long time ago, something happened."

25

"What?" Ash asked, and I didn't need the Link to tell me he was getting frustrated.

"I don't know," she admitted, carrying on quickly before Ash completely lost patience. "I told you, I'm one of three, what I can't tell you, one of my siblings may. Can I continue uninterrupted this time?" She nailed each of the men with penetrating ruby eyes. "Okay, that's better. So, as I was saying... a long time ago, something happened that rippled across space, impacting every planet, galaxy, and universe. At the time, it was feared the same thing would happen again, so it was decided we should be prepared. The Helyan Codex, the one Finnian told you to find us about, is a copy of symbols found carved into a cave wall on Earth many moons ago. It was older than anything anyone had seen before, and even though the swirling, delicate text was alien to them, a message of importunacy was laid out in the exquisitely detailed pictograms. Over the years, the Helyan Codex was passed from civilisation to civilisation, eventually ending up in the enlightened hands of the Tetrarchy. The Brotherhood of the Virtuous Sun was originally created to look after the Codex and to care for the person who would come when needed."

"And Shae's the person?" Ash asked.

"Yes, though we didn't know that until she was conceived."

"You're saying the Brotherhood's one and only purpose right from the beginning, was to protect Shae?" Ash continued.

"Yes, well, the key," replied Yana. "At the beginning, anyway. But it has grown and developed into so much more. If you take out their failure towards Shae, there's no denying the outstanding work they've done since their inception. I mean, look at you," she said, her question aimed at Ash. "I know you. I know what you have done and achieved. How the Brotherhood started should not diminish the work done. The work you have done."

"I guess," he said, but I had to work hard on my mental roadblocks to stop the confusion and pain overwhelming me. "Please, carry on."

"You said you found a manuscript page in the monastery?" she asked me.

"Yes, hidden in a wall safe."

"I believe this page to have come from the Helyan Codex. I know what you're going to say, that it doesn't look like it was written millennia ago, but every so often, when it threatens to succumb to the ravages of time, a copy codex is made and the previous one disintegrated."

"And you've never been able to read it?" I asked.

"We believe we have decrypted some, but not enough. We knew someone would come, but we didn't know when. It was also clear Earth was not alone, and whatever happens, would impact all races, so the first Tetrarchy agreed to provide three copies of the Codex to other worlds to ensure the message never got lost. Three incomplete versions."

"What does that mean?" I asked.

"It means they were all missing the same page. The page

that was kept at the monastery?" Ash said. "Right?"

"Right," Yana replied. "The original stayed on Earth, but I'm sorry, I can't tell you where the others went. I would if I knew, but I know they were supposed to be kept secret and safe."

"Supposed to be?" Ash asked.

"Good catch. Rumour has it, one of the alien planets entrusted with a codex, went through a bitter civil war, and their copy was… lost… stolen… liberated maybe." I'm sure she looked at Jared when she mentioned the word. "I believe, from what you've said, somehow the Khan brothers, or this 'Outsider' person you've mentioned, got their hands on it – or a copy of the copy, and that's how they found Tartaros."

"And that's how he knew about the codex, and my pendant," I said, putting two and two together. "But how did they know the Helyan Cube was in the underground secure area at the Palace of Palavaria?"

"That I can't answer," Yana said. "I don't know anything about cubes or pendants. Just the codex."

"So what else can you tell us about it?" I asked, hungry for any information she could give.

"We believe it contains the plans to stop whatever it was that happened at the beginning of time, from happening again. It tells of a person, who will be born when needed, and that she or he, it doesn't detail that, would be the person to stop it."

"So it's a prophecy?" Jared asked, rubbing his temples vigorously.

"No, it's not a prophecy," she said indignantly, fire flashing in her ruby eyes. "A prophecy is usually spouted by some unimportant person who takes notoriety from effectively foretelling something so vague that practically anything happening in the future could justify their prediction." She breathed deeply. "The codex…" she paused for effect, "is more of an instruction manual."

"For what?" I asked.

Yana copied Jarred in rubbing her temples and then ran her hands through her long bone-white hair, and just at that moment, she reminded me of Queen Sophia.

"We believe it's for a weapon," she replied. "And I think you are pivotal in making it work – whatever it is. We couldn't decipher enough to get more detail than that. I'm truly sorry. But…" She paused, thinking, while we waited. "May I see your pendant," she asked after a moment.

"Of course," I replied, taking it off and handing it over. She flipped it back and forth, studying the symbols and the blue stone.

"Can we—" Jake started, but Yana hushed him, holding her hand up at him.

"Have any of you heard of the Rosetta Stone?" she asked.

"Sure," Ash said. "Who hasn't? It was a stone found on Earth. Deciphering it led scholars to interpret other languages. It was literally the key to unlocking previously unobtainable knowledge."

"Exactly," Yana said, holding up the pendant.

"Finnian said I was the key, but what if he meant I had the key?" I looked around the room excitedly. "What else can you tell us?"

"That's all I have, I'm—" For a moment she froze, her un-blinking eyes staring into mine, like she was searching my brain. Then without warning, she reached forward and grabbed my wrist. Burning pain seared deep into my bones, her eyes rolled into the back of her head, and then she whispered, "The fall darkness again eight and shines."

Her eyes rolled back, and she let go of my wrist. Jared instantly took my hand, inspecting it for any damage, as Jake helped Ash off the floor.

"What happened?" she asked, dazed and confused.

"You don't know?" Jake replied. She looked up into his face, the anger still burning behind his eyes.

"Jake, I'm okay," I said.

"You sure?"

"Yes, it's fine. A little weird, and the pain was definitely excruciating, but it's passed."

"What the hell happened?" Yana asked again.

"You grabbed Shae's wrist, your eyes rolled back, and you said something that made absolutely no sense," Ash said. "Care to explain?"

"I would, but I have no idea," she replied, and I believed her.

"Is there anything else you can tell us?" I asked, slightly distracted by Jared, who was still holding my hand, rubbing my wrist gently with his thumb.

"That's all, but I'm one of—"

"Three. We get it," Jake grumbled. "If that's all you can give us, we should go."

"You're right, we should," Yana said as she stood. "It's not safe for her to be here. You must take better care of her, for if she falls, I fear so will we all."

"Okay, let's not get over dramatic," Jake said, "But you're not coming with us."

"I can help," she replied.

"How? You've already said you don't know what your siblings will look like."

"The same way I knew Shae. I'll know them if I see them."

"Okay, she comes," said Jared. "But not looking like that."

I watched, fascinated, as she started morphing back into her Human image, but banging on the door froze her mid-switch – her hair still straight and china-white at the ends, while the roots had turned black, and super curly.

"Hey, Marla," Stan yelled. "Show's in fifteen. You coming?"

"I'll be right up," she replied. "Head on without me."

"You okay?" He tried the locked door handle. "I

thought I heard voices."

"Just some friends. I'll be up in a minute."

"Okay, don't be late, you know what those crowds get like."

We listened to his footsteps disappearing up the hall, as Yana finished her transformation. But rather than the Marla we'd seen during the show, she looked completely different.

"Nobody's seen me like this," she explained, her voice different as well. "Let's go."

"What about the show?" I asked. "Won't you be missed?"

"Marla will. They'll cope. I was getting tired of the show anyway. I've got a number of different aliases around the resort. Shall we?" she said, waving a hand towards the door.

As soon as we left the changing room, Jake messaged the others to rendezvous back at the departure lounge asap. We walked through the aquarium, nobody giving Yana a second glance.

Ty and Connor waited in the lounge, but they both stood and came over when they saw us. Ty seemed extremely interested in Yana, deftly making his own transformation into the resident ladies' man.

"Well, hey there," he said. "What's a girl—"

"Zip it, pretty boy," she said, cutting him off. "I'm way out of your league."

Ty's cheeks darkened. "I get the message," he said, holding his hands up. "No harm, no foul." His dazzling smile was just for her, but at that point, the others arrived back.

"So you found the Harb—" Kaiser started.

"For the love of... seriously? And you're a covert unit?" Yana huffed. "Are you trying to get us all killed? Honestly, you lot I don't care about, but if she dies..." her dark brown eyes were serious, "it's game over."

"Is she...?" Kaiser asked Jake. He nodded. "Wow, I expected someone a little..."

"Older and wizened, with warts on my face and a cane to steady me?"

"Well, umm…"

"Don't sweat it. I'm just teasing you," she said. "Blondie, when's the next elevator?"

"You talking to me?" Connor spluttered, but then he looked at his watch. "Twenty minutes, give or take."

"Nothing sooner?" Jake asked

"There's a tour elevator leaving in five, but it stops so many times, the other one gets to the surface first."

"Well then," Yana continued, slipping her arm around Connor's. "We take the fast elevator. The last thing we want is to be stuck in a glass tube with killers on the loose. In the meantime, your one and only job is to protect Shae."

The elevator arrived on schedule, but the decanting party seemed like their only mission was to cause a scene, wanting pictures taken in front of the glass tube. A steward tried to move them on, but they brashly told him how much they'd paid for this experience, and they'd take as much time as they liked.

I could tell the Pack was getting antsy, so I wasn't surprised when Jake, followed by Kaiser, told them to shift, and when they didn't, they weren't given the choice. Indignant huffs and angry words filled the lounge as the group was physically herded away from the elevator doors so we could get in. As the steward passed Jake, I heard him whisper, "Thanks."

Another group had arrived during the incident, and tried to go on behind us, but Kaiser stood in the doors, blocking their entrance. I guess they felt waiting for the next elevator was easier than trying to push past him.

During the relatively short trip to the surface, we spread out around the seats and Yana purposely sat next to Connor; close enough to make him blush.

"What are you smiling about?" Jared asked. I nodded towards the couple.

"It's cute," I said. "And have you seen Ty's face?"

"Yes. I don't expect he gets too many knockbacks." Jared's smile matched mine, and he stretched out his arm along the back of my chair.

As we stepped out into the bright, natural sunlight of the afternoon, Yana stopped, closed her eyes, and lifted her face to the sun, basking in the rays. "It's a long time since I've seen natural daylight. I wish we could walk the promenade, but it's not safe. We should book the next shuttle to Arboribus."

"Way ahead of you," Ty said smugly. "We have tickets booked on the next one leaving at 2.30pm."

Jake checked his watch. "That's not for another half an hour," he commented. "Anything sooner?"

"They go on the hour," Ty explained.

"I don't like this," Yana said, looking around us. "Something doesn't feel right?"

"What?" I asked as her frown deepened.

"I'm not sure. It's like there's something in the air – something that shouldn't be here. Something out of place." She looked around us again. "We should move quickly," she concluded.

The way to the shuttle took us passed the stunning, aquamarine Grand Canal that fed the sea to the smaller waterways twisting around the resort.

"It's so beautiful," I said to know one in particular. "It's almost like—" Screams stopped me mid-sentence, and I looked around, trying to see what was causing such a commotion.

"Shae, look out!" Connor shouted and I turned just in time to see the bulk of the Goralite launching itself out of the grand canal. Connor barrelled into me, his shoulder pushing me to the side just as the Goralite attacked. I picked myself up, stunned and confused, watching as the creature pinned Connor to the path, all teeth and claws. But then he stopped, and sniffed the air, his head moving side to side.

The Goralite let go of his grip and Connor's limp body fell to the pavement.

I thought about a blast wave, but Connor was between us, and I felt sick, unable to draw my eyes from him. I vaguely heard shouting and turned my head to see Kaiser trying to hold back Jake, who was desperate to get to Connor, but now the deadly creature was padding the ground between us and him.

The Goralite sniffed the air again, and memories of the creature cave on 758-C2 came flooding back. "We have to go," Yana said, pulling at my arm, but I couldn't move – I couldn't leave because Connor needed me, because I could make him perfect again. By the time I realised the creature was heading straight at me, I only had enough time to push Yana out the way, realising what was going to happen next was inevitable. I worried more for the others, as the animal swatted them away like insects, but he it wasn't interested in them any further than getting them out of its path.

I tried to lift my hands to send a pulse of energy, but my arms were like stone. It felt like I was in slow motion mode, but no matter how fast or slow I was, the Goralite was faster. At the last second, I covered my face with my arms as the creature attacked, knowing that it wouldn't make a difference. I felt searing pain, weightlessness, and fear. Fear for Connor. Fear for all of them.

The warm water engulfed me as the beast plunged us both into the canal. For a moment, we surfaced, and a drew a gurgling breath before we went under again. I couldn't see anything but bubbles and blood, and all I knew was pain. Teeth dug into my shoulder and torso, more pain cascading through my body as we changed direction. I can't remember how long we were underwater, or even where we were, but I think that's when I couldn't hold my breath any longer.

I gulped for air that wasn't there, my lungs burning like

they were being ripped apart. Then a calmness shivered through my body, and I felt light, the pain no longer there. I felt tired, exhausted... and relieved. Relieved that this whole thing was over, that the others could go back to their lives.

That was the last thing I remembered, until the pounding on my chest roused me. I tried to breathe, big gulping breaths, but that only made me choke and I rolled on to my side coughing up water. Pounding on my back, though annoying, helped, and when there was nothing more to bring up, I laid on my back.

I felt the sting of a hypospray in my neck. And then another.

I lifted my arm to protect my eyes from the afternoon sun, trying to work out where I was and who was with me. It took me a minute to focus my brain, and I know I should've been worried that others would see the silver-blue glow that surrounded me like a soft blanket.

"Breathe," someone was saying, but I didn't recognise the voice. "That's it. Breathe deeply, get some air in. You were down there for some time." I looked up at the blue face, panic in his eyes. "How do you feel?"

"Just give me a moment to heal." It took a few minutes for all the holes and rips to repair. "Can you help me up?" I asked when I was almost done. My throat was sore and my voice croaky.

"Sure, but take it steady. You held your breath for some while. You're lucky I was able to get to you in time."

"I wouldn't say I was that lucky," I replied, watching the skin smooth over and turn a warm pink. Stan steadied me as I concentrated on the last bit of healing. "You... you know who I am?" I asked, as he didn't seem at all phased by my gift.

"Yes. I help the Harbingers." He didn't elaborate further.

When I was fixed and my brain no longer occupied with healing, my thoughts switched to the others. "Where are we?" I asked urgently. "How far are we from the others? I need to get back to them." I looked frantically around for clues.

"We're at the end of the East arm," Stan said. "Listen to me... stop! I know you're panicked, but you need to concentrate on me for a moment." He held my arms, and I finally gave him the attention he wanted. "The quickest way back to the hub is by the mag train that runs from the tip here to the centre."

"Okay, I got that," I said urgently, trying to pull away again.

"Shae," he said. "Pay attention. Someone set that Goralite on you. Someone is trying to kill you. Take the mag train, but be vigilant. You're in great danger."

"Aren't you coming with me?"

"No. I..." he paused to allow me to cough up more water. "I'm not allowed on the mag train. I scare the tourists, so management says." More coughing. "Those injections I gave you will help your body expel all the water you breathed in. It'll get better over the next hour or so."

I was barely concentrating, my mind replaying the horrific sight of Connor being grabbed in front of me. He pushed me out of the way. He saved me and I needed to get back to save him.

"I have to go," I said pulling my arms from his grip. I was already running when he shouted his reminder to be safe, stay alert.

I waited the four painful minutes for the train, my mind trying to work out if I could get there quicker by running, but the answer was a definite no. Even then, I was just about to bolt as the train came into view, I jumped in, willing the train to start. A couple got on behind me, their reaction a mix of disgust and bewilderment. I looked down to see what they were staring at, and I realised my shirt and trousers were riddled with teeth and claw holes. I didn't care, my only thought was Connor.

As the doors opened, I bolted through them, following the same path we had taken earlier, but when I got to where the attack happened, the place was crawling with medics and officers. Tents had been erected, and I couldn't see what was happening. People had gathered to gawp, and I pushed through them, trying to get to Connor.

An officer stopped me and wouldn't let me pass no matter what I said. I must've sounded like a crazy lady, and I was about to use a blast wave to get myself through when I saw Beck limp out of one of the tents.

"Beck," I shouted. "Beck! Over here." I waved and shouted until he looked up. He limped over, the bandage on his leg seeping blood. At first, it was as if he didn't recognise me, but then his vision cleared.

"Let her in!" he yelled. "Fucking hell. Let her in," he bellowed again.

"She with you?" the officer asked.

"Are you fucking kidding me? Of course, she is. Why the fuck else would I say let her in for?"

"In you go, miss," the officer grunted, turning the emergency tape off, so I could walk through.

Before I could say anything, I was engulfed by Beck, who tried to stifle the moan from the pain it caused. He set me down, just looking at me, dumbfounded.

"We thought you were dead. Fuck, Shae. Everyone thinks you're dead. You need to come with me."

"I need to see Connor," I replied, not struggling as he guided me towards the tents.

"You need to see Ash," he replied. "He's out of his mind."

"Connor first."

"Ash first," he corrected, but by that point we were in the first tent. Ash was sat on a plastic chair, his head in his hands. Jared stood to the side, his back to us. "Hey!" Beck yelled to get their attention. He didn't need to say any more than that.

Ash looked up with red, sad eyes, and it took a moment for comprehension to dawn. Jared turned, his eyes widening as he saw me, but he stepped out of the way, giving Ash a clear run.

Ash smelled of blood, and I would've body checked him had he not been holding me so tight. The pressure brought on another coughing fit, and he released me.

"I… I… how?" was all he could say, as he studied me.

"I'm ok," I reassured him, but the blast from the Link nearly wiped me out again. Pain, sadness, despair, all crashing into my brain at the same time. He grabbed me up again, and for the first time in my entire life, I felt his body shake as he cried silently. When he let me go, he motioned for Jared to come forward.

He didn't say anything. He just took my face in his hands, looking deep into my eyes. I reached up and placed a light kiss on his lips. "I'm okay. I promise," I whispered, but as I pulled back, the pale sadness still lingered on his face. "Oh my gods, Connor. I need to get to him. I need to…" my sentence trailed off as I looked into Jared's eyes. "No," I said, fighting back the tears. "No, he's okay. Nothing I can't fix." A lump in my throat made it difficult to talk.

"Shae," Jared said, and I just knew – I knew from the way he said my name. Just like he had when Finnian was murdered.

"No," I repeated, pulling away. "You're wrong, you have to be. I can fix him." As he reached out to grab me again, Ash stopped him, allowing me to pull back the tarp flap to the next tent.

Connor was on the floor where the Goralite had left him, a congealing puddle of blood staining the pristine white rock. Jake knelt, holding Connor's hand, while the rest of the Pack stood around him. I took a step forward, my blood cold in my veins. Kaiser was the first to turn and see me.

"Blue?" he said, causing the others to turn. "How?"

Jake was off his knees in a second, but he stopped just short of me. "Is it really you?" he asked.

"Yes."

"We thought…"

"I know," I said.

"How?" He reached out, examining the holes in my shirt and trousers.

"I need to get to Connor," I said, trying to pass him, but he kept shifting his body, like he was shielding Connor from me. "Jake, I need to get passed." His eyes reminded me of the pain in Jared's, and although I knew it to be true, I also told myself it couldn't be.

"He's gone, Shae," Jake said, his voice catching. "There's nothing you can do."

"I can try," I begged. "Let me try."

"It's no use. Dead is dead, remember?"

"He can't be. He saved my life, Jake." Tears streamed down my face.

"I know." He pushed my damp hair behind my ear and cupped my hot face in his hand, just like Jared had. "Come here," he said, trying to pull me into a hug, but I just couldn't. My body was stiff, unyielding.

"I have to try," I said. "Please. Please, let me do that. I need to know I've tried."

"Okay," he conceded before asking the medical staff to leave the tent.

I knelt next to Connor, not caring about the blood soaking into my trousers. His beautiful young face was pristine and undamaged, his eyes closed. He looked like he was asleep, and part of me took comfort in that. My breath caught in my throat as I pulled back the cover. The damage was extensive, and again, similar to the victims on 758-C2.

Jake knelt quietly beside me.

My hands shook as I placed them over his torso, and I tried to concentrate on the healing process, but there was nothing there. I tried again and again, tears falling on to his body. On to Connor. Eventually, Jake took my shaking hands in his and turned me away as Kaiser covered him back up.

This man, this amazing, kind, thoughtful man, had saved my life, and lost his in the process. In that frozen moment, the cost of my mission became all too clear.

I had done this to him.

I had killed him.

When Jake tried to help me off the floor, my legs felt like lead, and my knees like jelly. He scooped me up as I cried – cried harder than I think I had since Finnian's death.

"It's my fault," I kept saying through tears. "It's all my fault." I felt the hypospray in my shoulder, but only for a second before everything went dark.

26

The exotic floral aroma filled my lungs as I woke, and it was a moment before I remembered. Grief filled my heart, tears welled, and guilt flowed through my veins like cold water. The evening moonlight streamed through the open balcony doors, the sheer curtains dancing in the breeze. I didn't care.

I pulled the sheets up and cried myself back to sleep.

The next time I woke, the doors had been closed. I couldn't see Ash in the dark, but I knew he was there.

"Hey," he said quietly. "You awake?"

"No," I replied, trying to fight back the tears, and failing. Again.

"Okay," he said. "Is it alright for me to come over there?"

"No," I repeated.

"I'll be here when you need me."

"No."

"No? I don't understand." I felt his confusion through the Link.

"I need to be alone, Ash." My voice broken by sobs. "Can you give me that?"

"You sure?"

"Please," I replied, pain and grief overwhelming.

I heard the chair creak as he stood.

"Shae?"

"Save your breath, Ash. You're wrong."

"You don't know what I was going to say."

"You were going to say Connor's death wasn't my fault, but you're wrong. I failed him twice." Anger took over from pain – anger at myself.

"But—"

"That creature was after me, Ash. Me. Not Connor, or any of you. He was coming straight for me, and Connor pushed me away, put himself right in its path. It should have been me."

"I don't—"

"Don't say it, Ash. Don't you dare. If I hadn't dragged all of you into this, he would still be alive. And had I got to him quicker, I could've fixed him. Could have saved him." Grief took over from anger. "It is my fault. Please, Ash. Please just leave me."

"Okay," he said, his voice sad in the darkness. "I'll be downstairs if you need me. What about Jared and Jake?"

"What about them?"

"Do you want me to send either, or both of them in."

"No."

"Are you sure?"

"I can't face them. I can't face any of them." I pulled the sheets over my head as I heard the door open and close, but then I got out of bed briefly to lock the door.

I woke many times during the night, creatures and blood plaguing my dreams. I watched the sun rise through the patio doors, too sad to appreciate the beauty of it. I must've been running through the attack for the hundredth time as a knock on the door distracted me.

"Shae?" I didn't answer. "I know you're awake. Ash can feel it," Jared explained. "Can I come in?" I still didn't answer. "Please, Shae?"

"Leave me alone."

"I'm worried about you. Please let me in."

"I can't... I..." Words failed me. "No," I finally said.

"Alright, I'll leave you... for now. I'll be here if you need me."

"Thank you. And Jared?"

"What?" he replied, expectantly.

"I can't face anyone right now."

"I'll let Jake know," he said reluctantly.

Hours passed as I lay in bed, my guilt and grief overwhelming. I'd been devastated by Finnian's death, but one of the things that made it partway bearable, was that he'd been killed in the line of duty – defending the Monarchy. But Connor? Connor had died because of me. On a mission he wouldn't have been on if it wasn't for me. That wasn't bearable.

Occasionally, there was a knock on the door, and a call from someone I wasn't even listening to. I don't know how long it was until a pounding on the door brought me out of my sad reverie.

"Shae, I'm worried about you," Ash called.

"Go away."

"I'm telling you now," he shouted. "If you don't open this gods damn door, I swear I'm going to kick it in."

"Whatever," I shouted back.

"I'm not bluffing," he said, as if he was reading my mind. "This is your last warning."

"Leave me alone."

"I warned you," Ash said as the door reverberated with his kick.

"Okay, okay, Ash. Leave the door alone. I'm coming." I unlocked the door and headed straight back to bed, pulling the sheets back over my head. I felt the bed dip as he laid out beside me.

Silent minutes ticked on, and I wondered how long it

would be before he tried to convince me I wasn't to blame. Minutes turned to an hour, and still he hadn't said anything, but his breathing relaxed me somehow. Eventually I came out of my cocoon.

"I can't bear it," I said as he lifted an arm so I could get closer to him.

"I know," he replied, closing it around my shoulders. "I know," he repeated gently.

I cried and he held me. Cried until I had no more tears to spill, and it still wasn't enough. "I don't think I can do this anymore," I concluded after a while.

"You can," Ash replied. "As much as you don't want to hear this right now, you have to go on."

"I can't. And neither can any of you. If it wasn't for me, you'd be Primus, Jared would still be safe on the *Defender*, the Pack would be on some other clandestine mission, and Connor would still be alive."

"That's where you're wrong," Ash said sitting up and propping pillows behind his back, giving him eye contact for the first time. "If it wasn't for you, I would've been dead several times over. Jared would still be the green, stick-up-his arse Captain he was when we first met him, and the Pack… they would've been on some other dangerous mission, putting themselves in mortal danger every day."

I sat in silence as the sun dipped on the horizon and the late afternoon sun filled the room. "It's weird," I said, distracted for a moment. "Weird that we watch the same sun rise and set. Do you feel it?"

"Feel what?"

"The resort turning, spinning to make that happen… I thought I felt it when we first got here, but…."

"Shae, no one blames you for Connor's death."

"Do I count, because I sure as hell blame myself. Ash, can you do something for me?"

"Of course. Whatever you need."

"Can you go downstairs and tell everyone the mission's

over?" I sighed heavily. "I can't be responsible for any more death."

"Bullshit," Jake said, from the doorway, his arms folded across his chest. "Connor was a good man, and an excellent marine," his voice broke slightly, "and he came on this mission fully understanding the dangers involved. He was part of my team, my... family, and he died in the best possible way mud monkeys like us can – with his boots on. No one blames you, Shae, or holds you in any way responsible. The mission has to continue so Connor's death means something."

I got out of bed, and he met me in the middle of the room. Closer, I could see the sadness on his face, and even through his own pain, he was trying to alleviate mine. That was just one more thing to feel guilty about, and another reason why I loved him so much. I held my hand up to heal the deep gash, red and angry under some poorly placed med-strips, but instead, he reached up and took my hand in his.

"I'll give you guys some privacy," Ash said as he tactfully left the room. Once the door was shut, he held his other hand out and I put mine in it.

"I thought you were dead... we thought you were dead," he said, his voice breaking again.

"I'm sorry I put you through that."

"Hey, don't be! You're alive. That's what matters."

"And I'm sorry I couldn't save Connor. It all happened so quickly. I don't even remember what happened after... after he saved me. I need some air." Jake followed me out to the balcony, pulling two chairs together. We sat, and he took my hand again.

"After Connor, we couldn't stop it," Jake said. "All of us combined were no match for the animal. It was after you, babe. Pure and simple. You don't remember being flung against the wall?"

"No."

"Probably for the best," Jake said, a shudder running through him.

"Then what happened?"

"It grabbed you in its mouth, teeth ripping at your... blood dripping... and you were so limp. Lifeless. We still tried to get to you, all of us, but it dove into the canal and that was the last we saw."

I leant forward to wipe away the rogue tears that had escaped his red-rimmed eyes, but he pulled away rubbing them vigorously as he composed himself.

"I thought we'd lost both of you," he said. "Ash was beside himself. He said he couldn't feel you anymore. How? How can that happen if you weren't dead?"

"I think... I think maybe I was at one point. Maybe that's why he couldn't feel me."

"And Jared?" Jake continued quickly, trying not to dwell on my words. "I knew the hell he was going through, because I felt it too. You were gone and we couldn't follow, and Connor was there, and I... I should've tried to find you."

"There was nothing you could do, Jake. You thought I was dead – and you had Connor. He needed you, even in death. The Pack needed you."

"I don't think I'm useful to anyone at the moment, but one thing I can tell you is that no one, not one of the men downstairs, blames you."

"It's kind of you to say, but I don't believe you."

"You should, Blue," Kaiser said, and I turned to see all of them standing further down the balcony. "Because it's true."

My breath caught, and I had to swallow several times to get rid of the lump in my throat.

"See? Told you," Jake said, forcing a sad smile. He got up and helped me out of my chair as Beck stepped forward with a stack of shot glasses. He laid them out on the balcony wall as Ty filled them with Santian vodka. Silently, we each picked one up, leaving just one glass on the wall.

"To Connor," said Kaiser. "That boy could fly a dump truck if it had wings."

"To Connor," said Ty. "To the best wingman a guy could ever have."

"To Connor," said Cal. "I hadn't known him long, but long enough to know he cheats at poker."

"To Connor," said Jake. "Who will always, always be family."

"To Connor," we chorused before downing the vodka. The single glass sat untouched on the wall.

Ty filled the glasses again, and I noticed Jared lingering silently to the side. So did Jake.

"Connor's gone, but our mission's not over," Jake said. "A while ago, Shae and Ash told you this mission was dangerous, and they gave you all the chance to opt out. I'm doing the same thing right now," he said, his tone hard. "We can't change what's happened, and we're all grieving, but we still have a job to do. And the danger is all too real. So… anyone who wants to leave, now's your chance. No recrimination."

Kaiser lifted his glass. "I'm all in, Blue," he said before drinking. The rest of the Pack followed suit.

"What about you, Beck?" Jake asked.

"You know what? Who was I kidding? I was all in from the moment Ash and Shae busted me out of the Basement." He drowned his shot.

"Jared? I guess I don't need to ask," said Jake.

"No, you don't, but for total clarity, I'm in it till the end."

Jared and Jake downed their vodka at the same time.

"We'll that settles that," Jake said. "But as Jared just said, for totally clarity, does anyone here blame Shae for Connor death?"

"Jake!" I gasped, horrified.

"What? You need to know this, babe. You need to

believe it. You need to be one hundred percent on your game. Because, if you're not, you might as well just opt out yourself."

"Hey, tone it down," Ash said stepping forward.

"No. No, it's okay, Ash," I said, stepping between them. "Jake's right. I'm sad and I'm in pain, but so is everyone else. And a part of me will always blame myself for Connor's death. But if we're going to finish what we started, I need to get my head in the right place. Guys, do you mind giving me and Jared some time?"

"Sure, babe. As much as you need," Jake said, ushering the group down the balcony and around the corner of the house. I sat on the stone wall just a couple of meters down from Connor's full glass, and Jared came up close in front of me, his hands on my knees.

"What do you need," he surprised me by asking. "Whatever you want or need from me right now, I'll do it."

"I need you to make me forget the pain, Jared. Even for a short time. I need you to kiss me, to—" His lips were just as warm and soft as I remembered, and I allowed myself to feel safe in his arms as he held me as close as he could. His body was firm and hot against mine as I wrapped my legs around him. His tongue found mine, and his kiss was passionate, lighting the embers deep inside me. My hands wandered under his shirt, his skin shivering under my touch, and mine did the same moments later as his kisses travelled down to my neck and along my collarbone.

Jared's hands caressed my bottom, pulling me even closer to him, his hardness pressing against me. He pulled me off the wall and carried me inside, my legs still tied around him, our kissing even more passionate. He paused momentarily to lay me gently on the bed, but then his lips found mine again.

Jared sat up, still straddling me, and I undid his belt as he undid his shirt buttons, throwing it on the floor. My hands gently stroked his trembling skin before running my fingers down to his trouser buttons, undoing them one at a time until he was free of their constraint.

He grabbed the bottom of my top and pulled it up over my head, and his hands cupped my breasts. His lips were on mine again, his breathing shallow and fast, but then he stopped, pulling back.

"What's the matter," I asked. He sighed deeply, rubbing his temples briefly before running both hands through his hair. "Have I done… did I do anything wrong?" Worry and concern dampened the fire.

"No, no. God no," he replied, swinging one leg over so I could sit up. "You were… this was… God, why is this so hard?"

"I don't understand?" I said reaching out to him. He took my hand and held it to his bare chest.

"Can you can honestly tell me you want this. That you want me here and now because you're in love me—"

"I am, I do," I interrupted, but he carried on.

"Then I would love to explore every part of your perfect body," he said, leaning forward to stroke the bare skin just below my collarbone, causing goose bumps to appear immediately. He smiled briefly, then removed his hand. "But that's not why, not right now anyway. You want to feel something, anything, other than pain and guilt, and I want to help – I said I would – but I can't. Not like this. It feels wrong, like I'm taking advantage."

We sat in silence for a moment, his hand on my knee while I wrestled with my feelings.

"What are you thinking?" he asked.

"That maybe you're right."

"Damn it," he said playfully, the boyish grin appearing.

"That maybe I do want to feel something good, but is that such a bad thing?"

"Not always. But you and me? We were going to do this the right way, remember? I want to take you away, just us. No Pack or Ash. Just us," he repeated, and I knew exactly what he meant, because deep down I felt the same way. "I don't want you to look back and regret it."

"I would never regret being intimate with you, Jared. I'm just one hot kiss away from pulling you right back down on this bed." His grin widened. "But I can't disagree with you."

"Just one hot kiss, huh?" he joked, leaning forward to kiss me, but at the last minute, he diverted off and kissed my forehead instead.

"Do you think they'll ever be a right moment for us?"

"Of course," he said, pulling me into a hug. After a moment, I pulled back.

"Enough of that malarky, or I might just change my mind."

He sighed deeply again. "Come on," he said, pulling me off the bed and handing me my top. "Only way to stop this is to go back downstairs. Better than a cold shower any day."

"I know," I replied, handing him his shirt. "Hey, what happened to Yana? I didn't see her on the balcony."

"She stayed downstairs. Said she didn't want to get in the way."

"Jared?"

"Hmm?"

"I love you."

"I love you, too. Come on, you're making it way too hard for me," he said, taking my hand and leading me out of the bedroom.

Jake and Ash were chatting by the huge plexi-screen when we entered the lounge, the others sat around the vast dining table with Yana, studying what looked like a holo-map of Arboribus.

Ash crossed the room when he saw me. "You okay?" he asked. "I mean, given the situation."

"I'm functional," I replied as he bodychecked Jared.

"Buttons," he said quietly, standing in front of Jared so he could re-button his shirt correctly. Once it was done, all of us headed over to the table.

"Hey, Blue," said Kaiser, patting the chair next to him. "We're putting together a plan to find the next Harbinger."

"Yana's our best chance of identifying them," added Cal. "So, we're going to start and the centre and do a spiral grid search until we come across them."

"We're heading there first thing tomorrow," explained Jake. "No point in heading there now, we'll only get an hour or so into the search before we have to get the last transport back."

"Not the worst plan I've ever heard," I replied. "And I'm sorry we've lost a day because of me."

"I don't think anyone was in a rush to get out today, babe," Jake said kindly.

"Yo, hold up guys. Are we seriously not going to talk about the elephant in the room?" Beck said, causing everyone to turn and scowl at him, and I noticed Jake's hand drop to his thigh – the only time I'd been grateful of the no weapons rule. I guess he thought in for a penny, in for a pound, as he continued. "How the hell did Shae survive the creature attack? We all saw what happened."

"Hey, fuckface," Kaiser said, putting his arm across me like he was trying to protect me. "Ask that question again. I dare you."

"Calm down, gigantor," Beck blustered, "It's not even the most important question, and no one wants to ask that. Including me."

"Then why don't I ask it?" I said, shattering the rising tension. "Who set the creature on me in the first place? And how did they get my blood for the hunt? Oh, and in answer to your first question, Beck, I didn't survive. I died. But Stan brought me back; he saved me."

"Who the chuff is Stan?" Cal asked, tucking a rogue piece of hair back under his extortionately priced new beanie.

"He works with me at the aquarium," Yana explained.

"He's an Other, part aquatica, and an expert in Goralite behaviour, including hunting. If anyone could've got Shae away from the creature, it was him."

"The creature must've taken me through the canal to the open sea, where, somehow, Stan managed to get me away from the beast and take me to the surface. Whatever he did brought me back. The injuries, I then fixed myself."

"Do you think he was in on the attempt on your life," Ty asked.

"Never," Yana cried. "Stan would never. Plus, he's my custodian. He knows who I am, and he's just one of a network of people who protect the few remaining Harbingers."

"And he saved me, Ty. I think it's fair to say he wasn't involved."

"Then who?" Cal asked. "And if this creature hunts by blood, how the hell did they get yours?"

Silence filled the room for a moment.

"Yana," I blurted as I remembered.

"The Harbinger tried to kill you?" Beck asked, moving away from her.

"No, idiot. Yana tested my healing ability as double-proof of who I was."

"Of course," she said, recognition dawning. "I threw the tissue in the bin in my changing room. Someone must've got it there and then given it to the Goralite before setting it free."

"Well, I guess that proves one thing," Jake said. "We may not have seen anyone with scar tattoos, but even at a ridiculously expensive resort like this, someone is trying to get to Shae. Beck, Kaiser, I want you to go find Camille White and ask her how her investigation's going. Hey," he added as they got up to leave. "This is important. For Connor. Play nice, and don't fuck anything up."

"Sure, boss," Kaiser replied. Beck kept silent for a change, just nodding his understanding.

As the evening progressed, we finalised the plans for the next day, and were just concluding when Kaiser and Beck returned.

"Anything of use?" Ash asked.

"Nope, not really," Kaiser replied, rubbing my arm gently as he walked behind me to slump into an opulent armchair. "White said the security cameras had been disabled at the Goralite pen shortly after the morning aquarium show."

"Perhaps whoever did this saw you in the auditorium as I did?" offered Yana.

"Maybe," Ash replied, "but you knew who she was by her…"

"Aura?" Yana helped.

"Yes, aura. But whoever did this must've known her by sight," he continued.

"So, what if that was the case?" Jake said. "Someone recognising Shae, I mean. How did we get from there, to the attack? Nobody knew the test Yana did, or that Shae's blood would be in her room."

"And on that," Beck said. "White's put a look out order on Marla. She's worried you're either part of the crime, or an additional victim of it," he added, looking at Yana.

"Okay, so we have no facts here, just supposition," Jared summarised. "All we know is that someone recognised Shae, retrieved the blood sample from Yana's changing room, disabled the cameras in the Goralite pen, and then released it to track down Shae. That sounds like a more than one person job."

"Great," Jake huffed. "One person was bad enough, but multiple bad guys? Fuck me. I think tomorrow—"

"Don't say it," I warned. He looked surprised.

"What?"

"That I'd be safer locked up in the villa."

"Maybe you would," he replied, the tiniest hint of a smile. "But that's not all—"

"You were going to say? You were going to add that, in fact, you would feel more comfortable if I went back to wait everything out on the *Veritas*."

"Damn, you're good," Jake replied, the smile now obvious as he scratched at his stubble.

"And you two," I added, looking between Ash and Jared, "don't even bother. That's never going to happen."

"I didn't for a minute think it would," Ash replied, shaking his head knowingly. "Wasn't going to waste my breath. But... I am going to stipulate one non-negotiable point. And that's from now on, you don't go anywhere without everyone else. For your protection. Understand?"

"Yes," I replied, not even thinking about disagreeing.

The following day boasted more glorious weather, with promise of the same on Arboribus. The two other groups of holiday makers with us on the inter-planetary shuttle, were happy and excitable, planning their activities for the day. In comparison, ours was quiet and reflective.

The emerald planet was just as stunning as Paradism, in its own way. We were gifted more exquisite flower garlands as we left the landing pad, heading towards the very centre of the resort. Yana walked next to me, closer than I was comfortable with, while the others took 360-degree protective positions.

I strained my neck upwards, surprised that such a large, heavy structure would be safe high up amongst the thick trunked trees. Rooms and walkways had been fashioned along trunks and branches, higher and lower, one tree to another. It was both magnificent and mesmerising.

"This hotel is the dead centre of the resort," Yana announced, her new voice matching the image she'd decided to wear today.

"Can we avoid the use of the word 'dead' today, please," Ty said quietly.

"I'm sorry. Of course," Yana replied.

"So, we all know the plan," Jake said. "This time, we

stick together, and we stick to the search pattern we decided on last night. Yana, we're counting on you to identify the second Harbinger, so stay alert."

"I'm not one of your Pack, Colonel. You can't order me around," she replied, more fact than frustration.

"Today, you are," Jake replied. "And I can." She didn't disagree.

As we followed the spiral search plan, we passed more holiday makers chatting excitedly or studying maps and directions.

"Hold up," Jared said after a few hours of walking around. "Ten-minute break."

"We keep going," Jake replied, anger very close to the surface.

"Jared's right." Ash stepped in. "We can afford a few minutes," he added, passing me a bottle of water.

I sat on the moss-covered brick wall surrounding four or five holiday huts that were almost camouflaged by the greenery covering the walls and rooves. Jared sat next to me, and I handed him the bottle. He took a deep swig, then handed it back.

"When this is all over, I'm going to take you away from all this," he said quietly. "Somewhere nice and peaceful, where we can just relax. No mission or emergency, no Pack or Brotherhood. And definitely no danger."

"I'd like that," I said, resting my head on his shoulder.

"Time's up," said Jake loudly, winning a few inquisitive stares from other holiday makers. He lowered his voice. "We need to finish the main resort by lunchtime if we want to cover all the satellite resorts and activities by the time the last shuttle leaves."

I stood up and joined him, checking out the holo map he was studying. "We're going to find the second Harbinger, Jake."

"I know," he replied, planting an unexpected kiss on my forehead. "I worry that while we're looking for the

Harbinger, something dangerous is looking for you. I just want to protect you and keep everyone else safe."

"I understand. Connor was family," I added. "I can't imagine how difficult this is for you."

"Losing people under your command is something we all face, Ash and Jared too. But it never hurts any less. And for Connor, we were his only family."

"He had no one else?"

"No. His parents died not long before he completed at the Academy, and there was no one else. But I meant what I said yesterday. Connor died with his boots on, doing a job he loved, while trying to protect his family. To him, that would've been right. Honourable. That's what I take solace in at the moment." I put my hand on his arm, not sure if it would add any comfort, but he placed his hand over mine. "But…" his eyes darkened, "If I come across the person who did this, I might not be able to hold myself back."

"And neither should you," Ash said, and I realised everyone had grouped around us. "So, let's get going."

We finished our search grid a little after fourteen hundred, and we stopped briefly for sustenance.

"Well, that was a waste of fucking time," Kaiser said. "Scuse my language," he added looking at me. I smiled.

"We've only just started," Jared replied, rubbing his temples and squinting.

"What's the matter with you?" Jake asked, studying him.

"I've got a headache."

"Have you considered amputation?"

"Fuck you, Jake."

A ripple of laughter ran through the Pack, as I rummaged through Ash's backpack for a hypospray. I saw Yana out the corner of my eye, wondering why she was studying the interactive map attached to a large signpost, but then my thoughts returned to Jared.

"Why didn't you say something sooner," I asked as I held the spray to his neck.

"In the grand scheme of things, it didn't seem that important."

"It is. So tell me next time, okay?"

"Okay," he conceded.

"Where now?" Ash asked as I tossed the hypospray in the nearest bin.

"Now we follow the second part of the plan, out to the satellite resorts and activity centres, starting with the cave activities. Up and at it – we're moving on," Jake said.

"Wait," said Yana, not turning away from the map.

"We're shipping out, if you're coming with us," Jake replied, annoyance tinging his tone.

"Yes, I'm coming… just not there. Here." She pointed at the map. "We should go here."

"Hell yeah," said Kaiser as Yana tapped the icon for the extreme ziplining.

"We follow the plan," Jake said. "We go to the caves."

"Please yourself," she replied. "It's not just time you're wasting, but every second Shae's out here in the open, there's more chance she'll get injured… or killed."

"If you think—" Jake began, but Jared stepped in.

"Why do you think we should go to the zipline, Yana?" he asked, and I thought Jake was going to bust something.

"I don't know," she said honestly. "But I have this feeling deep down inside that I can't explain. I just know we should go there."

"Then we go," Ash said, as if he was making the final decision – which I guess he was, because that's what we decided to do.

27

We followed the signposts to the zipline centre, which turned out to be a shack at the base of the most enormous tree I'd seen in my life.

"Philips party?" a young woman sang, bouncing over to us while studying a holo pad. "Though your early, and we're only expecting four. Naughty, naughty," she added with a mock frown and wag of the finger, then laughed cheerfully. "No worries my lovely adventurers, there's room for all. But only for the fearless, for this is ziplining to the extreme." Ash tried to get her attention, but she was on a role. "Trees, rocks, caverns and waterfalls; you'll see them all this afternoon, but you better keep your eyes open, you really build up quite the speed." Jared tried to interject, to no avail. "Secure body-mods are allowed, but weak hearts are not, and each of you will need to sign our liability waiver before you can fly. There," she took a deep breath, "I think that covers it. Who's up first?"

She looked at our group expectantly.

Kaiser stepped forward, child-like awe in his eyes, but Jake coughed, and he stepped back, disappointed.

"We're not actually the Philips party," Ash said.

"No?" She looked almost as deflated as Kaiser did.

"No. We're just looking around, getting to know the place, seeing what you have to offer."

"Oh," she said. "Feel free to have a nosey around. If you're okay with heights, you could pop on up to the launch pad for a look see. And if you're not okay with heights… then this definitely isn't the adventure for you." Her smile was wide and genuine.

"Launch pad?" I asked. She looked up into the tree and we all followed suit. "I can't see anything. Just leaves and branches. Am I missing something?"

"Above these branches," she replied. "Much higher. This isn't called extreme ziplining for nothing," she added, back to her sing-song happy voice.

"How do we get up there," Kaiser asked, a ting of excitement in his voice.

"Through there," she replied, pointing to the base of the tree, and for the first time, I realised there was a hole on the trunk.

"Thank you," Ash said, as the actual Philips party arrived. "We don't want to keep you."

"If you like what you see, let me know and I can book you in. Thanks for visiting Arboribus, and I hope you have a fabulous day." And with that she was off.

We gathered around Yana, and for the first time I realised how quiet Cal and Ty were being. And Beck, for that matter. They'd hardly said a word all day and my heart went out to them.

"Anything?" Ash asked Yana.

"No," she replied. "It's definitely not her, thank gods. How annoyingly upbeat was she?" she added looking over to the Philips party.

"Have we wasted time?" Ty asked.

"No," replied Ash in contradiction to Jake nodding. "We had to check this place out anyway."

Yana looked back up into the tree. "Who's coming with

me?" she asked, looking around the group. "I bet you're up for it, big guy?"

"Sure as shit am," Kaiser replied, his eyes lighting up again.

"Okay, okay, hold up," Jake said, thinking. "This could just be adding to the time we've already wasted."

"Have faith," Yana said, and that was it – decision made. We were all going.

We stepped out of the bright sunshine into the middle of the tree trunk, where the air was cooler and smelled a bit like cedar wood.

"Fuck me, what the fuck is that?" Kaiser said, staring at the paternoster.

"Looks pretty obvious to me," Yana said, stepping forward, but Kaiser stopped her, looking concerned.

"That thing cannot be safe," he argued, but Yana wasn't entertaining him.

"You want to go extreme ziplining, but you won't get on the lift?"

"That's not a lift, it's a moving death box."

"Think of it like this," Yana soothed. "It's just a load of linked compartments that go around a belt at the top and the bottom. You step on when the box is about level with the floor, and you do the same to get off. No biggie," she added, stepping into one of the cubicals as it passed. "Just don't forget to get off at the top," she yelled back.

Ash and I stepped on the next compartment, and the others behind us. When we stepped out at the top, Yana was waiting.

"Did he get on?" she said, laughing.

"No idea," Ash replied, but as we stepped out the way so the others could disembark, we could hear his grumbling getting louder. Jake pushed him out of the compartment as they levelled with us.

"Okay," Jake said. "Let's make this quick. I don't want to be stuck up the top of a tree if anything bad happens."

"Well now it will," Beck moaned. "Coz you've just gone and god-damn jinxed us."

"Shut up, Beck," Cal said. "No one wants to hear your shit."

I think Beck was so surprised Cal had said something, he didn't give one of his renowned clap backs.

We followed a series of signposts to the zipline, crossing between trees, and walking along branches so wide you could easily walk two side by side. It was further than I'd expected. The slatted bridges swung gently as we walked. I stopped and closed my eyes as it rocked gently. It was... therapeutic was the only word I could think to describe it, but it was only a few seconds before Jake came up behind me, gently putting his hand on my hip.

"What's the matter?" he whispered.

"Do you feel it?"

"What?"

"The peace. Close your eyes. Feel the sway and listen to the trees – it's like being on a boat in the ocean. The trees sound like waves and the sway—"

"The boat," he finished for me. "Yeah, I feel it. But we need to go. I can't protect you out in the open like this."

"Okay," I agreed reluctantly.

There were two people at the launch pad, with one of them being strapped into a harness by an athletic looking attendant, and I wondered how many times he'd used the zipline himself. I continued to watch, fascinated, as the man then moved to the designated square. A moment later, a hook of some kind lowered from the roof, and the attendant pulled it down with a strong arm, attaching it to the back of the harness.

"Keep your arms tight into your body and legs together when going through any of the caves, but other than that, do what the heck you want. There are cameras at various intervals – photos will be sent to your rooms. You all good?"

"Yup," said the man, but his voice wavered.

"You sure?"

"Let's do it."

"Okay, on three… two… one… release."

The man disappeared instantly, leaving an unusually high-pitched scream as he left.

I turned to Yana. "I'm sorry. I'm not sure where else we can look for your brother."

"Oh, no need," she replied, smiling. "He's right there."

Everyone turned to look at the attendant, and he look startled, until he saw Yana. Then he looked anxious. He came over and stared at her for a moment.

"Yana?" he asked.

"Yes, brother," she replied, putting her hand gently on his chest. He returned the gesture, his hand light on her skin. They closed their eyes and touched foreheads, silent and still, and it was like our whole group held its breath.

Kana smiled as they separated. "Who?" he asked Yana.

"This one," she replied, pulling me forward. He stepped up close to me, very close, but I couldn't to pull away. His hands were soft on my cheeks, and as he ran them down under my chin and along my collarbone, I felt panic and euphoria at the same time. I saw Ash buckle, falling to the floor holding his head, and I wanted to get to him, but my muscles wouldn't work. Kana lowered his forehead touching mine, and I became overwhelmed with images on top of images, emotion on top of emotion. Love, hate, adoration, fear, arousal, birth, death, all layered on top of each other. I could barely stay conscious, and when he let me go, my knees buckled like Ash's had.

Jared caught me. He lifted me up easily and took me to a bench, lowering me softly. My head was clearing quicker than I expected, and I really don't know what made me, but I leant forward and kissed him. For a moment, he kissed me back, but then he pulled away, fear in his stunning blue eyes.

"Are you okay?" he asked, studying my face.

"I… umm, I'm… I…"

"She'll be alright in a couple of minutes," Kana said, but Jake suddenly had him by the throat, pushing him against the wall.

"What did you do to her?" he growled.

"It was a test," Kana said with difficulty.

"Jake?" Jared shouted. "Jake, let him speak."

"Fine," Jake grunted, releasing his grip.

"What was the test?" Ash asked, still looking bilious.

"I can't tell you," Kana said. "But she will be okay. If she was not the one, she would be dead by now."

"You tested her? Without her consent? Knowing that she could potentially die?"

"Of course, but my sister tells me she's the one, so I knew she would survive, yes?"

"I'm alright," I said, as Jared searched my face.

"Really?" he asked.

"Almost," I replied truthfully.

"What happened?"

"I don't know. I really can't remember much. What's wrong?" I asked as he continued to study my face.

"Your eyes."

"Blue?"

"Yes, but the colour's fading. They're mostly back to hazel."

"What did you do to me?" I shouted at Kana, getting up from the bench and taking a few wobbly steps towards him.

"I told you, it was a test. I really don't see what all the ruckus is about, you passed, and, see, you're eyes are back to beautiful hazel. That was your doing, by the way. The test had nothing to do with your eye colour – you made that happen all by yourself. But I'm far more interested in another question. What's with the symbiotic relationship you've got going on with him." He pointed at Ash.

"That's none of your business," Jake growled. "We need

to—"

"Boss," Ty said, cutting him off. "We've got company, and it ain't the Philips party."

Jake went to look back down the pathway. "Fuck," he said loudly before turning to Kana. "We need a way out, fast. There's at least six people heading this way, and I'd lay a wager they're not here for the ziplining."

"There's only two ways down from here," Kana said, his voice calm, even jovial. "And this is one of them." He pointed to the zipline.

"And what's the other?"

"Back that way." He pointed to the walkway.

"Looks like you're going to get the experience after all, Kaiser," Jared said. "Let's do it. Quickly."

Kana reached into the hut, pulling out harnesses and goggles. When we all had one set each, he threw the rest over the balcony.

"Don't want anyone following us," he explained.

"Shae, get that harness on quick," Jake shouted, keeping an eye on the walkway. "You're first."

"No. The Harbingers need to go first," I replied.

"I'm not debating this," he shouted. "Jared?"

"I'm on it," Jared replied, already strapped into his harness. I was still faffing with clips.

The incoming group were less than a tree away by the time Yana was stood on the square launchpad. "Listen carefully," Kana ordered Ash. "You pull the strap down, hook it over the harness here, and double secure it like this. Give it a tug to make sure it's okay, then press this button to launch. Got it?"

"Got it," Ash said, securing Yana's harness.

"Good, that's all correct. Only one thing left to do."

Ash pressed the button and Yana disappeared. "You're next," he said to me.

"No, Kana first."

Ash didn't argue as the fight started. He strapped in

Kana, only pausing to grab my wrist to stop me joining the others. "Come here," he said pulling me into the newly vacated pad and helping with the goggles. As he hooked me up, I turned and grabbed him.

"No one gets left behind," I said, as he pushed the button.

It felt like my stomach shot into my chest as I dropped, but then I was flying forward, warm air against my skin. I flew over treetops, then through them, little tunnels made from branches and leaves. Then I was back to open air, dropping quickly towards sheer rock, but at the last minute, I veered off towards the left and through a dark tunnel to the other side of the outcrop. I saw Kana, way in front, and I turned back to see who was behind me, but all I saw was rockface.

Kana dropped through the trees ahead and disappeared, so this time I was ready for the plunge. Floral scent with a hit of pine replaced the brisk fresh air from above the canopy, and as I flew through woods, and skimmed over rivers of the deepest blue, I felt exhilarated, like everything bad was being stripped away from me.

I didn't get that wet as I flew through a waterfall, but I don't think I would've cared if I was soaked to the skin. The flight continued over fields of brightly coloured flowers, and then veered left and started to slow. As I approached the landing point, the brakes kicked in, slowing me, and I felt bad that I'd loved the ride when the other were still in danger.

Kana unbuckled me and the hook disappeared into the roof. "The others will make it," he said with a certainty I wished I could share. We stood and waited, and eventually Ty came in to land. His face was a little banged up, but he didn't seem too bad.

"What happened?" I asked immediately.

"There were seven of them, but the saving grace was they weren't armed. Seems they heeded the no-weapon rule as well." As he finished, Cal came into view, and as we unhooked his harness, Beck was next. With each man who arrive, the injuries sustained were also worse.

Yana and Kana watched, mesmerised, as I healed Ty and Cal – then Beck after he landed. I searched the treeline, looking for the next person. The wait was agony, even though it was only a minute of two, but then we heard Kaiser before we saw him. Arms and legs splayed, and the biggest grin on his battered face as he landed. But as I healed him, a veil of seriousness fell over his face.

"It's brutal up there, Blue. We thinned the herd, but they're tough. Clearly well trained, and they had a mission. One of them tried to get Jake's harness of, but Ash took the guy out."

We all looked back to the treetops. Waiting was a bitch, but my stomach flipped as we saw Jared approach, but then my stomach flipped for a difference reason.

"They didn't have guns, but a hunking chunk of wood can be just as effective," Kaiser said as he supported Jared while Kana unhooked him.

Jared had taken a hell of a beating and healing him took more out of me than the others put together, and through all of that, I feared the worse for Jake and Ash.

"I wanted to stay," Jared said, "I told Jake to go next, but he insisted I did. Said he was pushing me off the launch pad whether I was strapped in or not."

"Sounds like Jake," Kaiser said, his voice proud.

"What about Ash?" I asked, not quite sure I wanted the answer.

"He's… he's doing okay. I mean, he was doing okay when I left. It'll be alright, Shae," he said, taking my hand as we went to watch the trees. Seconds felt like hours as we stood, in vigilant silence. "They'll be okay," he whispered into me ear as I leant against him, his chest warm against my back. He put his arms around me, and I wrapped mine around his, pulling them tighter until I couldn't get any closer.

"Someone's coming," Cal shouted, pointing at the trees.

"That's... that's not one of ours," Ty shouted, and in a heartbeat, Jared had swung me behind him.

"Get in the office," he ordered. "And the Harbingers. Now."

I did as ordered, without argue. The three of us hunkered down below the windows, but I couldn't help taking a peek. Jared and the others got ready to fight, but as the man came in to land, he didn't even have the strength to unbuckle himself. I grabbed a pile of bungees off the desk and left the safety of the office.

The man didn't struggle, and I thought that was a good thing because clearly Jake and Ash were still putting up a good fight.

"Kana?" I said as a man and woman walked out of the office. "Yana?"

"Yes, and yes," Yana said. "Thought it was prudent we change our looks."

"This isn't good." Kana studied the harness Kaiser had taken off the stranger.

"What isn't," Jared replied, but I saw his face cloud over with recognition. "There were no spare harnesses were there? You threw them over the balcony."

"What are you saying?" Ty said, though he knew exactly what it meant. I suspect he was just like me – not wanting to think about the consequence.

"How long does it take to get back to the start?" Jared asked.

"Longer than they will have," replied Kana. "If you... wait, what's that?" he asked pointing up to the trees. It was difficult to make out at that distance, but as the mass got closer, it was definitely two people – one clinging on to the other.

As Ash and Jake came into land, Ash's pain through the Link almost floored me. He'd held on to Jake the entire flight, but twenty meters short of the landing pad, he ran out of strength and Jake's lifeless body fell the short distance to the ground, hidden by brightly coloured flowers and bushes.

Ash swayed in the harness as the flight ended, and Jared was there in a second to help him, propping him up as he undid the straps. I tried to get close to heal him, but Ash pushed me away.

"Jake," he said. "Help Jake."

"In a moment. After you."

"No, now," he replied, and the fear rippling through the Link chilled my blood.

"Keep him safe," I told Jared, and as he nodded, I sprinted off after the others to find Jake.

If it was possible, my blood turned colder. The Pack had trampled the area around Jake, so it was easy to get to him, but I stopped up short, watching as Kaiser felt for a pulse.

"Is he…"

"I don't know," Kaiser replied. "I can't find a… no wait, I've got it. Faint, but it's there."

I knelt down on the squashed flowers, pinks and silvers tarnished with blood red. There were so many injuries, I wasn't sure where to place my hands, so I opted for his head and chest. I breathed in deeply, the sweet, soft fragrance of the flowers filling my lungs, and then I felt it. The tickly feeling warming the pit of my stomach before travelling up into my chest and running down my arms in pulses. My hands shimmered silver blue, and then the usual strands of dancing energy sparked to Jake's body. He started to glow, head and chest first, then bursting around the rest of his body.

I closed my eyes, concentrating hard, imagining him whole and unbroken. It took a while to heal Jake, and that in itself told me how bad it had been. When it was done, I took my hands away, a wave of fatigue hitting me like a sixty-tonne shuttle. But just as I thought I would collapse,

Jake sat up and put his arms around me.

"Thank you," he whispered as he held me tight.

"I guess things got a bit hairy up there," I said when he let me go. "When one of the bad guys came down, I thought something terrible had happened to you or… Ash! Oh, my gods, Ash," I gasped, desperately trying to get up, but my legs were like jelly. Kaiser, I think, slipped his hands under my armpits and hoiked me up, and Jake was already standing, ready to put a steadying arm around my waste.

Jared stood over Ash, who was slumped on one of the benches, his head in his hands.

"Glad you're ok," Jared said to Jake, taking over support duty whether Jake liked it or not. After giving me the briefest hug, he set me on the bench next to Ash. "You don't look good. I'm worried about you."

"I'm okay," I replied, suppressing the urge to put my head back and go to sleep.

"Your eyes are blue again," he continued.

"They are?" I frowned, looking over to Jake, but he shrugged.

"Thought you had enough to worry about without piling on, babe," he replied, before giving Jared a glare, but then Ash groaned, and my attention switched to him in an instant. I put one hand on his back, one on his chest, and repeated everything I'd just done with Jake, only this time, even though Ash was less broken than Jake, it took longer, and far more concentration. When Ash was part way healed, enough to bring him back to his senses, he tried to stop me, to push me away.

"No," I said succinctly, and he stopped fighting me. He knew me too well to fight a losing battle. When he was done, I surveyed the group, making sure I'd healed everyone, and when I was one hundred percent satisfied, I let the fatigue overwhelm me. I slid sideways, my head landing comfortably on Ash's thigh.

"We can't stay here," I heard Kana say through the fog

in my head.

"Well, we can't go anywhere at the moment," Jared replied. "Look at her. Look at what she's just done."

"The bad guys know we're here," Jake said. "I don't know about you, but I'd rather avoid Round Two."

"I get that, Jake, but we're going to draw even more attention walking through the resort carrying a passed-out female and dragging along a semi-conscious man in bungee ties."

"I know, I know," agreed Jake, frustrated and angry. "But one thing's for sure – we're sitting ducks here."

"We should go, I'm alright," I said, trying to sit up, but my head spun, so I gave it up as a bad idea. Ash stroked my forehead as the debate about what we should do next continued.

I don't think anyone had noticed Yana had disappeared until she pulled up in a resort-branded tour bus. "Did someone order a taxi?" she asked.

"Lady, I could kiss you," Kaiser said as he manhandled our prisoner onto the vehicle, stuffing him between seats out of sight. Jared picked me up, and carried me on, while the others took up seats around me.

"So?" Yana asked, turning to face us all. "Where are we heading?"

"Anywhere private; off the grid," Ash replied.

"I know somewhere," Kana added, making his way up front to sit by Yana. I've no idea where we went, or how long it had taken, but I jolted awake as the bus stopped.

"Sorry if I dribbled on you," I apologised, checking Jared's shoulder.

"Wouldn't care if you did," he replied, his beautiful blue eyes sparkling, and that reminded me.

"What colour are my eyes now?" I asked quietly.

"Hazel."

"And you're not just saying that, so I don't worry?"

"No. I wouldn't do that," he replied genuinely. When it

came time to disembark the bus, I wasn't sure if my legs would work, but it didn't matter as Jared gently picked me up. I rested my head on his shoulder and promptly fell asleep again.

By all accounts, while I was out of action, the others had interrogated our prisoner. Kaiser was apologetic as he explained to me that the man was just a hired hand from one of the other activities, paid generously to capture me.

"Capture? Not kill?" I asked. "You sure?"

"That's what he said, Blue. Not a bright spark, though. I don't think he had any idea who you are, just that someone was paying handsomely."

"That's a shame. I thought we'd finally caught a break."

"Sorry, babe. Not today," Jake said, joining us.

"What about Kana? What did he have to say?"

"Nothing."

"Nothing?"

"He wouldn't talk to us. Said he would only talk when you were awake," Jake explained.

"Well, I'm awake now."

"You sure? You still don't look great."

"Thanks a bunch," I huffed.

"You know what I mean," he replied. "You're exhausted. And don't try to deny it, I can feel it through the Link."

"Gods-damn Link," I grumbled, realising that I'd healed everyone in the room to some degree – except Yana and Kana. I wasn't too worried about Beck, Ty, and Kaiser, and even fixing Jared hadn't been that intense, but Ash and Jake were very different. Ash, I was used to, but Jake... I'd have to make sure my roadblocks were secure.

Jake ordered Beck, Cal, Kaiser and Ty to walk the perimeter of the shack, while the rest of us gathered on dusty wooden furniture. "What is this place?" I asked.

"It's the welcome hut for the rapids adventure, but it only gets used when the water levels rise, so it's empty half the year. It's out of the way. Private," explained Kana. "Shall we get down to business?"

"What do you know?" Jared asked.

"Yana's filled me in on everything that happened on Paradism. I'm not sure I can offer much more."

"Anything's better than nothing," I replied.

"True," he said. "Let's see what I can add. Yana's told you about the codex, yes?"

"Yes," I replied.

"And you found one page of it at the monastery?"

"Yes," I repeated.

"And it had some handwritten words on it?"

"Yes. Family, Honour, Courage," I replied while he surveyed the group before raising an expectant eyebrow at Yana.

"For fuck's sake," Jake grumbled. "This is going to take all day. We already know about the codex and it's cryptic prophecy."

"Not a prophecy, I told you that," Yana replied, her patience waning. "A prophecy is like a vague foretelling that—"

"Yeah, yeah, we get that," Jake interrupted her.

Kana turned his attention back to me. "It's important that you're clear on this. The codex is written as fact. It's more of a warning that something is coming, and also a list of instructions."

"Instructions for what?"

"For how to use the weapon."

"You've both mentioned a weapon now, but what is it, and where is it?" Ash asked.

"Ah, now see there's the problem," Kana said, causing Jake to huff again. "No one knew. Which is why some people who don't have the full facts, like your Khan brothers, refer to it as the 'Amissa Telum.' Which, in today's language, would roughly translate as 'lost weapon.' But actually, to make it work, you need two parts – the weapon itself, and the power source needed to make it work. The Helyan cube is the power source."

"So, basically, you're saying the codex is an incomplete manual on how to use the battery for a weapon no one has been able to find in many millennia. Fucking marvellous," Jake said.

"Did I say no one had found it?" replied Kana.

28

The atmosphere in room switched in a second.

"Have you heard of dualism?" Kana asked, infuriatingly changing subject.

"Of course," Ash replied. "Simplistically, it's two different sides of the same coin."

"Exactly," Kana said. "So as the Brotherhood of the Virtuous Sun was formed to protect the future from whatever it is that's coming, the Vex was born in secrecy to do everything within its power to make sure it does. Duality. Two sides of the same theory."

"And that's why they're trying to kill Shae," Jared asked. "To stop her from finding the lost weapon. The Amissa Telum?"

"Stop fucking around, and just tell us where it is," Jake added, but Kana's sudden laugh was unexpected.

"You don't understand," he said, cheerfully. "You don't need to find the Amissa Telum, you already have it... she's right here."

My stomach flipped. "But Yana said I was pivotal to making the weapon work – not that I was the weapon."

He reached out and held my hand, the soft scales warm against my skin. "You are the lost weapon, but you will need more to stop the coming."

"The cube," Jared said, and I wasn't sure if it was statement, or question.

"Correct," confirmed Kana. "But I am one Harbinger, and that's not part of my knowledge."

"Of course, it isn't," Jake said. "Because that would make things way too easy."

"Like it or not, that's all I can give you," Kana replied, his tone hardening, and when he stood, the red scales on his face and neck had darked.

"Kana," Yana said, her tone cautioning. "Kana," she repeated as the man faced up against Jake. "Kana!" she shouted, finally getting through, and the man stood down, his colour lightening again.

"Please," I said, overcome with weariness again. "Can we all just play nice while we make sure we've understood everything so far?"

"Okay, babe," Jake said, perching on the edge of the table, his arms still folded across his chest.

"Ash, will you do the honours, please," I asked as I sat carefully, my legs about to give way again.

"Sure," he replied, but I felt his concern for me through the Link. "The codex is a manual on how to use an ancient weapon against something that's coming – but we don't know what that is or when it's going to happen. Shae – the Amissa Telum – is the lost weapon, whatever the hell that means, but she needs the cube as some sort of energy supply. The pendant is a Rosetta Stone to help us read the codex, of which there are four: one on Earth, one lost, and two with another races, currently unknown. The Brotherhood has failed in its care of Shae, and the Vex are the anti-Brotherhood, solely created to stopping Shae from being the weapon, to which she is also the key. Have I missed anything?"

Silence filled the room.

"I think that about covers everything," Kana agreed.

"And neither of you can tell us anything about the cube? The one the Khan brothers were looking for at the Palace of Palavaria," asked Ash. They both shared a look before shaking their heads, and I believed them.

"So, what now?" I asked, but unexpectedly Kana's hand shot out, grabbing my wrist, and the searing pain drilled down to my bones. His eyes rolled into the back of his head.

"Vail and will unless become the true," he said, before releasing his grip.

This time, Jake and Jared joined Ash in feeling the pain through the Link, and when Jake got unsteadily to his feet, his face was murderous.

"Jake, stop," I cried. "Leave him alone. It's not his fault."

"What happened?" Kana asked, not taking his eyes of Jake. "What did I do?"

"You don't remember?" Ash asked.

"No, I…" he rubbed his head looking confused.

"It's okay," I said. "The same thing happened to Yana."

"Is that what I sounded like?" She asked. I nodded my head. "No wonder you thought I was crazy."

"It's done now," Ash said, unease strumming the Link. "What you said made as much sense as Lana, so let's not dwell on it." That last bit was squarely aimed at Jake.

"What do we do now?" I asked, trying to get the conversation back on track.

"Now we look for Lana," Yana said. "But it's getting dark. Too late to go to Infernum now."

"Agreed," said Jared, looking at me carefully. "And no point going back to Paradisum. We hold up here tonight and take the inter-planetary shuttle to Infernum first thing tomorrow."

"Agreed," Jake added. "But we need supplies, food,

water, clothes. Gonna draw the wrong kind of attention with all this blood."

"We can see to that," Yana said. "Nobody's seen these faces, we can come and go with ease."

"Good, then we have a plan," Jake said. "I'll set up security patrols with the Pack."

"Count me in," Ash said.

"And me," Jared added.

I opened my mouth to speak. "Not you, babe. Not tonight." I didn't have the energy to argue. In fact, I didn't have the energy to stay awake five minutes, let alone waiting for the Harbingers to come back.

Next morning came too quickly, and I protested as someone tried to wake me. "Already?" I groaned, not wanting to open my eyes. "Just another thirty minutes... fifteen? Five?" Jared laughed quietly.

"The sun's up. You know I'd let you sleep all day if I could, but the sooner we get back to the *Veritas*, the happier we'd all be."

"I know, but see? Nothing works," I said, relaxing my limbs like dead weight, but Jared lifted my shoulders and sat me up. "You're evil," I moaned.

"You've called me many things, but that? I'm wounded," he said, holding his hand to his heart.

"And I thought I was the dramatic one."

Jared held out his hand, and I reluctantly took it, but as he pulled me up, I felt lightheaded and queasy.

"Hey, are you okay?" he said, steadying me. He checked my eyes and felt my forehead.

"I don't know," I replied honestly. "I think I'm just still feeling all those heals yesterday. And that wrist burning thing whacks a hell of a punch."

He lifted my face to look in my eyes again, searching them for something. "I'm going to take you back to Paradisum."

"No," I challenged.

"Shae, you're pale and sweating. Your eyes are sluggish, and you can barely stand unaided. Jake can find the other Harbinger and bring her to us."

"That's not going to happen, Jared. Nobody puts themselves in danger for me without me being there."

"But—"

"This is my fight," I said, getting heated. "If you're not going to help me, then get the hell out of my way." He took his hands away from me and I lasted seconds before I collapsed. "I'm sorry, Jared. I didn't mean to be such a bitch."

"I do believe that's our first argument," he said, helping me up again. I looked at him and his boyish grin, and I returned it.

"Umm, if a recall, we've had several disagreements before."

"Yes, but not since we've been... well, since you realised staying away from me wasn't an option."

"Our first fight then? Didn't last very long."

"Must be my roguish charm," he said, laughing again.

"Jared?"

"Yes?"

"Happy birthday." I stood on tiptoes and gave him a kiss. It lasted longer than I intended as he slipped his arm around me, kissing me back. I didn't mind.

"I didn't think you'd remember," he said. "Things have been a bit full-on over the last week."

"Well, I did. And maybe tonight, we'll get a few minutes to slip away on our own to really celebrate it."

"It's a date," he replied, touching my face gently.

"I'm sorry though."

"What for?"

"I haven't been able to get you a present."

"Being here with you is the best present I could have – regardless of circumstance. Does that sound too cheesy?"

"Just cheesy enough," I assured him, resting my head on his shoulder as Ash walked in with a mountainous plate of food.

"Breakfast?" he asked

"You're a lifesaver," I replied, hungrily tucking in.

I ate half the plate in record time, and that was enough to make me feel marginally better. The three cups of coffee helped a bit more. By the time we were ready to move out, I felt at a solid fifty percent capacity.

"Just concentrate on where you need to go, babe," Jake said. "Me and the boys will do the rest."

"Thanks," I replied, going to give him a quick hug, but he was warm and solid, and I felt like he sapped all the weariness out of me. I felt I could stay like that forever, but then Ash called for the rollout and that was that.

We tried to look innocuous as we headed back though the central resort to the shuttle pad, but thankfully it was still early and there were only a few people out and about. We we're actually lucky for a change and a shuttle to Infernum was due to depart imminently.

We sat in the passenger cabin, ours the only group. "You don't both have to put yourselves in danger," I said to the Harbingers, who were wearing new faces again.

"Wouldn't miss it for the world," Kana said. "To be who we are again after all this time is…"

"Liberating?" Yana offered. They both laughed and then excused themselves to carry on catching up.

Jake sat at the table opposite me. "I don't like going into this situation blind," he said, looking between me and Ash, who was sat beside me.

"I've got to agree with Jake," Jared said, easing himself in beside Jake. "What?" he said as Jake stared to him in mock amazement. "It can happen," he explained. "Just not very often."

"Whatever," Jake replied, sounding like Beck.

"I think we all agree it's a shitty plan," I said. "But we all saw Yana get us to her brother just by looking at a map and getting the feels. All the planning in the universe can't match that. So, the plan is simple. Land, find the nearest map, and see what happens. End of mission brief."

"Still not the worst plan I've ever heard," Jake said, smiling. "One time, Con took us…" he trailed off, sadness clouding his eyes. I leant forward and took one of his hands.

"I'd like to know, if you want to tell us."

Jake coughed to clear his throat. "You sure?"

"If you want to."

Jake started the story, and when the Pack heard what was going on, they came over and added their usual flair until we were all breathless with laughter and Jake could barely finish.

"Thank you," he said to me after, as we got ready to disembark.

"For what?"

"For encouraging me to tell Connor's story. Why did you do that?"

"When Finnian died, I didn't handle it well."

"I know, I wish I could've been there for you. Ash said it was difficult for you."

"He was being diplomatic," I replied as Jake's forehead puckered. "The truth is, I didn't handle it at all, and it nearly killed me. Literally." Tears welled, but didn't fall, as I suddenly felt panic and fear from Jake through the Link. "I'm okay, everything was okay. I'm here and everything's fine. But it could've been very different without Ash and Francis. At the time I didn't realise it, but in my effort to forget my pain, I created new pain for those around me."

"What happened?" Jake asked quietly.

"A lot of avoidance and anger, then denial and guilt. But it all came to a head when I made the most ridiculous decision to go diving the reef alone one afternoon. Time went by, and I decided it would be alright to move away from the reef into open water. Only I didn't keep track of time, and I didn't realise how late it had got. Before I knew it, I was surrounded by waking Mantra sharks. Apex predators all looking for dinner."

"Fuck me, babe. You're okay now, so I guess things turned out okay. What happened?"

"Ash and Francis happened. They pulled me out of the water at the last second, and I think it was Ash's despair, and my very close death-call that brought me around. Anyway, there's a reason I'm telling you this, and that's because it took a close call like that to realise that the support I needed was there, around me, with me through all of it. And when we started talking about Finnian, about who he was, and what he did, rather than the fact he was dead, it made it easier. The pain doesn't go, but it helps. Connor was an amazing man, who did amazing things that other people don't get to hear about because of security levels, but here, amongst us, we can celebrate his whole life. And in time, maybe it will hurt a bit less."

"I love you so much," Jake said, before he even realised what he was saying. "I'm sorry, that was unfair of me."

"You don't need to apologise."

"It's just..." He paused, running his hands through scraggy, unbrushed hair, that seemed to be even more unruly than normal.

"Just what?"

"It's like you get me. You understand me and the Pack more than anyone I've ever met. You're one of us. I know you feel that deep inside."

"Jake, I—"

"We're leaving," Ash shouted across the cabin. "Let's go."

The searing heat and dry, cracked earth reminded me of Independence. I've never liked super-hot places, and my ability to deal with things was directly related to my energy levels. "Who the hell would choose to come here," I grumbled as Jared handed me a pair of sunglasses. And to top it all off, the T-shirt Yana had bought for me was a size too small and I felt conscious of its tightness, which didn't improve my mood any.

We found the nearest resort map and huddled around it, Yana and Kana front and centre. "Okay, so we've got the main resort ahead, semi-active volcanoes to the north—"

"What's a fucking semi-active volcano," Kaiser asked as we all turned to look at the smoke in the distance. "Surely it either is or it isn't."

"It means they're at the foreplay stage and haven't blown their load yet," Beck replied to a ripple of sniggering.

"Thanks for that graphic explanation," said Ash, "But technically you're correct. It means they're not dormant, but they haven't erupted either. The live volcanoes are a puddle-jumper trip west, effectively straight on, passed the resort."

"Don't tell me, that's where they do the lava surfing," Kaiser said. "Please don't tell me the third Harbinger is anywhere near there."

"Not really feeling anything," Kana said, but Yana seemed to be more interested in the resort.

"What do you think?" Jared asked.

"I'm not sure," Yana said. "I thought I felt Lana here." She pointed to an activity at the centre of the resort. "But then it was like she disappeared."

"Fucking hell," Ty said, shaking his head. "Had to be spelunking, didn't it?"

"Am I missing something?" Yana asked as the group broke into laughter.

"No, no, we're all good," I said, trying to get serious again. "Have you had any hits anywhere else?" I asked. She shook her head. "Then that's where we'll go first."

"Listen up," Jake said, his game face back in place. "We cannot have a repeat of the last two planets. We can't afford to have another run in with this Vex group, so stay alert and vigilant." He took a quick glance at me. "Shae's the priority, and she doesn't have the strength for any more healings this time, so let's do this quick but careful. I want a 360-protection deployment and heads on a swivel at all times. Let's go."

We took one of the travellators through the resort to the entrance of the main cave system, getting there in a fraction of the time walking would've taken. The shack was similar to the ziplining one on Arboribus, and there was a lady out front greeting guests with an eerily similar up-beat welcome and safety check.

"Feel anything?" Ash asked as the Harbingers surveyed the area.

"No, sorry," Yana apologised, looking deflated, but then she perked up. "Wait, I feel something. It's faint, but definitely something." She scoured the area again. "I can't see her, but it's like her essence is getting stronger. I don't understand."

"It's okay," Kana said, soothing her, but then she relaxed and smiled.

"Of course," she said, pointing at the group of people exiting the lift that took adventurers down to the caves. The attendant was busy with her group, collecting back in harnesses, helmets, and torches, and as we didn't want to cause a scene, we held back until the area was clear.

As we approached, she looked up and froze – just for a second before dropping the harness and rushing to her siblings. I hung back, not wanting to interrupt the reunion.

"What? Why? How are you here?" she spluttered. "It's been so long since we've been together. But you shouldn't be here, we shouldn't be together like this until…"

"She found us," Yana said. "She's here," she added moving the men aside so Lana could see me for the first time."

"For real? For sure?" Lana asked.

"For sure," Kana answered.

Lana took a step towards me, but Jared and Ash stepped in front of me like a shield, as Jake stepped in front of her to stop her advance. I had to go on tiptoes to see over their shoulders and I watched as she studied Jake. Not just a quick glance, but a proper head to toe bodycheck. She put her hand on his chest and closed her eyes for a moment and smiled as she took it away. She stepped around Jake, and he immediately put out his arm to stop her.

"It's alright," Yana said. "She won't hurt you."

Jake turned is head to look at us, and Ash nodded. Lana went up to Jared first, repeating the same thing she'd done with Jake, and when she was done with Jared, she moved to Ash. "Come," she said urgently. "We must get you all out of sight."

We followed Lana down a few corridors and into a room filled with stacked chairs and tables. "We'll be safe in here," she said. "Now, tell me everything."

Beck picked a chair off one of the stacks and put it behind me. "Sit," he said. "You look like you're going to keel over."

I let the others recap everything for the third time, and when Lana was caught up, she sat back in her chair, taking a moment to digest. "Then it begins," she said ominously, before pulling up her chair in front of me with a screech and sitting again – her knees almost touching mine. "So, you're the one."

"I thinks so," I replied. "I guess so from what's been happening."

"What more can I tell you, my siblings haven't?" she asked.

"The Helyan cube," I replied, and her eyes crinkled as she studied me further. "The one the Khan's found in the catacombs under the Palace of Palavaria. What can you tell us about it?" Lana laughed, the sound almost musical, and her scales rippled with colour. "What's so funny?"

"I'm sorry, child," she replied. "It's just I expected you

to be more prepared when you got to us."

"And that's funny how?" Jake chipped in, moving to stand behind me.

"Again, my apologies," Lana replied to Jake, before turning her attention back to me. "I meant no offence. We've waited so very long for you to come, and now you're here. It's magical, and you're... beyond amazing. Yana and Kana have told me of your abilities, Shae. You truly are a wonder."

"Thank you," I said, "I think." In all honesty, I was overrun with embarrassment – Lana was being so overwhelmingly flattering. She smiled and placed a delicate hand on my knee.

"The cube," she said, bringing us back to business. "What was it like?"

"It was kept in a wooden box, covered with those swirling patterns we now know are words. It was brushed bronze, some kind of metal, with the same patterns as the wooden box and this." I showed her my pendant, and her ruby eyes shone. "Oh, and there's something else. When Vanze took it out of the box, my chest started to vibrate, like right to my core. It took my breath away."

"How big was it?" Lana asked.

"Maybe this by this," I held up my hands, trying to make a square about five centimetres. "Is that about right, Jared?"

"Yes, about that. Maybe a bit bigger." He shrugged.

Lana nodded. "So, they're still separated."

"I don't understand," I said. "They?"

"Yes," she said, laughing softly. "What you saw was just one part of the Helyan cube in its entirety. You and the cube – the whole cube – are what's needed to drive back the coming darkness."

"Are you saying there are more Helyan cubes?" Ash asked.

"There's only one Helyan Cube," she explained. "But the one is eight."

"Now I'm losing track," said Jared, pinching the bridge of his nose.

Lana sat back in her chair. "The Brotherhood really has failed you," she said, before looking over her shoulder to her siblings, as if she was finally acknowledging what I have no doubt they'd told her about my preparedness.

"We've been through all this," Jake said, and I could feel his frustration through the Link. "She doesn't know. The Brotherhood did a shitty job. We have to accept that and move on. The longer we're here, the greater danger Shae's in. I'll go to hell and back to make sure no harm comes to her, but I'd rather avoid confrontation at this point with her so weak."

Lana cocked her head, and looked at him, like she was looking right into his soul. He shifted position and looked uncomfortable. "What Courage you have," she said before concentrating back on me. "As I've said, the cube you saw is one part of the Helyan Cube. Too long ago to remember, the cube split into eight identically sized pieces, and each smaller cube was separated to make sure it survived the ravages of time and be ready to use when needed. It was also to make sure the Vex didn't find it and destroy it."

"Vanze didn't know the full story, then." Jared said. "He thought the one in the catacombs was the only one. He had no idea there were more."

"Only a select few do," Lana replied.

"Where are they now?" Ash asked.

"They're spread far and wide. Four are split among the Tetrarchy, and as you now know, the one with the House of Palavaria is in the catacombs. One went to the D'antaran, one to the Ethileron, one is with the Hanson Republic, and the final one is with the Rhinorians. You will need to collect all of these to reconstruct the Helyan Cube. And mark my words, Shae, you will need all of them. And you'll need help." She looked around the gathered men.

"You want me to find all the cubes?" I said

dumbfounded, following her gaze. "I can't ask these men to keep putting themselves danger for me."

"You're not," Ash said. "I'm with you to the end. You're my sister. You really think I'd let you do this by yourself?"

Lana smiled. "You are Family," she said to Ash, and he nodded proudly.

"We're all family," Jake said. "I'm in."

"And me," Jared added "We've come this far; there's no way I'm standing down now." He looked around the group. "I think I speak for all of us when I say we're in this to the end, whatever that looks like. It's more than a duty, or a mission. It's like Jake said, we're family, and that means fighting for the people we love." The warmth of love I felt through the Link made me catch my breath.

"That's very Honourable of you, Jared," Lana replied.

"What do we do when we have all the little cubes," Ash asked.

"Not a clue," Lana replied. "That's what you need the codex for."

"Fuck me," Kaiser said, making us all turn towards him. "We have to find eight teeny tiny cubes, scattered across the universes, and then some ancient book to understand what to do with the fucking things."

"You want out?" Beck challenged.

"Fuck, no," Kaiser replied. "Just summing up the mission's all." His eyes crinkled as he laughed. "We do this together."

"Till the end," Cal added.

"For Connor," Ty said.

"Bring it on, Blue," Kaiser concluded.

"Well, I couldn't have put it better," Jake said, grinning like a proud father.

29

I worked hard to keep my mental roadblocks in place. Skilled at compartmentalising Ash's feelings, it was harder to stop Jake and Jared's from catching me off guard. I took a moment to centre myself and concentrate on the task at hand.

"Is there anything else you can—" I started, but Lana was too quick for me to react as her hand shot out and the inevitable pain buried deep into my bones.

"Will the rise the nine light," she said, her eyes white. After a moment, she shook her head, as if trying to clear it. "What happened?" She asked as Ash, Jared and Jake picked themselves of the floor.

"What happened?" Jake stormed. "You babbled a load of fucking nonsense and caused a shit-tonne of pain. Again. I mean, what is it with you guys?"

"I'm so sorry," Lana apologised. "I really have no idea what came over me. This happened with you two as well?" she added to Yana and Kana. They nodded.

"None of it makes any sense," Ash said. "None of you made any sense."

"Well, it doesn't sound like there are any answers

forthcoming about it, so we might as well move on," Jared added in his best diplomatic voice, still unsteady after feeling my pain through the Link.

"Is there anything else you can tell us?" I asked, keeping my arms clamped to my side. Yana and Kana shook their heads, though I noticed Lana didn't.

"You need to find all eight cubes and the codex," she summarised. "You'll definitely need the page the Brotherhood took from you. That page is probably one of the most important within the codex, which is why it came with you to the monastery. It was yours, Shae; it was always meant for you. Were you able to read it by chance?"

"No," I replied.

"Worth asking," she said, not surprised by my answer.

"Except for the handwriting at the bottom of the page."

"Really?" she replied slowly, dragging the word out. A smile appeared as if she knew exactly what I was talking about. "What did it say?"

"Family, honour, courage," I explained. "Nothing else. I thought it was some kind of family motto, or wise words to live by."

"Really?" she repeated slowly again. "Nothing springs to mind when you think of those words?" The question irritated me because she obviously knew exactly what it meant, and now she was looking around the men, as if she was expecting them to come up with the answer.

"If I knew the answer, I…" My sentence hung as I followed her gaze. "Fuck me," were the only words suitable.

"Babe! Language," Jake scolded, pretending to be shocked.

"Courage," I said, still looking at his smiling face, but then I moved my attention back to Lana, who was also smiling. "I'm right, aren't I?" She nodded, and I turned to Ash, next to me. "Family?" She nodded again. "Honour," I concluded, looking into Jared's handsome face.

"Now you understand," Lana said.

"No, that's not true," I replied, my mind bombarded with so many emotions seeping through the Link. "The words on the codex page were handwritten at some point before my birth. How? How did they know these three men would be the personification of those words? And what does that even mean?"

"Wait, so are you saying the three words on that paper are Jared, Jake and me?" Ash asked, standing and pacing.

"Yes," Lana said. "It all makes perfect sense."

"Well, I'm glad it does to someone," Beck grumbled.

Lana ignored him. "You were never meant to take this journey alone, Shae. You were always going to have support. Just as it was written you would come when needed, so it was written that three protectors would be drawn to you, to help you complete your task. It was fate, if you will. Family, honour and courage. It's no accident that the four of you came together. Your lives are intertwined – powerful forces have dictated that."

My head span, then fear took over.

"What is it?" Ash asked, my own fear mirrored in his eyes.

I could barely breath and my heart was beating so fast.

"Shae, what's going on?" Ash pushed, but I couldn't hear him. I stood, not wanting to believe. Jared came towards me, but I put my hand up to stop his advance. Eventually, I turned towards Lana.

"To be clear, you're saying these men are as much a part of my purpose as the cube and the codex and the—

"Stop it," Ash said sharply, grabbing my shoulders. "I know you, Shae. Please. Do not go down this rabbit-hole." Tears fell down my hot cheeks.

"I have to. I have to know."

"What's going on? Ash? Shae? What is it you have to know?" Jared asked.

I backed away from Ash and turned to Lana. "I'm right,

aren't I? If Ash and Jared and Jake are part of this whole gods-damn, fucking nightmare, they have no say in it either." Lana nodded her head.

"They are part of your journey," she confirmed, but that just made my blood boil more.

"And that's why we all felt so close together when we first met? Feelings of closeness... of intimacy... of love... were just some misunderstood—"

"No, that's not true," Jared said, heatedly. "I don't care about some stupid words on a bit of stupid paper. I know what I feel for you, and it's real. I love you. Please don't torture yourself like this, Shae."

"But how do you know?" I challenged, my cheeks burning. "How can you possibly know for a fact? Do you love me? Or is it just one big cosmic joke, and what you think is love is simply duty."

"Everybody out," I heard Jake say as I turned to see him ushering Beck and the Pack out the door, and when they'd gone, he came back to face me. "It's true that I've never felt anything even remotely similar to what I feel for you with anyone else." Jared huffed in the background. "But that's not because I'm linked to you for some upcoming apocalypse, it's because of you. The way you look at your feet when your nervous, the way you share yourself so openly with people, the way you will always help the underdog, and even your addiction to ice-cream is kinda cute. What I'm trying to say is that none of that has anything to do with some crazy Helyan prophecy."

"Still not a prophecy," Yana corrected.

"Still don't give a fuck," Jake replied. "But if it walks like a duck, and quacks like a duck, it's a fucking duck."

"Any idea what he's talking about?" Kana not so quietly whispered to Yana, but Jake nailed both of them with a glare.

He continued. "And you know what, babe? So what if some inexplicable force drew us all together? It brought us together, that's all. It didn't dictate how we feel about each other."

"Jake's right," Jared said, causing Jake to raise a questioning eyebrow. "If we are supposed to help you through all of this, whatever this is, then you know what? I'm totally fine with that. Just means you stuck with us." The boyish grin and the sparkle in those amazingly blue eyes would normally be enough. "Like Jake said, something unexplainable might have brought us together, but it didn't make us love you."

"Hey, we're stuck with Beck too, and I can tell you for a fact, I'm not loving him," Jake said, and the ridiculousness of it made me laugh. Briefly.

"I love you," Ash commented. "But I love you as a sister. A really, really, really, annoying sister. Which just proves we can all hold you in our hearts, and help protect you through all this, without actually having to fancy you. No offence. But that means whatever feelings Jared or Jake have, above and beyond that, are valid and true. Hey, come here," Ash added, pulling me into a hug. He didn't say anything else. He just held me while my mind settled. Eventually, he pulled away, and looked deep into my eyes before telling me everything would be okay. And I agreed because I wanted him to be right, but uncertainty, fear, and pain churned deep inside me.

I wiped away my tears and apologised for messing up Ash's top. He shrugged it off before turning to the Harbingers. "I'm almost afraid to ask this, but is there anything else?"

"Any more bombshells you want to drop?" added Jake.

The three of them looked between themselves before shaking their heads in unison.

"You have a treacherous road ahead of you all. You will need to be strong and unyielding, possibly in the face of what will seem insurmountable odds," Yana said.

"Have faith and trust in each other," added Lana. "And

remember, you have others with you to help you get to where you need to go. Don't underestimate their importance."

"Does that mean we really can't ditch Beck?" Jake joked, and I touched his arm lightly as I passed to go to the three Harbingers were standing.

"I have one more question," I asked seriously, before pausing to take a deep faltering breath. "The old woman from Phrayton. She said I would be betrayed. Could she mean what's already happened with the Brotherhood – with them not preparing me properly?" I knew I was reaching.

"I don't think so, child," Kana replied, his eyes darkening to a deep crimson red, and he looked sad.

"Do you know?" Ash asked. "Do you know who will betray Shae?"

The collective shook their heads. "I wish we could tell you," said Yana kindly. "But we can't tell you what we don't know."

After that, all that was left was to say our goodbyes and leave the Harbingers catching up on the many, many years they'd been separated.

We met the others back at the entrance to the caves, and although they were clearly on guard duty, they'd managed to rustle themselves up drinks.

"Here you go, Blue," Kaiser said, handing me a bottle of water. "And, umm… well, we were talking while you were still in there, and we just want say… just in case there was any confusion… we're with you, wolfpup. You couldn't get rid of us, even if you tried."

"I hear that," Jake said. "I've been trying to get rid of Beck since that first day on Dennford, but he just won't get the hint. So, we all might as well just accept we're in it together."

"That's very pragmatic of you, Jake," Jared said.

"Fuck you, Jared. It's bad enough being stuck with Beck, but you too? Fuck me." Everyone laughed, including

Jake and Jared.

"Can we pick up this mutual appreciation society back on the *Veritas*," said Ash. "I think we're done here, and I'd rather not stand around to be a target for the Vex."

"Agreed," Ty added. "The departure lounge for the orbital station is just south of here."

"That's a no-go," Cal said. "Shuttles from here only go to the orbital station around this planet, and there's no transport between the three stations. We're going to have to go back to Paradisum on an interplanetary, and then take the shuttle from there up to the *Veritas*."

"Well, ain't that just peachy," Kaiser grumbled.

"Okay, no point in arguing. That's just going to draw more attention," Jared said, shielding his eyes as he looked up. "Let's head back to Paradisum."

"And keep your eyes open," Jake added. "If those tattooed bastards are out there, I want us to see them, before they see us. Understand? Good. Let's roll out."

The walk back to the landing pad for the interplanetary was uneventful, thankfully. I was weary, and walking was far more of a chore than it should've been, but even heavier than my legs, was a sadness deep inside my chest. No matter what had brought us all together, and in spite of everything Ash, Jake and Jared had said, I still couldn't shake the thought that their feelings for me were artificial. And if that was the case, was the way I felt about them unreal too?

The heavy silence persisted as we took our seats in the shuttle, but eventually, Jake was the first to speak. "Correct me if I'm wrong, but I don't think there's anything back at the villa we need?" He paused to wait for any contradiction.

"Only Kaiser's swanky new clothes," Ty replied, but he was too close to the big guy to joke and earned himself a punch on the arm.

"So, nothing we need to go back for," Jake concluded. "I suggest we head straight to the orbital shuttle and back to the *Veritas*."

"Agreed," Ash added. "But let's not forget what happened on Paradisum. That Goralite is under control, but it doesn't change the fact that someone set it on Shae in the first place. Or that there was a second attempt on her life on Arboribus."

"Not to state the obvious," Jared said, "But we still don't have weapons, and while the same seems to be true about our bad guys, we need to be prepared."

The rest of the short trip was spent studying the resort map and the different ways we could get from one landing pad to the next. It wasn't far, but far enough to have several possible routes, and we agreed primary and secondary pathways, should anything happen. From there, we agreed a separate emergency plan, should we get separated.

I felt short walking between Ash and Jared, with Jake taking the lead. No one seemed overly bothered by us as we passed through the lounge, and those that were, were probably more interested in the way a group of men surrounded a lone female.

We didn't stop. For anything. Not even for Camille, who joined us just as we got near to the departure lounge for the orbital shuttle. She walked with us, matching our pace.

"I got a report there was a seriously intense-looking group on the incoming shuttle from Infernum," she explained. "Thought it might be you. And after what happened last time you were in my resort, I wanted to check everything was okay."

"We're peachy," Beck said, sarcastically. "Depends whether you've got that mutt of yours on a leash."

"The Goralite won't be a problem," she replied, eyeing him carefully, as if she was looking for any kind of reason to detain him for being a smart arse.

"You'll be glad to hear we're leaving," Jake said. "Next shuttle, and we're out of here."

"I've got to say, I'm not unhappy to hear that," she replied. "But until you're off the ground, you're still my responsibility, and I've placed my team around the entrances to make sure you leave in the same condition you arrived." Her face clouded over. "I'm so very sorry for the loss of one of your party," she continued. "As you instructed, your friend has been moved to the orbital station. I assume you'll be leaving as soon as you're back on your own ship?" Jake nodded. "Would you like me to radio ahead and have the coffin moved to your ship."

"Thank you. Please do so," Ash said, as the wave of grief from all the men overwhelmed my mental roadblocks.

"Ahh, her she is," Camille noted, as she watched the shuttle coming into land through the window. She stayed with us, right up until the point we stepped foot in the shuttle, and then she maintained watch at the entrance until the door was sealed shut.

The flight was smooth and there were only a handful of other guests finishing their holiday. It seemed a lifetime ago that I'd had the luxury of browsing the atrium for clothes, but now the shops went by in a blur as we walked with purpose back to the *Veritas*.

My thoughts were all over the place, barely able to comprehend everything that'd happened over the last few days, and all the things the Harbingers had said – including the words that literally made no sense. I rubbed my wrist absentmindedly, conscious there was no lingering pain or redness.

The first sign something wasn't right came about the halfway point. "Jake?" Ash said.

"I see them," he replied, stopping us in the middle of the vast atrium we were walking though. Holiday makers mingled among stalls, and sat at tables, eating food that smelled divine.

"Four, maybe five?" Jared said.

"At least seven," Ash declared. "Four in the shadows

ahead – 2 left, two right. Then one by the fountain, one by the coffee stand, and one pretending to read the resort map."

"Hate to correct you," Beck added, "But there's another two to our six."

"That's at least nine, and there's probably more we can't see." Ash concluded.

"Okay, we planned for this," Jake reminded. "Kaiser, Beck, you take the sides, and Jared and I will plough straight through the ones in front. And we don't stop. Ty, Cal, you stay in the rear and take out anyone that gets close. Ash, you don't leave Shae's side. Whatever happens, Shae's the priority. If we get split up, we meet at the *Veritas*. There's just one rule… don't stop. Everyone ready?"

"Abso-fuckin'-lutely," Kaiser replied for all of us as he cracked his knuckles.

"Then on my mark. Three, two, one, mark."

The second Jake finished counting, we ran, and the moment we did, so did they. A few seconds later, I caught a blur of activity in my peripheral as Cal took out the guy who'd been looking at the resort map. Then Jake and Jared ploughed through the four bad guys in front of us like a freight train. But then others joined, and I thought they were fighting against Jared and Jake until I recognised a face, and a frown settled across my forehead.

"Go," Jake shouted to Ash as we slowed and turned to help. "Keep going."

I tried to get back to them, but Ash caught the back of my shirt and dragged me along with him.

"Don't stop," he reminded me, and although I hated the thought of leaving everyone behind me, I sped up.

"Did you see that?"

"What?"

"I swear some of those guys who waded in were Luke's men from the monastery. But it looked like they were fighting on our side."

"It doesn't matter – just keep running."

We ran along the planned route to the *Veritas* – passing shops and bars, and people jumped out of the way as we barrelled past.

We weren't that far away when we turned a corner and literally ran into a couple more bad guys. Ash grappled with one, as I fought with the other. His bulk gave him some serious strength, and I buckled as his punch caught the side of my ribcage. A second to my gut left me winded, panting air, but each breath was like a knife under my ribs. I prepared myself for the next, but in that moment, he was bowled to the ground by Ash. No, not Ash. Luke. I stepped back, shocked, then tried to wade in to help Ash, who was now fighting two men.

"Get to the *Veritas*," he ordered. "I'll be right…" he ducked a punch, "behind you."

"But—"

"Go," he shouted.

I left him and Luke still fighting and ran, turning corners, and charging down corridors, before arriving at the hanger where the *Veritas* was waiting. Jake had given me and Ash the codes, and I waited for what seemed an hour for the ramp to descend.

"Shae, wait," Luke shouted as he entered the hanger, panting and gingery holding his side.

"Stay away from me," I ordered. The ramp was still too high for me to get on, but I mentally recalled where the nearest weapon was.

"Shae, just listen to me. I'm here to help you."

"Right. Of course, you are. That's why you tried to take me on Lilania."

"No, you're wrong. Well, yes, technically you're right. I was trying to take you away from the monastery, on the orders of Queen Sophia."

The ramp was almost down, but his words intrigued me. "Sophia?"

"There are those in the Brotherhood who've known your purpose from the moment you were born, and we wanted to prepare you. But a larger population felt you would attract more danger if they were to tell you the truth. So, we worked behind the scenes, guiding here, a nudge there."

"Finnian?"

"Exactly. He was part of our faction, and he worked hard to make sure you were as ready as possible without drawing the attention of the Supreme Primus."

"So back at the monastery?"

"It was clear things were going terribly wrong after Finnian died, and then we found out you'd started putting two and two together. Our group feared you'd do… well, exactly what you did do. We've been trying to catch up with you since."

"What did you mean about orders from Queen Sophia? Since when has the Brotherhood taken orders from the Tetrarchy?"

"Not the Tetrarchy, just Queen Sophia."

"You're not making any sense."

"You found the Harbingers, right? You know what you need to do next?"

I nodded cautiously, wondering how he knew what had happened. "Yes," I replied.

"Good. You need to come with me back to Earth."

"I'm not going anywhere with you," I replied, taking a step on to the ramp.

"You need to see Sophia. She has things she has to tell you."

"What I need, is to get on this ship, get some weapons, and go save my people."

"That's out of the question. You're coming with me."

"Like hell I am. You can—"

"Shae!" The voice stopped me mid-sentence. I stepped off the ramp and away from its safety to look around the side of the ship.

"Francis? How?"

"Easy," he said, pulling me into a bear hug until I could barely breath. "While Luke was tracking you, I was tracking him. And I managed to pick up the *Nakomo* on the way." I smiled, knowing she was back in safe hands. "It's good to see you," he said hugging me again. "Come on, let's go."

"Go where?" I replied frowning.

"The *Nakomo*. We can go back to the monastery and sort all this out with Noah. Everyone's beside themselves with worry."

"Really?"

"Of course. You're family. When you left the way you did, everyone feared for your safety."

"Don't listen to him. You need to come with me, Shae," Luke said. "The monastery is the one that kept you in the dark."

"You said compliant before," I reminded him.

"That's right," he replied. "And I stand by that," he added, glaring at Francis.

"Don't listen to him, Shae," Francis said, drawing my attention back to him. "He's not family. You need to come with me. Trust me, you'll be safe." I thought it weird he hadn't mentioned Ash.

"I'm sorry, Francis, but I can't go with either of you."

"You're making a big mistake," Luke said.

"Maybe, but it's my mistake to make."

As I finished my sentence, a group of four or five people silently appeared behind Luke, and I thought they were with him until one of them reached around and raked a knife through his neck. I jumped back, closer to the safety of Francis.

"Run," I cried, trying to push him away, but he didn't move. "Run, Francis. Come on... hey, what are you doing?" He held me by the wrist, tight enough to hurt.

"Let me explain, Shae," he said, as I looked into his eyes

for some kind of clue.

"We're beyond that," the stranger interrupted, wiping the blood off his knife on Luke's trousers before stepping sideways to avoid the pool of seeping blood. As he approached, his scar tattoos became more obvious and I tried to pull from Francis again, but his grip tightened.

"Someone better explain something," I pushed, anger now mixing with fear.

"Fine. All this," the man continued, waving his hand between his team, and then between me and Francis, "boils down to one thing… the boss wants you, so the boss gets you." He handed Francis a gun. "Let's be honest with the girl shall we, Frankie-boy. Your role in this has always been to stay close to her all these years, and then bring her to me when—"

"No," I gasped, looking at Francis, confusion and pain washing over me. "It can't be."

"Oh, it can be, and it is," the tattooed stranger confirmed.

My insides froze. He was lying. He must've been lying.

"Francis, tell me this isn't true. Tell me you're not part of this," I said, practically begging for him to say something that made sense.

"It'll be okay," he said. "Just do as Yeager says, and they won't hurt you. I'll make sure of that."

Every word was a knife stab to my heart, and I could barely think straight. And then Ash came charging into the hanger, bloodied and dishevelled, putting all of Yeager's men on alert – weapons immediately trained on him.

He stopped dead, arms up as if to confirm he wasn't a threat. "What's going on?" His forehead creased. "Francis? How did you get here?" Ash looked at the gun in Francis's hand, and the grip he still had on my wrist.

"Just great. Anyone else coming to join the party?" Yeager grunted. "I've had enough of this shit." He reached forward and grabbed my free arm, pulling me away from

Francis, and immediately Ash stepped forward.

"Don't involve yourself, Ash," Francis said quickly. "If you want to live through this, just walk away."

"What the hell's going on, Francis?" Ash repeated. "And you sure as hell better release her," he added, pointing to Yeager, who'd manoeuvred me so I was between him and Ash. The knife stung as it pricked my ribcage.

"Okay. Okay. You don't need to do that," Ash said, backing away, arms raised again.

"It's cute you think you have a say," Yeager mocked, before turning his attention to his team. "Okay, listen up everyone, we're moving out before anyone else decides to join us. And for fuck's sake, will someone deal with him."

"I'll do it," one of his men said, lifting his gun towards Ash, but Francis stood in his way. For a second I though he was seeing sense.

"I don't know what's going on, Francis," I said. "But whatever it is, we can work through it. You're my brother. I know you're not a bad—"

The shot echoed in the hanger, and my heart stopped. Ash crumpled to the ground, the gun still raised in Francis's hand.

My legs buckled.

I pulled on Yeager, trying to get to Ash, but he was strong and I couldn't move him.

I felt energy swirl in the pit of my stomach, and I prepared to release a pulse, but before I could do anything, Frances stood over Ash, firing a second shot.

My heart broke, the pulse extinguishing in a second.

Francis stooped down to feel for a pulse. "He's dead," he confirmed. As he stood, his pale face was unreadable for a moment before Yeager dragged me away.

I craned my neck back, cold with horror, and the last thing I saw before I felt the hypospray in my neck, was Francis covering Ash's face with his jacket.

ABOUT THE AUTHOR

British author, S.M.Tidball, has been writing since her teens, starting with poetry before moving on to short stories. Despite the challenges of being diagnosed with dyslexia, she has continued follow her passion, and now shares her epic vision of secrets, danger, and rebellion in the Helyan Series.

Books available in the four part Helyan Series:

Part One: Guardians of the Four
Part Two: Fallen Star
Part Three: The Trinity Planets

Don't miss out:

Follow on twitter: @SarahTidball

Like on Facebook: @SMTidball

Follow on Instagram: @SMTidball

Printed in Great Britain
by Amazon